Praise for the Blasphemy Series

"Laura Kaye shows her mastery of the BDSM world. I'm eagerly anticipating more in this bold new series!"

~ Cherise Sinclair, *NYT* Bestselling Author of the Masters of the Shadowlands Series

"Smoldering and sexy, Laura Kaye's Blasphemy series is everything I look for in a romance. Haunted heroes and strong heroines populate this one of a kind club and I can't wait to see the big bad Doms fall one by one."

~ Lexi Blake, *NYT* Bestselling Author of the Masters and Mercenaries Series

Mastering Her Senses
FIRST EDITION February 2017

Cover Design and Interior Format
© The Killion Group, Inc.

MASTERING HER Senses

LAURA KAYE

Hot Contemporary Romance by Laura Kaye

Blasphemy Series
HARD TO SERVE – A HARD INK CROSSOVER
BOUND TO SUBMIT
MASTERING HER SENSES
EYES ON YOU

Raven Riders Series
HARD AS STEEL – A HARD INK CROSSOVER
RIDE HARD
RIDE ROUGH
RIDE WILD

Hard Ink Series
HARD AS IT GETS
HARD AS YOU CAN
HARD TO HOLD ON TO
HARD TO COME BY
HARD TO BE GOOD
HARD TO LET GO
HARD AS STEEL – A RAVEN RIDERS CROSSOVER
HARD EVER AFTER
HARD TO SERVE – A BLASPHEMY CROSSOVER

Hearts in Darkness Duet
HEARTS IN DARKNESS
LOVE IN THE LIGHT

Heroes Series
HER FORBIDDEN HERO
ONE NIGHT WITH A HERO

Stand Alone Titles
DARE TO RESIST
JUST GOTTA SAY

Dedication

To all those searching for their light in the dark…

Chapter One

QUINTON ROSS WAS IN HIS happy place.

Standing behind the bar at Blasphemy, the club he co-owned with eleven of the coolest assholes he'd ever known, he surveyed the roomful of wonderfully kinky people wearing a whole lotta nothing. Totally his jam.

And the fact that he'd get to *play* with one of them later? Seriously, a man's life didn't get any better.

Well, having a submissive of his own...that could be better. Theoretically.

Except he'd never found someone with whom he felt like he fired on all cylinders. Someone who was into the same kinky play he was, but wasn't looking for a twenty-four/seven arrangement, because that wasn't his style either. Someone who loved the outdoors the way he did, and for whom a fun weekend consisted of camping and hiking and maybe even an afternoon of skydiving. Someone who didn't mind stepping outside their comfort zone, whether that was in the bedroom or traveling to a new place where maybe you didn't even know the language.

Syncing that way with someone was harder than it seemed.

But, whatever. He had a great life as it was. He never lacked for company or partners around the club, and no submissive ever left him anything but fully satisfied. He made damn sure of it.

"Hi, Master Quinton," came a feminine voice from further down the counter.

He turned to find a blond-haired woman with a sleek, silver prosthetic arm leaning against the marble of the ornate bar. Kenna

Sloane. And right behind her stood her big mountain of a Dom and one of Quinton's best friends, Griffin Hudson. "Aren't you looking lovely tonight, Kenna," Quinton said with a smile as he made his way to where Griffin was sliding into a seat and pulling Kenna's slim hips between his legs. "And am I wrong or is this some snazzy new hardware?" He nodded at her arm. She'd lost everything below her right elbow while serving with the Marines in Afghanistan. If she and Griffin hadn't been fuckin' fated, Kenna might've been Quinton's kind of woman.

Adventurous. Brave. Willing to push life to the extremes.

But they *were* fated, something the diamond on her finger and the platinum collar with its unique interwoven knot sitting at the hollow of her throat both indicated. Loud and clear.

Kenna smiled, so much more comfortable here at the club—and seemingly in her own skin—than she'd been when she and Griffin had first reconnected a few months back. "I have a couple different sockets. And a girl has to coordinate," she said, holding it up to the almost sheer sparkling silver halter top she wore.

Chuckling, Quinton nodded and clasped hands with Kenna's Dom. "Master Griffin, how the hell are ya?" Their wrists bore matching leather cuffs with embroidered Gothic M's. Every Blasphemy Master—the experienced Dominants who owned the club and took turns running and monitoring it—wore one.

"Never better, my friend. Never better." The skin crinkled around Griffin's dark eyes as he spoke, his smile coming a million times easier than it ever had before. Quinton guessed that was what happened when you were not only able to correct one of the biggest mistakes of your life, but find a submissive who was also your soul mate in the process.

Lucky fucker.

"I know that's true," Quinton said, winking at Kenna. She ducked her chin but was smiling bright enough to light up the whole room. And that was saying something, given the size of Blasphemy. Located in the renovated remains of an old church, the massive rectangular nave formed the central part of the club. Filled with lots of seating and play areas, it had a soaring ceiling, massive stained-glass windows all around, and a performance and demonstration stage where the altar had once been. Themed rooms and other private spaces stretched off from the main floor. In addition to the very private and exclusive Blasphemy, the public front of their business—Club Diablo, a three-story dance club in a renovated warehouse—stood across a courtyard.

And Quinton provided hands-on management over it all.

He'd been with the clubs from the beginning, and had used his savings and the money he'd made selling a small but successful bar of his own to purchase his ownership stake in Blasphemy. The deal got even sweeter when his partners had offered him the job of managing the bars and all the food service at both clubs. Food, drink, and sex all tantalized the senses and therefore were equally high up on the list of things he loved, and always had been. Given his prior experience, he pretty much had full control of the operation. Just like he liked.

Griffin placed an order for him and Kenna, then asked, "You have a scene set up tonight?"

Quinton got busy making their drinks and shook his head. "No," he said with a grin. "But I'm looking forward to the thrill of the hunt."

Griffin chuckled. "Good luck with that."

The quip on Quinton's tongue died when a flashing red light under the bar's edge caught his eye. An emergency in one of the rooms. He glanced at the tag over the light to determine which one, then slammed the drinks down in front of his friends harder than he'd intended. "Shit, G, sorry. Emergency in the dark room. Get someone to cover?" he said, moving without waiting for an answer. He knew Griffin would have his back.

Quinton moved as fast as he could without calling undue attention. Their members knew that the Masters and a team of other Doms who worked as monitors responded to all sorts of problems around the club. Some were as mundane as an equipment malfunction and others more delicate situations involving disputes between players in a scene. Hell, a few months ago, Quinton had responded when Kenna broke down during a bondage scene, and Griffin had called for help extricating her from his intricate ropework. Sex at the extremes was bound to run into a few issues, which was why consent and safety were hallmarks of BDSM and Blasphemy itself. But none of them wished to distract players from their pleasures with worry or curiosity, either.

Off the main floor, Quinton picked up his pace as he moved

down the long hallway off of which most of the themed play rooms were located. The dark room was at the far end. Master Wolf came up beside him. "Hey, man," he said.

Quinton gave him a nod. "Didn't know you were on tonight, Wolf. Good to see you."

A little taller than Quinton, the guy had dark blond hair, the brightest green eyes you'd ever seen, and a chiseled Scandinavian face that turned heads all over the club. "Running the security control room. Relieving Isaac because the baby's sick," he said, referring to Isaac Marten, their head of security operations, who had a two-month-old son.

"Damn. Sorry to hear that," Quinton said as they closed in on their destination. The dark room was actually a series of three interconnected rooms. In the center was a pitch-black bedroom, accessed only through two changing/waiting rooms on either side of it—one of which let out into this hallway, and the other which let out into a different hallway so that the players couldn't run into each other before or after the anonymous scene. The dark room was very popular, and given Quinton's interest in sensory deprivation, it was one he'd used many times.

He heard someone in distress before they even got inside.

Quinton and Wolf burst through the door to find one of the monitors trying to calm a woman curled on the floor, gasping like she couldn't breathe. She wore a slinky bronze dress that bared most of her legs.

"What happened?" Quinton asked, grabbing a blanket from a shelf and going to his knees beside her. He tucked the soft fleece around her.

"I don't know," the monitor said. "I sounded the alarm but she told me not to call an ambulance."

"She just freaked out. I swear. Hard anything happened between us," a shirtless man said from the doorway to the dark bedroom.

Quinton hadn't even noticed him there, but Wolf was already questioning him. He nodded to the monitor, a Dom in his forties, and then peered up at Master Wolf. "You all clear out. Debrief him and get his information."

"You got it, Q," Wolf said, motioning the other men out into the hall. "Call if you need help."

As they left, Quinton brushed the woman's shoulder-length

brown hair back off her splotchy face. "We need to get your breathing under control or I have to call an ambulance."

"No…no…I…it's…" Clenching her eyes, she shook her head and growled as if in frustration.

Damnit, he needed to do something for her. The part of him that needed to care and soothe decided. He scooped her off the floor and carried her to the couch. Everywhere they touched, her pulse hammered against her skin. If this was a panic attack, it was one of the worst he'd ever seen.

He sat with her in his lap, the blanket still wrapped around her, and cradled her so that they were facing each other. "Breathe with me, little one. Do you hear me? Look at me and breathe with me." Striking hazel eyes with flecks of gold cut to his. Almost familiar…

Focusing, he exaggerated one breath, than another, and another, until she struggled to match her rhythm to his.

Satisfaction rolled through him as the woman's body calmed. Her breathing evened out. Her pulse slowed. Her muscles lost their tension.

"That's it. That's good. Just watch me and breathe with me. Don't stop. We'll kick this thing, don't you worry." He stroked his hand over her hair, wanting to soothe her. The color was so rich it almost matched the bronze of her dress. Her hair was beautiful and soft. As was the rest of her, all golden skin and pretty curves. Her weight felt good in his arms. She turned her face into his hand, just the littlest bit, and he stroked her hair again. A jagged scar ran along her forehead and into her hairline over one eye.

The scar triggered the oddest thought: *That wasn't there before.*

His gaze cut back to those eyes. Hazel with the gold. And he suddenly knew he'd seen them before. Years ago. Right here at Blasphemy. A name clicked into place.

"Cassia?" he asked. Cassia. As in Cassia Locke, a submissive he'd flirted with quite a few times and was once supposed to play with… but she'd stood him up the night of their scene.

"Y-yes, Sir," she whispered. "H-hi, Mas-ter Qu-quinton."

So she recognized him, too. Did she remember that night? He shook off the thought. Their history wasn't something to deal with just then.

"Hi yourself, kid." He gently scratched his fingertips against her scalp and concentrated on taking slow, deep breaths that she mimicked. Studying her, Quinton noticed another scar on her right shoulder. Her hair was much longer than the almost boyish style she used to wear. Finally, Cassia went limp in his lap, and her ease unleashed a satisfaction in his blood. "Feeling better?"

She gave a long sigh, the sound exhausted and defeated. "As better as I can feel after utterly humiliating myself. Sir."

He shook his head. "No such thing happened. Not as far as I'm concerned."

Her gaze skittered away.

"Did I tell you to stop looking at me?"

Cassia's eyes snapped back to meet his. "No, Sir."

Her obedience unleashed even more of that satisfaction. The attraction of BDSM, to him, was as much about the psychology of it as the physicality of the acts. Her reaction—that obedience—represented an ingrained instinct, a need to serve, a desire to surrender. And that fucking heated his blood.

He arched a brow and nodded. "Good girl."

She shifted in his lap, but kept her eyes on his. The movement reminded his body that he'd been planning to find a partner for later, but he locked that shit down tight. First, because she'd been through something tonight he didn't entirely understand. And second, because given that she'd stood him up and never bothered to follow up to explain, he wasn't sure what to make of her anyway. Which meant he needed to know.

"Now, tell me what happened," he said, nailing her with a stare. "And tell me the truth."

Chapter Two

COULD THIS NIGHT SUCK BIGGER *donkey balls?*

That was the tenor of the thoughts running through Cassia Locke's head as she stared at the man who'd just willed her out of one of the worst panic attacks she'd had in a long time. A Dom who was also the sexiest man she'd possibly ever known in her entire life. And that was saying something given the guys her biker brother, Jagger, hung out with....

"Cassia?" Master Quinton arched a brow over light brown eyes that could sometimes appear almost hazel, and other times, darker. It took everything she had not to squirm under that stern *Dom look*, especially since it hadn't been that long since she'd returned to the BDSM club scene after everything that'd happened. She'd nearly forgotten how powerful a look like that could be. And it didn't help her that Cassia was kind of a big Chris Pratt fan, especially after that whole riding-a-motorcycle-with-dinosaurs thing in his last movie, and Master Quinton could've played the actor's seriously hotter stunt double.

Here she was, a basket case the first time she'd seen him after two years.

"I had a panic attack," she said. Story of her life. Lately. She freaking hated it, which was why she'd come tonight. She'd had to at least *try* to move past everything that'd happened.

That eyebrow arched a little higher. He shifted her on his lap so that he could lean over her, his totally lickable face coming closer. The position made her utterly aware of the fact that she was draped over, and now, sorta under him, too. "*And?*"

Swallowing hard, she wet her lips with her tongue, and her stomach gave a flutter when Master Quinton's gaze temporarily tracked the movement. "And…I'm sorta…scared of the dark." Understatement of the century, right there.

For a moment, his expression didn't change, and then all at once his eyebrows cranked down and his face was a mask of confusion. Frowning, he glanced back toward the dark room's door, the obvious question so clear on his face. "Uh…"

"Yeah," she said. "I'm so fucked. Sir."

He scratched his chin. "There's, like, a whole story you need to be telling me here."

Cassia huffed out a breath, and gave the most rote description that she could muster. "I was in an accident. I got trapped in a cave collapse during a research expedition. It took about twenty-four hours for all my light sources to die. After that, I was in the dark."

"Jesus," Master Quinton bit out. "How long was 'after that'?"

An uncontrollable shudder racked through Cassia's body. "Three more days." Four days trapped, three in utter pitch blackness. Her Walkie-talkie had been damaged in the cave-in, and her cell had no service underground, of course. So all she'd been able to do was wait for someone to notice her team hadn't returned on schedule and send help. On top of it all, she'd been alone with the bats and the bugs and all manner of things she couldn't see, because the cave-in had separated her from her two teammates, and she hadn't known if they'd survived. She hadn't known if *she* was going to survive, either. Turned out, they hadn't. She'd been the lucky one.

Not that it always felt that way, not when Cassia could no longer do the job she'd trained for and loved. And especially not when she felt stuck and scared and *trapped*. Still.

Master Quinton raked a hand through his short brown hair, hair that had that casually messy look others paid for and she suspected was all natural with him. "I'm…I'm sorry that happened to you." He heaved a breath and tilted his head. "Can I ask what you were doing in a cave? Is it too hard to talk about?"

"No, it's okay," she said, appreciating the concern. "I'm a geologist with the U.S. Geological Survey. Or, at least, I was. A geologist too afraid to, you know, enter the earth isn't exactly…" Her words trailing off, she shrugged.

Cassia still worked for the USGS, just not doing the thing she most knew and loved, which was investigating the earth science of the planet's caves. In the wake of the accident—and her new fears—she'd been transferred from the headquarters in Virginia to the Chesapeake Bay Water Science Center here in Baltimore.

"Damn." He stroked her hair again, and it was such sweetness. She remembered that about him, how he could be sweet and playful and funny, too. Cassia found it endearing. And sexy. "So, given all that, why did you go into the dark room?"

"I was hoping…I don't know. I thought maybe if I could connect the darkness to something else—to, um, sex—that…maybe…" She sighed. "It was stupid."

Master Quinton's head tilted and he stared at her like he was looking inside her mind. "Actually, I think it could be genius. Except you jumped right into the deep end of the pool. Without knowing how to swim. Or wearing a life vest."

"Well, I'll never know now, I guess." Because no way could she try that room again. Not when she hadn't made it even five minutes. And for most of those she thought she was going to explode out of her skin, the urge to flee or scream or cry had been so strong.

"Are you in therapy for all this?" he asked.

Cassia pushed the blanket off her arms and scrubbed her hands over her face. What therapy *hadn't* she tried? Hell, she'd even given hypnosis a try. "I was. For a long time. Nothing worked. Or, at least, not enough." Which was why she slept with a light on. And hadn't seen a movie at a theater in more than two years, because you never knew when the screen might go all the way dark. And used the flashlight on her cell phone so much that she carried two extra portable charging devices with her to recharge it. It all felt so ridiculous. But she couldn't help the terrifying associations that her mind had made with the dark.

A big, warm hand wrapped around her wrist, pulling it away from her face. Master Quinton stared at the ribbons on her wrist cuff, the ones that indicated what a submissive was or wasn't willing to do. "Why don't you have a phobia ribbon on here?" he asked, a dark cloud rolling in over his expression.

Oh. Oh, shit. "Because…because…"

"I want you on your knees. *Now*."

The command sent her heart into her throat. Cassia moved as

quickly as she could, pushing off of him and going to the floor. Apparently, she was even more fucked than she thought, but she forced herself to concentrate on getting into position—knees spread, hands on her thighs, back straight, head down—and holding it as he rose in front of her.

"Head. Up," he said.

Cassia lifted her gaze.

His eyes absolutely blazed down at her. After being wrapped in the blanket—and in him—the air felt cool against all the skin her little dress bared. She nearly vibrated in anticipation. "Do you understand that BDSM is based on trust, and that without complete honesty and full disclosure, that trust cannot be had?"

"Yes, Sir," she said. Oh, damn. She hadn't meant to lie, exactly, she'd just been *determined* to beat this thing. And how could she do that if no one would help her try? Still, guilt slinked through her belly at the thought of how her behavior might've affected the Dom she'd gone in the dark room with. She hadn't meant to deceive or put anyone else in a bad situation, but she also hadn't been fair to him, had she?

"And do you understand that when there isn't trust, people get hurt, physically, emotionally, or both?" He nearly glared, and it was kinda intimidating, but also strangely hot. This wasn't a side of Master Quinton she'd seen before, but it was clear by the hardening of her nipples and goosebumps racing over her skin that she didn't dislike it.

"Yes, Sir, I do."

He crossed his arms, and the muscles of his biceps, bared by the black tank top he wore, bulged deliciously.

That man gave some seriously good arm porn. *Focus, Cass.* Right.

"And do you realize that in failing to request a phobia ribbon *and* in entering the dark room when you knew you had a fear of the darkness, you represented yourself as being willing to do something which you, in fact, are not willing to do?"

"Yet," she said without thinking.

"What did you say?" He crouched in front of her, those eyes darker now. Dark and intense. It was the kind of look a Dom gave you when you deserved to be punished.

Cassia almost wished he would. Emotion whipped up inside her. Frustration. Despair. And fear, too, which stirred up some anger, for good measure. "*Yet*, Sir," she bit out, her voice trembling from the sudden whirlwind inside her. "I understand I didn't handle this right. I thought…I just thought about it all wrong. But I wasn't trying to deceive, I was trying to force my brain to give up this fucking ridiculous and irrational fear because…because I hate it! I hate being such a damn coward all the time! I'm…I'm stuck, and I just want to…get *unstuck*…and live again!" She hadn't meant to raise her voice, nor had she intended to cry. But she felt tears swimming in her eyes, threatening to fall.

Master Quinton caught a bit of the wetness with his big thumbs, and then he cupped her face in one hand. "Dude. You're kind of a badass, and you don't even know it."

She rolled her eyes. "More like a dumbass."

He bit back a smile, even as he arched a brow. "Did you just roll your eyes at me?"

"Um."

"There's only one right answer, little one."

"Yes, Sir." Cass's shoulders fell.

He nodded. "Do it again and I will find fun and varied ways to punish you. Fun *for me*. Got it?"

Now she was the one biting back a smile, because that *almost* tempted her to do it. All of which was amazing given how awful she'd been feeling just a moment before. "Yes, Sir."

"Good. Now, I have to ask. Why didn't you come to me with all this? Or one of the other Masters?"

"Oh, uh…" She swallowed as her thoughts raced. "Well, first, because I figured you were maybe pissed at me for not showing up that night. And second, because if you're still into the sensory deprivation scenes you used to be into, I'm the last person you'd want to play with. Now."

His eyes narrowed. "You deciding for me what I want?"

Cassia gasped. She couldn't stop screwing up tonight, could she? "No, Sir. It's just that. You like to play with senses, or at least you used to, and I'm terrified of one of mine. So, I just thought—"

"That's part of your problem. You're thinking too much." Rising again, he turned away. And then he paced.

She had about a million questions on the tip of her tongue, but she held them, because he'd put her on her knees to prove a point. There were rules to follow. And right now, that included her keeping her mouth shut. It was one of the things she loved about being a submissive—surrendering to another person's will could be so damn…freeing. And she needed some freedom from her own mind just then.

Finally, Master Quinton came to sit on the couch in front of her, his elbows resting on his knees and his hands laced in front of him. "Maybe I could help you."

"You…want to help me?" Cassia asked, hope and fear and anticipation and excitement flooding through her.

"Yeah. I mean, I have some thoughts. And I'd need to know a lot more to come up with a plan," he said. "And, of course, it'd all be no-strings-attached—"

"No strings attached?" Cassia asked, trying out the words and deciding they made a lot of sense. After everything she'd been through, she needed to get comfortable with herself. And the last thing she needed was the complication of trying to build something with someone else when she was still trying to rebuild herself—and not even sure it was possible.

"I just mean, I wouldn't expect anything more from you outside of our arrangement. And vice versa. Though, obviously, if you don't want me—"

"I do. Want you. Your help, I mean. I want it. Sir." Cass slammed her lips together to cut off the stream of nonsense she couldn't help. She was just so stunned.

Master Quinton chuckled. "Uh huh."

She chuckled, too. "And no strings attached…I think that makes the most sense for me. I'm not looking for a relationship right now. Not with all of this going on."

"Okay, good," he said. "I'm not either. So we're on the same page. But there's one more thing I need to know."

"Anything," Cassia said. Never in a million years had she thought this would happen. She'd just assumed playing with Master Quinton wasn't even a possibility, not after everything.

"Why'd you stand me up the last time we made plans to play? And why didn't you ever get in touch after?" Master Quinton's expression was neutral, *carefully* neutral, she thought, but she could've sworn something flashed behind his eyes. Hurt? Anger? Cass hated that he might've felt either. In truth, she'd thought about letting him know what'd happened, but she'd been messed up for a long time, and by the time she was more herself, she'd been sure Master Quinton had written her off.

"I'm truly sorry about all that," Cassia said, willing him to believe her. "I never meant to flake on you. I'd made that date with you as my own personal celebration from returning from the research trip."

His eyes went wide. "Wait. Are you saying…"

"Yes, Sir. The day I was finally rescued from the cave was the day I was supposed to be here. With you."

Chapter Three

QUINTON HOPED HE WASN'T ABOUT to make a huge-ass mistake.

After talking to Cassia for several more hours the night they'd reconnected, he'd spent the past week reading, making plans, talking on the phone with Cassia, and getting a handle on her interests and limits. He'd bounced ideas off of Masters Griffin and Kyler, the two Blasphemy Masters with whom he was closest. He'd sought the advice of Master Alex, who worked as a psychiatrist. And he'd even reached out to Master Hale, the one of the twelve of them who owned the biggest share of Blasphemy. For reasons none of them fully understood, he didn't play as much anymore, but Quinton figured he'd owed it to the man to keep him in the loop.

And tonight was the night. Quinton's first scene with Cassia.

Truth be told, he was a little nervous. But he was also really freaking excited. Because if what they did worked, a woman was going to get back the life she wanted, and he'd have played a role in that. Christ, a part of him still couldn't believe what Cassia had been through—or that it explained why she'd not shown up for their scene two years before. In his mind, he heard Jack Nicholson from *A Few Good Men* saying, *Don't I feel like the fucking asshole?* Because back then, Quinton had been pissed. And here she'd been hurt. And while she hadn't followed up after the fact, neither had he. So, yeah, on some level he *had* been the fucking asshole.

But hopefully, he'd make up for that now. And, in the process, they were going to push things to some extremes that had his blood pulsing with anticipation.

But, first, baby steps.

Surveying the room he'd set up over the years specifically for sensory deprivation scenes, Quinton made sure—again—that he had everything ready that he might need. And then he went to find Cassia.

She was already waiting for him at the bar. Fifteen minutes early. He liked that. He liked it a lot. Not just the eagerness, but the demonstration that he could count on her to be in this with him.

Quinton came up behind where she was seated on one of the high chairs at the ornate bar and spent just a moment appreciating the beautiful, bare expanse of her back in the sheer black dress. *Dress* might've been too formal a word for it, actually. Which made him appreciate it even more. Leaning in, he spoke close to her ear. "It's good to see you, Cassia."

She gave a little gasp and shivered, and when she turned to him, she was smiling. Her gaze wandered over his shoulders and chest before settling on his face. "It's good to see you too, Master Quinton."

He leaned in closer. "Is it now?"

"Yes, Sir," she whispered, a hint of shyness in her expression as she offered him her wrist. "I rectified this, and I apologize for the error in my judgement, again."

Pleased to see the black-and-red phobia ribbon on her cuff, Quinton smiled and held out a hand. "Very good. And your apology is accepted, little one. Now, come with me."

Nodding, she grasped his hand and slipped off the stool. Hand in hand, they made their way through the lighter Tuesday-night crowd on the main club floor. Instead of heading toward the hall of themed rooms, Quinton guided Cassia to a stairwell that led downstairs, where just two playrooms were located—the dungeon and the sensory room, both of which were completely soundproofed.

He led her inside the largely utilitarian-looking room with its concrete floor and gray sound-proofing on the walls and locked them in. "We're going to talk a little first," he said, leading her to a leather couch at the side of the room. He sat first and peered up at her. "I want you in my lap, Cassia."

She lowered herself slowly, carefully.

Quinton hauled her against him. Her chest to his. His face close.

Her ass against his cock. "I want to feel you."

A beautiful pink filtered into her cheeks. "Yes, Sir."

They'd gone over some of what he wanted to discuss by email, but that didn't mean he wasn't going to be sure. "What are your safewords?"

"Green for *go* or *I'm good*, yellow for *slow down*, and red for *stop the scene*," she said.

"I need you to use them, Cassia, and use them honestly. We're going to start slow, and what we're trying to do here is going to take some time. We're essentially trying to retrain your senses. Right now, you're blinded by fear in the darkness. I'm going to blind you with pleasure."

Her mouth dropped open. "That...that sounds good."

Quinton chuckled, loving how game she was for all this. And respecting the hell out of her for it, too. Without getting too specific, he'd talked about some of the things he thought might have a chance at doing just that, so he knew just how far she was willing to go.

And it was pretty damn far. His kinda girl.

"Yes, it does." Slowly, he pressed a finger to her lips. Instinctively, she kissed it, but he wanted more. "Suck it. Make it wet."

On a quick intake of breath, she did exactly what he said—opened her mouth and sucked in his finger to the middle knuckle. Her tongue bathed his skin, sending blood to his cock. But this wasn't about him. Not tonight.

When he was satisfied with her response, he withdrew, and drew the wet, shiny point of his finger down her neck to the thin strap of her dress. From there, he traced the loose, low neckline of the dress. Down over the mound of one breast, and back up over the swell of the other. Until he was at her mouth once more. "Again," he said, watching her mouth oval around his finger. Then he repeated the teasing, pulling the fabric down more in the process. "Close your eyes and silently count. When you reach ten, you may open them."

With a little shiver, she obeyed immediately. And that slayed him, a little bit, it really did. The trust despite the great well of vulnerability he knew she had. He rewarded her by baring a breast and drawing his fingers around her nipple, gently stroking and pulling.

Her eyelids flipped open, the hazel reflecting desperation back at him.

Watching her closely, he bared the other breast, and her dress pooled around her waist. "Again, little one. Eyes closed and count to ten." He tormented the other breast and studied her face, watching for any signs of panic, but also taking in how pretty she was. High cheekbones. Full lips. The scars that proved she was a survivor.

Swallowing hard, she opened her eyes, a little smile playing around her lips.

"Good," he said, giving her the praise she deserved. "We're going for more now. When your eyes are closed, imagine you're looking at something or some place that makes you feel safe and secure, that makes you feel good. Okay?"

Studying him, she nodded.

He laid her back against the edge of the black leather couch and leaned in over her. "Then this time, count to twenty-five. Go."

Her lids fluttered closed, and Quinton replaced his exploring fingers with his tongue. He licked and sucked at her neck, the sensitive tendon of her shoulder, her breasts, zeroing in on her nipple until he drew it into his mouth. Jesus, she was sweet.

"Twenty-five," she whispered on a gasp.

"Very good," he said, rewarding her with more praise each and every time, until she could hold her eyes closed for a count of sixty and was starting to drive him insane with the way she was squirming in his lap. She was ready for more. Leaning in, he pressed his mouth to her ear. "Are you aroused, Cassia?" He didn't really need to ask, but getting her talking was one small part of getting her out of her head.

"Yes, Sir," she whispered.

His tongue flicked over the shell of her ear. "Are you wet?"

"Very," she said, her head falling to the side as her hand fisted in his tank top.

Then she was definitely ready for more. "Then rise and undress. I want you standing in front of the wall." He pointed to the far side of the room, where a set of chains dangled from the ceiling. "It's time to begin."

Cassia couldn't stop shivering, but it was the good kind of trembling. For once.

Because of Master Quinton.

He'd barely touched her, really, but it was the way he'd done it. Guiding her through the darkness behind her closed eyes so that she'd never felt the full impact of the fear stalking around the edges of her mind. Instead, he'd proved to her again and again that he'd still be right there even if she couldn't see him.

Smart, smart man. And *damn* if smart wasn't sexy as hell.

As she undressed and moved to the stark concrete wall, Cassia burned for more. More of his calloused touch, more of the commanding rumble of his voice, more of that intense masculine gaze. It's been a long time since she'd done a full scene, and never once since the accident.

All of which made it feel like she might vibrate right out of her skin, like she couldn't possibly bear the anticipation of it, like it was her very first time.

She took position, back to the wall, with her legs spread, her hands at her side, and her head down. And then she waited.

Finally, *finally*, Master Quinton appeared in front of her. His bare feet stuck out beneath the frayed hems of his jeans. She hadn't realized just how sexy feet could be before that moment. It almost made her smile.

"Reach up and grasp the bar," he said in a low voice.

Releasing a shaky breath, Cassia found a spreader bar hanging above her with an open cuff on each end. The metal was cool against her palms, and the position totally exposed every part of her to Master Quinton's gaze. Which unleashed nervous butterflies inside her because it had been a long time since she'd last been this open, this trusting with another person. But then she realized she could study him in return.

And, holy hell, if she'd thought his feet were sexy, that was nothing compared to the rest of him. He stood there wearing a pair of obviously well-loved blue jeans, his leather Master's cuff, and nothing else. Somehow, that was hotter than if he'd been totally nude. Master Quinton was defined without being ridged, muscular without being beefy, and he had an absolutely fascinating black tribal tattoo that wrapped around the right side of his ribs—fascinating because it disappeared beneath the waistband of his faded jeans.

"Very nice," he said, his voice deep and gravelly. "You look beautiful like that, open and available to my every whim."

Another shiver raced over Cassia's skin. "Thank you, Sir."

"This scene is going to be about learning where the edge of your tolerance is, Cassia," he said, drawing out her name in a way that made her think of him licking her skin. "Are you ready?"

"Yes, Sir," she managed. At least, she hoped she was. No, dammit, she *was*.

With a nod, he held up a circle of sheer black lace. "Then you'll wear this for me," he said. Not a question, but she nodded anyway. In a quick movement, he slipped the soft fabric around her head. The stretchy lace was black, but largely see-through. It gave the illusion of darkness, without being dark. He peered down and met her eye-to-eye. "Where are you right now?"

"Green, Sir."

He nodded and ran his knuckles gently down her cheek. "Brave girl."

Cassia's reply was cut off as she gasped, because Master Quinton had pressed a vibrator against her clit.

Fisting his hand in the length of her hair, he brought their faces close. "Come as fast and as often as you can." The vibrations intensified.

"Oh, God," she moaned. Because she was already close. From his teasing on the couch. From the fear that already had her body and mind wound tight. From the tormenting sensations.

"Close your eyes, Cassia," he whispered. "Close them and just *feel*."

Oh, God, she did. She closed them. But he held her grounded in the moment. With the warmth of his face against hers. With the tight, commanding hold of his hand in her hair. With the vibrations shoving her hard toward release.

It was the best she'd felt in longer than she could remember. The lightest. The most free.

And that...that was a lot.

Suddenly, she was right there. On the edge, then falling fast. A moan ripped out of her as the orgasm tore through her, her first at another person's hands in so, so long.

"Don't let go," Master Quinton growled. "Because you're not done yet." The vibrator pressed more firmly between her legs. "I want more."

"Oh, shit," she gasped, shaking her head but holding on tight, just like he'd commanded.

"Blind with pleasure, remember?" The tone was smug, as was the chuckle that followed when she repeated her curse. But she could hardly hold that against him when she was already close again, especially as he released her hair and took to tormenting her nipples instead. One and then the other. Biting squeezes that rocked through her like an electrical charge. Palming the head of the vibrating massager, it was almost as if he were cupping her pussy as he pressed it tighter against her clit. And then he moved it in slippery, taunting circles. "I want my fingers *dripping* with your pleasure."

The sensations were destroying her restraint, but it was the blunt words that did it. Eyes clenched tight of her own accord, Cassia came again, and again, before she nearly crumpled as the aftershocks of the orgasms wracked through her.

Master Quinton caught her with an arm around her waist. "Good. So fucking good." He hugged her against his bare chest, and she soaked in his heat. "Do you need a break?"

"No," she said, breathing him in. Soap, spicy aftershave, and something all Quinton. "No, I'm good, Sir."

He pressed a kiss to her hair. "Good. Because we're just getting started, baby girl. Put those hands back up."

Lust drunk, Cassia chuckled as she reached upwards. "I don't know if I can."

"Oh, you can," he said, eyebrow arched in a sexy smirk. When she was in position again, he held up another circle of black lace. "Ready for more?"

She shuddered. "Yes, Sir." The second layer of lace slipped over her head, as sheer as the first, though together, they obscured more of her vision.

"Good?" He stroked a hand down her ribs, making her squirm.

Smiling, she nodded. "Green, Sir."

"Mmm. Green is good." Master Quinton stepped out of her line of vision, and all she knew was the odd cranking sound that echoed in the room. Like a spigot turning on.

He returned to stand in front of her, and sure enough, he held a hose with a strange hand-held shower head on the end. The kind with multiple settings...

The evil Dom nailed her with a stare. "Have you ever used a shower head to make yourself come, Cassia?"

Heat roared over her face, which was really frickin' ridiculous given that she was naked and he'd just given her three orgasms, but the question—and that hose—had just taken her by such surprise. "Um. Yes, Sir."

He gave her a playful smile—part smirk, and part sex on a stick—and nodded. "Was hoping you'd say that." He held the shower head near her lips and twisted a nozzle until water trickled out in a slow stream. "Drink."

Cassia sucked the lukewarm water into her mouth. As she did, some dripped down her front. But she didn't mind, not when his gaze blazed at the wetness falling from her mouth and running down her neck, over her breasts…

"More?" he asked.

"No, thank you, Sir." She licked her lips.

He made another adjustment, and the water hit her belly more firmly. Not a hard spray yet, but a soft shower. And warmer now. "Water is going to be our friend in this little endeavor, Cassia. I want to build a strong sensual association to it, for you."

Warmth rained down over her breasts, her belly, her hips. Ticklish, soft, and comforting, too.

"I want you to associate water with feeling good…" The spray passed over her mound, and she gasped. He trailed it down her legs, down her thighs to her knees to her feet—and then back up again. "I want water to be calming and relaxing, to help get you out of your head and your fears." Using a little black remote he pulled from his pocket, Master Quinton dimmed the lights. Between the lowered lighting and the layers of black lace, it seemed much darker in the room. Dark enough that he was mostly a silhouette before her. Cassia's heart tripped into a sprint, and her mind flirted with the desire to flee.

Gritting her teeth, she tried to resist, and then she moaned, "Yellow, Sir."

The room brightened just a little, but it was enough to help hold the panic at bay. And then the stream of water hit her clit. She went up onto tiptoes as she clutched at the bar above her.

"That's it," he rasped. "I'm here. And you're safe. And you're going to come to please me."

Master Quinton held the water *right there*. And then he turned up the pressure. "Don't think, Cassia," he bit out. "*Feel*."

She did. God help her, it was nearly all she *could* do. The spray was almost harsh now, and it nailed her where she was neediest and most sensitive. The water stimulated her senses as it ran down her legs, dripped and splashed against the concrete floor, and drilled into her clit in an inescapable, delicious torture. "Oh, oh, Master Quin—"

The orgasm stole her ability to speak, to think, to breathe. And then he prolonged it by turning the pressure up yet another notch. Cassia screamed her way through two more orgasms, sure she was losing her mind, her sanity, her very self.

The pleasure was so overwhelming, when she'd been adrift in a sea of utter shit for so long, that it was...almost...too much. *Toomuchtoomuchtoomuch.*

On a moan, Cassia broke into a sob as wrenching as it was unexpected. And all she knew was that she wasn't alone. And that, right now...that was more than she'd had in a long time.

Chapter Four

QUINTON CAUGHT CASSIA IN HIS arms as she nearly crumpled to the ground. Part of him had expected this, so he'd been prepared to move when she finally broke.

Wetness be damned, he carried her to the leather sofa where they'd sat earlier, settled them into a corner of it, and pulled a blanket to wrap around her. Given how high he'd taken her, it wouldn't have been surprising for any submissive to achieve the kind of intense subspace that could lead to a marked emotional release like this. But he'd suspected that Cassia's trauma might make those reactions even more intense.

Which just meant he'd need to be there for her every step of the way.

Exactly what he planned to do.

Holding her against his chest, Quinton eased the lace blindfolds from her head and stroked her hair. Finally, her tears quieted to sniffles and occasional shudders.

"Wow," she finally managed, peering up at him with eyes so bright they were almost green. "I'm sorry for losing it."

"Nothing to be sorry for. Just rest, Cassia," he said. "Let your mind shut down if you need to. I've got you. And I don't have anywhere else I need to be other than right here with you." He always felt that way towards the submissives who gifted him with their service. It was his duty to provide aftercare for them. And with Cassia, it felt especially important, because he knew she was struggling with something bigger and deeper than most.

She reached up and gently, softly stroked the side of his face. "Sweet man," she said in a sleepy voice. Her eyelids sagged shut.

He didn't know if it was the satisfaction of having given her pleasure, the ease reflected in her gaze and her body, or those words, but, sitting there with this warm, sated woman in his lap, Quinton felt ten fucking feet tall. And he was overcome with a sudden *yearning*. For someone who'd make him feel that way all the time. Not just like a Dominant, but like someone's *Master*.

The distinction wasn't one that he'd given that much thought to during his years in the lifestyle. That is, not until his two closest friends at Blasphemy had collared submissives of their own over the past couple of months. First, Kyler Vance, the proud commitment-phobe, had collared Mia Breslin, despite the fact that she'd turned out to be his boss's daughter, something that had almost ended them before they'd even started. And then Griffin got the second chance he'd always wanted but never dared hope for with Kenna.

On some level, Quinton was aware he held a piece of himself back. And he didn't need a shrink to know why. Growing up, he'd had a front-row seat to a grade-A dysfunctional marriage. He'd seen the fighting and the apathy, and how two adults could lead separate lives even though they'd lived in the same house. From one particularly nasty fight before they'd divorced, his mother's words still sometimes rang in Quinton's ears: *I never should've settled for less than everything*. He'd expected his father to yell something mean in return, but what he'd heard instead left a bigger impression: *No, you shoudn't have. And neither should I.* His dad had moved out the next day.

So Quinton wanted the real thing. He wanted the everything. And he'd never been entirely sure it existed.

But Kyler thought he'd founded it, and so did Griffin.

Quinton peered down at Cassia, his thoughts a mess of wants. After a while, his gaze locked onto the scar on her face. They should've been together just as she'd been suffering that injury. That she'd gotten hurt wasn't his fault, and there wasn't a thing he could've done to stop the accident from happening, but that didn't change the odd niggle of guilt he felt. At the very least, he could've checked in, followed up, helped her sooner.

Coulda, woulda, shoulda.

Even though it made no sense, he had the oddest thought: *Next time, I'll be there to protect her.* Except that wasn't their deal here, was it?

On a stretch, Cassia's eyelids fluttered open, distracting him from examining the strange impulse any further.

"Hi," she said, a sleepy, warm smile shaping her beautiful face.

"Hi, yourself."

"Was I out long?" she asked, just a hint of self-consciousness in her expression.

He shook his head, wanting more than anything to have her at ease around him. Always. Why did she make him feel that way? Was it a desire to make up for what he hadn't done before? He didn't know. "Not too long. How do you feel?"

She hesitated for a moment, and he could see that she was really reflecting on the question rather than giving the rote *fine* that so many people might've. He appreciated that. "I feel…good. A little tired. But, also kinda energized from...everything." Pink filtered into her cheeks.

"Everything being the seven orgasms?" He arched a brow.

The laughter that spilled out of her lit him up inside. "Pretty much," she said. "But it was more than that, too. I mean, don't get me wrong. That was *amazing*." They both chuckled. "But for the hour I was with you, I didn't think…of everything that happened. I was just…me. The old Cass." A sheen of glassiness made her eyes sparkle as she peered up at him.

The old Cass. He liked the sound of that, for her. He tucked a strand of rich brown hair behind her ear. "I'm glad." Quinton didn't want this to end tonight. Not yet. And then he thought of something fun that would keep it from having to. "I've got an idea and I want you to say yes."

Her eyebrow arched over a confused expression. "Uh, okay. Is it… are you ordering me to say yes? Sir?"

Quinton grinned. "Not unless you want me to." Really, he wanted her to say yes because *she* wanted to.

Cassia bit her lip. "Well, I think we both know that I like when you order me around."

"I'll never get tired of hearing you admit that," he said, smirking.

She laughed. "So what's your idea?"

"Get dressed and come dancing with me," he said. "Here, at Blasphemy."

Putting her finger to her lips, she affected an *I'm thinking about it* smile. "Hmm. Let's see…that's a yes."

Satisfaction tore through his gut. "There's a catch, though."

"Which is?"

He held up the double layer of black lace she'd worn before. "I want you to wear these while you're doing it."

Cassia stood with Master Quinton in the shadows at the edge of the dance floor. Her gaze ran over the stage where they sometimes did demonstrations, the soaring vaulted ceiling, and the moving, swaying bodies clad in every variety of play wear—leather, lace, PVC, and more.

Finally, she forced herself to meet the Dom's dark, searching gaze. Nerves made it hard to do. Why it should feel any different now to wear the blindfolds, Cassia didn't know. Without the distractions created by him tormenting her body, would she be able to tolerate the way the lace obscured her vision? And if she couldn't tolerate it, would she freak out in the middle of the dance floor? In front of all these people?"You're thinking too much again," Master Quinton said.

She couldn't even deny it. "I know, Sir."

"Unless I tell you otherwise, you can drop the *Sir* when we're not in scene. I've never been a stickler for the protocol. How's that sound?"

That sounded…good, easier. Part of her yearned for the service and satisfaction of being a submissive, but right now, she felt a little overloaded. From what they'd done and the newness of being back in the lifestyle after so long away. So his offer felt like it relieved a pressure valve inside her. And, damn, she really appreciated that, appreciated that he seemed—once again—to know what it was she might need. "I like that, thank you."

He nodded and gave her a crooked grin, and then he stepped in close. So close that she could feel his heat. Since she'd literally slept up against all that heat, maybe feeling it now shouldn't have been so startling, so appealing, but it was. Because she knew just how good it felt. "Now, tilt your head back."

She did, and her hair fell away from her face. He slipped the blindfolds over her head. Taking a deep breath, Cassia peered around her. Colored and white lights flashed through the lace, which in a strange way highlighted the darkness around the flashes. The blindfolds also brought to life her other senses. Against the louder backdrop of the music, she heard voices—talking, laughing, cries of ecstasy from somewhere in the distance. The bass beat echoed up through the floor so that she felt it in her body. The heat of the spotlights passed over her.

Master Quinton's big hands settled on her shoulders, and he leaned in. "Doing okay?"

"Yeah," she said. "Was just…making sure."

"Me, too," he said. He took her hand, his grip big and firm around hers. "Come on."

The music shifted just as they made their way into the center of the tight, pulsing crowd. The song had an intense, driving beat that drew more people to the floor. Cassia grinned as the press pushed them closer together. She gave herself over to the energy and the music and the heat radiating from a hundred other bodies. And just danced.

And so did Master Quinton. Trying to watch him move made her suddenly glad for the blindfolds. She might not be able to see details, but he couldn't see her watching him, studying him, admiring the way his hips moved and enjoying the smile that communicated the comfort he had in his own skin.

Not to mention, from what she could make out, the man moved like a freaking dream. Like, you could just look at him on a dance floor and think, yup, that man has to be good in bed. Which had her wishing at least a little that things had gone further between them tonight, even though a big part of her was grateful that he'd only taken it as far as he had. She'd really appreciated that he'd made the scene sexy and satisfying and intense, even when it was also about moving them toward a specific goal—making her more comfortable in the dark.

That she also liked Master Quinton was just icing on the cake.

He moved in closer and pressed his lips to her ear. "Tell me something about you, Cassia." Grasping her hand, he spun her and settled her back to his front.

Which made it damn hard to think. Especially when he gripped her hips and moved them together. Especially when all his hardness rubbed against her ass and his breath fell on her neck, along with a trail of soft, teasing kisses.

"Tell me something," he said again.

Forcing herself to think through the haze he cast over her mind and body, Cassia debated. What could she tell him that he didn't already know? Once, she'd considered herself adventurous and daring, but she couldn't help but think that the cave-in had changed all that. Maybe forever. Before tonight, the best she'd felt since the accident was when she'd...

There. *That* was something.

Turning enough so that he'd have a chance of hearing her, she said, "I like to ride motorcycles."

"No shit?" he said, appreciation plain in his voice. "Do you own one?"

She shook her head. "My brother does. He's in a club in Frederick. I ride one of his whenever I visit him."

"I'm more of a fast car guy, but bikes are pretty badass, too," he said.

Cassia turned in Quinton's arms, excitement bubbling inside her. "Then you would totally love my brother. He runs the Green Valley Race Track. Have you ever heard of it? Stock-car races, demolition derbies, that kind of thing?"

"Heard of it? *Girl*, I've been there many times. I freaking love racing."

Grinning, Cassia nodded and leaned in so Quinton could hear her. "Then you know my big bro's track. Well, it's his club's place, but he manages everything about it. The races are a blast." And Jagger loved running the track, too, almost as much as he loved being a part of the Raven Riders club that owned it. Cassia used to go up there all the time for the weekend races, but she hadn't gone as frequently since everything happened. Which made her suddenly miss him.

"Damn, that rocks," Quinton said, his tone making Cass wish she could see his expression better, because he sounded a lot like a kid learning about a new toy.

And that gave her an idea... "You know, I could take you up there some time. Maybe meet some of the drivers. See the race from the pit. I'm sure Jagger would give you a behind-the-scenes tour. And if we went early enough, we might even be able to get you a turn driving on the track. If you think watching is fun, driving is a total trip."

Through the mask, Cass could just make out the oval of Quinton's mouth.

"I mean, of course you don't have to. I just thought—"

His mouth came down on hers. The kiss was an overwhelming full-body experience. His tongue colliding with hers. His hard muscles pressing close. His hand sliding into her hair.

It was fantastic, even though it ended way too freaking fast.

"When?" he asked, not even trying to hide how excited he was.

Cassia laughed, dizzy from the lingering heat of the unexpected kiss and delighted at Quinton's enthusiasm. "I'll call him and see when would work best."

"You'd do that?" he asked. "Because that would be fucking awesome."

Still smiling, she was already thinking of what she would say to Jagger—about the visit, the favor, and the man she'd be bringing along. On the surface, her brother seemed easy-going and laid back. And he mostly was. But he still had a protective streak a mile wide. And Cassia hadn't brought anyone around for a long time.

Even though she was already determined to make this happen, she couldn't help but have a little fun with Master Quinton. "Hmm. I *think* I'd be willing. I mean, maybe I could use a little encouragement, though."

His grip in her hair tightened. "Could you now?" he asked, his voice dropping. The music shifted gears, slowing down into something sensual and gritty, the lyrics full of dirty innuendo. "And what kind of encouragement might you need?"

"Oh, I don't know," she said, her breath catching as Master Quinton hauled her closer, close enough that she could feel, against her belly, that his cock had hardened. And that thrilled her, the knowledge that she aroused him. Sexy and powerful weren't things she'd felt in a long time, but as his hard-on bumped and grinded against her, she felt both. And, damn, that was something after everything she'd been through.

"I do," he said, his mouth at her ear again. And then his fingers tugged at the lace around her eyes. She was almost sad that he was removing it, except then it got *darker*.

Cassia gasped. He hadn't removed the lace, he'd *folded* it, doubling its thickness, and nearly obscuring the light altogether. She clutched at his thick biceps.

"Hold on to me. Just like that," he said, his arms coming around her, one hand palming the center of her back, the other settling on the swell of her ass.

Competing reactions exploded inside her. Anxiety, fear, and panic threatened. Those she expected. But there was also anticipation, desire, and excitement, too. It was an overwhelming, disorienting cocktail.

"Where are you, Cass?" he asked.

"Um..." She swallowed, hard. "Yellow, Sir," she said, feeling weak at the admission.

He kissed her, soft and sweet and approving. "Good girl," he said. "Always want you to be honest with me. If it's too much, squeeze my shoulders three times. Otherwise, no talking."

"Yes, Sir," she said, knowing that they'd just slipped into a scene without him having to tell her. And that helped tip the scales toward the more positive reactions he'd unleashed. Because her body was a live wire waiting to see what he had in store for her. Why had she teased him again?

Words rumbled into her ear. "There's a couple right behind you. Almost touching you. The man is dancing behind the woman, and he's pulled up her skirt." Cassia's heart tripped into a sprint. Master Quinton squeezed her ass with one big hand as they danced, his body tight against hers. Other bodies bumped against them, too, against her elbow, her heel, her hip. "She was naked beneath," he continued, "and her pussy is bare. The man is teasing her, rubbing his fingers over her lips without really hitting her clit. The look on her face is pure torture."

Each word painted a new stroke of color against the blackness of her eyelids—and over all the most sensitive places of her body. Her nipples. Her neck. Her clit. Cassia shivered as the image Quinton described came to life in her mind's eye.

Slowly, Master Quinton dragged his tongue up the column of Cass's neck, adding to her own torment. And then his lips were at her ear again. "He's fingering her now. Forcing her to keep dancing while he does it." He swallowed thickly. "Aw, fuck, Cass, he's making her suck her own wetness off his fingers. Off his *dripping wet* fingers."

Cassia moaned at the vivid picture she now had, and at the rough arousal in her Dom's voice. His lust stoked her own, made her wish that *they* were the ones doing what he described.

Quinton licked the shell of her ear, unleashing goosebumps all down her neck and shoulders. "He's taking his cock out now. Lining it up between her legs… Oh, yeah, he just slid into her from behind. Right here on the dance floor."

A whimper spilled from Cassia as heat roared over her body. Suddenly, she could barely stand the thin fabric of her dress against her skin.

"Mmm, like that idea, do you?" Quinton said, his dirty words a secret the music helped them keep. "Looks like she does too, the way her Dom is taking her right here in the middle of all these people, all of them watching her, touching her. Can you see it, Cassia? Can you see him fucking her?"

She gave a fast nod, almost forgetting not to speak. But, *God*, she wanted to. She wanted to *beg*.

For Quinton. For his touch and his tongue and his cock.

"Yeah, I know you can. You can see his fat cock sliding deep. I bet you can even *feel* it."

Jesus, she was going to come. She was going to come from his words alone.

On some level, she knew what he was doing. And she freaking adored him for it, for the way he'd put light in the darkness with just his voice. But she was too invested in the story to think about it. She needed more. She needed it all.

The music changed again, faster now, and intense. Master Quinton's hands roamed until both of them cupped her ass. He squeezed and lifted, his actions reverberating between her legs. Making her want to grind. Making her need to.

She was almost ready to plead for him to continue when more rough words spilled into her ear again. "The man…he invited others to touch the woman while he fucks her. A male sub just knelt on the floor, and he's eating her right there in the middle of everyone, tonguing and sucking and licking at the wetness the man's cock draws out. God, Cassia, can you imagine what that would be like?"

The sound she made was almost pained. Because she could. God help her, she could imagine what it would be like to be impaled on Quinton's cock while another man devoured her clit. Wetness slicked the tops of her thighs around the thin thong she'd worn.

"Yeah, I knew you could," Quinton said. "Fuck, I bet you'd come so hard."

"Master Quinton," she moaned, breaking.

He gave her a hard swat on the roundest part of her ass. "Quiet, little sub. We're not talking right now. We're watching this couple next to us fuck. And, damn, he's fucking her so good, Cassia. She's so damn wet."

Cass rubbed her thighs together as they moved, absolutely desperate now.

"I think she's gonna come," he said, his breath hot against her ear. "And if you can get there, just from this, you can too." He shifted her so that his leg nudged between hers, just the littlest bit.

It was everything, but it wasn't nearly enough.

Cassia cried out in her desperation.

"Oh, fuck, Cassia. She's coming. She's coming so hard. And her Dom is too. While all these people watch."

His words had turned her into pure animal need. She was still listening to him. Of course she was. But she was also trying to move her body against him. Starving for even the smallest amount of friction she could find from his thigh, from her own. Jealousy of the other woman's release seethed through her.

"His come is dripping down her thighs," Quinton growled. "And he's showing it off to everyone, how he owns her inside and out."

Her head spinning from the pleasure drenching his voice, she dug her fingers into his muscles and rocked against him as hard as she could. Her clit bumped his thigh in one single, devastating impact.

Cassia came on a scream that the music swallowed. And then Master Quinton did as well when his mouth sealed over his. He kissed her hard, rough and claiming and domineering.

And even though the orgasm eased the worst of the greedy, red-hot lust flooding through her, it wasn't enough. She needed more. She needed to be the one impaled on his fat cock, coming on it, taking everything he had to give.

She was just barely aware of the music changing again, this time into a lighter techno dance song with a fast beat.

Master Quinton pulled his lips from hers. "Thank you for dancing with me, Cassia."

Did he imagine she was capable of speech just then? She licked her lips and nodded. "Thank you, Sir," she managed, her voice a raw scrape.

Hand in hand, he guided them off the dance floor. Her mind and body were still reeling as she followed him on unsteady legs. Because he'd not only rocked her world with the power of his voice, but every bit of the anxiety she'd felt when he'd first doubled her blindfold was now entirely gone. She wasn't even sure if the couple he'd described actually existed, but that had never been the point, had it? He *made* them exist in her mind, and in doing so, fought her fear.

It shook the ground beneath her feet, because that...that was *power.*

After everything she'd been through and everything she'd tried, she knew it was. Which made her wonder: how long was this no-strings-arrangement going to last? Because some part of her already regretted that it might end. It was probably a ridiculous thought after just one night, and no doubt it was just her banked lust talking.

Finally, Master Quinton guided her to sit and removed the blindfolds. "How are you?"

Her gaze raked over him. His hair was a little damp with sweat. His face was flushed. His eyes, dark fire.

And even sitting down, there was no denying that his cock was rock fucking hard. The bulge filling out the front of his jeans was pronounced.

"I asked you a question, Cassia."

Her gaze cut back to his, and she was so busted. "I'm...good, Sir. Kinda shell-shocked. And still really freaking horny."

He grinned and nailed her with a stare. "Good. You're not to have any orgasms until we meet again."

She gaped, then pretended to look at the watch she wasn't wearing on her wrist. "I'm free in five minutes. You?"

Master Quinton burst into a big belly laugh that might've made her laugh, too, if she hadn't been so serious. But she was. The orgasm she'd just managed to have from that brush against his thigh hadn't nearly satisfied the deep burn she had inside.

"You're going to be a lot of fun, Cass," he said, with a smugness she kinda wanted to hate but couldn't because it was too hot and playful. "How about Tuesday night?"

Chapter Five

GOOD THING NO ONE HAD ordered *Quinton* not to orgasm until he and Cassia were together again, because he wouldn't have been able to follow the command.

Only three days had passed since their first night together, and he hadn't been able to restrain himself from replaying the scenes they'd done and jerking himself off every single time. Twice, that first night after she'd left Blasphemy.

Orgasm denial was a *bitch*. Which made him feel delightfully evil as he wondered if Cassia had obeyed his command. Oh, the fun he'd have if she hadn't. Actually, he was going to have fun either freaking way.

Because, somehow, despite the fact that he'd never taken his cock out of his pants that night, those scenes had turned his blood molten. And he didn't see cooling off anywhere in his immediate future. Not with Cassia around.

Quinton had carefully prepared the scene they'd played out in his sensory room that night, but the dance floor…that had been pure chemistry at work. And the fact that they'd both gotten so hot proved that their equally matched dirty minds got off on the exact same things.

Put that together with learning that Cass loved motorcycles and race cars, and he was well beyond intrigued.

Which was maybe a problem, given what he'd proposed and she'd accepted.

No strings attached. That makes the most sense for me right now….I want that, too.

The memory of her words kept him grounded in reality, and that was a good thing. He didn't need promises of forever to have a good time, and never had. The thought had Quinton thinking about the fun he'd have *tonight*. He surveyed his preparations in the sensory deprivation room. He'd been debating trying out two different scenes tonight, but had finally come down on the side of overwhelming Cassia's senses.

He hadn't tried anything quite like this before, and he was looking forward to it.

Just like last time, he found Cassia sitting at the bar waiting for him. Master Leo was slinging drinks and smiling at Cass in a way that made Quinton feel possessive. Maybe even a little territorial. Especially when she laughed so freely in response to whatever it was he was saying, no doubt charming her with those unique eyes, one blue and one green. More than a few subs had gone crazy for the guy's look, but not nearly as many were into his darker brand of play.

And, damn, Leo wasn't the only one who'd noticed Cassia.

Because Master Wolf was sitting at the bar next to her. Master Wolf, who got off on voyeurism and exhibitionism and whose actions had inspired the scene that Quinton had shared with Cass on the dance floor.

Quinton came up between them, his arm around the back of her chair. "Hello, Cassia. You're looking lovely," he said, drinking in the flowy white halter dress that tied behind her neck and left the entirety of her back bare.

Though she'd already been smiling at whatever the other men had said, her whole face lit up when she looked at him, and damn if that didn't make him feel good. "Hey, there you are, Master Quinton. And thank you."

Wolf turned on his stool and they clasped hands. "Q, how the hell are ya?"

"I can't complain," he said, his gaze cutting to Cassia. "In fact, I think tonight is going to be fucking awesome."

When she spoke, Cassia's voice had a huskiness that hadn't been there just a moment before. "Master Wolf and I were just talking about Sweden."

The other Dom nodded. "Turns out Cassia and I have a friend in common. How random is that?"

"Oh yeah?" Master Quinton asked, the possessiveness easing off a little so that he could relax, especially as he clocked the just-friendly vibe between them.

Cassia nodded, her expression excited. "A couple of years ago, I got to go on this incredible research trip to the Coral Cave in Sweden. It was only discovered in the 1980s, so there's a lot of uncharted territory down there. Researchers from all over the world have led expeditions exploring it. While I was in Sweden, I also visited the country's largest cave, which is open to the public. And Master Wolf is friends with a geologist who works there." Wolf nodded as she spoke.

Quinton couldn't help smiling at her enthusiasm. "Can I just say how much I love a woman who gets excited over uncharted territory?" He arched a brow.

She laughed, just like he hoped he would. "Is that so, Sir?"

"Uh huh," he said, grinning like an idiot now.

Shaking his head, Master Wolf clapped him on the shoulder. "On that note, I'm off to do…something. Or someone." He winked, and then his expression went mischievous. "Maybe I'll see you two on the dance floor again later."

Quinton slipped into the other Dom's seat as Cass gasped. "Wait. Was he…I mean…did you…"

"Yup." He grinned as she squirmed in her seat and her cheeks pinked.

"Well. Okay, then," she said, her eyes wide. "Is it hot in here or is it just me?"

"Oh, it's *definitely* you," he said, allowing his gaze to wander. Over the deep V of her neckline, over the way the short skirt revealed the soft expanse of her upper thighs…

She finished the last sip of her drink and turned to him until her knees touched his thigh. "Can I tell you something, Master Quinton?"

"Always."

Those pretty hazel eyes were full of heat as they met his. "It's interesting knowing that what you described to me that night was real. But I…"

"What?" Hanging on her words, he tucked a strand of silky bronze behind her ear.

"I still think the image is hotter if I imagine the man...was *you*."

Aw, hell, yeah. He leaned in, knowing she liked his voice in her ear, his breath on her skin. "And that, little sub, makes you my new favorite person. My new favorite person who I just might like to reward for offering such a nice fucking compliment." He pulled back just enough to meet her gaze again, and the need there rushed heat over *his* skin. "But I gotta ask you something first."

"Yes, Sir?"

"Did you touch yourself, Cassia? Did you make yourself come since we were last together?" He wasn't sure whether he wanted her to have broken down or held out.

A fast shake of her head. "No, Sir. Even though it was hard as hell," she said with a laugh.

"Mmm, then you definitely deserve a reward. Let's go."

The adrenaline rush had Cassia shivering, and they hadn't even started yet. Naked, she stood in the center of the room, feet apart, hands at her side, head down. And waited.

Finally, Master Quinton came to her, his feet bare again under the ragged hem of the worn blue jeans. His voice was soft, soothing. "Look at me, please."

She lifted her gaze, struck all over again by how freaking sexy this man was.

"Sensory deprivation is the ultimate mindfuck, Cassia. Which is why I love it." His grin was pure seductive confidence. "And it can be achieved in all kinds of ways. By depriving your senses, as we did the other night. Or by *overwhelming* them. And that's what we're going to try tonight. Both the lack of stimulus and the overstimulation of the senses can make it difficult for your brain to process what it's experiencing. And that's what we want, to trip up your brain's current way of thinking."

She nodded, appreciating how thoughtful he was about all this. It didn't sound like this was just a kink to him, though it was definitely that. But it also sounded like he enjoyed the *challenge*. "Yes, Sir. That makes sense."

"Good." Slowly, he walked around her, just the tip of one finger dragging against her skin. Her stomach, her ribs, her spine. "I want to push you a little further tonight, Cassia. In *every* way. What do you think of that?" He returned to stand in front of her.

Cassia shivered again, her imagination running wild. Would he fuck her tonight? She'd dreamed of nothing but that in the three days since she'd last been here. "I want to try, Sir."

"Brave girl." Gently, he pressed a kiss to her mouth. "Pretty girl."

Her heart did a little flip. She knew they were just having fun together, just doing scenes, but she couldn't help but think that whoever got to have this man as their own would be one lucky sub.

Why couldn't it be me?

He didn't give her time to debate the thought, because just then he said, "The only time you're allowed to speak is if you need to use your safeword. Otherwise, no talking. Understood?" She nodded. "Then let's begin."

Silently, he guided her to a huge piece of dungeon furniture that took up much of one wall. The St. Andrew's cross was shaped like an X, and Master Quinton helped her step up onto the short, elevated platform at the bottom of it. He secured her feet there with cushioned cuffs that held her in place even though she barely felt them. Pressing himself to her back, he secured her hands to the top of the X next, so that she stood spread-eagled, her back to the room, her face towards the wall.

A thrill of anticipation raced through her.

A thrill he ratcheted up when he blindfolded her just like he had the other night, with the room-darkening double layer of lace. And she found herself glad he hadn't folded it over like he had on the dance floor because, next, a pair of heavy headphones settled over her ears, deadening the world around her. Little sight. No hearing.

Tingles cascaded over her skin, and her heart tripped into a sprint. Those same warring reactions erupted inside her. The threatening panic and the equally strong excitement. Like being held at the crest of a roller coaster's highest hill but knowing any second you were going to fall down, down, down.

And then Master Quinton began his true assault.

Dragging something light and soft down her spine, over her ass, and up her arms, her whole body shuddered. He teased and tickled her on and on, until she thought she couldn't stand it anymore. Until she was hypersensitive and squirming. Having lost two of her senses, Cassia's sense of touch was absolutely *alive.*

Which she felt even more acutely when the sensations changed. Now, something icy hot slid down the backs of her thighs, then slowly, lazily up the insides. And then his tongue was on her back, licking up her spine and leaving its own trail of wetness behind. Gasping, she tried to go up onto her toes when the ice met the heat of her core just as his teeth nipped at the tendon along her shoulder. It was so much, it was almost *too much*. But damn if the overload of sensation wasn't keeping her from focusing on the blackness against her eyes.

And, oh God, he didn't let up.

Because just as she started to get used to the sting of the ice, it changed again. Flaps of leather landed against her ass, biting her skin with warmth and surprise. A flogger, if she had to guess. But what kept her so off kilter was that he alternated his strokes with the ticklish drags of what felt like a feather, delivering the blows of both at irregular, unpredictable intervals so that she couldn't anticipate, couldn't expect, couldn't brace or prepare or breathe.

She was just sensation, and it was like her skin was a live wire, flush with a hot, pulsing energy. Cassia shivered nonstop. Her nipples were hard points. And her clit ached for the attention he was delivering everywhere else.

Sound flooded her ears. A rainstorm against a lonely violin. Together with the physical sensations, she totally understood what he meant by overwhelmed. All at once, her brain swam in an attempt to make sense of the physical, the visual, the aural until she was nothing *but* those competing sensations.

For just a moment, the violin quieted, amplifying the rain shower in her ears.

And out of nowhere, her mind conjured the blackness of the cave, and the dripping, splashing, flowing sounds of the water that were her constant companions while she'd been trapped...

The sound sucked her into memories she tried to forget, and the scene fed into her growing disorientation. The cuffs were the rocks that caught one of her ankles. The soft blows of the flogger were the outcroppings of rock she stumbled into in the darkness. And the rain was the *dripping dripping dripping* water...

Red red red red red red... "Red!"

Light and sound sucked her out of that cave, out of the memory.

"Hang on, Cass. I've got you," came a voice. Master Quinton. Oh,

God, he was here. And then he had her in his arms, wrapped in a blanket and pressed against all his heat.

"I...I...where..."

"It's okay. Just take a minute," he said. His hand stroked over her hair.

Blinking away the last vestiges of the darkness, Cassia struggled to get her bearings. They sat in a heap on the floor in front of the cross, and he held her in the cradle of his lap. Finally, she focused on his face, and it was his eyes that grounded her. Blazing with emotion and regret. She struggled to swallow, to slow her breathing, to reorient her brain against the confusion. "I'm...sorry."

"Please don't be," he said, pressing his forehead to hers. "Never apologize for something that's not your fault, especially when it's *my* fault. Damnit, I pushed you too hard, Cassia. Are you okay?"

"No." She shook her head, struggling to think, to speak. "I mean, yes, I'm okay. But you didn't push me too hard," she said a little breathlessly. Cassia forced a deep inhale and exhale. "It was the rain. It was just the rain."

For a moment he frowned, and then his eyes went wide. "Aw, hell. There's water in caves. I'm an idiot."

There was something about the sarcasm in his self-deprecating words that eked a smile out of her. Maybe because it was clear that he was so upset and she wanted to make him feel better, even though she was the one lying in his arms and trying to shake off the last tendrils of the panic attack. "An exceedingly hot one, though," she managed.

He froze, and a million emotions seemed to flash across his expression, like he didn't know which part of what she said to react to first. "Did you just agree that I'm an idiot?"

She bit back a smile. "Did you just ignore that I called you hot?"

Finally, he grinned too, and gave a little reluctant chuckle. "I totally did *not* miss that, cheeky little sub." The smile faded again. "I really am, sorry, Cassia. I should've known—"

"No, Sir. Really." She grasped his hand and pressed a kiss to his palm. "And I was just teasing. You are *not* an idiot, and this was no one's fault. I'm not sure *I* would've known the sound of the running water would impact me that way. I loved the scene you did with the hose—that didn't bother me at all. And I've never freaked out during a storm. I was enjoying myself until it just suddenly became too much."

On a not fully believing sigh, he nodded.

"We're done for tonight, aren't we?" she asked, suspecting the answer, then seeing it in his expression. She hated that she might've disappointed him. She'd certainly disappointed herself. Cassia wanted to be stronger than this. She *should* be stronger than this.

"With that scene, yes. I don't think either of us are in the right head space for mind-fucking right now."

"You have quite the way with words, Sir." She grinned, remembering the way just his words had made her so hot. "But I guess you're right."

Wearing a crooked smile, he winked. "Always a safe assumption."

"Is that right?" His humor was infectious.

"Mmhmm. Besides, there are plenty of other ways to make you come." Her mouth dropped open at the promise of his words, and he leaned in and kissed her cheek, then nuzzled her there. "Dirty talk works for you, doesn't it?"

Heat bloomed over her body. There was no sense denying it, not after the other night. "Yes, Sir."

"I like that. I like that that your body is so responsive to having your senses heightened." He made a low hum of approval as he kissed her throat. "Do you still trust me?" he asked, the echo of that hesitance still plain on his face.

The question reached inside her heart. "Aw, Master Quinton. Of course I do. Honestly, during the time we've spent together, I've handled darkness better than at any point in the past two years. You didn't mess up with me, I swear."

Gently, slowly, he cupped her face in his hand, and then he drew her in. The kiss was languid and deep, soft but exploring. And hot. It was freaking hot. "Your bravery is a fucking turn-on for me, you know that?"

Cassia liked that. She liked it a lot. It made her feel strong, and she adored that he could give her that feeling with just a few words. And after everything else that'd happened tonight. "If you say so, Sir."

"I do." He arched a stern brow, which slowly slid into a grin. "And I'd still like to make you feel good, if you're up for it."

"I am."

He smiled, and man, she really dug that about him, how freely and often he smiled and laughed. He could turn on the stern Dom in an instant, but his normal operating mode seemed to set to light-hearted and easy-going. "Good. Because I have an idea."

"You do?"

"Mmhmm."

She couldn't begin to imagine the universe of this man's ideas, but she was definitely game to explore them. "Then lead the way."

Chapter Six

QUINTON WAS GOING TO MAKE this night up to Cassia. And he was going to make it up bigtime.

For fuck's sake. He'd been caving before—twice. Once in a rock cave with a club in college a million years ago, and once he'd swam and snorkeled in an underground *cenote* while on vacation in Mexico.

He should've anticipated this problem. He should've taken better care of Cass. But at least now he knew that building a positive association for her with water was even more important, because it was clearly a trigger for her fear of the dark.

Regret weighing on him, he retrieved a cream-colored robe and slippers from a cabinet. "Wear these," he said. As she slid it on, he gathered up their clothes.

Cassia hugged herself and ran her hands over the plush chenille. "I hope you don't mind, Sir, but you're never getting this back."

He laughed, enjoying that she took pleasure in such a simple thing, and making note of it, too. "Is that right?" He joined her where she stood by the couch.

"Yup. Would it help if I licked it?"

Quinton froze. "Excuse me?"

Grinning, she tilted her head and peered up at him. "You know, people say when you lick something you've claimed it."

Oh, he was going to enjoy the *hell* out of what he had planned, all right. He crossed his arms. "And just how widely do these people apply this licking-equals-ownership principle, Miss Locke?"

Cass gave a coy shrug. "Personally, I take it on a case-by-case basis."

"Oh, girl," Quinton said, grinning now, and really appreciating how her good humor helped him shake off how badly he'd felt moments before. He'd probably never forgot the terror that had warped her voice when she'd called out her safeword over and over. "You are in so much trouble."

"I am, Sir?"

"Uh huh," he said, lowering his voice as he stalked toward her.

Laughing, she backed up until he had her pinned against the door. And damn she was pretty, vibrant and full of interesting layers he increasingly wanted to expose one by one by one. For a long moment, he just stared—and then he sprang, hoisting her over his shoulder in a fireman's carry that had her screaming and guffawing and grabbing him in all sorts of fun places.

He swatted her on the ass for good measure.

"Oh, my God, Sir!" she cackled. "Put me down."

"You don't give the orders around here, little subbie," he said, totally pleased with himself as he carried her out the door and down the hallway. Midway, he keyed a code to open a non-descript door. It took them into a back passageway only the Masters and Dungeon Monitors could access, allowing them to move quickly through the facility in case of emergency, or to remove a problematic player if someone got out of hand. It was rare, but it did happen. All of which Quinton explained to Cass as they moved—though not why he was taking her. *That* was a surprise.

Next, he called the elevator and placed her on her feet once they were inside.

"Have you ever gone on a tour of a museum or a historical site where there are ropes or chains that close off parts to the touristy rabble?" she asked.

Quinton chuckled. "I guess so."

Cassia braced her hands on her hips. "I *always* want to be a rebel and sneak behind those ropes and see the secret parts."

He grinned, getting her meaning. "You're totally digging the behind-the-scenes thing right now, aren't you?"

"Yes!"

"You are delightfully easy to please." He nailed her with a playful, appreciative stare. Because he really liked that about her. Cassia Locke found pleasure in small things, and was adventurous, curious, brave, pretty...

Damn, the list of things that intrigued him about her grew every time they were together, didn't it?

"Come on," he said, taking her by the hand and leading her out of the elevator. He loved the feel of her at his side. A realization that suddenly made him wish he *always* had the privilege of that feeling. Not just of a woman's company, but of her companionship, her constancy, her being there for him the way he'd be there for her.

The togetherness and sense of belonging of a relationship.

Damn, his desire for those things nearly blind-sided Quinton, it was so strong. Or maybe it was just that he'd never felt anything like it before.

And Cassia was bringing it out of him like no one ever had, like he wasn't even sure was possible.

Two stories above the main part of the club, Quinton led her to the Masters' private lounge. "Wait, please." When she nodded, he disappeared inside. The main room was a long rectangle with one-way glass overlooking the club that occupied the old church's nave. With all its dark mahogany paneling, plush carpeting, and overstuffed leather furnishings, the lounge resembled an old-school gentlemen's club. Next, he ducked into the locker room, which had showers in addition to several private saunas and Jacuzzis. Fortunately for Quinton, the entire space was empty.

Score.

He opened the door to retrieve Cass only to find her in the waiting position. Kneeling with her knees spread, her hands behind her back, her shoulders back, and her head up. And, *fuck*, her submission, so readily and beautifully given, was a heady thing. It really fucking was. He hadn't even intended his words as a command, exactly, but as an obviously well-trained submissive, she'd taken them that way. Of course she had.

Quinton held out his hand. "Rise, pretty girl."

She came to him with a smile.

"*That*," he said, eyeing the floor where she'd just been. "...was incredibly sexy. And very much appreciated."

She ducked her chin, but not before he saw on her face the pride at his words. "Thank you, Sir. It was for you, of course, but if any of the other Masters were here, I also didn't want to make you look bad by just slouching around out here."

Her submission *and* caring how she reflected upon him? Wow. Quinton had to clear his throat. "Well, I love you on your knees, but you're not bad just slouching around either." He winked.

And Cassia laughed, just like he hoped she would. "I'll remember that, Sir."

He showed her inside, and watched as she moved right to the glass wall. He'd spent more than his fair share of time people watching from up here, a pastime that was part of why he enjoyed bartending, too, so he couldn't blame her one bit. It *was* fascinating to see so much of Blasphemy at once—all the best and the most natural and the most depraved of human interaction at a glance. And, during the day, their elevated position provided an absolutely glorious view of the old church's stained glass.

Quinton came up behind her. Directly below was the huge iron-and-marble circular bar where he spent so much of his time. "Mmm, maybe sometime I'll take you right here, up against this window, your breasts pressed against the cold glass." She didn't necessarily know it was one-way…

Cassia's breath hitched. "Is that your idea, Sir?"

He pressed his lips to her ear. "Not tonight, little one." Taking her hand, he guided her to the locker room, then through it to one of the private Jacuzzis. It sat flush with the floor and had tiled steps down into the shallow tub. He adjusted a few knobs, and the bubbling water came to life. He turned to her. "After what happened earlier, I'll completely understand if you prefer to do something else. I just want to make you feel good. So, no blindfolds and no darkness, just pleasure. Do you feel up to that?"

"I think that sounds incredible," she said. "I love hot tubs."

Brave woman, once again. "Well, all right, then. Go ahead and get in. I need to make one further arrangement." When she slipped into the water, he stepped out of the room and called the club's food service to order a tray of refreshments for them to share. "How's the water?" he asked when he returned.

"Ah-mazing," she said, submerged almost to her chin with her head resting against the curved tile.

"Good." He unbuttoned his jeans and shoved them down over his hips.

Cassia's mouth dropped open.

Quinton grinned, and tugged the denim all the way off until he stood before her naked as the day he came into this crazy world. "Damn, girl, you know how to make a man feel ten feet tall."

Her lips snapped shut. "I, uh..."

"Don't pick up your jaw on my account. I mean..." He waded into the water.

She rolled her eyes. "My jaw did *not* drop."

"Oh, Cassia. Did you just roll your eyes at me, little one?" He moved until he stood right in front of her. The water bubbled just below his hips, leaving his half-erect cock exposed and nearly at her eye level.

A fast shake of her head as her eyes went wide.

"No? You didn't just roll your eyes at me?" He donned a well-practiced stern expression and affected an ice-cold stare, even though Quinton was totally enjoying himself. "Because I know I was quite clear on what the consequences would be if you did."

"I'm sorry, Sir," she said, holding up her hands. "I won't do it again."

"Sit on the edge of the tub, Cassia."

"Sir—"

"*Now.*"

Slowly, she complied. And he enjoyed every goddamned second of the water sluicing off her body. Over her breasts, her nipples, the curve of her belly. Lower...

"Feet up on the edge next to you. Legs open." He arched a brow.

Releasing a shaky breath, she got into position, and fuck if she wasn't a vision. Pretty little cunt open to his view. Rivulets of water running over her skin. A flush in her face and anticipation in her eyes.

"Wider," he said.

She let her knees fall to the sides.

"Just like that." Without another word, he sank in the water to his knees right between her thighs, cupped her ass in his hands, and planted his mouth around her clit. He sucked and licked and nipped, worrying his tongue over her nerves and then plunging deep inside her. Drawing out her arousal. And, *fuck*, she tasted like a dream. Salty and clean, sweet and feminine.

Cassia was panting and cursing and grasping at his head, her fingers on one hand twisting in his hair. And he loved it. Her desperation and her need and her loss of control.

He met her gaze and reveled in the pleasured-soaked expression on her face. Mouth slack, eyes hooded, gaze not quite focused. "You will come five times. You will concentrate on nothing but coming until you have done this. You will give your orgasms to me as fast as you can, without holding back for any reason. And you will count them out and thank me for every one."

"Oh, God," she whimpered.

Quinton smirked, his cock almost all the way hard now. Because he fucking *loved* eating pussy. "Fun for *me*, remember?" Obviously, she was going to enjoy this, right up until she started begging him to stop. He didn't wait for her reply before he dove back in. Quinton absolutely feasted on her, sucking hard on her clit and mercilessly strumming it with his tongue until she was panting and thrusting her hips into his mouth and then holding her breath. He felt the contractions before she even spoke.

"One, Sir. One. Oh, God. Thank you, M-Master Quinton," Cassia cried as her whole body shook around the first orgasm.

"Again," he ordered, his mouth still pressed to her core. The higher she managed to go, the harder he got and the deeper the ache of want that settled into his balls. This time, he fucked her with his tongue and ground his nose against her clit, going at her ruthlessly until she was babbling and shaking.

A knock at the door.

"Come in," Quinton said, lifting his head.

A male submissive entered carrying a tray of covered dishes. Perfect timing.

"Place it right here." Quinton gestured to the floor beside Cassia. "Please stay until she comes twice, then you may leave."

She gasped, but he knew from their conversations before anything started between them that she was open to public play. And, certainly, her reactions on the dance floor had proved she enjoyed it.

"Why don't you tell him what you did, Cassia?" Quinton said.

Her gaze cut uncomfortably to the lean male, standing there barechested and wearing only a pair of nearly sheer black biker shorts that barely hid his cock. "I rolled my eyes at Master Quinton."

The submissive pressed his lips together in a mock pout and shook his head.

"Yes, you did," Quinton said, giving her a wink before devoting himself to her pussy once more. And, what do you know, that second orgasm came intriguingly fast, with the handsome young sub standing there, providing her pleasure with an audience. She cried out the number and her gratitude.

He didn't let up for a second.

Tilting his head, he came at her clit from the side, so that he could lick back and forth over it instead of up and down.

"Oh, *fuck*," she moaned, her thighs shaking now. "I can't...I can't..."

Quinton didn't bother arguing with his voice. He commanded instead with his lips and his tongue and his teeth and his whole face. *Come. Come now.*

"Oh, God, Master Quinton, I...I..."

With both hands, he reached up and grasped her nipples in a teasingly tight pinch and then he used his mouth even harder.

"Oh, oh Jesus, three. Three, Master Quinton, thank you," she managed, though the words were all nearly a jumble. The desperate satisfaction in her voice nearly made him come right there.

The door clicked shut as the other man departed.

Going for four, Quinton added his fingers, easily sinking one, then two, into the tight sheath of her slick core. His cock throbbed in anticipation of feeling that sensation for itself. Some time. Shaking, Cassia reclined back on her elbows, like she was unable to hold herself upright anymore. Male satisfaction surged through Quinton, egging him on. Sucking her clit into his mouth, he finger fucked her in a steady rhythm, his fingers curling upward when he went deep, stroking a spot inside her that made her squirm and gasp and close her eyes at the goodness of it.

"I want it all over my hand this time, Cassia," he said, staring up her body from his position between her thighs. He worked his tongue and his lips and his fingers and that spot until she was rasping out her orgasm and her thanks, her juices spilling down his fingers and into his palm, her whole body shuddering. "There it is. One more."

"Please, Master Quinton. I can't do it. It's t-too much," she said, her voice wrecked.

"One more, Cassia. Legs wider, and lay all the way down."

On a moan, she did as he asked. Quinton slid his come-slicked fingers to the tight rosebud of her asshole. He eased his middle finger in, working it until she could take one knuckle, two, then after a minute, nearly all of it. And, oh yeah, he wanted his cock there, too.

In every part of her. *Owning* every part of her. When he was satisfied she could handle him there, his mouth returned to her pussy. And he ate her like a man who hadn't had sustenance in *days*.

She came on a scream, her ass pulsing around his finger while her whole body shook. It was fucking glorious, her gift of submission, her words of gratitude, her pleasure, her shattered satisfaction.

When her body calmed, he eased his finger free of her, and then he dragged the flat of his tongue lazily over her clit, his eyes on hers every time. Just licking.

Her hips jerked on every stroke. "You're…you're licking me," Cassia said breathlessly, a small smile playing around her mouth.

"I'm claiming you, like you said." The words caught him a little off guard. He'd meant them in the same vein as the joke she'd told earlier, but they'd come out sounding a helluva lot more serious than that. The words *felt* right, but Quinton also worried that, in saying them, he might've crossed a line of expectations they'd both made clear. So he waggled his eyebrows like a cartoon villain. "You can have the robe, but your clit is mine."

Cassia chuckled.

Attempting to cover the strangeness his words had made him feel a moment before, he lifted her off the edge of the tub and eased her into the hot water again.

She squeaked as she lowered her hips into the bubbling water, and Quinton chuckled.

"You might be evil, Master Quinton, anyone ever tell you that?" she asked, her expression amused even as she shifted, obviously trying to get used to the water's intensity against her probably over-sensitive clit.

"Evil genius, maybe." He winked. "Now, I'd like to feed you, Cassia. Will you let me?"

"Yes, Sir," Cassia said, her body limp after the glorious assault of Master Quinton's tongue. If cunnilingus was an Olympic sport, the man would easily win the gold. Jesus.

"Lay your head back and close your eyes."

When she did, metal clanged lightly against the tile. She could almost picture him removing the lids from the serving dishes, water running off of all those well-defined inked muscles. His cock bobbing at the water's edge, thick and just long enough that she'd probably have to manage a little of him down her throat in order to take him all.

"Keep your eyes closed and open your mouth," he said in a low voice.

Warm and sweet and creamy…melted chocolate.

"Bite."

Cool strawberry juice mixed with the chocolate next.

Oh, man. Five orgasms *and* chocolate-covered strawberries. Master Quinton was kinda blowing her mind. He really was.

He fed her a second strawberry.

Actually, he'd *already* blown it—when he'd said he was claiming her. Looking up at her from between his thighs, that wicked mouth wet with her arousal, those words had reached inside her chest and set her heart to flight. But it had been a joke. Of course, it had. And it *was* funny. Or it would've been, if parts of her hadn't wanted him to mean it for real.

Which was an odd reaction given that she'd been convinced at the start of all this that she didn't want a relationship. Not with how messed up she'd been. Scratch that. Not with how messed up she *still was*. Her reaction to the scene earlier proved that.

So, she remained convinced that a relationship didn't make sense for her.

Even with all of Master Quinton's yumminess.

"More?" he asked.

"Yes, Sir."

Sweet and rich, the flavors were so much more intense with her eyes closed. She also found that she concentrated on them more, *enjoyed* them more, without the distraction her eyes might've provided. Delicious.

She'd eaten five when he invited her to open her eyes again. He had a smudge of chocolate on the corner of his mouth, and Cassia couldn't stop looking at it. Wanting to taste the flavor off his skin.

"Normally, I'd say that orgasms, a full belly, and this relaxing hot water would make me want to sleep," she said.

"Normally?" Sitting an easy arm's reach away, his knees touching hers, he arched a brow.

"Well, Sir," she said, shifting closer. His gaze tracked her movements with interest. "You have a spot of chocolate on your mouth, and it's distracting me from that sleepy feeling."

"Is it now?"

She nodded. "Uh huh."

"Maybe you should do something about it."

Grinning, she leaned in. Licked and nibbled at the corner of his mouth until the chocolate was gone. A little noise of pleasure—or maybe want—rumbled from his throat, urging her on. So she didn't retreat. She ran her lips and tongue over his jaw, his ear, his neck.

"Finding more chocolate?" His big hand curled into her hair.

"No, Master Quinton. Just you."

"Fuck, Cass."

The raw need in his voice lanced desire through her—a desire to please him the way he'd pleased her. They might not be heading for a relationship, but as a submissive, she had a soul-deep need to please and satisfy her partner, and Cassia wanted to give as much as she got.

"May I please keep going?" she asked, peering up at him.

He gave a nod, then rose up out of the tub like some kind of a water god. "All yours." Quinton arched a brow over hungry brown eyes as he leaned back against the tile. He braced his hands behind him, much as she had before.

And there he went again, making her heart do strange things over words he surely didn't intend the way she heard. But she wasn't thinking about that now. Not when she had six-plus feet of wet, hot, naked man sprawled out in front of her.

Cassia moved to stand between his spread thighs. She braced her hands against his thick muscles there, and adored the groan that spilled from him. Slowly, she dragged her fingertips upwards, over his hips, over the flat plane of his stomach, to his chest. She stepped closer, and his close-trimmed pubic hair tickled her thighs.

Holding his gaze, she kissed his chest. Once, twice. And then licked over one hard nipple. She explored him slowly, lazily, even though everything inside her was ravenous for the hard cock jutting out against her. Every so often, she glanced up at him.

His eyes were on fire watching her, and she loved every second of it.

Kneeling, her breasts settled against his cock, and that had them both groaning.

"Fuck, Cassia, I want your mouth."

Excitement shivered over her skin. From the command, from the hot need in his tone and his eyes, from the bead of pre-come sitting on the fat head of his cock.

"Yes, Sir," she said, sucking just his tip. Which gave her a delicious idea. For several long moments, she focused all her attention *just* at the tip. Sucking it, flicking her tongue over his head, plumbing the hole to taste more of his salty arousal.

His hand fisted in her hair. "Christ, girl. Take all of it," he said, his voice almost a growl.

And that raw desperation nearly undid her. She inhaled his cock, taking it straight to the back of her throat in one rough stroke.

Master Quinton shouted at the change in her technique, both of his hands grasping her head and holding her down. "Jesus God, Cassia. Hold it, baby. Just let me feel it all the way inside you." His hips jerked, shoving him a few precious millimeters deeper. And then he did it again. Cassia needed to breathe, but she needed to make him fall apart more. Finally, on a guttural moan, he let her up.

She gasped for air, but didn't hesitate to dive back in, sucking him on a fast, deep in-and-out that had his cock hitting her throat each and every time.

"Yeah, baby. That's it. Take it all. Every fucking time."

He opened his legs wider, making more room for her to get closer. And that was when she felt a forceful flow of water right near her thigh. Aroused again, she shifted, and the jet blasted into her clit.

On a moan, she rocked her hips into the wet friction and held herself down this time, impaling her mouth on him again and again.

His hand came down on the back of her head, a firm pressure that told her to hold the position. "Are you fucking yourself against a jet, Cassia?"

She moaned her answer.

"Good. I want you to come when I do. And I want you to drink down everything I've got."

She wrapped her arms around his hips, forcing him as far into her throat as she could take him.

He shifted his hips, going deeper, pushing her limits. And then Master Quinton came, his voice a gritty scrape of satisfaction. "Fuck, take it, baby."

The words set her off, too. Working to swallow his release, she screamed around his cock as the water battered her sensitive clit.

But she wasn't wasting a single drop of him, not when this was the first time she'd ever been able to serve him this way.

Gently, his hands drew up her face.

Peering at him, at all that sated male satisfaction, Cassia smiled. "Thank you, Sir."

Without warning or a single word, he hauled her into his lap and kissed her. His hand cupped her face, holding her to him, and his tongue surged deep. For some reason, she heard his voice again, from before.

I'm licking you.

And she felt that same urge to be claimed that she had when he'd actually said it.

But of course, it was hard not to feel that way given everything they'd shared, right? It was just the haze of lust and release coloring her reactions, making her a little more sensitive to everything in the moment. Totally normal.

Maybe.

Probably. But still, Cassia needed to be careful. She didn't want to screw this up by getting in deeper than she could handle.

Chapter Seven

AT CASSIA'S REQUEST, THEY AGREED to try the sensory overload scene again on Thursday night.

Master Quinton had been hesitant, but it hadn't been the scene so much as a specific part of what he'd used to overwhelm her that had caused her breakdown. If he removed the sound of the water, Cassia was convinced that she could handle it. At least, she wanted to try.

Which was how she found herself spread-eagled and cuffed to the St. Andrew's cross again, a double layer of lace over her eyes and the headphones heavy against her ears.

He tormented her body with alternating sensations again, though not the same as before. He dripped what she thought was melted wax down her back and over her ass. He drew a spiky Wartenberg wheel over her skin. And he spanked her with a flat, leather paddle. Winding her tighter and tighter until she thought she might burst.

And then the music started in her ears, only different. It was the song from the dance floor. The one that had been playing when Master Quinton had told her to close her eyes and listen to his voice. Driving and sexy and seductive.

It shoved her *hard* toward release. But she couldn't ask for it. She couldn't beg, even though she wanted to, because she wasn't allowed to speak.

Cassia couldn't do anything but *wait* for Master Quinton to set her free.

It was a delicious torture.

One that became even more intense when another song began to play on top of the one they'd danced to. The first had been a faster alternative song, but the new one was heavier rock. The beats, lyrics, and rhythms competed and intertwined, making it impossible for her brain to concentrate on just one—making it impossible for her brain to concentrate on *anything*. And even though she knew that was the point, her mind couldn't take on that kind of analysis when so many sensations competed. The first song, the second song, the darkness, the paddle, the prickly traces of that wheel.

Pressure fell against her clit. His fingers circled once, twice...

Cassia's orgasm detonated as if the touch had been a command.

And just like a bomb, the explosion left her disoriented. She couldn't tell what was up and what was down with the world spinning and her body floating.

She thought she heard Master Quinton's voice, but that couldn't be true over the music. She thought she saw colors, but somehow, could still feel the stretchy weight of the blindfold. She thought... she wasn't sure *what* she thought...

Finally, she just gave in to the chaos, into the peacefulness, into the nothingness, and let it carry her away...

The next thing she was aware of was Master Quinton's brown eyes. "Talk to me, Cass."

"Hi," she whispered.

A slow smile drew up over his mouth. "Hi. How are you feeling?"

"Good," she said, unable to hold back a sudden yawn. "I'm sorry. Was I sleeping?" She realized he had her in his lap on the big leather couch in the outer room where he always took her.

"Just a little," he said, stroking her hair. "You fell pretty deep into subspace at the end of the scene, so I told you to rest. Do you remember us talking about that?"

She searched her thoughts, but, no, she didn't. "No, Sir. Really?"

"You were very out of it, so I'm not surprised," he said. The little touches he gave her felt soothing, calming, and it was like he *needed* to touch her. Needed to soothe and calm.

She adored it. "That was...it was really intense."

"Intense good or intense bad?" He tilted his head and nailed her with an assessing stare.

Cassia thought back over what she could remember. The disorientation. The disconnection. The floating. "It was good," she said. Then stronger, "It left me feeling totally freed. And even though I knew it was dark, behind my closed eyes I could perceive colors. And I feel like…" She grappled for the words as the significance of that began to sink in. "…like there's hope that I could learn to apply that in other situations. To know there's color and light even in the dark."

His smile was so sweet. "That's great, Cassia. I'm glad it left you feeling so hopeful. That's…" He nodded, emotion plain on his face. "I'm happy for you."

Lacing her fingers with his, Cassia brought their joined hands to rest against her heart. "And I'm grateful, Master Quinton. I don't know if any of this will have lasting results, but hope is more than I've had in a really long time. So even if it doesn't, that means a lot."

He kissed her then, and it felt different from any other kiss they'd ever shared. It was soft and slow, but urgent. Tender, but demanding. It was sexy and hot and arousing, but more than anything, it felt *intimate*.

It felt like strings attaching.

At least, it did to Cassia. It'd only been about two weeks since they'd started playing together, but damn if the old crush she used to have on him years ago wasn't rearing its head again. Or maybe this was all new now. Growing up like a spring bud through the recently thawed earth, having been watered by the intensity of everything they'd shared during this short time.

And Cassia wasn't sure what to think of that. All at once, it worried her, excited her, scared her, and left her wishing she was as brave as Master Quinton thought she was.

Because she *didn't* feel that brave, she changed the subject. "So, I have a surprise for you, but it might be too short notice."

His expression seemed to register the changing of gears, but then he just smiled and let her get away with it. "Oh, yeah? I love surprises."

"Good," she said. "My brother says Saturday could work for a visit to the Green Valley Race Track, if you're available. If we get there before two, you can drive the track. Then the races start at seven."

"Oh, damn. Yeah? That sounds awesome. I'm supposed to work the bar Saturday night, but if I can get Master Leo to switch with me, you're on."

"Okay, great," she said, smiling at his enthusiasm. Knowing he was so excited about it totally made the grilling Jagger had given her when she'd called worth it. She'd been prepared for it though. After all, she hadn't been there for months, and now her first time back, she was bringing a guy. A guy *friend*, but still. "If you can't switch, I'll ask Jagger for another date. There are races most weekends."

"Jagger, huh? That's a cool name."

"Well, his real name is Jackson, but he's kind of a genius on the guitar. I don't even know for sure how young he was when people started calling him that, but it's pretty much been his name as long as I can remember." Affection filled her as she spoke about her brother.

Things hadn't always been great at home growing up. Their mother tried, but after their father split, they had trouble making ends meet. Seven years older than her, Jagger had picked up the slack at a series of odd jobs until he found the Raven Riders and then work at their track. Her grades had been good enough to earn some scholarships, but Jagger had otherwise been responsible for putting her through school.

Cassia owed him so much.

"No shit? I play, too, but nowhere close to good enough to be nicknamed for a rock star," he said with a laugh, his tone full of that self-deprecation she found so endearing.

Excitement had her pushing herself into a sitting position in Master Quinton's lap. "Seriously? You play?"

He held up his hands and shook his head. "I dabble on the acoustic. Have for years. But the emphasis is on *dabble*."

Cass grinned. "Still, that's so awesome. You and Jagger are going to get along great. I can just tell."

Chuckling, Master Quinton nodded. "He sounds like good people, so I'm sure we will. What did you tell him about me, anyway?"

"Just that you're a friend with a crazy obsession for fast cars, which he totally respected, by the way."

He nodded, and for a moment she could've sworn that something regretful passed behind his gaze. But then he smiled again. "Sounds about right. Well, let me twist Master Leo's arm and see if I can make this happen."

"Sounds like a plan," she said.

"Good. Then let's get you cleaned up."

"Okay," she said. "And thank you, again, Master Quinton." Cassia pressed a soft kiss against his lips, and then he helped her rise.

The blanket fell into a heap as she rose, and she leaned down to retrieve it.

"Freeze," he said. "Stay just like that." Bent at the waist, she braced her palms on her knees as his hands ran over her back, her ass, her thighs. His touch was soft and caressing, but still heated her blood. "Just admiring all this wax against your gorgeous skin. Almost hate to see it go."

She peered over her shoulder. "I'll wear it for you if you wish, Sir."

Dark eyes flashed to meet her gaze. "Is it uncomfortable?"

She shook her head, because the pleasure she'd get from putting that interested look on his face would far outweigh the annoyance of tolerating the tight weight of the wax for a little while longer. "Tell me to wear it for you."

He arched a brow, his tongue dragging over his bottom lip, and then he nodded. "Keep it on for me, Cassia. Until you get home. Wear it because you know it pleases me."

"Yes, Sir," she said, arousal stalking over her skin again.

He squeezed her ass one last time. "Very good. Then get dressed and we'll head out to the bar. Leo's on, so I can ask him about the schedule tonight."

Fifteen minutes later, they were standing at the crowded bar, waiting to get Master Leo's attention while they chatted with two people Master Quinton introduced as Master Griffin and Kenna. The couple was a study in opposites—Griffin was a big guy with dark hair and olive skin, while Kenna was shorter than Cass and lean, with fair skin and golden blond hair. But the way they looked at each other and the beautiful jewelry-style collar Kenna wore made it clear what they had in common was far more important. As the men fell into conversation, so did Cass and Kenna.

"Are you new here?" Kenna asked. "I haven't seen you around before the last couple weeks."

"I used to belong a couple years ago, but I had an accident and didn't come for a while. Just started back," Cassia said.

"Wow," Kenna said with an easy smile. She held up her prosthetic arm. "I could've given almost the same exact answer. I joined right after Blasphemy opened, and then about a year later I enlisted in the Marines and this happened. I re-joined the club at the end of the summer after five years away." She spoke about her amputation like she was totally at peace with it, and it made Cassia wish she could be the same way.

"Wow is right. Thank you for your service, Kenna. My accident wasn't anything as honorable. I got trapped alone in a cave-in for a few days and now I've got a thing with the dark," Cass said, putting herself out there in a way she usually didn't with new people. But if Kenna could do it, she should be able to, too.

Kenna's eyes went wide. "That sounds terrifying, Cassia. But I'm glad you're back. And from what I understand, you're in very good hands with Master Quinton."

Cass's smile was immediate. "Yeah, I think so."

The other woman grinned and leaned in. "He's so nice. I'm glad to see him settling down with someone."

She inhaled to correct her, but was interrupted by Master Quinton kissing her cheek. "Good news. Master Leo and I are trading Saturdays, so I'm all yours."

"Oh, that's great," Cassia said, torn between excitement that their day together was going to work out and concern over letting Kenna think there was something more serious between them than there was.

But she never got the chance to say anything more to the other submissive, because just then, her Dom guided her away into the crowd.

A spot opened up at the bar, and Master Quinton drew them into it so that they could lean against the cool marble. "You okay?"

"Yes, of course. Better than, because you are going to love the track. And now *I* get to be the one to share all the behind-the-scenes stuff with you."

His laughter chased away the last of her weird mood. She'd just be sure to talk to Kenna the next time they ran into one another. "Yes, you do. So, what time should we leave on Saturday?" he asked.

Master Leo appeared in front of them. "Sorry to interrupt."

"No worries," Quinton said. "I was just telling Cassia the good news."

The dark-blond-haired Dom nodded, and Cassia was struck again by the mesmerizing uniqueness of his different-colored eyes. "I went into the system to update the schedule. Are you still doing that demonstration next Saturday night? Is that going to work if you're tending bar?"

Demonstration? Master Quinton was doing a demonstration?

Competing reactions flooded through Cassia. Regret and jealousy that he'd be playing with another submissive. Irritation at herself for feeling that way. Resignation, too, because *of course* he could play with other people if he wanted to. Her head started to spin at the whirlwind of emotion. They'd never agreed to be exclusive, and they'd specifically discussed keeping what they were doing no-strings-attached.

The memory of the intimate kiss they'd shared flashed through her mind. The one that had felt like *all kinds of strings*.

"Oh, hell," Quinton said. "I forgot about that…" His gaze cut to her for a moment, and he shook his head. "Don't worry about it. I'll figure something out."

"Okay," Master Leo said. "Can I get you two something?"

The way he eyed her made her feel exposed, like he'd seen something in her reaction that she hadn't meant to reveal. Cass felt twitchy and restless, full of fight or flight. "No, thank you. I should probably be heading home soon."

"Oh, okay. Of course," Master Quinton said, his expression a little concerned, like maybe he'd picked up on it, too. Which made Cassia really need to get out from under all these too-observant Dom gazes. At least for a little while. Until she could pull herself together. It had been a very draining and emotional night, after all. "I'll walk you out."

They threaded through the crowd until they found themselves at the women's locker room door where she'd stowed her purse and coat. "So, about the time on Saturday? What do you think?" he asked.

She forced a smile. "How about eleven? That'll have us up there by noon and give us a few hours at the track before things get started."

He nodded, his gaze running over her face. "I'll pick you up at eleven sharp. Okay?"

"Sounds great," she said, desperate to bolt and itching to remove the evidence of their time together from her skin.

"Tonight…tonight was a privilege, Cassia." He leaned in and kissed the corner of her mouth.

She didn't know how to respond. Because the words were sweet and kind and felt…meaningful. But he hadn't kissed her *on* the mouth like he had before, and he had plans in the not-too-distant future to play with someone else. So her mind was a jumble. And, oh, for crap's sake, all this intellectual masturbation over what he said and did and what it meant was one of the reasons she hadn't wanted a relationship in the first place!

"Good night," she finally managed.

Slipping inside the locker room, Cassia knew at least one thing for sure—she had some major string snipping to do before Saturday.

Chapter Eight

QUINTON PARKED IN FRONT OF Cassia's apartment at five minutes before eleven, eager to see her. Eager to make sure she was okay after the way she'd rushed out of Blasphemy on Thursday night. He'd texted her twice yesterday to check in on her, and her replies had seemed perfectly normal, but his gut kept giving him checks that cautioned him that maybe she was telling him what he wanted to hear.

Her apartment took up the second floor of one of Baltimore's ubiquitous row houses. Her door stood at the top of an interior staircase. Quinton knocked and waited.

"Yay, there you are," she said as she opened the door. Wearing a big, open smile, Cassia looked beautiful in a pair of jeans tucked into a pair of brown knee-high boots, and a flowy ivory V-neck shirt that emphasized her creamy skin and the long column of her bare throat. Her street clothes covered a lot more skin than what she wore to the club, of course, but she was still every bit as appealing to him.

"At your service," he said, giving a wink.

"I think that's my line." She gestured him in with a smile.

Quinton chuckled, his tension melting away as he took in her happy, easy-going mood. "This is a great room," he said, surveying the large rectangular living room with big, airy windows all around. To one side sat a breakfast bar with a pass-through to what looked like a smaller kitchen. With its overstuffed furniture and stacks of books everywhere, the room was comfortable and inviting, feminine without being girly. He could easily imagine a lazy weekend here, stretched out on the couch watching movies or eating pizza out of a box on the glass coffee table. The thought caught him off guard.

"I got pretty lucky with this place," she said. "Good neighbors, safe street, lots of light. Want the nickel tour?"

"Sure," he said, curious to learn more about her. "I'm a big tipper, too."

She chuckled and gave him an amused look. "I've heard that about you."

Quinton couldn't help but laugh. His concern that Cassia wasn't okay after the other night seemed completely unfounded.

Cass led him to the galley-style kitchen. "It's small, but I've never been too much of a cook anyway. I mean, I love to eat, but I'm just as happy with a bowl of cold cereal or soup and sandwich. Both of which seem like the finest filet mignon after eating pre-packaged kits while out in the field."

"I love to cook," he said, a little outraged on behalf of the world's finest steak. "I'll make you a filet that'll keep you from comparing it to cold cereal. Not sure what kind of tenderloin you've been having, woman."

She laughed and shrugged. "Remember me? Easy to please, over here. But you're on."

He followed her deeper into the apartment. She'd made a tiny room into an office that was dominated by a huge desk with a large flat-screen computer monitor. Bookcases filled one whole wall. And there were funny geology sayings on bumper stickers and postcards and little signs everywhere:

Don't take geologists for granite!

Geologists are the schist!

Don't expect perfection from geologists – they all have their faults.

And Quinton's favorite, for obvious reasons: *You can test my hardness if I can test your cleavage.*

Grinning, he pointed to that one where it hung over her desk. "Cleavage?"

She shook her head. "Leave it to you to notice that one. Cleavage is the tendency of a mineral to break along flat planar surfaces typically due to weaknesses or deformities in its structure."

He waggled his eyebrows. "It turns me on when you talk about flat planar surfaces."

Cassia smirked. "You have no idea how hard it is not to roll my eyes right now."

He arched a brow and loved it when she laughed.

"What are these?" he asked, stepping up to picture frames hanging on the wall.

"Different research trips," she said, joining him. She pointed to the images as she spoke. "This was a week-long trip through Western Maryland. This was Mammoth Cave in Kentucky. And this one's the Endless Caverns in Virginia, and this one." she said, gesturing to another frame, "was a trip to an unknown cave a photographer stumbled on in Vietnam just two years ago." On the adjoining wall, she excitedly pointed out a picture of herself with a green glow in the background. The Northern Lights. "This was from the trip to Sweden," she said, continuing on to point out some of the interesting features captured in the shots. Quinton really enjoyed hearing her talk about something she obviously loved.

Even more strongly than before, he wanted to help her do that work again.

"You've probably gone places on this earth that not too many others have," he said. Her adventurous spirit was one of the things about her that called to something inside him. And damn if that list wasn't getting longer with every minute he spent with her.

"I know," she said, leading him into the hall again. "That has always been one of my favorite things. And this is my bedroom."

Decorated in greens and blues, the space was big enough to fit a queen-sized bed, two night stands, and a chest of drawers. He dragged his gaze away from the bed, which encouraged all kinds of ideas he didn't need to be having right now, and surveyed the room. More framed photographs covered the dresser.

When she saw him looking, she led him over. "Jagger and me, when we were younger. And this is him more recently." She handed Quinton the pictures.

While Cassia's hair had some reddish tones in it, her brother's was a darker brown, but he saw the resemblance in the eyes and shape of their faces. In the more recent shot, he sat on a motorcycle and wore a vest with multiple leather patches. Cass sat on the bike behind him, her chin resting on his shoulder. Quinton had already been able to tell they were close just from how she talked about him, but now he could see it, too.

"Do you have any brothers or sisters?" she asked.

Putting the frames down again, he nodded. "One brother. Taylor. Just had a little girl a few months ago, so I'm an uncle, too." When she congratulated him, he added the part that totally kicked ass every time he thought about it. "And you know the best part? Besides the baby, of course?"

Cassia smiled. "What's that?"

"They named her Quinn." He grinned like the proud-uncle idiot he was.

"Oh, my God. That's so awesome. Now you have to be the coolest uncle who ever lived."

"Fuck, I know. I'm already planning out the next eighteen years."

She shook her head. "I'm sure you're going to rock it. She'll be lucky to have you."

Talking about his niece, and hearing Cass give him such easy, ready praise, had his brain going in some weird directions. Like, what it might be like to have a kid of his own someday. Like, what kind of pride he'd feel if he were a father himself.

Which then had him wondering if Cassia wanted kids...

And all things considered, that was cart about a million miles before any horse that might or might not exist. For fuck's sake.

No strings attached, remember?

Right.

Back in the living room, Quinton stopped Cassia with a hand on her hip. "Before we go, in case it needs to be said, I don't expect any sort of Dom/sub protocol during the trip. We're just Quinton and Cass today, okay?"

Her expression went soft as she nodded. "Quinton and Cass. Okay." Damn, he had to admit, he really dug the sound of his name on her lips. The sound of their names *together*, if he was being honest. Which took him right back to that fucking horse and its runaway cart.

Before long, they were on the road in Quinton's Land Rover. It was an easy drive up I-70 to Frederick. Suburbia gave way to farm fields and mountains just donning their fall foliage. Mostly, they made easy small talk as they went, and Quinton appreciated how comfortable it was to just sit with her in silence, too, music filling the car, the view flying by. But there was also something he'd been wondering.

"How did you get into the lifestyle, Cass?"

Her gaze swung to him as she shifted in her seat. "A roommate in grad school introduced me to it," she said. "Mary had already been a submissive for a few years and was in a relationship with her Dom. When I found out about them, I was immediately intrigued. Something about the idea of being dominated just hooked me. Mary invited me to a play party, and the first couple times I just watched. But even that was enough to realize that I was a submissive, because I got more turned on watching than I'd ever gotten having vanilla-only sex with my boyfriends." She shrugged. "I mean, don't get me wrong, vanilla sex can be awesome sometimes, but I realized I need more than that."

As she spoke, Quinton glanced between the road ahead and Cass's thoughtful expression, and damn if her answer didn't resonate with him. He didn't need the formalities of BDSM all the time, either. And he didn't have to play the role of a Dominant to be dominant in the bedroom, because that was who he was. But he absolutely needed it to be a part of his sex life; he craved the extremes, too. And he loved that Blasphemy gave him a way to bring so many of his interests together.

"How about you?" she asked. "Do you mind me asking?"

Giving her a smile, he shook his head. "Course not. I owned a bar of my own before I worked at Blasphemy, and a friend of mine was deep into the lifestyle. He rented the bar out a few times for private events, and that made me realize that some of what I was already doing in my sex life was very much in line with BDSM. So I learned more. Got more involved and studied with a few experienced Doms, a couple of whom are other Masters at Blasphemy now. When plans for our club came about, a bunch of us were already friends and knew each other well enough to know we shared a vision that we could bring to life at our own place."

"It's really kind of life changing when you find other people who get you that way, isn't it?" she asked.

"That's the truth," Quinton said. "I think that's what all of us are looking for, inside of BDSM or not. To be understood, to find our like-minded tribe, to be accepted and belong, no matter what."

"Wow."

He peered over at Cassia, and the affection on her face nearly made him do a double-take. "What?"

She turned her gaze out the passenger window, and he hated the loss of her eyes on him. "That was really beautifully put. That's all." A moment passed, and she continued. "How did you get into sensory deprivation?"

"Because I'm kind of an evil fucker and I like to torment submissives with pleasure." In a nutshell. He grinned.

"You don't say," she deadpanned.

"Admit it, you love me when I'm an evil fucker."

"I'm struggling with that eye roll thing again," she said, trying to suppress her smile but not quite succeeding.

"Oh, *please*, Cassia. Lose. That. Struggle."

The bloom of pink that rose on her cheeks was the sweetest reward.

"Uh huh," he said, enjoying himself and this conversation more than he had in a long time. "And, anyway, I'm kind of an adrenaline junkie. I enjoy things at the extremes, and sensory deprivation can definitely be that."

"You showed me at least a little of that the other night," she said.

"Mmm, and I enjoyed every minute of it," he said, nailing her with a stare.

She shifted in her seat and reached to turn up the fan on her side, filling Quinton with all kinds of satisfaction that she might be getting hot and bothered over there. But it also made him need to know something about their time together today.

"No pressure whatsoever, but I need to know what you do or don't want in front of your brother. I know you told him I was a friend, so..."

"Oh. Um." Awkwardness suddenly filled the Rover's cab. "I guess, I don't know. I mean, I know we're not together, so..."

Aw, hell. He regretted her discomfort, and his gut really hated the declaration about where they stood. Because it was true. But it also wasn't. Or maybe he was just rethinking where he wanted them to be? More importantly, what did Cassia want? Did she still prefer to stick to the original terms of their agreement?

As they passed the first sign for their exit, the one that meant they were only ten minutes out from arriving, Quinton knew they didn't have enough time to do justice to the conversation they increasingly needed to have. Or, at least, he needed to have it. If he was being honest. And as a man, let alone a Dom, he owed her that much. Anyway, perhaps today in front of her brother wasn't the time to make a change even if she were amenable.

Making sure his tone was casual and light, he said, "Keeping things friendly is fine, Cass. I just didn't want to overstep or do anything to embarrass you. Okay? I'll keep my hands to myself. Promise." He gave her a wink, wanting to dispel the weirdness his question had caused.

Finally, she chuckled. "Okay. No hands. Got it."

Of course, that left his brain conjuring up all the parts that *didn't* include...

Off the highway, Cassia guided them until the big speedway came into view. Sitting at the base of a mountain, the long oval track surrounded by stadium stands filled a huge field. Parking lots stretched in two directions around it. A huge mural filled one whole exterior wall with the words *Green Valley Racing* painted in green over a waving black-and-white checkered flag. A handful of bikes and cars sat close to one of the main entrances.

"Jagger's club owns all this. Has for years. The club president's grandfather inherited it decades ago, and now the Raven Riders operate it as their main source of income." She leaned forward and peered out the windshield. "You can just make out the clubhouse up the mountain. See?"

Sure enough, a big building that looked like a mountain inn sat amidst the trees high above the track.

Quinton turned into the parking lot. "Seems like a big operation for a motorcycle club."

"From what Jagger says, it is. But the Ravens aren't a typical club. They offer protective services mostly for women and children in some sort of domestic violence situation, sometimes working directly with the authorities, and sometimes at the request of the victims themselves." She grinned and waved. "Oh, there's Jagger."

Before Quinton had a chance to process the magnitude of what the Ravens did, they parked and got out. Cassia rushed towards her brother and gave him a hug that had them both laughing.

"Been too long, Cass," the man said. Wearing a cut-off jacket with Raven Riders MC insignia on it, he had a wavy mess of brown hair, a little longer now than it had been in the photograph, and eyes a shade darker than his sister's golden-flecked hazel.

"I know," she said. "I'm glad this worked today. Jag, I want you to meet Quinton Ross."

Quinton held out his hand. "Hey, Jagger. Thanks for having me. I've been to the races a few times, so I'm looking forward to seeing behind the scenes."

Jagger returned the shake, his expression friendly but his eyes calculating, observing. Not that Quinton minded. He didn't have a sister, but he could still imagine how he'd view anyone she might bring home. *Not* that Cassia was bringing him home, exactly. For fuck's sake, they really needed to have that conversation so Quinton didn't end up hitting himself over the head with a frying pan over all this angst. On the other hand, there was something a little awesome about maybe being interested enough in someone to actually feel the angst, too. He couldn't deny that.

"Nice to meet you, man. Welcome to Green Valley. Cass tells me you like fast cars, so you've come to the right place." Jagger glanced back and forth between them. "You two want to go up to the club and grab some lunch first, or head right to the track?"

Quinton looked at Cassia, and both of them spoke at once. "Track." The echo had them both laughing, which had Jagger's gaze ping-ponging between them again. The guy was totally clocking that they weren't just friends. Quinton could see it in his eyes.

"Guess that's settled, then," Jagger said. "Come on in."

Oh, holy crap, Cassia thought. *Jagger totally knows I'm sleeping with Quinton.*

It had been in her brother's gaze. In the arched brow he gave her as they turned towards the track. In the fact that Jagger had planted himself between the two of them as they walked.

So much for that painfully awkward *we're just friends* conversation they'd had in the car. Still, it was probably good that they'd had it, because it helped remind Cass what they were, and what they weren't. Which was good, because she'd spent thirty-six hours pep-talking herself into being ready to spend the day with Quinton in a completely *we're just friends* way.

Jagger led them past the ticket office and into one of the main hallways. They crossed the concourse where all the concessions were located and walked out into the stands. "Crazy how peaceful it is in here when it's empty," her brother said.

"Yeah, because during race time you can hardly hear yourself think," Quinton said, his tone approving and engaged as he surveyed the big oval.

"True enough." Jagger turned to Quinton. "So, do you want to *ride* or do you want to *drive*?" Cassia saw the answer on Quinton's face before he spoke.

"Damn, if I can drive, I want to drive," Quinton said.

"That's what Cass thought you'd say. Let's get you oriented and suited up, then. There's someone I want you to meet." Jagger started down the steps, and they followed.

"Have I thanked you for this lately?" Quinton asked in a low voice. The raw appreciation in his gaze made her belly go on a loop-the-loop.

"No need," she said, just happy that he was enjoying himself. She'd really wanted this day to be fun and stress-free. It'd been a long time since she'd had a day like that herself, and sharing it with her brother and Quinton made it even better. No matter what Quinton was to her, she knew she'd always care about him for wanting to help her.

At ground level, she followed the guys through a tall gate that separated the stands from the field. Two stock cars sat waiting, one red and white and the other green and black. A driver wearing a matching racing suit leaned against the red one. Cassia had met some of the drivers on other visits, but this guy was new to her.

Jagger shook hands with the man. "Thanks for doing this today, Mason."

"Any friend of yours is a friend of mine, Jagger. Always. You know that. I'm Andre Mason," the man said, a slight southern accent to his voice. "Nice to meet y'all." After introductions were made, Mason continued, "Who's driving?"

"I am," Quinton said, and then his gaze cut to her. "You joining me?"

"Nope," she said. "This is all for you. I can take pictures and catch up with Jagger while you're out there."

What followed was about forty-five minutes of orientation for Quinton. She and Jagger sat in the beautiful fall afternoon air in the stands just outside the fencing. Jagger shared stories about some of the Ravens she'd gotten to know over the years and pointed out upgrades he'd implemented at the track. Meanwhile, Mason went over operating the car, explained the safety equipment, and reviewed the track rules. Quinton was attentive and easy-going as the two men spoke, and his attention being focused elsewhere allowed her the chance to admire him without getting caught.

And, damn, he was just as appealing to her in a pair of black jeans, a brown Henley, old brown boots, and a chunky silver watch on his wrist, as he was in the worn blue jeans he usually wore while doing a scene.

"You sure you don't want to ride with him?" her brother asked, his voice full of a smug knowing.

"No," she said, realizing she'd been caught after all. "I've been out with you before. This is for him."

"For him," Jagger said. "Mmhmm. And how about you? You for him, too?"

She waved him off.

"I'm serious, Cass. Just how serious are you two?"

Cassia shook her head and told the truth. "We're not serious." He gave her a look. "I mean it, Jag. We're not together. You know I'm not ready for anything."

He shifted in his seat next to her. "Why not? It's been two years since the cave-in. I know it's been hard sometimes, but it's clear there's something going on here." His chin jutted toward the field, where Quinton was getting fitted for a racing suit.

He zipped up the black, gray, and white suit, and Cassia about swallowed her tongue. Because Quinton was hot no matter what, but something about that suit gave off a vibe that worked for her. It worked for her *a lot*. Enough that her heart picked up the pace and arousal stirred inside her. Turning toward her, Quinton held out his arms in a silent *what do you think*?

She gave him a big thumbs up.

"What were you saying about nothing going on?" Jagger asked, amusement in his voice.

Cass rolled her eyes at him, and then had to bite back a smile when she thought of all the times today she'd been tempted to roll her eyes at Quinton just to see what he'd do. "I didn't say there was nothing going on, just that we're not serious." There. That was fair.

"But you want it to be," he said, his fingers moving over his thigh in a silent progression of chords. She'd gotten so used to that little quirk of his that she didn't always even register it anymore. But if

Jagger wasn't playing, he was thinking about playing, or humming, or tapping out a rhythm. He'd always been like that.

She looked back out at the track so her brother didn't see the answer in her eyes. "I don't know, Jagger. Really. I don't."

"I don't like you being alone, Cassie," he said, using the nickname she'd had as a girl. "I want you to be happy."

She turned to her brother, and met his gaze straight on. "I know. And I appreciate that. But, you know, I could say the same thing about you."

He shrugged one big shoulder. "I have the club."

"That's not the same and you know it," she said. They'd been down this conversational road before. Being stubborn was a quality they shared, unfortunately.

On a sigh, she looked back to the track and found Mason fitting Quinton with his HANS device, U-shaped safety equipment that rested over the driver's shoulders, providing an anchor system that attached to the helmet and kept the driver's head from getting whipped around in the event of a crash.

Finally it was time to climb in and strap up.

Cassia rose to her feet. "Have fun!" she called.

Quinton gave her a wave from the driver's seat of the green and black car, and then Mason climbed into the red-and-white car in front. The engines roared to life, and she could almost imagine the huge grin on Quinton's face.

Mason pulled out onto the track first, and Cassia had done or watched this enough times to know how it would work. The instructor would set the speed by leading about four car lengths ahead, and with each successive lap, he would increase the speed and the size of the car-length gap.

Soon, it seemed like they were flying. Cassia cheered and waved and took about a million pictures and a couple short videos, too. She wanted Quinton to remember this day because she knew that she would. She lost track of how many laps they did, but after about twenty-five minutes, Mason led them back into the pit.

Without a second thought, Cass took off down the steps and through the gate. When Quinton cut off his engine, she ran to his stock car, grinning from ear to ear.

He pulled himself out, something that she could've watched him do a hundred times, and tugged off his helmet. His hair was damp around the edges and his smile was about a million watts. On a *whoop*, he wrapped an arm around her waist and spun her in a circle. "That was awesome, Cass. Damn. That was just the best." He placed her back on her feet.

Laughing, she clapped her hands together because was so happy for him. Really, she was just *happy*. Realization hit her like she'd walked cartoon-style into a wall. She was happier than she'd been… in two years. Maybe more. Because of Quinton.

She wanted to kiss him and hug him and maybe even climb him. But despite the little victory dance they'd shared, they *had* agreed to be hands-off today, and that was beside the whole no-strings attached thing with which Cassia finally had to admit she was failing miserably.

Quinton went right up to Jagger. "If there's ever anything I can do to repay you, just ask, Jagger. This was fantastic."

"Glad you enjoyed it. I get out there every chance I get. Now who's hungry?"

Before long, they were parking in front of the Raven Riders clubhouse, a long, two-story log building with a covered front porch that stretched the whole width. Even with a few motorcycles in the lot and the club's four-bay chop shop across the lot, the place still looked like the old-school mountain inn it had once been. And the view down the mountain and into the valley was just stunning.

Cassia had been there many times, but it had been about six months since the last time. She regretted that because she used to come all the time.

She used to do—and be—so many things.

And she wanted it all back. She wanted herself back, too.

Inside, Jagger gave Quinton a tour of the main floor. "This lounge used to be the inn's lobby. That's the original check-in desk," he said, pointing to a long, ornate wooden counter that ran across the back wall. Over it, the club's motto—*Ride. Fight. Defend.*—was carved beautifully into the thick wood molding. Jag led them into a large, adjoining room. "And this is the rec room." A huge bar filled the long, front wall, and leather couches and pool tables took up much of the rest of the space.

Quinton ran his hand over the carved bar top. "This is a beauty. Amazing craftsmanship. I would've loved to have had something like this in my first place."

a bar?" Jagger asked.

l place in Baltimore. Did a good business. Locals, I'm in on a bigger club with some partners and run the bars and all the food service for it." Quinton's pride and pleasure in his work was clear in his voice. Cassia hadn't realized just how much of the operation he was responsible for, and found herself developing a new respect for him. Not to mention that competence was damn sexy.

"People are always hungry and thirsty," Jagger said.

"No doubt about that," Quinton said, laughing.

Her brother led them down a back hallway. "Dare's the club president. Let me see if he's here. I'll introduce you." He knocked on a door at the very end.

"Yeah?" came from inside.

"Got a minute, boss?" Jagger asked.

"Come in. Hey. What do you need, Jagger?" he said from his seat at the covered desk.

Cassia popped out from around her brother. "Surprise!"

Dare's normally serious expression split into a grin as he hauled himself from the chair. "Cassia Locke. Damn, kid, where have you been hiding yourself?"

She gave him a quick hug, but made sure not to squeeze him too tight. Something bad had gone down at a race over the summer, and Dare had gotten shot. "Nowhere at all. But I'm glad to get up here for the day," she said, turning. "Dare, this is my friend, Quinton. He just got to take one of the cars out onto the track."

The men shook hands, and fell into an easy conversation about racing, cars, and bikes. With shoulder-length brown hair and dark eyes, Dare had always had a bit of an intimidating aura about him, but despite having been shot, Cassia couldn't help but think he appeared more relaxed than she'd seen him in a long time. But what captured her attention even more was how easily Quinton fit in with Jagger and Dare. She had a fleeting thought—and then it came back around for another pass and parked itself right in the center of her chest: she didn't want this to be the last time she hung out with Jagger and Quinton at the same time.

Not that she had any idea what to do with that little gem.

"I don't mean to cut things short," Jagger said, "but I need to grab a bite to eat before I have to get back down there. You all ready?"

They said their good-byes to Dare and agreed to find him at the races tonight, and then Jagger led them back through the clubhouse and into the big mess hall. Two long lines of tables filled the central space in front of a huge floor-to-ceiling stone fireplace.

"If you liked the bar, you might enjoy their kitchen, too," Cassia said. "It's a cool mix of this old rustic architecture with modern amenities. A bunch of their guys often come here for mealtime, so they usually cook for as many a couple dozen people on the weekends, fewer on the weekdays." They pushed through the swinging door into the big space.

"Hey, Jagger," a blond-haired Raven said. Standing at the counter, he was building a sandwich, the fixings spread all around where he worked. Maverick Rylan, Dare's cousin and the club's second-in-command. "Whoa, Cass. Where the hell have you been?" he asked with a grin.

She released an exasperated breath. "Everyone keeps asking me that."

"That's because the last time you were here, the dinosaurs still roamed the Earth," he said with a smirk, amusement flashing in the darkest blue pair of eyes she'd ever seen.

She threw a glance at Quinton. "That," she said pointing at her brother's smart-ass friend, "totally deserves an eye roll. You gotta give me that."

Laughing, Quinton introduced himself, and the conversation quickly turned into a major sandwich-building party that once again went like Quinton had known these men forever. They ate together in the mess hall, and then Maverick treated them to a tour of his custom bike shop across the way. As five o'clock neared, they made their way back down to the track, where Cassia introduced Quinton to as many of the Ravens as she could.

And then the setting sun stretched long shadows across the ground and those roaring engines thundered as the races began.

By then, Cassia was nearly burning with the need to touch Quinton. The day had been a study in denied desire as they'd laughed, joked around, shared the amazing thrill of him getting to drive, and now sat next to each other, their thighs unintentionally resting against one another, as the pack of stock cars roared around the field.

Cass wanted so much more than that. She wanted to kiss him and straddle him and grind herself again him. She wanted to burrow her hands under his shirt and dig her fingers into his muscles. And she wanted him all over her, too.

But what did he want? She didn't know. So she stared hard at the races because if he saw her face—her eyes—for even an instant, he'd know.

She was dying for him.

A roving vendor went by calling out *Popcorn for sale! Get your popcorn!*, and Quinton held up his money to buy a big tub. "Want some?" he asked, holding it towards her.

"No, thanks," she said, finding it hard to sit still, not just because of how much she wanted Quinton, but also because nervous energy flowed through her. If she fessed up to what she was feeling, would it change things between them for the worse? Would it end the arrangement they'd come to? After all, he'd been clear that he wasn't looking for a relationship.

He nudged her arm with the bucket. "Cass, you sure?"

"Yeah," she said, eyes still straight ahead. Her thigh wouldn't stop bouncing now.

"Cassia, look at me," came his deep voice right in her ear.

On a deep breath, she complied. And let him see what he would.

He stared at her hard, and she knew exactly when it registered. Because his gaze went molten.

Finally, he leaned in close. "As soon as we're out of here, this no-touching thing? All bets are off."

Chapter Nine

QUINTON HAD AN AMAZING DAY—AND it was all thanks to Cassia.

It was one thing to click with someone sexually, and another to click with someone socially, and yet another to find someone so easy to talk to that it was effortless. But it was magic to connect with someone that way on every level.

He had that with Cass. He had all the cylinders firing. Just like he'd always wanted. Quinton had it in spades.

And it made him fucking *yearn*.

For more. For a chance. For the everything his parents apparently hadn't had but both had wanted.

Everything, with Cassia.

Especially when she looked at him the way she'd been doing for the past hour—like she wanted to possess him. Heat and need had been radiating off her so brightly that Quinton had been sporting a hard-on most of that time, his mind absolutely alive with all the things he wanted to do to her and experience with her.

As good as the day had been, he was nearly ecstatic when they said their good-byes and made for his Rover.

Of course, they weren't going anywhere fast. Not with a thousand other race fans pouring out of the lot at the same time. With each slow crawl toward the exit, Quinton could've sworn that the temperature in the vehicle ratcheted up. He was almost sure he could hear her galloping heart, and without question he could hear the shakiness of her exhales, the shifting of her clothing against the leather seat as she moved, and the bouncing of her foot against the carpet.

Baby girl was wound *tight*.

And all that unhelpful realization did was wind him even tighter.

Finally, *finally*, they pulled out onto the road, and within five minutes' time, they were back on the highway, flying east towards Baltimore.

The tension in the car took on a physical presence, and neither of them said a goddamned thing. It was almost as if speaking or moving or even breathing would explode the whole thing to pieces, until all that was left was raw animal need.

Christ, Quinton had never felt this kind of high-voltage sexual energy before, and definitely not in an otherwise platonic situation. But he was right on the fucking edge, and no more than a hair's breadth from falling over.

From the passenger's seat came the thick sound of a swallow, and it immediately unleashed a memory in Quinton's mind. Cassia, deep throating his cock while he sat on the edge of the Jacuzzi. She'd been aggressive and relentless and extreme, impaling herself on his length again and again, holding herself there until she had to gasp for breath. She'd shoved him hard and fast toward his orgasm until it had been irresistible.

Much like he was feeling right now.

"Master Quinton?" The soft words, spoken at barely more than a whisper, were like a crack of thunder inside the car. *Master* Quinton. He hadn't needed the title to know where her mind and body were, but it licked fire over his skin to hear it nonetheless.

"Think carefully before you say another word, Cassia. Because I'm holding on by a very thin fucking thread over here." His tone was harsher than he'd intended, but it was taking some serious effort to rein in his baser needs. Because, Jesus, he felt like a tiger pacing in a cage.

Silence followed, and Quinton heaved a breath.

Just twenty-five more minutes and they'd be back to her place.

"Master Quinton, *please*."

Fucking hell.

Without giving it another thought, he jerked the wheel to the right, pulling off on the exit ramp they'd just come upon. After a long straightaway, the exit emptied into a big, mostly empty parking lot in front of a small brick rest stop. He parked, cut the engine, and stalked around to the passenger's door. Wrenching it open, he leaned into the breach. "This isn't how I wanted to do this, Cass."

"I know, but I need it." Slowly, she lifted her gaze to his, and her expression was pure, blatant hunger. "And you do, too."

"Get out of the car," he said, his brain planning and debating. An older couple came out of the building and made for their car further down the lot. "Not here." Taking her by the arm, he pulled her along a side walkway that quickly fell into darkness as they moved away from the street lights lining the lot. Behind the rest stop, the sounds of the traffic were distant—as was the whole rest of the world. Or so it seemed. He boxed her in against a tall security fence, the kind that looked almost like prison bars, nothing but the moon through the trees casting any light. "You want to be fucked, Cassia? Where anyone might hear us? Where anyone might see us? Out here in the darkness?"

"Yes, Sir," she said, her voice thick with lust. And, Jesus, the fact that she was right there with him in this was making Quinton insane.

"Yes, Sir, *what*?" he bit out, roughly tugging open the buttons on her jeans and shoving the pants down over her hips to hang at her knees.

"Yes, I want to get fucked. Right here. In the open. In the dark."

"Take out my cock," he said. Her hands went to work immediately, and so did his. While she freed him from the denim, he retrieved a condom from his wallet. He almost couldn't open it, his hands shook so bad from the torture of her tight strokes around his length. "Grab onto the bar above you," he said as he sheathed himself.

She did, and the picture of her hanging from the gritty metal, half naked in the shadowy darkness, the occasional sounds of cars and voices just footsteps away, destroyed every remaining vestige of his better judgment.

Quinton tugged her hips out away from the fence, bent his knees, and guided his cock between her legs. Her readiness was immediately apparent as his pumping knuckles met her wetness. Gripping her ass hard, he found her center and buried himself to the hilt. Her moan was as loud as his pleasured grunt as they collided, all desperate lust.

"Use your safeword if you need me to back off, Cassia. Come as often as you can. And be as loud as you dare," he rasped, giving her a moment to adjust. "Understood?"

"Yes, Sir," she said, her speech almost slurred with the thrill of what they were doing.

And then he let himself off the leash. With his fist gripping one of the metal bars for leverage, his hips flew against her, his pubic bone crashing into her clit on every thrust. The fence rattled from the force of the fuck, and the position caused her tight cunt to fist his cock on every in and out. He shoved his jeans down further and stepped closer, grinding himself deep, deeper, until he was riding her clit and making her scream out an orgasm into the cooling night air.

"Fuck, yes, Cassia." He pulled out, but kept his hands on her hips to steady her. "Turn around."

Breathing hard and moving like she was drunk, she clumsily gave him her back and gripped the fence. "Please," she whispered. "Please, please."

He forced her to bend at the waist and then he drove his cock right back in. "God, that's good, baby. You take me so good. Just feel me, Cassia." Gripping the back of her shirt, he tugged it upwards as far as it could go, and then he folded the hem of it over her head so that it covered the top half of her face—playing with her senses, and pushing her just a little.

She cried out and ground herself backward into him, and that was all the reassurance Quinton needed that she was on board with where he was taking them. And knowing that she was good with it filled his balls with the need to move. His hips slapped against hers, the fence rang out a rhythmic *clink*, and Cassia babbled a nonstop stream of curses and pleas.

He hunched himself around her. "What do you see, little one?" he rasped against her shoulder. "Tell me what you see."

When her words came, they were halting and gritty, breathy and uneven. "Us…us fucking. In the dark. So dark."

"Yeah. Tell me more." He curled his arms around her shoulders, bringing them closer still, stroking faster and staying deeper inside her cunt.

"You're holding me…so t-tight, and it's making all those muscles…pop out along your back and side, under your ink," she said.

"Oh, God. The way your ass clenches." Her head fell against her arm, outstretched in front of her where she held onto the fence.

"More," he said, driving punctuated thrusts into her as the picture she painted came to life, making him see them as she saw them. A savage need crawled down his spine, telling him he didn't have much time left before he lost control.

"Oh, God, I'm gonna come again, Master."

"*More*," he growled, her lust-fogged mistake bringing out the most pronounced possessiveness he'd ever felt in his life, for a submissive only used the title *Master* alone for the one who owned her.

"And my wetness is...running down my thighs...and *oh fuck I'm...c-coming!*"

That was the end of Quinton. He drove deep as his orgasm nailed him in the back, and just as his body started to pulse with it, he withdrew, ripped off the condom, and shot his release over her ass in wet stripes. "Jesus fuck, Cassia. Now mine is too." The sight of his come marking her, temporary as it was, filled him with utter carnal satisfaction.

And the need to make the claiming more permanent, too.

When his body stilled, he fell heavily atop her spine and pressed a kiss between her shoulder blades. "You okay, baby?"

"So much better than okay," she said, her voice wrecked.

Heaving a deep breath, Quinton got himself upright again, and then he gently slipped the soft cotton of her sweater off her head. "Let me clean you up." He tugged off his Henley and used it to dry her as best he could.

After she did up her jeans, she fell back in a well-used heap against the fence.

Long seconds dragged out as they just stared at one another. In that moment, when she'd just given him something so profound and amazing, Quinton knew he needed to lay how he was feeling on the line.

But then she yawned so big it made her laugh. "Sorry. I think you fucked me into oblivion."

He grinned, feeling ten kinds of triumphant at the satisfaction and contentment rolling off of her. Because of him. "Well, I ain't never gonna apologize for that."

She shook her head. "And I won't ever want you to."

See? Perfection.

But talking could wait, because first, he needed to take care of her. "Come on, Cass." He took her hand in his. "Let's get you home."

The next thing Cassia knew, Quinton was opening the door to the Rover and lifting her out of her seat. She came awake enough to protest, but he just shook his head and carried her to the top of the steps that led to her apartment door.

"I gotta get the key," she said, fumbling for her purse.

"I found it before I woke you up." Gently, he placed her on her feet, but kept one arm around her waist to steady her as he unlocked the door.

She stepped inside, and he hesitated at the threshold. But Cassia wasn't having that, not after everything they'd shared, and everything she hoped they still might. She fisted her hands in the T-shirt he'd changed into at the rest stop, and looked him right in the eyes. "Stay."

Soul-deep happiness flooded through her when he nodded and came in. They grabbed some water and headed back to her room, and then they took turns in the bathroom before meeting again at her bed, where she was pulling on a tank top and a pair of boxers.

"This okay?" she asked, looking down at herself.

"Whatever makes you comfortable, baby," he said, pressing a kiss to her cheek. "You mind me naked?"

She gave him a look. One that stopped just this side of turning into an eye roll. "Is that a trick question?"

Quinton chuckled. "Get your sexy ass in bed, woman."

Grinning, Cassia climbed in on her side, and he got in on the other. They met in the middle, and she was just about to burrow into all that naked muscle along his side when she looked back to her nightstand, where the mini-lamp she always slept with remained on.

"Leave it on if you want. It won't bother me," he said.

She read the sincerity on his face, and that meant the freaking world to her. But then she thought about how brave Quinton thought she was, and she remembered the colors he'd painted in her imagination with just his words, and Cass felt the excitement and hope that still flowed through her from the fact that she hadn't gotten very anxious at all about what they'd done in that darkness on the side of the highway, even when he'd covered her eyes.

And for the first time in two years, she turned off that light and laid down in her bed. In the dark.

"You sure, baby?" he whispered.

And, damn, how amazing was it to have someone there with her in the darkness, helping her battle what she'd so long struggled to conquer on her own. "Yeah," she said, shifting to lay her head on his shoulder and pressing herself into the delicious nook along the side of his body. "I'm sure."

He kissed her hair. "Put your leg up on me. I want to feel more of you."

She did, bringing her core up close against the hard muscle of his thigh.

"Yeah," he said, tone utterly content.

Exactly how she felt, too.

With one exception. Tomorrow, when they woke up, it was finally time to lay it all out there. She wanted more, with Quinton. She maybe wanted everything with him. And it was time to be the brave woman he believed her to be and tell him.

Chapter Ten

WHEN MORNING CAME, CASSIA WANTED to pretend like she was still asleep. But of course, her infuriatingly too-observant no-strings-attached, just-friends Dom saw right through her.

"You ain't fooling me, Sleeping Beauty," he said, sounding way too freaking awake.

"Call me in an hour," she said, shifting onto her other side.

Quinton's big, warm body followed. "Nuh uh. I've been awake for thirty minutes. I require the attention of one incredibly beautiful, adventurous submissive. I'm needy like that."

She chuckled at the self-deprecation in his tone, and nearly glowed from the compliment, too. "Is that right?"

"Yup. How ya like me now?" He kissed her ear.

And even though she very easily could've followed this banter where it was leading them, like into round two of the best sex any two human beings had ever had, Cassia decided to woman up before she let that too-perfect segue get away.

Turning in his arms, she met his gaze. "Actually…I like you a lot."

His smile changed, as if he'd caught on to the shift in her own demeanor. "We need to talk, don't we?" Quinton asked.

"I was hoping we might," she said, a tendril of nervous anticipation stirring up butterflies in her belly. Had he wanted to talk, too?

"I know we said—" she began, just as he said, "I've been thinking—"

They chuckled, laying so close together that she had no way to hide from him. And she didn't want to, either. Cassia was done hiding—from herself, from the dark, from the world. So she took a leap and let the words fly. "I know I said I didn't want a relationship, and that we agreed to keep things no-strings attached, but I..." She shook her head. "I didn't know everything our time together was going to make me feel." She forced herself to look him in the eyes. "For you."

He cupped her face in his big hand. "Fuck, baby. Are you saying what I think you're saying?"

Her chest filled with a funny pressure that threatened to consume her. "That I'm kinda feeling some strings? And I'm hoping you might be open to exploring where they lead? If that's what you're thinking, then yeah." She nearly held her breath.

Or maybe it was just that he stole it. Because Quinton's mouth came down on hers in a searing, soul-scorching, life-giving kiss. He moaned low in his throat as he rolled her under him, and then finally, slowly, he pulled his mouth away. "I want that, too. Christ, I've been feeling it for a little while now. Yesterday, I knew I wanted to talk to you about it, and then after last night... Shit, Cassia, I feel like we're pretty fucking perfect together. So, yeah, I'm open. And I'm feeling those strings, too."

"Oh, my God. Really?" she said, unable to hold back a smile. She had to blink away the happy tears that surprised her when they flooded her eyes. "I was scared I was going to ruin everything."

"Never," he said, brushing away the stray wetness with his thumbs. "But there's one thing I need if we're going to give this a go."

"Of course," she said, peering up into his dark eyes. God, he was gorgeous, the morning light falling over his sleep-mussed hair, a little growth of scruff on his face.

"I want us to be exclusive, Cassia." Grasping her hand, he brought it to his mouth. "In case this helps make my intentions clear..." He licked her palm and straight up her middle finger.

Cass laughed, utterly tickled about how this conversation was going after everything she'd feared. "Did you just lick me to claim me?"

"Damn straight."

"So do I get to lick you back?" she asked.

"Baby, I really wish you would." He made a big show of rolling onto his back and pushing off the covers, baring himself to her gaze.

And damn, her bed had never looked better than it did at that very moment, with his ink, cut muscles, and hard cock laid out on display. Just for her.

She undressed and crawled toward him, then settled on her knees between his spread thighs. But before she got lost in his body, she had to know for sure. "What about the demonstration you have to do?"

Quinton folded his arm beneath his head and peered up at her. "That's what upset you the other night, isn't it? Why you left so fast?"

"I didn't like the idea of you playing with someone else, but I know you have to do stuff like that for the club," she said.

"I don't do anything I don't want to do, Cassia. The next demonstration I'll do, if you're open to it, will be with you."

The sheer relief she felt would've taken her to her knees if she hadn't already been there.

Releasing a shaky breath, Cass smiled. "Good. Then consider this my claiming." Leaning down so that the dark hair on his thighs tickled her breasts, she tongued him from the base of his cock to the fat tip.

His body surged beneath her, his hips thrusting closer, his back arching. And it drove Cassia on to claim more of him. With a fist around his root, she sucked him deeply, taking his cock to the back of her throat again and again, just like she already knew he liked.

But as good as it was, it wasn't enough. She wanted to claim more of him. All of him, if he'd let her. So Cass crawled up his body until her legs straddled his hips. Reaching into the nightstand, she retrieved a condom from a new box she'd bought when she started back at Blasphemy. Not that she'd ever imagined all this. Cassia held the little square package up.

He laced his hands behind his head, the picture of relaxation. Except for the hard cock jutting up between them, of course. "Whatever you want, Cassia, you are welcome to have," he said in a low tight voice.

Holding his gaze, she rolled on the latex, and then, bracing a hand against his hard chest, she centered herself over his cock and lowered herself until she'd taken every thick inch. "This is claiming you, too."

His hands flew to her hips, gripping and tugging as she rode him. The façade of relaxation quickly melted away, unmasking Quinton's commanding dominance. "Fuck, Cass. Ride me. Use me. Take everything I've got."

She gave herself over to the pursuit of pleasure, grinding, fucking, faster, harder. Long, pleasure-drenched minutes passed where they spoke only with their bodies, the sounds of their movements filling the room. Her skin slapping against his, the mattress shifting beneath them, their labored breaths and his throaty groans. "Quinton, oh God."

"Want you to come on me, Cass. I want you to come on me *now*." His fingers dug into her hips, a silent, stinging command.

It was exactly what she needed. Just three more aggressive strokes and she was coming, crying out, collapsing against his chest as the sensations wrung her out and left her raw.

And then she was on her back, all that dominance pinning her down. He drew her wrists above her head and pressed them into the mattress, and then Quinton was riding her, slow and deep and relentless.

"Feel like I've been looking for you, Cassia. For so damn long. And now that I've finally found you, I don't want to let you go."

That might've been the moment she fell in love with Quinton Ross. "Good. Don't. Not ever."

He dropped his head against hers, and his breaths rasped across her lips. Eyes open. Watching. Looking. Even with everything they'd already done, it was one of the most intimate moments of her life.

"Come in me, please," she whispered. "I want to feel it."

Immediately, his hips hammered harder, and then his eyes clenched shut as the orgasm rocked through him. "Aw, God, Cass," he growled, his cock jerking inside her. If nothing else ever worked to help her tolerate the darkness, the memory of how his gorgeous face looked in that moment, shattered by the pleasure he'd found in her, just might've done the trick. Because, damn.

When his body eased, he released her hands, and she immediately brought them around his big shoulders. "Don't go yet. I like the way you feel on top of me."

On an appreciative moan, he settled his face against the side of her neck and let her have his weight. "Keep saying things like that and we'll never get out of this bed."

Cassia chuckled. "That wouldn't be so bad."

"No, it would not," Quinton said in a low rumble.

It was after eleven when they awakened again, and their growling stomachs made food a dire necessity. The night before, she hadn't known what to expect when she'd invited Quinton to stay, but the day turned out to be perfect. They followed up the mind-blowing declarations and sex with an amazing lunch at Quinton's favorite diner, over which they discussed more about their relationship. Namely, they agreed that neither was interested in a twenty-four/seven arrangement. They would follow D/s protocol when at Blasphemy, other clubs, or play parties, and during all scenes. And, finally, that Quinton could initiate a scene outside of Blasphemy with her consent. With each agreement, Cassia felt nearly giddy with the realization that this was really happening between them.

That there was really, truly a *them*.

And even though she hadn't expected that, or even thought she'd wanted it, back at the start of all this, it felt good. Right. Like she was finally all the way out of that cave and living again.

After lunch, they played tourists, browsing the Inner Harbor and the funky boutiques in Fells Point. As darkness fell, they enjoyed a fantastic dinner in Little Italy, only to come full circle when they fell into her bed again that night and explored one another's bodies until neither of them could stay awake for one more minute.

It was the second night she'd slept in the dark.

On Monday morning, it was hard to say good-bye. They stood kissing for long minutes by her door, and she didn't want to let him go. But at least he didn't seem eager to leave, either.

"I'm tending bar every night but Tuesday and Thursday this week," Quinton said, his arms around her waist, "but I'll save you a seat at the bar in case you ever find yourself wanting to drop in and keep me company." He waggled his brows, and it made her laugh.

"Ooh, will my reserved seat have, like, a little black velvet rope across it?" she asked.

"Is that more likely to make you want to come visit me?"

Chuckling, she shrugged. "Well, it couldn't hurt."

"I'll see what I can do about some rope for you then, little one." He arched a brow that told her he had more in mind for that rope than just reserving a chair.

Annnd now she really didn't want him to go. "I'll keep the invitation in mind, then."

Shaking his head, he kissed her. "So, scenes on Tuesday and Thursday nights sound good to you?"

With him? Always. And even better was the knowledge that they weren't *just* about those scenes, or about her phobia, or about the sex. Not anymore. "Sounds amazing. I'll see you tomorrow night at the club then?"

He tilted his head. "Feels like forever, doesn't it?"

Man, she adored him for being the one to say it. "Kinda."

"I know, but I close tonight. Depending on how busy it is, the earliest I'd probably get out of there is two A.M. With how early you have to get up for work, it doesn't make any sense for me to come over."

Begrudgingly, she nodded. "Okay, well, text me when you have a minute and let me know how your day is going."

"You, too." Quinton gave her another long, deep kiss. The kind that was a promise of so much more. "Have a good day, baby."

She was still smiling as he jogged down the steps and out the front door.

What she wanted to do was curl into sheets that still smelled of him and them and sleep the day away but, alas, duty called. She grabbed a quick shower and threw on work clothes, and then she was out the door herself.

Still, it was the best Monday morning she'd had in years. Cassia felt happy and hopeful, like being with Quinton had plugged her back into the rest of the world after a long, lonely time away.

And those feelings meant so much to her. They meant everything. And they were all because of Quinton.

Tuesday night had taken about fifty-two years to arrive. At least, that's how Quinton felt as he sat with a couple of the other Masters at a grouping of couches near the bar waiting for Cassia to arrive.

"You doing all right tonight, Quinton?" Master Jonathan asked.

"What?" he asked distractedly, his gaze pinging between his friends and the locker room door, his knee bouncing in anticipation. "Oh, yeah, great."

"Dude," Master Cruz said. "What is your deal? You are wound tight as shit."

Quinton chuffed out a laugh. Sometimes, being friends with a bunch of Dominants could be a pain in the ass. The fuckers were too damned observant and good at reading people. Jonathan and Cruz were long-time best friends who'd served in the Navy together, and they often shared women in menage scenes the submissives here raved about, from what Quinton had heard. It was hard to get anything by these two. What one didn't pick up, the other always did.

"I'm good," he finally said. "Just waiting for Cassia to get here."

"Cassia? That another new sub?" Cruz asked, raking a hand through his short, dark hair. "Haven't heard that name before."

A flash of possessiveness swept through Quinton. Which just proved that Cruz was right—he *was* wound a little tight. But apparently that's what happened to him the first time he was going public with an exclusive relationship. "She used to belong to the club a few years back, and she's been coming again the past few weeks." He eyed Cruz, and then his blond-haired friend, too. "I'm seeing her."

"No shit?" Cruz said, an incredulous expression on his face.

Jonathan's face split into an easy smile. "For real? Good for you, Q."

Making that admission got easier the next time, when Griffin and Kenna joined them a few minutes later. Being a former Marine meant that Kenna traded regular barbs with Jonathan and Cruz over their naval service, which allowed Griffin to grill him about Cassia.

"Finally settling down with someone," Griffin said, the smug smile on his face making it clear he was busting his chops. Just a little.

Not that Quinton really minded. "It's all new, but it looks that way."

"Good," Griffin said. "About damn time, Q. Personally, I wouldn't have it any other way. Hope it works out for you two. Life's too fucking short to live it alone."

He didn't want to get ahead of himself, but Quinton agreed. Now that he was walking down this path, he didn't want to have to turn back. Not when he'd never been convinced he'd find someone who matched all his needs and interests as well as Cassia did.

Just then, he saw her across the club. She wore a black sheath dress that plunged low in the front and had a flowing, uneven short skirt. As always, she was sexy and beautiful, but it was the smile that lit up her face when she finally noticed him that was the real punch to the gut. Man, that one look took his breath away.

Quinton rose from his seat as Cassia approached. When she finally reached him, she bowed her head. "Good evening, Master Quinton."

He lifted her chin with his fingers. "Good evening, Cass. You look great."

"Thank you, Sir," she said, gifting him with a pretty smile.

And even though he could tell she was glad to see him, he sensed some nerves from her, too. It brought out his need to take care of her. So despite being eager for the scene he'd planned, they could take their time. "Sit with me," he said, sinking back down into the couch.

"Would it please you for me to sit next to you on the floor or the couch, Sir?" she asked.

Just the question had his cock stirring in his jeans. Possessing a sub of his own took the experience of being a Dom to a whole new level. "At my knee, little one."

Gracefully, she lowered herself into a kneeling position on the floor, her warmth pressed against his calf, her eyes on him. Jesus, her submission was beautiful to him. And the fact that the other men were looking on with approval—and interest—heightened the whole experience and made him start to realize how much he'd been missing.

But Quinton kept his attention on her. "Did you have a good day?"

She rested her chin on his knee. "Yes, Sir. My team finished a draft of a big water quality report, two days ahead of schedule. So it was a very good day."

He stroked her hair, pride flooding through him. "Congratulations."

"Thank you, Sir." Her smile faded a little. "May I tell you something, Master Quinton?"

The seriousness of her tone had him sitting forward, getting closer to her. "Of course. Are you all right?"

"Yes. I just feel like I should tell you. I tried to sleep with the lamp off again last night, but I couldn't do it. Not without you there."

He stroked his knuckles against her cheek, her admission pleasing him because he could tell it hadn't been easy for her to make. "Thank you for telling me, Cassia. One day at a time, you know? And you're going to have good days and bad days, too. But you've already come a long way."

"I know, Sir." She brushed her cheek against his thigh, as if touching him comforted her. And damn if that wasn't a heady thought.

"Next time something like that happens, please text or call me. Understand?" he asked, regretting their very different work schedules. "Even if we can't be together in the moment, I still want to be there for you."

"Yes, Sir."

He nodded, enjoying that their conversation seemed to be relaxing her. "Good. And little one?"

"Sir?"

"You may call me Master alone," he said, eager to hear her claim him that way, too. The way a submissive referred to the Dominant who owned her.

A gorgeous pink bloomed across her cheeks, and a satisfied smile shaped her lips. "Yes, Master."

Raw masculine need seared his blood to hear her say it, and he had to shift in his seat to accommodate his growing hard-on. Her gaze tracked his movements, settling on the bulge filling out the front of his jeans. Staring, she licked her lips.

"*Cassia*," he said in warning.

"Sorry, Master," she said, though her eyes belied the words. He arched a brow, a silent promise to remember this later.

For a few moments, the other Doms pulled Quinton into a conversation about some renovations they'd been considering for Blasphemy. The church that formed the main part of their structure had been built in the 1910s and in a state of some ruin when they'd first acquired it, so it pretty much always needed something. While he spoke, he enjoyed Cassia's quiet, attentive presence at his side. He reveled in it, in fact.

Her hand settled on his thigh. And that was the first time he noticed it—her wrist cuff had changed. Of course it had. He'd made the arrangements for it himself. But in the excitement of seeing her and being with her in public, he'd momentarily forgotten. Gone was the white *unattached submissive* cuff with its colorful ribbons indicating her interests and limits, and in its place was the dark red cuff of an *owned submissive*.

Quinton's submissive.

He'd never before put that cuff on someone's arm.

And it made him suddenly eager to get Cassia alone. He threaded his fingers between hers, holding her hand on his thigh so he could see that cuff. When he finished speaking to the other Doms, he pulled her fingers to his mouth and pressed a kiss to them. "It's time to play, Cassia. Are you ready?"

The banked heat in her eyes suddenly flared. "Very, Sir."

"Good. Then rise." Once again, she moved with grace.

And he just watched. When she was standing before him, he smoothed his fingertips up her thighs and under her short skirt. His fingers encountered the thin straps of a thong.

"From now on, no more panties when we're at the club," he said, peering up at her.

"Yes, Sir."

"Take them off." He held out his hand.

She didn't hesitate for even a second. Despite the audience they had, Cassia reached under her skirt, bent at the waist as she removed and stepped out of them, and placed the scrap of black in his hand.

Her obedience cut the last strings of his restraint. Tucking the panties in his pocket, he rose, well aware of the attention of the other men, but paying it absolutely no mind. As was only right. Someday, Cass would be ready for a public demonstration. Given her reaction to what they'd done on the dance floor and behind that rest stop, Quinton suspected she'd even enjoy being watched by a crowd. But not tonight. Tonight, she was his and his alone.

"The minute we walk through the door of the sense-dep room, I want you naked and kneeling," Quinton said, peering up at her. She nodded. "Good. Let's go."

Chatper Eleven

CASSIA HAD NO IDEA WHAT Master Quinton had planned, but whatever it was, she wanted it.

She wanted his dominance and his commands and his wonderfully dirty mind.

She wanted it all, with him. And that had never been more clear than when she'd knelt at his knees among all his friends and passersby in the club. She'd always received pleasure from being in service to another, but the pride and heat and approval in Master Quinton's gaze as she'd knelt there had spoken to something within her soul. The stress from the day, her nervousness about being at Blasphemy for the first time as *his* submissive, the fear that her confession about sleeping with the light on would disappoint him—all of it melted away kneeling at his feet.

After a few moments, he came to stand in front of her. "Rise, Cassia. And present yourself for my inspection."

In the quiet and stillness of the room, a thrill whipped through her belly. She got into position with her feet spread, breasts thrust outward, and hands laced behind her head.

Wearing only those worn jeans again, this time with the top button hanging dangerously open, he hummed appreciatively. "I want to see what's mine," he said, slowly circling and touching her. Coming in front of her again, he met her gaze. "I want to *use* what's mine. Every part."

Oh, God. Her nipples were immediately erect. She shivered.

He chuckled. "You like that idea, too."

"Yes, Sir," she said, for there was no point denying it.

"Good, because I want to push you tonight, Cass. Are you open to that?" His dark gaze flashed with arousal and need, but she saw the concern there, too. He wouldn't push her further than she could handle. And if he did, all she had to do was use her safewords and he'd back off. She had complete confidence in that because he'd done it before. And after all they'd shared, and the progress she'd made, she wanted to try. For him. For herself.

"Yes, Master. I am."

"Brave girl." He pressed a kiss to the corner of her mouth. "I'm going to play with your senses. I'm going to play with the darkness. And I'm going to play with your ass." He arched a brow.

Heat roared over her at the thought of all that might mean, and her heart tripped into a sprint.

"Let's push up against those boundaries, Cass, but don't let yourself get to the point of a panic attack. Do you understand?" She nodded. "Good. Then give me knees and elbows."

Arousal flooded through her as she moved for him, getting onto her knees, her legs spread, and then sinking her upper body lower yet, until she was resting on her elbows. She felt his gaze like a physical caress, even though he hadn't touched her.

And then he did. Two swats fell against her ass. "Arch your back further, Cass. Open yourself up to me." She did. "There it is," he rasped. A vibrator sounded out in the quiet, and then those sensations fell between her legs.

Cassia cried out, her whole body going taut at the contact.

A smack fell across her ass, this one stinging where the others had just been meant to catch her attention. "Be still," Master Quinton said. "And do *not* come until I give you permission."

A whimper spilled from her lips. Orgasm denial was so not one of her strong points. But she would not fail. Not at *this*. So as he tormented her clit with the thick head of the vibrator, Cassia gritted her teeth and counted breaths and traced the tiny lines in the concrete floor. *Anything* to distract herself from what her Master—*her* freaking Master—was doing to her body.

Cool liquid dripped against her ass. His touch jolted through her as he rubbed the slick wetness against her rear hole. It had been a long time since she'd taken anything there—anything more than his finger, at least—but something about the dirty decadence of ass play had always gotten her off in the past. So when he slid a finger into her, she heaved a deep breath and submitted to his desire.

"Good girl," he said. "Just breathe and feel, Cassia."

God, all she could do was feel. His finger sliding in and out of her hypersensitive asshole, the strokes teased and pushed against the ring of muscle there, all while the vibrator stimulated her pussy and made her drip. And then he added a second finger. Cass moaned at the stretching sensation, her brain racing through the possibilities of where he was taking this. Would he take them all the way? Her cunt contracted at the thought, revealing that no matter the discomfort she might feel, it aroused her, too.

Jesus, it was making her burn.

"One more, baby," he said from his position behind her. "Take it for me."

Her whole body shook as he eased a trio of his thick fingers into her asshole. "Oh, fuck, Master. Oh fuck." Fleetingly, she wondered if he was going to incorporate his trademark sensory play. Not that she needed it to enjoy what was happening. Not at all.

"Don't come," he bit out, sliding those fingers deep. His other hand pressed between her shoulder blades. "Upper body to the floor and use your hands to hold your ass open for me."

Shaking and dripping and needier than she'd ever felt in her life, Cassia shifted into the new position, her face and shoulders against the cool concrete, and her hands reaching back to grasp her cheeks.

"Christ, that's hot, Cassia. I'm going to reward you so good. Just hold on a little longer." Pulling the vibrator away, he fucked her with those three fingers again and again. Going deep and turning his wrist to vary the sensations. Even without the attention to her clit, she was on the verge of giving in to the desperate, alluring promise of release.

After several long moments, he eased his fingers free of her, and Cassia cried out at the loss. "Master," she gasped.

"I know, little one. We're not done yet. We're not done by a long shot."

Something hard nudged against her asshole, and then pushed in. It opened her wider and wider and wider until she wanted to scramble away from the pressure, and then the plug was all the way inside her, filling her and making her moan.

"Yes, good girl. Rise, Cass."

She almost couldn't make sense of the words. Shaky and needy, she forced herself onto her feet again, though without as much of the gracefulness with which she normally tried to move. And, oh hell, the fullness was so much more pronounced when she took a step, moving to face him again.

And then she *was* facing him—facing a man who looked as painfully aroused as she felt. His cock made an impressive bulge in the front of his jeans. His eyes were dark fire. His muscles were tense and his jaw tight. "Where are you, baby?"

"Green, Sir."

He nodded, his gaze hungry and approving. "Then follow me."

At the back corner of the room, Master Quinton opened a door, leading her into a dark dressing room. He turned on the light, revealing a sink, a shower, and a metal-looking wall with another door, this one raised off the floor and oval in shape. It reminded her of a hatch you might see on a ship. He closed them into the small room, and then opened the hatch.

Light spilled into the breach, revealing a larger-than-usual tub.

"It's a flotation tank," he explained. "The water is very high in salt content, so it makes you float. In fact, you can't sink. Between the buoyancy and the consistency with your own temperature, most people lose the ability to perceive their body while they're floating."

Cassia inhaled deeply and wrapped her brain around what he was laying out. She knew where he was going with this without him having to tell her, because there weren't any visible light fixtures inside the tank. "So, if you were in the water in the darkness...you'd be totally deprived of your senses." Just saying that out loud made her belly flip-flop. And she'd wondered if he intended to incorporation sensory play...

Be careful what you wish for, apparently.

"Exactly," Master Quinton said. "This, Cassia, is the ultimate mindfuck. But it's also very freeing. And if you lay totally still, you won't hear the water either. It'll be totally silent inside."

"Okay," she said, her pulse kicking up under her skin. "I'll try, Sir."

He took her chin in his hand. "You don't know how much that pleases me. But we're going to start out with light, baby."

The breath she unleashed nearly made her light-headed. "Oh. Okay."

He kissed her ear, then spoke in a whisper. "Brave fucking girl.

Get in and lay down."

God, the way he could build her up with just a few uttered phrases. Holding on to the door frame, she stepped into the shallow water. Not quite knee deep, it was warm to the touch, which made it easy to immerse herself as she lay back long-ways.

Master Quinton was right, she couldn't help but float. The water held her up from head to toe, just surrounding her face but not anywhere close to covering it.

"How's that feel?" he asked, peering in through the open door.

"Really good," she said. "It's kind of a weird sensation. Being totally weightless."

"Yes, exactly. It's good for sore joints and muscles, too," he said, his tone more conversational. And then that tone changed, becoming more commanding again. "Now, take a deep breath, Cassia." She did, blowing it out long and slow. The water cradled her body in warmth, even though it was hard to perceive it against her skin. She moved her toes just to be able to feel a part of her body. "Be still."

"Yes, Sir," she whispered.

"From here on out, no talking, except for safewords. No moving. And I would like you to try to close your eyes and keep them closed if you can."

She did, and the nothingness was suddenly and utterly encompassing. Her heart beat thundered, and it was the oddest thing because she heard her pulse in her ears against the water there.

For a long moment, she just floated in the quiet, and she had the strangest thought that she could fall asleep there, perfectly suspended, almost disassociated from any awareness of time or space.

And then Master Quinton said three words. "Do. Not. Move."

She was just wondering why he'd repeat the command when it started.

Vibrations.

Inside her.

She couldn't help the whimper that ripped out of her, or the way her muscles flinched against the erotic onslaught. The water rippled around her.

Jesus. It was a vibrating butt plug. And it put a match to the embers of arousal he'd ignited earlier. It only took a few precious seconds to make her desperate because the sensation was intense, powerful, penetrating. She couldn't perceive her hands or her arms or her feet or even her breasts. The combination of the sensory deprivation with the plug reduced her to her basest nature—to the nerves and need between her legs. To that plug in her ass and the way it was making her lose her mind.

And she was, she was losing her mind and herself and her control. But he hadn't given her permission…

Ohgodohgodohgod.

"Come. Come freely. As much as you can," came her Master's gritty voice.

Soaring with the granted freedom, she shouted out the orgasm, and the sound was echoed within the tank. Her whole body shuddered and shook, on and on and on, causing her to make waves. It was one of the most intense orgasms of her life, in part because all the deprivation took away every single other thing she might've perceived or paid any attention to.

Breathing hard, she opened her eyes and tried to get her bearings.

But then the vibrations became more intense and the light dimmed.

Cassia cried out, already on edge, completely disbelieving that she could handle another release of that magnitude again. She clenched her eyes tightly shut, trying to brace against the assault, but it was like the vibrator had become an extension of her cunt and her ass, and it wrung another orgasm out of her whether she thought she could handle it or not.

The vibrations strengthened again, and she had no time at all to adjust. She'd *entirely* become carnal sensation, and the third orgasm exploded her into pieces. Her eyes flew open as she screamed and shook, and the light was much dimmer than it had been, almost so dim that it was hard to perceive. And between the deprivation and the darkness and the maddening elation and drain of the orgasms, it was suddenly all too much. "*Yellow, Sir. Please, yellow.*"

The vibrations shut off, and Master Quinton was right there, helping her up, pulling her into his arms. "I've got you, baby."

"Holy fucking shit," she said, her body still shuddering. "Sir."

He chuckled. "You did so damn good."

"I…I…" She swallowed hard, struggling to pull herself together. She was floating right on the edge of subspace. It was enough to make her feel pleasantly drunk but nowhere near the emotional shattering she'd experienced before.

"Take a deep breath, Cassia," he said. "Pace your breathing with mine."

For several long moments, she did just that, reveling in the feel of him, the way he cared for her, and his small, tender attentions. Finally, she had to tell him. "I think I could've handled the dark, Master. I really think I could've gotten there," she rasped.

Master Quinton nodded. "And you will, but not tonight. Your words said *yellow*, but your tone said *red*, Cass. Which meant you did just what I asked you to do—used your safeword before you got to the point of a panic attack." He kissed her forehead. "I'm proud of you."

Beaming at the praise, she let herself be wrapped in an oversized bath towel and guided out of the tank.

"Brace your hands on the sink and bend," Master Quinton ordered. When she did, he gently removed the plug and dropped it in the sink for cleaning. An aftershock wracked through her, and as much relief as she felt to have it out, she also felt utterly empty.

A whimper spilled out of her.

"What is it, little one?" he asked, pulling her to face him again.

The affectionate concern in his gaze undid her. "Too empty, Master."

"Cassia—"

"Too empty," she whispered, shaking her head and pleading with her eyes.

"You need me," he said, eyes burning.

Oh, God. She did. It seemed like it should've been impossible after everything he'd just done for her, but she did. "I need you."

When he stepped back from her, she whimpered at the loss and at what she was sure was going to be his argument against going further. And then he stepped out of his jeans and turned on the shower. He crooked his finger, beckoning her to come to him.

Dropping the towel, Cassia crossed the small space, her gaze dropping to where his cock jutted out towards her.

"How do you want to be filled, little one?" he asked, his voice a low scrape.

"However it would please you, Sir," she said, relief racing through her veins at the question. Because it meant he wasn't ending things between them for the night.

"No. Answer my question. Say the words."

She didn't think. She didn't debate. She didn't even consciously choose. Her answer was pure instinct and need. "I want you to fuck my ass, Master." Because it was the only place she hadn't yet had him. And she didn't want there to be a single part of her he hadn't claimed.

"Jesus, Cassia. You're a fucking dream to me. Do you know that?" he asked, backing her into the warm, streaming water.

"And you make me feel as strong and brave as you think I am, Sir."

He cupped soap in his big hands and rubbed her whole body down, washing away the salt that was already making her skin feel tight. And then he treated her hair to the same attention, scratching her scalp with his fingertips until she was nearly purring at the goodness of it.

"Stand and face the wall, Cassia." Master Quinton turned off the water as she obeyed, and then he retrieved something from the cabinet over the sink. Her insides shook with the need to please him as little noises sounded out from behind her. The tearing of a condom wrapper. The wet slicking of lubricant.

After a moment, wet fingers fell against her asshole. She jumped at the touch, but almost immediately she eased into being explored there again. Because she wanted it so damn bad.

Master Quinton tugged out her hips, and his height allowed him to take her right there up against the wall. He lined his cock up with her ass and penetrated her inch by bone-meltingly good inch. She moaned at the stretching fullness. It started with a stinging pain that almost felt intolerable just before it became decadently good. Despite the way the plug had opened her up, it took a few minutes before he could go deep and set a faster pace, and she adored his patience and the way he took care not to hurt her.

"So fucking tight, Cassia." She could only moan her assent. "Every part of you is mine," he rasped in her ear.

"Yes, Master," she said, loving the sentiment. Loving...him. "Every part." Would he hear what she wasn't saying?

He didn't give her a chance to wonder any further, because just then, he picked up the pace of his strokes, hammering his cock into her ass deeper, harder, faster. He wrapped his arms around her, anchoring his grasp around her throat and her breast, and let his hips nail her mercilessly and frantically, as if something inside him had snapped.

"Touch yourself," he growled. "Make yourself come while I take your ass."

Her hand slid down the wet wall. On a moan, she followed his command, her fingers immediately circling hard against her clit. And despite the intensity of those earlier orgasms, the slick friction shoved her toward the edge. The desperation and urgency of his movements, the shockwaves of his thrusts inside her, and the way his breathing sawed in and out of his lungs, all pushed her harder. But she wasn't falling until he did.

"Can't last, Cassia. Can't last because you fucking *own* me, too."

His words, those beautiful, soul-bearing words, did her in. "Coming, Master. Oh, God, I'm coming."

As her release pulsed through her in a long, rolling wave, Master Quinton nailed her in a series of punctuated thrusts then buried himself to the hilt on a broken shout. "Fuck, baby. Fuck." His cock jerked inside her over and over.

It was all she could do to remain upright.

But he didn't let her fall. Of course, he didn't. Master Quinton cleaned her up a second time, and then he wrapped them both in fresh towels and carried her out to the couch where they'd so often sat together. They talked and relaxed for a long while, completely comfortable and at ease together. No matter what they did—however extreme or normal—Cassia always felt like they fit, and that wasn't a feeling she'd had this strongly ever before in her life.

She adored it. And Quinton.

He came home to her house again that night. And once again she slept without the lamp.

Because this incredible, handsome, adventurous man she'd found—*he* was her light in the dark.

Chapter Twelve

EVERYTHING HE AND CASSIA HAD shared on Tuesday night had been so amazing that Quinton had barely been able to sit still on Thursday in anticipation of seeing her again. Which was maybe why he found himself at a jewelry store. Just browsing.

At least, that's what he was telling himself.

Except, he was clearly browsing for something in particular, because the case in front of him was filled with rather stunning diamond choker necklaces. He knew he wanted diamonds. The hardest of the gemstones. Absolute gorgeous brilliance created under pressure.

Just like Cassia.

"May I help you?" the woman behind the counter asked.

And just like that, he knew the answer. He was doing this. Because it felt right. Because *she* felt like the everything he'd been looking for but never truly believed he would ever find.

He considered more than a few pieces, felt their weight in his hands, and imagined each and every one around Cass's neck. Until he found the perfect one.

Now it just remained to decide when to give it to her.

Quinton chuckled at himself as he had to resist the urge to drive to her right this fucking second and place the collar around her neck. Damn, he had it bad.

And he was absofuckinglutely okay with that. More than, in fact.

Quinton couldn't pinpoint the exact moment that it'd happened, but he knew he cared for Cass as more than just his submissive—

though that meant a fucking lot all by itself. Maybe it had been on the dance floor the night of their first scenes. Or maybe it was the way she'd followed him, so trusting despite her vulnerability, around the back of that building off the side of the highway. Or maybe it was the way she'd surrendered to his every dirty whim the other night. Or, perhaps, it was any one of a million times she'd faced her fears and beat—or weathered—them, finding solace and comfort in his arms again and again.

This necklace was him wanting to show her all of that. And letting her know that he wasn't just thinking about the next scene or the next week or the next month that they'd be together. He was thinking about them forever and for everything.

So it felt a little like fate when, twenty minutes after he left the jewelry store, his cell rang showing Cass's name on the caller ID. He grinned, hoping she was as excited as he was about tonight.

"Cassia. To what do I owe this pleasure?" he asked by way of answering, a big stupid grin on his face.

"Hi," she said, her voice sounding all wrong. "I'm afraid I have bad news."

"What's wrong?" he asked, freezing as he got out of his car in the lot at Blasphemy.

"My body has been possessed by a vomit monster. Either that, or I'm sick," she said.

"Damn, I'm sorry. Are you home?" A gut-deep need rose up to take care of her in *every* way she needed. And that told him a lot, too, about where he was with her.

"Yeah. I got home from work a few hours ago. I'm sorry I didn't call sooner, but I won't be able to make it tonight." Her voice was scratchy and croaky.

"Baby," he said. "Why are you apologizing?"

"Because I hate to disappoint you," she said.

Because I hate to disappoint you, Master.

She hadn't used the D/s title, but he'd heard it in her tone. Loud and clear. And even though her voice was a train wreck, the sentiment reached inside his chest and tugged at things. Tugged at them *hard*.

Christ, he was in love with this woman.

Christ. He was *in love* with this woman.

"Baby," he said, gentler this time. "You never could. Now, hang tight, I'll be right there."

Twenty minutes later, Quinton was knocking on her door. He hated that she'd have to get up to let his ass in. At some point he'd need a key. Because his brain was apparently unable to stop thinking of ways to make this thing he'd found with Cassia permanent.

The door eased open, and it was quite possible that the wood was all that held her upright. She was sheet white, had dark circles under bloodshot eyes, and stood hunched over.

"Hi," she said, hanging back from him. "Really glad you're here, but don't wanna get you sick."

"Don't care about that," he said, taking her in his arms and pushing the door shut. She was warm to the touch. "Damn, Cass, you're hot."

She tilted her head back to look at him. "I know, right? So hot."

He chuckled. How many times had she made him laugh these past weeks? Her sense of humor was just one of the many things he loved about her. "Come on, funny girl. Let's get you back in bed."

"Oh," she said, ducking her chin. "I, uh, have been laying out here. I kinda got sick in the bedroom earlier and trying to clean it up . . ." She shook her head. "I'll deal with it later."

"Okay. No worries." Damn, he was really glad he'd come. Quinton led her to the couch, and she immediately curled into a pile of pillows up against the corner. Crouching, he covered her with a blanket. "What can I get you?"

Her eyelids were already heavy. "Just you," she whispered.

"You got me, baby." Understatement of the century. "Sleep now."

He knelt there until her eyes closed, and then he went foraging. He grabbed a bottle of water and found the Tylenol in a cabinet, along with a little stockpile of chicken noodle soup. Maybe she'd be able to stomach that later. He placed the water and meds on the coffee table for when she woke up.

Then he checked on her bedroom. The sour smell hit him before he walked into the room, and no way was he leaving it like this. Quinton opened a window, letting the cool fall air stream in, and then he made quick work of removing the dirty sheets and emptying the trash can she'd made it to. The tour she'd given him his first time here meant he knew that she had a little laundry set-up in a hall closet. As quietly as he could, he dropped the sheets into the washer and got that going. Finally, he found clean bedding in a linen closet and got a couple wet rags from the bathroom to clean the carpet.

There wasn't a thing glamorous about any of it. But life and love were fucking messy sometimes, and the beauty of it all was in making someone else's life better with kindness and care. On the face of BDSM, it was the submissive who was the one in service. But the reality was that service was at the heart of who and what a Dominant was, too. Like most Doms, Quinton was hard-wired with the need to take care of those he cared about, and certainly, of the one he loved. In every way she needed. In *any way* she needed.

To take care of Cassia.

It was why he'd wanted to help her with the phobia that was the result of her accident. It was why he'd so often denied his own arousal when it was clear she'd gone as far as she could in a scene. It was why he *loved* eating pussy and got off on giving orgasm after orgasm. And it was why he'd made her bed and gotten on his hands and knees to scrub puke out of a carpet.

Footsteps pounded down the hall, and then the retching started.

Quinton was at Cass's side in a moment. He held her hair back as her whole body convulsed over the toilet with every heave. Fuck, he hated that he couldn't do more.

Finally, it passed. She flushed the toilet and attempted to stand.

"Come here, baby," he said, helping her up and to the sink. "Get some water. But maybe not too much."

Nodding, she rinsed her mouth with a few handfuls, and then she just sagged against the counter. "Thank you," she said, meeting his gaze in the mirror. "I know this sucks, but will you stay with me?"

He smirked. "Try to make me leave."

That eked a small smile out of her.

Quinton stayed the rest of the day. She slept on and off, and finally the vomiting stopped long enough that she attempted a cup of tea. When that stayed down, she tried a little of the broth from the chicken noodle soup. They watched *Ferris Bueller's Day Off* because that seemed totally appropriate to the situation and it made her laugh. And then he stayed the night, too, holding her as her fever broke and she moaned and shifted in her sleep.

And even though he regretted how bad she felt and wished he could weather it for her, he felt a kind of peace in his chest at getting to be with someone this way. At getting to be with Cassia this way.

Through the good and the bad. Because that was love.

Cassia might've thought she'd died if it wasn't for the hot expanse of man sprawled naked beside her on the bed, the early morning light casting shadows across his body that highlighted all his hard ridges and angles. His cock stirred despite the fact that he remained asleep. She wasn't remotely in any shape to do anything about that, but it sure was nice to look.

Maybe this was heaven?

Actually, there was no maybe about it.

Quinton had spent his whole day with her. He'd fed her, held her hair while she threw up, cleaned up her puke, and did her laundry. If that wasn't heaven, she didn't know what was.

What she did know?

She loved him. She was *in love* with him.

But was it too soon to tell him?

It hadn't even been a week since they'd agreed to be exclusive, and here she was imagining forever.

Pulling herself out of bed, she stumbled to the bathroom. At least the nausea was gone. Except now she was the human equivalent of a wet noodle. And that was being generous.

Back in the bedroom, she found Quinton in a stretch that highlighted every gorgeous muscle. All the way hard now, his cock bobbed against his stomach.

"Damn, I wish I was up to doing you right now," she said.

His belly laugh made her smile. "You can do me any time, baby."

He held out an arm, and she crawled in against him. Cassia loved the way his arm curled around her shoulders, pulling her in tighter. "Thank you for yesterday."

"Not a thing," he said. "How are you doing?"

"Better. I'm just kinda trashed from it."

He nodded. "You're not going in to work, I hope?"

"I don't think I could make it out the front door," she said. Disappointment stirred in her belly. "Which means I probably won't be up to visiting you at Blasphemy tonight."

Quinton made a sound low in his throat. "I'm thinking about

finding someone to cover me."

She shifted to brace her chin on his pecs. "You don't have to do that, Quinton. I'm a lot better. And the way I feel, I think I'm just gonna sleep."

"You sure? I want to take care of you." He tucked her hair behind her ear, his gaze so full of affection and concern.

And damn if his words didn't reach right into her heart. "I appreciate that so much. If I need you, I promise I'll ask."

Quinton heaved a breath like he wasn't entirely convinced. Finally, he nodded. "Okay, but I have a request."

"Sure." After everything he'd done for her, what *wouldn't* she give him?

"Would you consider giving me a key to your apartment, Cassia?"

A warm pressure bloomed inside her. "Consider it done."

"You sure? I know it might seem a little fast, but if you need something, I want to be able to get to you."

"Completely sure," she said. *It might seem a little fast...* If he thought it was fast to be swapping keys, it was definitely too fast for her to be telling him she loved him... "I have extras in the kitchen drawer."

"Okay, good. And this weekend, if you're feeling up to it, I want you to come to my place." He shrugged with one big shoulder. "I can't wait too much longer to get you in my bed, baby."

Happiness tingled over her skin. "I *really* hate that I'm sick right now."

He chuckled. "What can I do for you before I have to head to the club today?"

Aw, how freaking sweet was he? "Just being here is everything."

Quinton tilted his head, those brown eyes absolutely blazing. "Everything, huh?"

She nodded, and they spent the next three hours lazing in bed. Talking, touching, laughing. They ate soup and crackers together at her little kitchen table, and Quinton once again promised to cook for her when she was better.

Cassia hated to see him go. But she was also exhausted. In between dozing off, she answered the messages he sent checking in on her. And, just as she'd expected, when evening rolled around, she was in absolutely no shape to try to go out. So she sent him maybe her twentieth text of the day and said good night.

Lying in bed, Cass stared at the little lamp on her nightstand, its golden glow casting a low light over the corner of the room. Ridiculously, she felt almost like David facing off with Goliath as she debated, then finally resolved to *try*. She turned it off.

Darkness fell over the room.

Her heartrate picked up. Anxiety prickled across her skin.

Cass forced her eyes closed.

What do you see, little one?

Quinton, laughing like an idiot at Ferris Bueller. Quinton, his expression shattered as he came. Quinton, peering up her body, his mouth hovering over her core, his lips wet with her arousal. Quinton, taking care in a million different ways.

For the first time in two years, she fell asleep alone. In the dark. And was okay.

Chapter Thirteeen

CASSIA ARRIVED TO BLASPHEMY ON Saturday night absolutely giddy. Giddy to see Master Quinton, giddy to tell him about her silly-but-significant triumph, giddy to just *be his*, and have everyone know it.

The place was packed as it always was on the weekend, and the club was a feast for the senses. A driving, chanting music hummed over the crowd, cries of pleasure rang out, and people in every state of dress—and undress—danced and kissed and more. The soaring columns and towering ceiling made the space feel ethereal despite the press of bodies.

Cass made her way through the madness to the bar, and sure enough, Master Quinton had reserved a seat for her. A placard with her name sat in front of a stool. It wasn't a black velvet rope, but it made her feel a little gooey inside all the same.

She slipped onto the stool, her gaze immediately finding Master Quinton at the far side. He wore black jeans that hugged his fine ass and a black tank that showed off those delicious shoulders, and she reveled in every moment that she got to study him.

Damn, that man was *hers*.

As if he'd heard her, he turned, and the smile that lit up his face when his gaze landed on her made her feel like she might float up to the top of the vaulted ceiling. He finished with one more customer, wiped his hands on a rag, and stalked her way.

She couldn't stop grinning. "Hello, Master."

"Damn good to see you, little one." He winked. "Get up here and give me a proper greeting."

She looked at him and eyed the flat marble in front of her. "You want me to…"

He smirked. "Uh huh."

A thrill fluttered through her belly, but she didn't hesitate. Carefully, she shifted so that she was kneeling on the stool, and then, one knee at a time, she crawled up on the bar. Just like he'd commanded, she hadn't worn panties under her little red dress, so no doubt she was giving people a show. But she didn't care, not when he was smiling like that. Finally, she knelt on the bar top. Knees spread and waiting. Before Master Quinton.

A low hum rose up as people took notice of them, but Cassia didn't pay it any mind, because her Master suddenly looked like he might bend her over the bar and fuck her right there in front of everyone. And she would've loved every second of it.

He came right up to her and grasped her face in both of his big hands, and then he kissed her like she was the water he drank and the food he ate until she couldn't think, couldn't move, couldn't breathe—and was half convinced she didn't need air as long as she had him.

Applause. People were applauding.

She couldn't help the grin or the heat that flooded her cheeks when he finally pulled away.

"Now *that* was a proper greeting," he said, his smile pure smug sexiness.

"I'll remember that, Master." And she would. If he thought she wasn't doing this every time she came from here on out, he had another think coming.

"How you feeling, baby?" He braced his hands on either side of her knees against the bar top.

"A lot better. Still a little tired, but good." She smiled. "And guess what?"

"What?"

"I slept in the dark last night. And I was totally fine." The grin was so big it almost hurt her cheeks.

He cupped her face in his hand. "You are so much more than fine I can barely stand it. Proud of you."

She nearly beamed. "I still missed you, though."

"Mmm." He let his gaze drag down over her cleavage, her spread thighs, and then he lifted it again. "Missed you, too. In fact, I want you to stay right there for a bit so I can look my fill."

"Yes, Sir," she said.

He backed away, eyes on her, until he finally had to turn his attention to a customer. She loved watching him work, and it also helped to center her against all the attention still pouring her way. Maybe it wasn't usual to see a sub sitting on the bar? What did she know? But she kinda loved it, too.

Because Master Quinton kept paying her attention however he could. Throwing her a playful wink. Giving her a kiss as he passed her by. Placing his hand on her thigh when he served someone right near her.

It was fun and sweet and making her freaking crazy.

She wasn't sure how long she'd been kneeling there when he finally let her down onto a stool again, and she was excited to see Master Griffin and Kenna just by the bar in the crowd. How funny that Cass had worried about leaving the other submissive with the wrong impression the last time they'd chatted—only for that impression to now be true. Cassia waited for Master Quinton to be able to talk and then asked, "Master, may I have your permission to speak to Kenna?"

"If Master Griffin agrees," he said. "Unless I request otherwise, consider yourself free to speak and socialize while I'm working."

"Thank you, Sir," she said, slipping from the stool. She approached her new friends and waited for the other Dom's attention.

His dark eyes finally swung her way, and he gave her a smile. "Ah, Cassia. Hello."

"Good evening, Master Griffin."

"Are you feeling better?"

The question caught her off guard for a moment, because how did he...realization flooded through her. Master Quinton must've told him, which meant that he'd talked about her. "Much better, Sir, thank you."

"I'm glad to hear it." He glanced to the bar with a humored, approving expression. "You've been keeping your Master company, I saw."

"Yes, Sir," she said, unable to hold back a smile even as heat warmed her cheeks.

He turned to Kenna. "Would you two like to visit for a while? I need to get things ready."

"I'd love that, Sir," Kenna said, her smile immediate. Cass was so glad to see that. Two years of having largely dropped out of life meant that she didn't have that many close friends. And Kenna seemed like someone she could really like. Her Dom gave her a lingering kiss, and then disappeared into the crowd. "That man," she said, her gaze full of heat and love.

Cassia chuckled. "Yeah."

"He's totally wound up over a new suspension we're using tonight," she said, her hand rubbing over her prosthetic. "It's a little more demanding, but I can totally handle it."

"Master Griffin specializes in rope bondage, is that right?" Cass asked.

"He's a freaking genius at it," Kenna said, her expression going soft with affection and pride. "He's never once hurt my arm, but whenever we try something new or we do a demonstration, he always worries."

"He sounds like a good Dom, then," Cass said.

Kenna nodded. "Are you staying for our demo? We go on at ten."

"Wow, I'd love to see that. I'll ask Master Quinton, but I bet he won't mind."

They talked for a long while, the bar area getting more and more crowded around them. Kenna pointed out some of the others she'd gotten to know at the club and told hilarious stories about her nephew. They traded stories from their travels, and shared tips on where to find fun club clothes.

Every so often while they spoke, Cassia would peer back toward the bar and catch a glimpse of Master Quinton, wanting to remain aware of him in case he wanted her back on her stool again. But he was absolutely slammed every time she looked.

Finally, Master Griffin retrieved Kenna, who gave Cass a hug before she left. It made Cassia smile because she really felt like she'd found a friend, and who didn't need that? Especially because it was always good to have someone who understood this lifestyle with whom you could talk.

Threading her way back to the bar, Cass searched for Master Quinton, but he wasn't behind the bar. Instead, Master Wolf was there, scrambling to keep up with the orders that were coming in.

She slipped onto her stool, surprised it was still free, and wondered where her Master had gone.

After about ten minutes, Master Wolf caught sight of her sitting there and made his way down. "Master Quinton said he'll be back in a little while."

"Oh, is everything okay?" Cassia asked, unsure if it was appropriate for her to question.

"I think so. He has a demonstration tonight. They usually take thirty to sixty minutes, depending," he said, matter-of-factly.

Demonstration? The word hit her like a punch to the gut. "Isn't it Master Griffin who has the demonstration tonight?"

The Dom shrugged. "They're both on the schedule." Someone down the bar called his name. "Sorry, duty calls," he said to her with a wink. "Let me know if you need anything."

Need anything? Like maybe a heart transplant?

The room suddenly sucked in on her in a confusing, deafening swirl. Master Quinton...was still doing the demonstration? After... after...*everything?*

Cassia couldn't even make it make any sense.

And as she tried, her body started freaking out. Racing heart. Shallowing breaths. Spinning room. She'd lived with panic attacks for two years, so she didn't have to wonder what was happening.

Head down, she forced herself to breathe through it. *Deep inhale.* There had to be a mistake. *Long exhale.* There had to be some misunderstanding. *Deep inhale.* But wouldn't Master Wolf know? *Long exhale.*

Quinton couldn't be doing this. She shuddered, unable to get another deep inhale. He just couldn't. Not after everything they'd said and done and shared.

She wasn't sure how long she sat there, but she was trying to hold out, to hold on, to wait for him to return and *prove* that he wasn't off somewhere playing with someone else.

Nausea rolled through her at the thought. Pain squeezed her chest, from the growing anxiety, from her heart threatening to break. Part of her just couldn't believe it, but Master Wolf had just been so matter-of-factly confident about it.

"Hey, Cass, are you okay?"

The question, coming from right in front of her, nearly made her jump. Her gaze cut up and landed on Master Wolf's concerned face.

No, she wasn't okay. She really, really wasn't.

If she stayed here, she was going to cry. And if she cried, she wouldn't be able to convince anyone that she was okay. She didn't want to fall apart in front of all these people, and she certainly didn't want to do or say anything that would embarrass herself, or Master Quinton.

But if he really was doing a demonstration, she couldn't be here when it was done, when people might be talking about it or wondering, after their earlier very public display of affection, why she hadn't been the one to do it with him.

"Um, yeah. Yes, Sir. I'm…I was sick…I guess," she said, swallowing hard. She pressed a hand to her forehead. The next sentence that came out of her mouth wasn't a lie. "Just starting to feel unwell again."

He frowned, his brow coming down over a bright green gaze that locked onto the cuff on her wrist. "Maybe I should find Master Quinton," he said, slowly, like he was trying to put together a puzzle.

A fast shake of her head, and her words spilled out in a rush. "Please don't bother him with this. You guys are so busy in here tonight. I'll send him a text, but can you just let him know, uh, that I had to go?"

He stared at her, and she could almost see the debate playing out across his face.

"Please, Sir?"

He gave a single nod. "Are you going to be okay getting home? Do you need a ride?"

"Oh, no," she said, slipping off the chair. "But thank you." With a weak attempt at a smile, Cassia finally escaped.

She barely saw the crowd or remembered leaving the building or knew how she got home.

All she knew was the fear that maybe she and Quinton weren't everything she'd thought they were, and the pain of a heart that had already given itself away.

Sitting on her living room couch, she studied her phone, and then she finally typed out a message.

Hello, Sir. Waited for you, but started feeling unwell. Hope you have a good night.

There. Done.

Were they done?

Cassia forced a deep breath and blinked back the tears that wanted to fall. But she wasn't letting them. Not yet.

Maybe, just maybe, there was an explanation here. Because never in a million years would she have believed that the man who licked her hand and declared that he wanted to be exclusive would go back on his word.

Quinton rolled his shoulders and tried to shake off the frustration of the confrontation he'd just broken up. He'd cut an occasionally problematic Dom off from more liquor, but still had a bad feeling in his gut about the guy's demeanor. So about fifteen minutes after the Dom had called Quinton an asshole and wandered away from the bar, he'd gone in search of him.

He would've gone sooner if business hadn't been so booming. He *should've* gone sooner.

Because he found the guy harassing a male submissive he'd played with a few times, and not taking the younger man's *no* for an answer.

Quinton had tried to talk the Dom down, but the guy started getting belligerent—and then he got right up into Quinton's grill.

Thing was, Quinton had been trying to help the sonofabitch save face in front of the sub until that moment, but that had been his line in the sand. He'd dismissed the submissive, and the Dom had lost his shit and taken a swing that had split Quinton's cheek bone. The fucker.

Not even sure where they'd come from, Masters Kyler, Jonathan, and Cruz were suddenly there, helping Quinton bodily remove the guy from the club. He was done around here.

It felt like for-fucking-ever since he'd seen Cassia kneeling so pretty for him on the bar. And he hated how long he'd left her alone.

Swinging around the counter, his gaze searched. A bald-headed man sat in the stool Quinton had reserved for her. Frowning, he went up to where Wolf was making a trio of cocktails. "Hey, man. Sorry. You seen Cassia?"

Something flashed in his friend's eyes. He placed the drinks in front of the customers and pulled Quinton aside. "Yeah…wait. What happened to your face?"

Quinton waved him off. "Cassia?"

Wolf's expression was grim. "Yeah, I saw her, and I think I fucked something up."

"What the hell are you talking about?" Quinton asked, concern roiling through his gut. On top of the fight still snaking through his blood, he was right on the edge.

"Did you have a demonstration tonight?"

For a second, Quinton didn't know what the hell Wolf was talking about, and then it was like he'd been clobbered upside the head. He hadn't removed it from the schedule. Quinton had gotten Griffin to replace him, but he'd never gone into the schedule and removed his name from the calendar. "Please don't fucking tell me you told my submissive I was off playing with someone else."

"Jesus, Q. I didn't know. I didn't know she was yours or that the schedule was wrong."

"Aw, Christ," Quinton said, a sickening tightness squeezing his gut as he looked out over the crowd. "Where is she?"

"She left. Twenty minutes ago. Said she wasn't feeling well." Wolf's expression was like someone had just ran over his puppy. It wasn't the guy's fault. No, it was all Quinton's. His own carelessness had caused this mess—and the likelihood that Cassia was sitting at home right now believing he was balls deep in another woman.

God, would she really believe that of him? After everything?

She'd left, hadn't she?

"How can I make this better?" Wolf asked.

"Not your fault, and not your responsibility," Quinton said. "This is all on me. But can you handle the rest of the night?"

"Yes. Not even a question. Go make this right."

He was already moving. Looking at his phone, he saw her text message, and the formality of it was like a knife to the gut, cold and impersonal and capable of lots of messy damage.

As soon as he got where it was quieter, he called. Voicemail. "Damnit," he bit out.

Quinton was desperate to get to her, to fix this, to make sure she was okay. To make sure *they* were okay. And to make sure she knew everything she needed to know so that something like this could never happen again.

Chapter Fourteen

CASSIA WASN'T SURPRISED WHEN THE knock finally came, but the fact that he knocked set off a little pang in her chest. He had a key, after all. Her Master would've used his key.

Right?

GodGodGod. This mess of feelings, this angst, this uncertainty, *this pain*—all of it was why she hadn't thought she was ready for a relationship. Because she barely felt like she could stand and cross the room from the weight of it.

But she did, and then Quinton was standing in front of her.

Sexy and handsome and—

"Oh, my God, what happened to your face?" she asked. A nasty cut split open his left cheekbone, and it was already swelling and bruising around the corner of his eye.

He stepped into the apartment and closed the door. "You think I care about that when you believe I broke my word and did that demonstration?"

The question stole her breath and made her head spin. Did that mean he didn't? "I…I…didn't know what to believe. Actually, I thought I did know, and I tried to hang on to that, but Master Wolf was so certain."

"Christ, Cass," he said, coming right up to her. "With everything going on this week, I forgot to take it off the schedule. So that's my fucking fault. And I'm sorry for not being more careful."

"You didn't…" Her voice was no more than a whisper as relief rushed over her like a tsunami.

"No. I didn't. But you left," he said, his voice stern.

She nodded and swallowed thickly. "I just...I panicked. If it was true, I couldn't be there. I couldn't hear people talking about it. And in public wouldn't have been the place to speak about it with you anyway," she said, hugging herself and ducking her chin. "I had to get out of there. I'm sorry."

"I said we're exclusive, Cassia." He cupped her face in both of his hands and forced her to look at him.

"I know, Sir." The first of her tears finally fell. From the adrenaline let-down. From the relief. From the guilt she felt at ever doubting him in the first place.

He caught the tears with his thumbs and his lips. "But what I didn't say was this. I didn't play with someone else—and I *couldn't* play with someone else—because I'm fucking head over heels in love with you."

After the whirlwind of emotion tonight, her brain froze, like she couldn't quite process the words. And then they were sinking in, sinking *deep*, hitting her in every scared, cold, lonely place she'd ever had. And completing her.

"Oh, my God. You do?"

His eyes were dark fire. "I do. So now you know. Now you never have to doubt. I am yours and you are mine, and we are each other's. And there's no one else in this. Ever."

It was exactly what she'd needed to know. "Oh, God, I *am* yours, Quinton. And I love you, too."

"Fuck, that's what I wanted to hear." On a moan, he kissed her. He kissed her as if he could mark her with his hands and his tongue and his lips. And he could. He already had. She would never be the same.

Whispering words of love and devotion over and over, he walked her back the hallway to her bedroom. He shed their clothes piece by piece, until they were both naked and completely bare to one another.

He flattened her palm against his chest and held it there. "Yours, baby. Do you understand?"

"I do," she whispered, so overwhelmed with love for this man.

Quinton placed his big hand against her chest. "Mine."

"Yes," she said. "All yours."

He laid her out on the bed, and then he crawled up over her and reached for the drawer of the bedside table.

Cass grasped his arm. "I don't want anything between us. Not anymore."

"Are you sure, Cassia? I get tested regularly, and I'm clean, but we could get a new round of tests together first so you can be sure."

Smiling, she took his face in his hands, because after everything, she needed him to know. "I trust you, Quinton. And I'm sure."

His cock penetrated deep, skin on skin for the first time, and he gave her those life-giving, soul-healing words all over again.

"Love you, Cassia. Love you so fucking much."

Her hips surged under him as his body and his declarations wrung pleasure out of her. "Oh, Quinton. Oh, Master. I love you, too."

Finally, his release shook through him, and he moaned as he moved through it, giving her everything he had. She held her man in his arms, almost stunned at how joyous she felt.

They fell asleep with him still on top of her, still inside her.

And then he woke her up again, already moving inside her. Again and again, all night long, they came together. He claimed her, and she claimed him.

In the morning, they showered and dressed, and then Quinton turned to her with a nervousness she didn't understand.

"Come with me to my house."

She'd been dying to do that, so her answer came easily. "Okay. I'd love to see your place."

Fifteen minutes later, they pulled into the garage of a newer apartment building downtown. The elevator took them to the tenth floor and spilled out into a small lobby with only four apartment doors. He opened one of them, and she stepped into a sleek, modern apartment filled with leather and dark-finished woods and warm accents that managed to be stylish and inviting at the same time. It had a stunning view of the harbor and a killer kitchen.

"Quinton, this is amazing," she said, admiring the view.

He watched her walk around his space. "I've never liked this apartment more than I do right at this moment," he said, giving her a little smile that seemed loaded with significance.

"Oh, yeah? Why's that?"

"Because you being here makes it feel like a home."

She froze, because that was seriously the sweetest thing anyone had ever said to her. "Keep saying things like that, Quinton Ross, and you'll never get rid of me."

"Actually, that's what I'm hoping," he said, coming right up to her and making her heart trip into a sprint.

"What do you mean?" she whispered, butterflies taking up flight in her belly until she thought she might lift right off the ground.

He stared at her a long moment, as if he were debating, and then he swallowed. Hard. "Undress and kneel for me, Cassia. Right here and right now."

Quinton carried the boxes out of his bedroom and found Cassia kneeling in the middle of his living room, naked and gorgeous and absolutely everything he'd ever wanted.

He stood before her. "Look at me, please."

She lifted her gaze, her eyes full of awareness that something significant was happening between them. And she was right. Because Quinton had never done this before. He opened the large velvet box.

He crouched before her, wanting to look her eye to eye, wanting her to know exactly what she meant to him. "Cassia, I want you as a woman, and I want you as my submissive. I want to claim all of you, and I want to give you all of me." Glassiness suddenly shimmered in her pretty hazel eyes. "I want to care for you and cherish you and pleasure you. I want to spend my days and my nights with you. I want everything with you."

He lifted the choker so she could see it. It had a wide, flat platinum band, and where it met at the hollow of her throat sat a large diamond heart. The store had modified the clasp so that it was shaped like a lock.

"Cassia, would you do me the honor of wearing my collar?" he asked, emotion planting a knot in his throat.

"Yes, Master. Nothing would make me happier than being yours." She blinked as a tear fell, and laughed as her happiness bubbled over.

Coming behind her, he draped the choker around her neck, and then he secured the lock clasp. The little *click* sounded like forever in the making, and when he stood in front of her again, he was overwhelmed at the sight of the collar—*his* collar—around Cassia's beautiful throat.

And that was only the first of his plans. The first of the ways he wanted to claim her.

"I have something else I want to give you," he said, the mix of arousal and unusual nerves wreaking havoc with his gut. Because Quinton knew he was going fast. But apparently, that's what happened to a man when he claimed his woman and wanted to nail down all kinds of forevers.

"You do?" she asked, awe in her voice as her fingertips traced the diamond at her throat.

He held out his hand and helped her rise, and then he drew the flat, rectangular box from his pocket.

Fuck, he hated being nervous. It made him chuckle, even though he was dead fucking serious about the words on the tip of his tongue. He opened it, revealing another heart-shaped diamond, this one dangling from a key chain. He held it out to her.

Cass grasped the loop, and her gaze lifted from the two keys hanging there to him. "Master?"

"I know this is fucking fast. And maybe a little crazy. But I want you here. With me. Would you consider making my apartment our home? Would you consider moving in with me?" he asked.

Her mouth dropped into an oval, and her gaze latched onto the keys.

As the seconds stretched out, Quinton thought he might crawl out of his skin. Too fast. It was too damned fast. "Aw, hell, I haven't even shown you the rest of the—"

"Yes."

He almost swallowed his tongue. "Yes? Did you say yes?"

She laughed, and the sound lit him up inside. "Yes, it's fast and it's crazy and I'll move in with you."

"Holy shit, Cass," he said, hugging her and spinning her around. "Holy shit." Words spilled out of him in a fast jumble. "You can change whatever you want. Do whatever you want. Make it yours."

She kissed him and laughed and held him tight. Had his place ever heard so much laughter? Quinton determined right then and there that it always would. Every day.

"We'll figure it out," she said. "But maybe, you know, since I live here now and all, you could show me the rest."

"Yeah? Of course," he said, his head spinning from getting everything he wanted. And so much more. For a moment, he just stared at her standing there, naked, wearing his collar, holding *their* key, and agreeing to walk this life together with him. It made his heart race and his cock turn to steel. "Baby, I was thinking. Maybe this tour should start with the *bedroom*."

She arched a brow and tried to bite back a threatening smile. "Wherever you lead, I'll follow, Master. Always."

Which was the moment he threw his submissive over his shoulder, walked her back to their bedroom, and kept her there all night long.

About The Blasphemy Series

12 Masters. Infinite fantasies...
Welcome to Blasphemy

Books in Series

Hard to Serve
Bound to Submit
Mastering Her Senses
Eyes on You – Coming July 11, 2017

EYES ON YOU

SHE WANTS TO EXPLORE HER *true desires, and he wants to watch...*

When a sexy stranger asks Wolf Henrikson to rescue her from a bad date, he never expected to want the woman for himself. But their playful conversation turns into a scorching one-night stand that reveals the shy beauty gets off on the idea of being seen, even if she's a little scared of it, too. And Wolf loves to watch.

In the wake of discovering her fiancé's infidelity, florist Olivia Foster never expected to find someone who not only understood her wildest, darkest fantasies, but would bring them to life. As Wolf introduces her to his world at the play club, Blasphemy, Liv finds herself tempted to explore submission and exhibitionism with the hard-bodied Dom even as she's scared to trust again.

But Wolf is a master of getting what he wants—and he's got his eyes set on her...

Acknowledgments

BOOKS ARE NEVER WRITTEN ALONE, and that was definitely the case with *Mastering Her Senses*. I have to offer the biggest thanks to three people in particular. First, to my friend Lea Nolan, who cheered me on and allowed me to plot parts of the book out with her over our table at Panera. Second, to my friend Christi Barth, who critiqued the book for me and caught all kinds of things that made it shine. And third, to my publicist extraordinaire, KP Simmon, who was always there with a word of support and encouragement. Thanks to all three of you ladies, you were a big part of me getting this one done!

I also have to thank my Heroes and my Reader Girls, whose enthusiasm for Blasphemy is such a delight and motivation. You guys rock my socks!

And without question, I have to thank my husband and daughters, who allowed Mom lots of weekends and nights away to get this done. I couldn't do it without their love and support.

And, finally, thanks to you, the readers, who take my characters into your hearts and let them tell their stories over and over again.

~LK

Need More Masters?

Meet Master Griffin in BOUND TO SUBMIT!
Now Available

Chapter One

AS KENNA SLOANE STOOD ON the stage in front of the applauding audience, one word kept echoing through her brain.

Fraud.

Fraudfraudfraud.

Keeping the smile plastered on her face, she looked out over the ballroom full of women from a local business and professional organization.

Since being medically discharged from the United States Marine Corps two years before, Kenna had become something of a motivational speaker. She didn't feel particularly motivational or inspirational, for that matter, and she certainly hadn't set out to be any such thing.

It had started when her physical therapist at Walter Reed asked her to speak a few times to the new amputees. And then her nephew's teacher invited her to speak to his school assembly around Veteran's Day. One of the kid's fathers turned out to be a reporter for the local paper who pushed her to do a story until she finally agreed. Though the *Baltimore Sun* wasn't just any local paper. It was big. And so was the story. After it ran, the invitations came in from all over. And though some part of her always resisted agreeing, another part wondered how she could consider turning them down.

Because she was alive when others weren't. She could share their stories when they couldn't tell them themselves. She could perhaps offer other veterans and their families the hope that was so hard to grasp onto in those early months after a serious injury.

It was her duty. One way she could continue to serve. The *only* way she could continue to serve.

The long minutes after her speech passed in a blur of congratulations on her talk and introductions to dignitaries in the audience.

"Thank you for your service, Miss Sloane."

"Fantastic speech, Kenna. Truly inspirational."

"You're a real survivor, Miss Sloane. Thank you for sharing your story."

Kenna was grateful for everyone's appreciation—being thanked for her service and sacrifice meant a lot. But it was also hard to hear sometimes.

Hard to hear because so often—too often—she felt like such a damn fraud.

Everyone thought she'd adjusted so well—to the loss of her career, to the loss of her best friend in the Corps, to the loss of her right forearm and hand—but on the inside, she felt like a disaster. Grief, regret, guilt. And so much pain that sometimes she had to give into the promising lure of the narcotics her doctor prescribed.

She *should* be stronger. She should be able to fight all this. She was a damn Marine—and always would be, whether she still wore the uniform or not. At least, that's what she tried to remind herself.

"How did it go?" Sierra asked through the car speaker phone not five minutes after Kenna pulled out of the hotel's downtown Baltimore lot. Her sister was one of the few people who understood even a little of the inner turmoil Kenna tried to keep hidden from the world.

"Fine. Good. It was a nice crowd," Kenna said, her hands at ten and two on the steering wheel. One hand real, the other hand part of her myoelectric prosthesis. The hand was matte black and connected to a black and silver forearm shaft that cradled and covered the small stump of forearm that remained. Her gaze dropped for just a moment to the way the almost skeletal-looking fingers wrapped around the wheel.

Be thankful for what you have.

Because the prosthetic's cost of over fifty thousand dollars had been mostly, and generously, covered by a foundation.

"You there, Kenna?" Sierra asked.

"Yeah, sorry. How's Jake?"

"He's good," her sister said, a smile clear in her tone. "He lost a tooth at school today and I'm waiting to make sure he's asleep so I can play tooth fairy."

As Kenna maneuvered through Baltimore traffic, she couldn't help the small smile that crept up her face. "How much does a tooth earn these days?"

Sierra chuckled. "I'm giving him two bucks. The little bugger's losing teeth so frequently lately that I'm half convinced he's yanking them out for the cash. How was physical therapy? Didn't you have an appointment this morning?"

And there went that smile. Kenna didn't question the effectiveness of physical therapy—the muscles in her residual limb were stronger, which enhanced her ability to control the movement of the prosthetic—it operated in part based on the electrical signals her remaining muscles generated. She also had more mobility in her right shoulder, and her neck and upper back pain had improved a lot.

But physical therapy also left her arm fatigued and her body emotionally drained. And an intense session always seemed to exacerbate her phantom pain for a night or three after.

"It was fine. Good." Kenna merged into the right lane and turned.

"That's the same thing you said about your speech," Sierra said, her tone easy-going but obviously concerned.

Despite the light touch her sister tried to use, the comment still tripped Kenna's shorter-than-usual temper. "What the hell do you want me to say, Si? That I'm exhausted? That I'm randomly driving around right now to avoid going home because I know the second I lay down the phantom pain will start, and I'll have to grit my teeth through it all night in order to resist downing more pain killers? Which don't always work anyway. That I'm terrified that the pain will never go away and I won't be able to carry it, *and* I'm terrified that it will go away and how can I deserve that when George is dead? That every time I give a speech it makes the fear worse because now all these fucking people think I'm some kind of hero which means when I finally crash and burn they'll all know I never deserved their praise and applause in the first place? Is that what you want to hear?" By the time Kenna finished the tirade she was breathing hard and shaking, her eyes dry as always. Why couldn't she have a good cry and feel better like a normal person?

The phone was quiet long enough that Kenna wondered if she'd dropped the call. And then her sister spoke. "That's exactly what I want you to say. That and whatever else you're *really* feeling. Pull over."

"What?"

"Pull over. I want you to be safe and you're driving upset right now."

On a huff, Kenna made her way to the side of the street and parked illegally in front of a fire hydrant. "Okay," she whispered, smoothing her hands over her black dress pants.

"I'm not a stranger, Kenna. You don't have to put on an act for me. I'd know you weren't in a good place even if you did so don't waste your energy on it. I'd love for you to talk to me, but you don't even have to do that. You can just be silently miserable with me if you want. Or you can rant at me. Whatever you need, I'll do for you. And if you don't know what that is, I'll just be with you until you figure it out." Another long pause. "Okay?"

"Okay," Kenna said.

"Do you want to talk about any of what you just said?" Sierra asked.

Kenna gave a humorless chuckle. "Nooo."

"Fine. But I will say this, I didn't know Georgia as good you did, obviously, but I knew her well enough to know she would kick your ass for torturing yourself about her death. And you *know* that's true. Even if you can't feel it yet, you have to know it. She would not have wanted you beating yourself up on her behalf. She would've hated that for you."

A squeezing pang tugged in the center of her chest. Georgia Kern had been Kenna's friend from the first day of basic training, and they'd quickly become close. "I know that's true, but I…" She shook her head, the sadness of the loss washing through her for the millionth time.

"I know," her sister said.

Kenna and Georgia, or Ken and George as everyone had quickly taken to calling them, had both volunteered for the Female Engagement Teams, or FETs, small, specially trained groups who served alongside male infantry units in the Middle East. In their FET, they'd worked as cultural advisors and liaisons, communicating especially with the women and families their units encountered. She and Georgia had loved their jobs, loved being central to the mission of the infantry units, loved getting to serve in such a fundamental and intense way.

And then George hadn't made it when another of the guys in their unit, Evan Burrell, had triggered a forty-pound IED during a patrol. Kenna had been walking on the other side of George, the force of the blast enough to throw Kenna up in the air, spinning her body like a helicopter blade. She'd been close enough that the explosion had ripped skin and muscle off her arm, and the way she'd landed had done the rest of the job of destroying the arm she eventually lost, despite multiple surgeons' efforts to save it.

One of the doctors had said that Georgia being there had probably saved Kenna's life and, after he'd left the room, she'd vomited despite having nothing in her belly. Somedays, knowing she was alive because someone else had died was more guilt than she could bear. Especially when that someone had been her best friend.

"I'll call you tomorrow, Si, okay?" Kenna said.

"No you won't," Sierra said with absolutely no judgment. "But I'll talk to you soon."

After driving around for another hour, Kenna finally returned to the small studio apartment she'd managed to find when she'd been discharged. She'd been living off of her savings, her disability, and the honoraria she received from her speaking engagements, so the five-hundred-square-foot place was the most she could afford. Sierra had wanted her to bunk in her guest room, but no way had Kenna wanted to force her less-than-cheerful self on her sister's little family.

She was so used to removing her prosthesis that the process barely took thought anymore. She released the suction, removed the limb and plugged it in to charge, and rolled off the protective sleeve and cleaned it for the next day's use. And then she climbed into bed.

Hours later, she remained wide awake, her eyes glued to the dark ceiling overhead, ghosts of every kind making it impossible to fall asleep.

Tonight, the phantom pain was the worst of those ghosts. The pain made her arm and wrist ache despite the fact that she didn't still have those parts. It was an ache that felt like, if she could *just* massage the muscles and joints, it would feel better. It was a pain that sometimes felt like an itch she could never scratch, or pins and needles that would never go away.

But there were other ghosts, too. *"Quit yer bitchin'."* Georgia's voice. One of her favorite sayings when anyone uttered a gripe about anything. Kenna supposed that imagining her bestie wanting to kick her ass over the poor-me routine was better than remembering the sound of her screams when that IED had detonated.

On a sigh, Kenna sat up and turned on the light. Her gaze went right to her prosthesis, laying on her night stand and plugged into the charging unit. She had to find a way to become more than what'd happened to her, more than what she'd lost. If she could just get out of her head, maybe she could get free of the pain, of the grief, of the guilt.

Get out of your head, Kenna. Stop thinking. Just feel what I'm doing to you.

Kenna gasped.

Where had *that voice* and *those words* come from? Heat ran over her skin, a phantom sensation of another kind. A sensation from a distant, lust-drenched moment, and caused by a man to whom she hadn't spoken in years.

Griffin Hudson.

Her lover. Her Dominant. But never her Master. He hadn't wanted to claim her for keeps.

She'd fallen in love with Griffin, and when she'd finally told him, they'd ended up in what turned out to be the most awkward conversation *ever*, which had essentially boiled down to him not being interested in a committed relationship. He hadn't been unkind about it, just honest, but it had still left Kenna reevaluating everything. Because things with Griffin hadn't worked out, and working as a paralegal had left her absolutely certain she didn't want to go to law school, as her parents had badly wanted her to do.

She'd needed something more meaningful, something deeper, something *real*. She'd needed a change.

A change that had led her to a calling she hadn't realized she'd had until she'd made the commitment and become a Marine. Kenna hadn't told Griffin. She hadn't seen the point. She'd just enlisted. And she'd never regretted it for a moment—and still didn't. Being a Marine could be grueling and exhausting, but the comradery, mission, and service had resonated deep inside her in a way she never would've predicted. For a long time, she'd still grieved the loss of Griffin, but the Marines had been like someone turning the light-bulb on over her whole life.

So why was she thinking of Griffin now?

"I'm sorry. How long was I out of it?" she asked.

Arms around her shoulders, Griffin cradled her tighter against his muscled chest and smiled down at her. "About a half hour. Close your eyes and rest. I'm in no rush."

Kenna pressed her fingers to her mouth as her thoughts churned and realization finally set in. That memory of Griffin taking care of her had come after a particularly intense scene that had left Kenna flying so high she'd all but lost consciousness. Subspace, they called it, and with Griffin, she'd achieved it quite a lot. Nothing got her out of her head or sent endorphins racing like it.

"Oh, God," she whispered out loud. An idea took route that threatened to shake up her whole world—for better or worse, she didn't know. "Would it work now?"

That was only the first of the questions that came to mind. Would it work? Could she still engage in the bondage she'd once loved with an amputated arm? Was Blasphemy even still open? She'd met Griffin when the exclusive BDSM club had first opened six years ago. They'd frequently done scenes together for just over a year before she'd gone and gotten feelings for him that he didn't return. And if Blasphemy was still open, was Griffin himself still there? Was he still unattached? Could she even begin to think about playing with him again, after everything that'd happened in the five years since she'd left Baltimore? Would she be up to finding a new Dom instead?

"Oh, God," she said again, shaking her head at this madness. "What the hell am I even thinking?" But as she settled back in bed, she had to admit that during the minutes she'd spent thinking about Griffin, she'd *almost* forgotten about everything else.

About Laura Kaye

LAURA IS THE NEW YORK Times and USA Today bestselling author of thirty books in contemporary and erotic romance and romantic suspense, including the Blasphemy, Hard Ink, and Raven Riders series. Growing up, Laura's large extended family believed in the supernatural, and family lore involving angels, ghosts, and evil-eye curses cemented in Laura a life-long fascination with storytelling and all things paranormal. Laura also writes historical fiction as the NYT bestselling author, Laura Kamoie. She lives in Maryland with her husband and two daughters, and appreciates her view of the Chesapeake Bay every day.

Learn more at **www.LauraKayeAuthor.com**

The Hard Ink Series
Five dishonored soldiers
Former Special Forces
One last mission
These are the men of Hard Ink...

Hard As It Gets (Hard Ink #1)

Trouble just walked into Nicholas Rixey's tattoo parlor. Becca Merritt is warm, sexy, whole-some—pure temptation to a very jaded Nick. He's left his military life behind to become co-owner of Hard Ink Tattoo, but Becca is his ex-commander's daughter. Loyalty won't let him turn her away. Lust has plenty to do with it too. With her brother presumed kidnapped, Becca needs Nick. She just wasn't expecting to want him so much. As their investigation turns into all-out war with an organized crime ring, only Nick can protect her. And only Becca can heal the scars no one else sees.

Hard As You Can (Hard Ink #2)

Shane McCallan doesn't turn his back on a friend in need, especially a former Special Forces teammate running a dangerous, off-the-books operation. Nor can he walk away from Crystal, the gorgeous blonde waitress is hiding secrets she doesn't want him to uncover. Too bad. He's exactly the man she needs to protect her sister, her life, and her heart. All he has to do is convince her that when something feels this good, you hold on as hard as you can—and never let go.

Hard to Hold On To (Hard Ink #2.5)

Edward "Easy" Cantrell knows better than most the pain of not being able to save those he loves—which is why he is not going to let Jenna Dean, the woman he helped rescue from a gang, out of his sight. He may have just met her, but Jenna's the first person to make him feel alive since that devastating day in the desert more than a year ago. As the pair are thrust together while chaos reigns around them, they both know one thing: the things in life most worth having are the hardest to hold on to.

Hard to Come By (Hard Ink #3)

When a sexy stranger asks questions about her brother, Emilie Garza is torn between loyalty to the brother she once idolized and fear of the war-changed man he's become. Derek DiMarzio's easy smile and quiet strength tempt Emilie to open up, igniting the desire between them and leading Derek to crave a woman he shouldn't trust. Now, Derek and Emilie must prove where their loyal-ties lie before hearts are broken and lives are lost. Because love is too hard to come by to let slip away…

Hard to Be Good (Hard Ink #3.5)

Hard Ink Tattoo owner Jeremy Rixey has taken on his brother's stateside fight against the forc-es that nearly killed Nick and his Special Forces team a year before. Now, Jeremy's whole world has been turned upside down—not the least of which by kidnapping victim Charlie Merritt, a bril-liant, quiet blond man who tempts Jeremy to settle down for the first time ever. With tragedy and chaos all around them, temptation flashes hot, and Jeremy and Charlie can't help but wonder why they're trying so hard to be good…

Hard to Let Go (Hard Ink #4)

Beckett Murda hates to dwell on the past. But his investigation into the ambush that killed half his Special Forces team and ended his Army career gives him little choice. Just when his team learns how powerful their enemies are, hard-ass Beckett encounters his biggest complication yet—his friend's younger sister, seductive, feisty Katherine Rixey. When Kat joins the fight, she lands straight in Beckett's sights … and in his arms. Not to mention their enemies' crosshairs. Now Beckett and Kat must set aside their differences to work together, because the only thing sweeter than justice is finding love and never letting go.

Hard As Steel (Hard Ink #4.5)

After identifying her employer's dangerous enemies, Jessica Jakes takes refuge at the compound of the Raven Riders Motorcycle Club. Fellow Hard Ink tattooist and Raven leader Ike Young promises to keep Jess safe for as long as it takes, which would be perfect if his close, personal, round-the-clock protection didn't make it so hard to hide just how much she wants him—and al-ways has. The last thing Ike needs is alone time with the sexiest woman he's ever known, one he's purposely kept at a distance for years. Now, Ike's not sure he can keep his hands or his heart to himself—or that he even wants to anymore.

Hard Ever After (Hard Ink #5)

After a long battle to discover the truth, the men and women of Hard Ink have a lot to celebrate, especially the wedding of two of their own—Nick Rixey and Becca Merritt, whose hard-fought love deserves a happy ending. But an old menace they thought long gone reemerges, threatening the peace they've only just found. Now, for one last time, Nick and Becca must fight for their al-ways and forever.

Hard to Serve (Hard Ink #5.5)

To protect and serve is all Detective Kyler Vance ever wanted to do, so when Internal Affairs investigates him as part of the new police commissioner's bid to oust corruption, everything is on the line. Which makes meeting smart, gorgeous submissive, Mia Breslin, at an exclusive play club the perfect distraction. Their scorching scenes lure them to play together again and again. But then Kyler runs into Mia at work and learns that he's been dominating the daughter of the hard-ass boss who has it in for him. Now Kyler must choose between life-long duty and forbidden desire before Mia finds another who's not so hard to serve.

The Hearts in Darkness Duet

Hearts in Darkness (Hearts in Darkness Duet #1)

Two strangers. Four hours. One pitch-black elevator.

Makenna James thinks her day can't get any worse, until she finds herself stranded in a pitch-black elevator with a complete stranger. Caden Grayson is amused when a harried redhead dashes into his elevator fumbling her bags and cell phone, but his amusement turns to panic when the power fails. Despite his piercings, tats, and vicious scar, he's terrified of the dark and confined spaces. Now, he's trapped in his own worst nightmare. To fight fear, they must reach out and open up. With no preconceived notions based on looks to hold them back, they discover just how much they have in common. In the warming darkness, attraction grows and sparks fly, but will they feel the same when the lights come back on?

Love in the Light (Hearts in Darkness Duet #2)

Two hearts in the darkness…must fight for love in the light…

Makenna James and Caden Grayson have been inseparable since the day they were trapped in a pitch-black elevator and found acceptance and love in the arms of a stranger. Makenna hopes that night put them on the path to forever—which can't happen until she introduces her tattooed, pierced, and scarred boyfriend to her father and three over-protective brothers. Haunted by a child-hood tragedy and the loss of his family, Caden never thought he'd find the love he shares with Makenna. But the deeper he falls, the more he fears the devastation sure to come if he ever lost her, too. When meeting her family doesn't go smoothly, Caden questions whether Makenna deserves someone better, stronger, and just more…normal. Maybe they're just too different—and he's far too damaged—after all…

The Heroes Series

Her Forbidden Hero (Heroes #1)

Former Army Special Forces Sgt. Marco Vieri has never thought of Alyssa Scott as more than his best friend's little sister, but her return home changes that...and challenges him to keep his war-borne demons at bay. Marco's not the same person he was back when he protected Alyssa from her abusive father, and he's not about to let her see the mess he's become. But Alyssa's not looking for protection—not anymore. Now that she's back in his life, she's determined to heal her forbidden hero one touch at a time...

One Night with a Hero (Heroes #2)

After growing up with an abusive, alcoholic father, Army Special Forces Sgt. Brady Scott vowed never to marry or have kids. Sent stateside to get his head on straight—and his anger in check—Brady's looking for a distraction. He finds it in Joss Daniels, his beautiful new neighbor whose one-night-only offer for hot sex leads to more. Suddenly, Brady's not so sure he can stay away. But when Joss discovers she's pregnant, Brady's rejection leaves her feeling abandoned. Now, they must overcome their fears before they lose the love and security they've found in each other, but can they let go of the past to create a future together?

Printed in Great Britain
by Amazon

57852042R00088

Menton

le Guide

Musées
Monuments
Promenades

PRÉFACE

Boutros Boutros-Ghali

Ancien secrétaire général de l'Organisation internationale de la francophonie

Ancien secrétaire général de l'Organisation des Nations unies

Menton

MA VILLE EST UN JARDIN

ÉDITIONS DU PATRIMOINE

CENTRE DES MONUMENTS NATIONAUX

Coordination

JOSIANE TRICOTTI
Animateur de l'architecture et du patrimoine

Les auteurs

AMORETTI Louis Nicolas
Professeur ès lettres honoraire
Menton et les écrivains

AMORETTI-LÉONELLI Françoise
Directrice de l'école municipale d'arts plastiques
Villa *La Tête du Commandant*

ARELLANO ALONSO Almudena
Agent du patrimoine
Musée de Préhistoire régionale
Les Rochers rouges et les grottes de Grimaldi (Vintimille)

BILAS Charles
Architecte, artiste peintre
Architecture du XXe s.

CAPERAN-MORENO Louis
Historien, service du patrimoine
L'Histoire de Menton
Le Guide de Menton : itinéraires 1 à 6

GHERSI Rolland
Président de la Société d'art et d'histoire du Mentonnais
Castellar

IMBERT Michel
Guide conférencier du patrimoine
Gorbio

MONNIER Yves
Professeur au Muséum d'histoire naturelle de Paris
Les jardins

MONTELATICI Gilles
Président de la Société des amis de l'Orient
L'Orient et Menton

MOULLÉ Pierre-Élie
Attaché de conservation du patrimoine
Musée de Préhistoire régionale
Les collections d'archéologie du musée de Préhistoire régionale

RIDÈS Jacques
Vice-président des Amis des musées et de l'opéra de chambre de Menton
Le festival de musique

ROSSO Lucien
Professeur d'enseignement artistique
Conservatoire municipal de musique, de danse et d'art dramatique
Architecture du XXe s.

TRICOTTI Josiane
Historienne de l'art
Animateur de l'architecture et du patrimoine
Service du patrimoine
Le Guide de Menton : itinéraires 1 à 6

VIALE Huguette
Conservateur de la bibliothèque municipale
Les collections de la bibliothèque

ISBN 978-2-85822-827-0

Menton demeure tout d'abord associé, dans mon esprit, à la villa *Maria Serena* qui surplombe la mer...

Je ne parlerai ni du palais Carnolès, ni du musée Jean-Cocteau, ni de l'église Saint-Michel, ni de tant d'autres monuments, musées et jardins d'exception, en un mot je ne parlerai pas de la richesse et de la diversité du patrimoine de la ville de Menton que vient détailler et promouvoir ce petit ouvrage.

Car Menton demeure tout d'abord associé, dans mon esprit, à la villa *Maria Serena* qui surplombe la mer avec majesté. C'est dans ce lieu magnifique, à quelques encablures de la frontière italienne, qu'a vu le jour, en 1972, l'Académie mondiale pour la paix.

J'ai eu l'honneur de contribuer à la création de cette institution qui se donna pour président René Cassin, le père de la Déclaration universelle des droits de l'homme. Et c'est ainsi que Menton reste, encore aujourd'hui, pour des centaines de jeunes auditeurs de toutes les régions du monde le lieu où l'on vient se former à l'art du dialogue et de la négociation.

Sans doute n'y a-t-il aucun hasard dans cette association élective, puisque Menton porte avec fierté le témoignage vivant et vibrant de sept siècles d'art et d'histoire. Un témoignage émouvant, car l'on ne peut s'empêcher, à la vue des créations de l'homme qui ont pu traverser le temps, de songer à la brièveté de la vie. Quelques décennies à peine, de l'enfance à la vieillesse, à la mort...

Et pourtant ces quelques décennies savent être parfois si riches et si intenses qu'elles transcendent l'humain. Mais entre ces deux infinis de grandeur et de petitesse, il est une autre leçon : celle que les femmes et les hommes du monde entier, malgré leur diversité, appartiennent à la même famille, empruntent le même chemin, partagent le même destin.

BOUTROS BOUTROS-GHALI

Sommaire

l'Histoire

le Guide

Le centre historique

Du Vieux-Port à l'hôtel Adhémar de Lantagnac

« Le Rêve babylonien »

Des Rochers rouges à la vieille ville

À l'ouest de Menton

De la place des Victoires à la villa Carla

Le centre-ville

Les collines du pays mentonnais

Aux alentours de Menton

l'Histoire
de Menton

• • • Au commencement...

Au commencement était la mer. Et la montagne. Puis l'homme vint, et son témoignage perdure. Il est présent sur le site niçois de Terra Amata où *Homo erectus* apparaît il y a 400 000 ans environ. On le retrouve dans les grottes des Rochers rouges, à la frontière franco-italienne, avec *Homo sapiens,* vieux de 37 000 ans. Il se manifeste dans les milliers d'inscriptions rupestres du val des Merveilles, à l'est des Alpes-Maritimes, vers 4000 av. J.-C. Il s'affirme encore, à la veille de notre ère, dans les vestiges de camps ligures ou d'*oppida* romains. Et quand est érigé le Trophée d'Auguste, sur le site de La Turbie, six ans avant notre ère, ce monument commémoratif marque l'achèvement d'une épopée. La *pax romana* s'impose sur toutes les terres en bordure de la Méditerranée.

Ci-dessus : *Les Rochers rouges.*

Toutefois, aussi loin que l'on remonte dans le temps, Menton ne se révèle être ni une fondation grecque, tels Monaco, Nice et Antibes, ni une glorieuse cité romaine à l'instar de Cimiez ou Fréjus. Pressés par les vents de l'histoire, les Grecs ont oublié le golfe de la Paix ; quant au *cursus*, l'efficace poste impériale romaine organisée par Auguste, elle n'a laissé qu'un souvenir sur notre territoire : la Via Julia Augusta.

Ci-dessous :
En haut : *Le Trophée d'Auguste.*
En bas : *Le site de Puypin.*

L'Empire romain se fragmente peu à peu sous la pression des invasions barbares. Entre le Vᵉ et le Xᵉ s., le haut Moyen Âge succède à l'Antiquité ; il donne naissance à l'Occident.

Sur ces périodes reculées, notre région est encore bien avare de documents ; il faut attendre les années 972-979 pour qu'ils nous informent de l'expulsion des Sarrasins grâce au succès remporté dans les Alpes par les armées du comte Guillaume de Provence.

• • • Menton, des Vento aux Grimaldi

À partir du XIIe s., on assiste à un nouvel élan du dynamisme politique local, dû aux ambitions rivales de la commune de Gênes et des comtes de Provence sur le comté de Vintimille. Les Génois étendent à ce moment-là leur autorité sur la « rivière du Ponant ». Ils contraignent les comtes de Vintimille à leur remettre châteaux et places fortes, qu'ils leur rétrocèdent en fiefs moyennant l'hommage vassalique. C'est le cas, en 1146, de Puypin, première agglomération mentonnaise, dont la localisation précise n'a jamais été attestée.

Sceau de Charles Ier Grimaldi († 1357), seigneur de Monaco.

LA SEIGNEURIE DES VENTO : 1262-1346

Au XIIIe s., pour la première fois, Menton est mentionné dans des archives. Sa fondation serait due au déplacement de Puypin près du littoral (1249-1269). La convention d'Aix, signée par le comte de Provence et la république de Gênes (21 juillet 1262), reconnaît Puypin et Menton comme possessions de Guillaume Vento, noble génois. Celui-ci décède en 1279, laissant la succession à son fils Manuel, qui inaugure une ère de paix relative.

En 1290, Manuel donne à la cité ses premiers statuts, qui constitueront la base législative et judiciaire de la seigneurie jusqu'en 1516, mais il meurt en 1302, sans descendance directe. De nombreux prétendants vont alors s'opposer, jusqu'au rachat de la ville et des droits afférents, le 19 avril 1346, par Charles Ier Grimaldi, fils de Rainier Ier, amiral de France et seigneur de Cagnes. Sept mois après la cession, les Vento remettent officiellement les clés du château et de la cité entre les mains de son nouveau possesseur, dont l'étendard fuselé d'argent et de gueules (rouge) est hissé au sommet de la forteresse.

En 1355, Charles Ier – le premier des Grimaldi à porter le titre de seigneur de Monaco – agrège à ses domaines la seigneurie de Roquebrune.

LA SEIGNEURIE DES GRIMALDI : 1346-1524

L'acquisition de Menton se situe à un moment difficile de l'histoire monégasque. Les guerres civiles génoises, prenant appui sur la confrontation entre deux factions rivales – les guelfes (favorables au pape) et les gibelins (partisans de l'empereur romain germanique) –, conduisent à l'expulsion des Grimaldi en 1357, année de la mort de Charles. Monaco – à l'exception de

Généalogie de la maison Grimaldi

	Otto Canella • ? - av. 1143 Consul de Gênes en 1133	
	Grimaldo Canella • ? - ? Consul de Gênes en 1162, 1170, 1184	
	Oberto Grimaldi • ? -1252 Commissaire de Gênes en 1188	
	Grimaldo Grimaldi • ? - ap. 1257 Membre Conseil de Gênes en 1237, 1244	
	Lanfranco Grimaldi • ? -1293	
	Rainier Ier • v. 1267-1314 Amiral de France en 1304	
	Charles Ier • ? -1357 Seigneur de Monaco en 1331	
	Rainier II • 1350 -1407 Seigneur de Monaco en 1357	
Ambroise • ? - v. 1433 Coseigneur de Monaco de 1419 à 1427	**Antoine** • ? - ? Coseigneur de Monaco de 1419 à 1427	**Jean Ier** • 1382-1454 Coseigneur; seigneur de Monaco en 1427
		Catalan • ? -1457 Seigneur de Monaco en 1454
	Claudine • 1451-1515 *Épouse Lambert Grimaldi en 1465*	**Lambert Grimaldi** • 1420 -1494 Seigneur de Monaco en 1458
Jean II • 1468-1505 Seigneur de Monaco en 1494	**Lucien** • 1481-1523 Seigneur de Monaco en 1505	**Augustin** • ? -1532 Seigneur de Monaco en 1523
	Honoré Ier • 1522-1581 Seigneur de Monaco en 1532	
Charles II • 1555-1589 Seigneur de Monaco en 1581	**Hercule Ier** • 1562-1604 Seigneur de Monaco en 1589	
	Honoré II • 1597-1662 Seigneur, puis prince de Monaco en 1612	
	Hercule • 1623-1651 *N'a jamais régné*	
	Louis Ier • 1642-1701 Prince de Monaco en 1662	
	Antoine Ier • 1661-1731 Prince de Monaco en 1701	**Jacques de Goyon de Matignon** • 1689-1751 Prince de Monaco *sous le nom de* **Jacques Ier** du 29-12-1731 au 8-11-1733
	Louise Hippolyte • 1697-1731 *Épouse Jacques de Goyon en 1715*	
	Honoré III • 1720-1795 Prince de Monaco en 1734	
	Honoré IV • 1758-1819 Prince de Monaco en 1814	
Honoré V • 1778-1841 Prince de Monaco en 1819	**Florestan Ier** • 1785-1856 Prince de Monaco en 1841	
	Charles III • 1818-1889 Prince de Monaco en 1856	
	Albert Ier • 1848-1922 Prince de Monaco en 1889	
	Louis II • 1870-1949 Prince de Monaco en 1922	
	Charlotte • 1898-1977 *Épouse Pierre de Polignac en 1920*	**Pierre de Polignac** • 1895-1964 *devenu* **Grimaldi** *par mariage*
Antoinette • née en 1920	**Rainier III** • 1923-2005 Prince de Monaco en 1949	
Caroline • née en 1957	**Albert II** • né en 1958 Prince de Monaco en 2005	**Stéphanie** • née en 1965

Dessin reconstituant la physionomie que Menton pouvait avoir au Moyen Âge. Menton, bibliothèque municipale.

Menton, défendu par son fils Rainier II – est rattaché à Gênes jusqu'en 1419.

Après avoir recouvré Monaco, Jean Ier, petit-fils de Charles Ier, se rapproche de son voisin le duc de Savoie à qui il inféode la moitié du territoire mentonnais le 19 décembre 1448. Avant de disparaître en 1454, Jean Ier établit des règles successorales fondamentales pour la maison de Monaco : la succession se fera par les enfants mâles, selon l'ordre de primogéniture, ou, à défaut, par les femmes sous réserve que leurs descendants prennent le nom et les armes des Grimaldi.

Sceau de Lambert Grimaldi (1420-1494), seigneur de Monaco.

En 1465, Claudine, petite-fille de Jean Ier, épouse son cousin Lambert Grimaldi, coseigneur d'Antibes et de Menton, à qui elle abandonne les rênes du gouvernement. Mais, en 1466 et 1468, Menton se rebelle contre son autorité, si bien que le seigneur décide, le 18 mars 1477, de mettre le siège devant la ville, où il entre neuf jours plus tard. La paix revenue, les concessions faites à Philibert de Savoie en 1489 affaiblissent le pouvoir de Lambert, qui cherche à négocier un véritable protectorat avec la France. Charles VIII et le duc de Savoie reconnaissent la souveraineté pleine et entière de Monaco à Lambert. Ce dernier s'éteint en 1494 ; il est inhumé dans l'église Saint-Michel de Menton – une dizaine d'années auparavant, il avait présidé à la fondation du couvent de la Madone de Carnolès. Lui succède Jean II, époux de la fille du duc de Savoie, Antoinette, qui est désormais l'héritier des seigneuries de Monaco, Roquebrune et Menton. À peine assoit-il son autorité qu'il s'engage aux côtés de Charles VIII – prétendant à la souveraineté du royaume de Naples – lors des premières guerres d'Italie. En témoignage de gratitude, le roi de France accorde le droit de mer pour Monaco et le privilège d'un libre commerce avec la Provence.

Les subsides tirés de ses expéditions italiennes permettent à Jean II, dès 1503, de faire restaurer le château de Menton, déjà reconstruit en 1276, mais sévèrement endommagé lors du siège de 1477. Dans cette somptueuse demeure, la nuit du 10 au 11 octobre 1505, Jean est assassiné par son frère Lucien Grimaldi.

Les Mentonnais prêtent alors allégeance au nouveau seigneur. Mais Louis XII, qui succède à Charles VIII au trône de France, prend prétexte du meurtre pour rompre ses liens avec Lucien ; quelque temps après, il s'en rapproche de nouveau et tient à réaffirmer l'indépendance de Monaco par la prorogation du protectorat français en 1512. Au cours de son règne, Lucien Grimaldi noue des alliances, entretient de multiples relations économiques et va jusqu'à conclure un accord maritime avec Florence, représentée par Machiavel, qu'il reçoit en 1511 au château de Menton. Lucien s'attache également à l'organisation de ses seigneuries et promulgue, le 27 mai 1516, de nouveaux statuts destinés à réglementer la condition et les biens des Mentonnais.

Lucien Grimaldi (1481-1523), seigneur de Monaco en 1505. Archives du palais de Monaco.

Cependant, l'émergence de Charles Quint sur la scène politique européenne remet en cause l'équilibre de la région. Les Français sont chassés du Milanais et de Gênes. Empereur germanique, roi d'Espagne et de Sicile, Charles Quint envahit la Provence. Le 22 août 1523, Lucien meurt assassiné par son cousin Barthélemy Doria. Son frère, Augustin Grimaldi, évêque de Grasse, assure la régence et prête attention aux exhortations de la chancellerie impériale. L'année suivante, Monaco est intégré dans le protectorat espagnol, avec Menton et Roquebrune.

LA VIE ÉCONOMIQUE À MENTON SOUS LE RÈGNE DE LUCIEN GRIMALDI

Lors de la proclamation des statuts de 1516, la population de Menton est évaluée à environ 1 000 personnes. Les habitants se réunissent en parlement pour traiter les affaires intéressant leur communauté. L'économie est toujours fondée sur la culture vivrière (céréales et culture arbustive) et l'élevage, mais une nouvelle activité prend son essor : l'agrumiculture. L'importation des céréales et du vin, l'exportation toute naissante des oranges, à la fin du XVe s., entraînent le développement du cabotage. Menton se transforme en un petit centre de redistribution où les marchands des bourgs voisins viennent s'approvisionner et vendre leurs productions.

• • • Le protectorat espagnol : 1524-1641

Le protectorat espagnol sur Monaco, Roquebrune et Menton va durer plus d'un siècle, conforté, de 1559 à 1610, par la puissance et le prestige intellectuel de l'Espagne, alors à leur apogée. Pour les trois seigneuries, cette protection se déroule sans heurt, mais, de 1610 à 1641, l'omnipotence hispanique commence à fléchir face à une France sortie des guerres de Religion. La situation se dégrade, notamment en raison du mécontentement monégasque à l'égard de l'Espagne, à qui il est reproché de ne pas remplir tous ses engagements. On s'achemine vers la rupture.

Antoine Manchello, retable de l'église Saint-Michel, 1565.

LE GOUVERNEMENT D'ÉTIENNE GRIMALDI

En 1532, lorsque disparaît Augustin Grimaldi, son neveu Honoré n'a que dix ans. Les représentants des trois seigneuries confient la régence à Nicolas Grimaldi et à un Conseil, dévoués aux Espagnols, mais – *de facto* – c'est Étienne, frère de Nicolas, qui exerce le pouvoir. Énergique, déterminé, il devient le seul maître, malgré la présence du résident impérial dépêché par Charles Quint.

L'ère de paix qui s'ouvre sous l'autorité d'Étienne se poursuivra jusqu'au début du XVIIe s. Elle favorise une réelle renaissance artistique, comme en témoigne le retable du peintre monégasque Manchello, commandé en 1565 par la communauté de Menton pour orner l'église Saint-Michel ; cette œuvre montre saint Michel entouré de saint Jean Baptiste et de saint Pierre, lequel porte les attributs de la papauté.

À l'appel de Pie V, qui fonde la Sainte Ligue, Philippe II d'Espagne unit ses forces à celles de Venise, de Gênes et du Saint-Siège pour aller livrer la dernière croisade. Quatorze Mentonnais s'engagent et montent à bord des deux galères appartenant aux Grimaldi. Le 7 octobre 1571, se déroule dans le golfe de Lépante, à la sortie

Chapiteau au monogramme des Grimaldi, dans le couvent de la Madone.

Honoré II, prince de Monaco. Archives du palais de Monaco.

Honoré II
1597-1662

HONORÉ II est seigneur de Monaco, Menton et Roquebrune de 1604 à 1632, puis prince de Monaco jusqu'en 1662. Honoré II avait pris le titre de prince dès 1612, mais celui-ci n'a été reconnu qu'en 1633 par la chancellerie espagnole.
HONORÉ II est aussi marquis de Campagna, chevalier de la Toison d'or (1624), duc de Valentinois, marquis des Baux, comte de Carladez et seigneur de Saint-Rémy (1641).
À MENTON, la place qui porte son nom a été inaugurée le 28 septembre 1975. La ville doit à ce prince bâtisseur l'église Saint-Michel, les couvents des Capucins et de la Madone, le Bastion et le percement de la rue Neuve (actuelle rue Bréa).

du détroit de Corinthe, la bataille décisive qui met en déroute la flotte ottomane commandée par Ali Pacha. L'un des survivants, Barthélemy Pretti, en rapporte deux lances turques et un drapeau dont la hampe est aujourd'hui utilisée comme croix processionnelle par la paroisse Saint-Michel.

LE PRINCE DE VALDETARE
ET LES DÉBUTS DU RÈGNE D'HONORÉ II

Après la souveraineté d'Honoré Ier, son fils Hercule accède au pouvoir. À la mort de ce dernier, en 1604, lui succède son propre fils Honoré II, encore mineur, dont la tutelle est confiée à un oncle maternel, le prince de Valdetare. Très lié au gouverneur espagnol du Milanais, Federico Landi de Valdetare adopte une politique hispanophile qui aboutit à un renforcement du protectorat. En 1605, les Espagnols placent à Monaco leur propre garnison. En 1615, au cours d'un déplacement dans ses seigneuries, Honoré II constate que les protecteurs se sont transformés en occupants et qu'ils commettent de nombreux excès. Cette situation conduit le prince à être attentif aux propositions françaises. Les négociations entreprises avec la France aboutissent à la signature du traité de Péronne le 14 septembre 1641. Monaco, Menton et Roquebrune passent sous protectorat français; ils y resteront un siècle et demi. Deux mois après le traité, dans la nuit du 17 au 18 novembre, Honoré II et ses sujets mentonnais et roquebrunois chassent de Monaco la garnison espagnole, qui, six jours plus tard, est remplacée par 500 soldats français.

• • • Le protectorat français : 1641-1701

Le protectorat français connaîtra deux phases distinctes au cours desquelles les événements tendront peu à peu à altérer l'esprit et l'application du traité de Péronne. La période de 1641 à 1701 apparaît comme l'âge d'or des relations avec la France, au point que l'on a pu la qualifier de « Grand Siècle monégasque ». Puis, de 1701 à 1792, les relations se dégradent et compromettent les structures profondes de la principauté.

LE DÉVELOPPEMENT URBAIN

L'extension urbaine de Menton est liée à l'accroissement de sa population. De 1611 à 1620, elle compte 1 250 habitants; à la fin du XVIIe s., elle atteint le chiffre de 1 720.

Au début du règne d'Honoré II, Menton a conservé l'aspect d'une bourgade médiévale, mais un secteur moderne prend forme avec la rue Longue, où se dressent l'hôtel Pretti de Saint-Ambroise et le palais princier. Au sud, le cap Saint-Sébastien voit se développer de nouvelles constructions. Afin de protéger les habitants de ce faubourg, Honoré II fait bâtir le Bastion, qui sera achevé en 1639. En 1618, une rue est percée pour donner accès au couvent des Capucins. C'est la première extension de la ville vers l'ouest. Témoin de ce développement, l'église Saint-Michel, édifiée à partir de 1639, est ouverte au culte en 1653 et consacrée le 8 mai 1675.

Barthélemy Puppo, retable de la basilique Saint-Michel.

Le sursaut religieux, qui marquera tout le XVIIe s., provoque l'épanouissement de la vie séculière et régulière. Trois couvents d'hommes voient le jour. En 1615, le souverain fonde celui des Capucins ; en 1640, les pères réformés s'installent dans celui de la Madone ; en 1694, des prêtres mentonnais fondent une congrégation qui s'établit à l'Annonciade. Par ailleurs, la renaissance artistique perceptible dès la fin du XVIe s. se poursuit au siècle suivant. Horace de Ferrari peint trois retables pour Saint-Michel ; Barthélemy Puppo y signe deux autres peintures, en 1650 et 1670.

Louis Ier (1642-1701), prince de Monaco. Archives du palais de Monaco.

Outre ces évolutions, le trait dominant de la période réside dans le renforcement de l'autorité princière, qui s'affirme avec Honoré II, puis avec son petit-fils Louis, qui lui succède en 1662. Dès le commencement de son règne, Louis Ier, filleul du Roi-Soleil, s'intéresse à la réforme des institutions. En 1671, il crée le Magistrat des citrons, un conseil qui veille à la cueillette et au commerce des agrumes. Sept ans plus tard, il promulgue de nouveaux statuts, nommés « le Code Louis ». Si le prince ne parvient pas à fondre les communautés de Monaco, Menton et Roquebrune dans un même cadre juridique, il sait maintenir une remarquable harmonie dans les liens qui unissent la principauté à la France.

• • • Le protectorat français au XVIIIe s.

Au cours des règnes d'Antoine Ier (1701-1731), de Louise Hippolyte (1731) et de son époux Jacques de Goyon de Matignon – qui devient prince de Monaco sous le nom de Jacques Ier (1731-1733) –, puis de leur fils Honoré III (1733-1792), on assiste à la dégradation des conditions sur lesquelles reposait le protectorat français, c'est-à-dire la suprématie militaire du protecteur et la valeur stratégique du protégé. La prépondérance française en Europe faiblit lors de la guerre de Succession d'Espagne (1701-1714); elle subit même un coup d'arrêt avec le traité d'Utrecht, signé en 1713, qui met fin au conflit. De plus, avec les perfectionnements techniques – en particulier ceux que connaît l'artillerie –, Monaco perd de son importance stratégique.

Ci-dessous:
– *Antoine Ier (1661-1731), prince de Monaco.*
– *Marie de Lorraine, épouse d'Antoine Ier.*
Archives du palais de Monaco.

LES GUERRES ET LES CRISES

Durant la guerre de Succession d'Espagne, Antoine Ier, qui accède au pouvoir en 1701, observe une neutralité agissante en faveur de la France. Mais l'impérialisme britannique est en pleine phase d'ascension. Les Anglais font leur apparition en Méditerranée et, dès 1712, prennent l'habitude de croiser le long du littoral et d'y accoster. En 1732, le curé de la paroisse rapporte que la place du Cap est appelée « la place des Anglais ».

Ci-dessus:
– *Honoré III (1720-1795), prince de Monaco.*
– *Marie-Catherine de Brignole-Sale, épouse d'Honoré III.*
Archives du palais de Monaco.

Pendant la guerre de Succession d'Autriche (1740-1748), la politique de non-ingérence adoptée par Honoré III se veut plus stricte à l'égard des belligérants. Ses motivations tiennent à la gravité du conflit; les troupes violent la neutralité monégasque et envahissent le pays à tour de rôle, selon l'issue des batailles.

Le relâchement de la protection française a valu à la principauté de connaître deux sévères échecs. D'une part, lors du traité d'Utrecht, Antoine Ier avait été contraint de rendre l'hommage vassalique au duc de Savoie Victor-Amédée II – devenu roi de Piémont-Sicile –, pour les onze douzièmes de Menton (cet hommage n'avait plus été rendu depuis 1523). D'autre part, en 1760, Monaco est amputé des deux tiers de son territoire lors de la délimitation des frontières avec le royaume de Piémont-Sardaigne – le duc de Savoie avait échangé, en 1720, la Sicile contre la Sardaigne. La partie continentale du royaume de Sardaigne était alors constituée du Piémont, de Nice et de la Savoie.

À tous ces conflits, à toutes ces guerres qui s'égrènent tragiquement au long du siècle viennent s'ajouter huit épidémies: la peste (1721), la variole (1731), les fièvres

(1735), de nouveau la variole (1746, 1752, 1760, 1766, 1772). Enfin, cinq crises de subsistance frappent la population mentonnaise (1704-1705, 1709, 1765-1766, 1778-1779 et 1783-1784).

LE DÉVELOPPEMENT ÉCONOMIQUE

Au XVIIIe s., Menton a totalement abandonné la vieille économie médiévale et tire sa richesse de trois formes d'activités : l'agriculture (agrumiculture et oléiculture), le négoce et le cabotage. L'agriculture repose sur les agrumes (citrons et oranges), l'olivier et, accessoirement, sur le mûrier et l'élevage des vers à soie. Au cours du siècle, l'huile devient la deuxième production destinée à l'exportation. L'agrumiculture et l'oléiculture donnent naissance à des ressources dérivées : la distillerie et la menuiserie (tonnellerie et ébénisterie). L'exportation de fruits et d'huile d'olive ayant de plus en plus pour origine l'ensemble du Midi, les négociants sont conduits à élargir leurs activités en y joignant d'autres spécialités. Les échanges nécessitent l'établissement d'une « maison de commerce », forte d'un dense réseau de correspondants établis dans les places du pourtour méditerranéen. En ce domaine, Marseille occupe incontestablement une place prépondérante dans la région. De plus, l'essor du commerce a stimulé celui de la marine locale à qui l'on confie les chargements sur une petite distance. Pour les expéditions lointaines, la règle est d'affréter un bateau en partie ou en totalité.

Plage de la Grava. Menton, musée des Beaux-Arts.

LE DÉVELOPPEMENT DE LA CITÉ

L'accroissement de la population mentonnaise n'a jamais cessé malgré les guerres, les épidémies et les crises. À partir des années 1760, l'essor démographique s'accélère ; de 2 565 âmes en 1761, on passe à 3 300 en 1786. Cette augmentation du nombre d'habitants se conjugue avec une forte expansion économique et provoque l'éclatement des anciens remparts. La ville poursuit son développement commencé au siècle précédent. Le gouvernement princier et la commune lancent alors d'importants travaux : réalisation d'une voie carrossable pour relier Menton à Monaco, aménagement de la route de la vallée du Careï. En ville sont aménagées la rue

Saint-Michel et la place Honoré-III. À partir de 1753, Honoré III fait construire le grand escalier communément appelé « les Rampes ». Enfin, en 1779, sont bâtis des aqueducs pour acheminer l'eau depuis le Sourgio. Par ailleurs, l'ordonnance souveraine du 14 décembre 1701 organise l'enseignement et crée un collège. Parallèlement, on assiste au déclin du mouvement artistique. L'école mentonnaise de peinture, qui a connu un bel épanouissement au XVIIe s., ne voit surgir qu'un peintre notable au début du XVIIIe, Jean Augustin Vento. À la même époque, Monaco ne connaît que deux artistes de talent: Dominique Joseph Bressan et Jean Horace Sigaldi. Quant à l'architecte monégasque Emmanuel Cantone, il édifie le campanile mentonnais entre 1701 et 1703.

Les Rampes et la basilique Saint-Michel.

À la veille de la Révolution, la caractéristique principale des Mentonnais est la vivacité. Leur naturel ardent et emporté, leur énergie, conjugués à une relative grossièreté, s'accompagnent parfois de quelque brutalité, en particulier lors des conflits qui opposent le pouvoir princier à l'évêque de Vintimille, de 1750 à 1755.

Au terme d'un long règne, Honoré III a eu le mérite d'œuvrer de façon louable pour le développement économique en favorisant le commerce, la circulation des personnes et des marchandises. La création de quelques industries procure à ses sujets de nouvelles sources de revenus. Cependant, vivant le plus souvent éloigné de ses États, coupé de ses sujets, le prince ne mesurera pas la portée réelle des événements qui éclatent dès 1789 dans la principauté.

• • • De la Révolution au rattachement à la France : 1790-1861

Le règne d'Honoré III, qui avait débuté en 1733, semble figé dans son lourd passé, avec des institutions vieillies, mal adaptées aux besoins d'une société en mutation. Depuis quelques années, les idées révolutionnaires qui circulent en France trouvent un écho favorable dans la principauté, notamment à Menton, où la garnison française contribue à les diffuser.

LA RÉVOLUTION MONÉGASQUE : 1788-1793

Dès le 10 juillet 1788, le peuple monégasque, par la voix de ses syndics, présente ses revendications au prince. Quatorze jours plus tard, Honoré III accède à ses désirs. Le processus révolutionnaire est enclenché.

Les 8 et 11 février 1790, les syndics et l'assesseur de Menton sollicitent la réforme des institutions communales et l'accession de tous leurs concitoyens à l'exercice des droits électoraux. Le 25 février, le prince accorde aux Mentonnais la constitution d'un conseil communal. Les 18 et 26 mars, les institutions sont étendues à Roquebrune et Monaco. Paralysés par des difficultés économiques et des rivalités de personnes, ces conseils fonctionnent mal ; à la fin de l'année 1791, Honoré III supprime ces nouvelles institutions.

Plan de Menton (1811). Menton, Archives municipales.

Le rapport de force entre modérés et extrémistes évolue dans un sens contraire à ce qui se passe à Paris. Le 20 avril 1792, la France déclare la guerre à l'Autriche. Le 29 septembre, les hommes du général d'Anselme franchissent le Var et occupent Nice. Le 22 octobre, un bataillon occupe Monaco. Grâce aux événements extérieurs, la faction révolutionnaire l'emporte. Au début de janvier 1793, la société populaire abat les armoiries des Grimaldi et fait voter la déchéance du prince. La République monégasque est née. Dans sa séance du 14 février 1793, la Convention nationale annexe la ci-devant principauté, qui est rattachée au département des Alpes-Maritimes.

Le quai Bonaparte. Menton, musée des Beaux-Arts.

L'ANNEXION À LA FRANCE : 1793-1814

Alors que le mouvement extrémiste cherche à fondre la principauté dans le bloc français, on assiste au développement d'un certain particularisme qui tend à un patriotisme local. Deux éléments lui donnent vigueur : le sentiment religieux et les difficultés de ravitaillement que les modérés ne manquent pas d'exploiter, provoquant ainsi un mouvement réactionnaire.

Le 2 mars 1793, la Convention réclame des prêtres le serment civique, mais la municipalité et la société populaire refusent d'afficher le décret. Plus de 80 % des prêtres émigrent en terre génoise. Le 16 mars, les Mentonnais s'opposent à l'envoi, à Gênes, de l'argenterie des édifices religieux. Ce mouvement n'est pas homogène et contribue à provoquer une rupture entre Menton et Monaco où se manifeste un patriotisme opposé. La population mentonnaise saisit l'occasion pour rompre toute subordination vis-à-vis de la cité monégasque. Le corps municipal souffre alors d'une instabilité chronique et son action est souvent inspirée par la société populaire. En trois ans, Menton compte six municipalités et cinq maires différents ; il faudra attendre le Consulat, puis l'Empire pour que les institutions communales se stabilisent avec la nomination, au poste de maire, le 19 pluviôse an IX (8 février 1801), de Jérôme André de Monléon, fils de l'ancien gouverneur monégasque de la ville et chef de file des modérés mentonnais.

Porte de la maison, rue Bréa, où le général Bonaparte demeura en 1796.

De 1793 à 1814, les municipalités se succèdent, composées de propriétaires (rentiers ou cultivateurs), d'hommes de loi et de négociants. Quant au petit monde des gens de la terre et de la mer, des artisans et des journaliers – qui constituent la majorité des sans-culottes –, il est exclu de la gestion communale.

En l'an II, sur une population de 3 300 habitants, on relève 149 Mentonnais qui ont choisi d'émigrer. Si elle est peu importante, cette émigration touche l'ensemble des catégories sociales : clergé, noblesse, bourgeoisie, mais aussi gens de la mer et journaliers. Dans le district de Menton, la vente des biens nationaux débute en floréal an II (avril-mai 1794). La municipalité n'applique la mesure que contrainte par l'Administration. Sous le Premier Empire, proclamé le 18 mai 1804, le Bastion est cédé à la commune, ainsi que le château. Quant au domaine de l'Annonciade, il est acquis en 1808 par Jérôme André de Monléon lui-même.

LA VIE ÉCONOMIQUE ET SOCIALE SOUS LA RÉVOLUTION ET L'EMPIRE

De nombreuses crises jalonnent les périodes révolutionnaire et impériale : 1790, 1793, 1808-1809, 1810 et 1811. Celle qui survient en 1814 remet en question le difficile équilibre entre production, exportation et importation. À ces crises s'ajoutent les effets du blocus anglais, qui plongent une grande partie de la population dans la misère. En 1793, les autorités révolutionnaires tentent de supprimer le Magistrat des citrons au nom de la liberté d'entreprendre et de commercer. Mais, rapidement, on revient à une réglementation afin de soustraire les cultivateurs des spéculations des négociants. L'agriculture connaît de grandes difficultés. La liberté du commerce et la concurrence des produits en provenance de la Ligurie, le blocage des prix, les intempéries, la sécheresse sont autant de facteurs qui pèsent sur les échanges. Depuis 1793, les cultivateurs ont la possibilité de triturer leurs olives dans les moulins de leur choix, dont la municipalité encourage le développement. En 1810, 19 moulins sont en service dans la commune. Mais le commerce des huiles est lui-même en danger : maladies des oliviers, mauvaises récoltes successives, interdiction d'exporter à l'étranger, chute des prix due à l'intégration de la Ligurie dans les territoires de l'Empire. Quant au cabotage, il devient de plus en plus malaisé en raison du blocus. Seuls les bâtiments danois, qui observent une politique de neutralité, mouillent dans les eaux mentonnaises.

Ernest Louis Lessieux, Le Pont Saint-Louis. *Menton, musée de Préhistoire régionale.*

Néanmoins, la crise économique favorise nombre de travaux d'intérêt général – une ombre toutefois : ni la Révolution ni l'Empire ne sont parvenus à créer un établissement scolaire capable de transmettre la culture française.

Afin d'assurer le désenclavement de Menton et de faciliter les relations avec Nice, la Ligurie et l'arrière-pays, le gouvernement napoléonien entreprend la réalisation d'un vaste réseau routier. Les travaux de la grande corniche débutent en 1806. Après avoir contourné la ville par le bord de mer en 1812, les ingénieurs des Ponts et Chaussées effectuent le franchissement du torrent Saint-Louis grâce à un pont de pierre achevé en 1818. De 1803 à 1813, on restaure la route Menton-Sospel-Tende, nécessaire aux liaisons commerciales avec le Piémont.

Tout au long de cette période, la municipalité doit faire face aux problèmes du logement et du ravitaillement des armées. La ville souffre du passage des soldats et subit vols, exactions et maraudages. Le tirage au sort et la conscription se révèlent fortement impopulaires, tout comme les trop fréquentes restrictions.

LA RESTAURATION DES GRIMALDI : 1814-1848

Par le traité de Paris du 30 mai 1814, la principauté monégasque renoue les liens qui l'unissaient à la France avant le 1er janvier 1792 ; elle est placée sous son protectorat. Honoré IV, malade, donne délégation à son frère Joseph pour présider à la restauration du prince légitime à Monaco. En juin 1814, Joseph balaie vingt années d'administration française et rétablit l'Ancien Régime. Dès janvier 1815, il est remplacé par le fils d'Honoré IV, Honoré Gabriel. Celui-ci, duc de Valentinois et pair de France, administre la principauté au nom de son père, puis il accède au trône en 1819 sous le nom d'Honoré V.

Honoré V (1778-1841), prince de Monaco. Archives du palais de Monaco.

La principauté ne connut certes pas la période des Cent-Jours (20 mars-22 juin 1815), durant laquelle Napoléon tenta de restaurer l'Empire, mais elle en subit les conséquences. En effet, le second traité de Paris, signé le 20 novembre 1815, place Monaco sous le protectorat du royaume de Piémont-Sardaigne sans que n'aient été consultés ni le prince ni les habitants. Honoré V doit réorganiser son administration. Il supprime les lois remises en vigueur par Joseph et décide l'application des Codes français. Menton est doté d'un gouverneur et de trois consuls pour diriger la commune, mais aucune assemblée représentative n'est élue.

Menton, l'Italie et l'Espagne

« J'AI PASSÉ une journée à Menton, c'est une petite ville très curieuse qui m'a fait penser à la fois, à l'Italie et à l'Espagne. »

PROSPER MÉRIMÉE

En novembre 1815, Honoré V institue la gratuité de l'enseignement ; Menton retrouve son école primaire et son collège. Le souverain fonde l'hôtel-Dieu de Carnolès et, en 1822, autorise les religieuses à ouvrir un établissement scolaire pour jeunes filles.

Dans le domaine économique, la situation est redevenue critique. Les ressources qu'il était possible de dégager à l'époque prérévolutionnaire n'existent plus désormais. Reste évidemment le commerce extérieur, qui s'appuie sur le savoir-faire local, l'huile et les agrumes, mais il est réduit ; n'étant plus protectrice, la France interdit les importations en franchise. De plus, les conséquences des gels successifs en 1811, 1813-1814 et 1815-1816 se font douloureusement ressentir. En février 1817, des émeutes causées par la faim ont lieu devant l'église Saint-Michel. Les difficultés économiques sont accentuées par les mesures fiscales imposées par Honoré V, conduisant à la suppression de la taxe foncière à laquelle se substituent des impôts indirects s'appliquant tant aux importations qu'aux exportations. Par ailleurs, afin d'assurer l'approvisionnement en blé, il en confie le monopole à un particulier peu scrupuleux.

En janvier 1820, l'hiver rigoureux ravage les campagnes mentonnaises. Cultivateurs et négociants sont ruinés. Des émeutes éclatent en mars 1821, réprimées par les troupes dépêchées par le gouvernement de Turin pour rétablir l'ordre. Le 7 mai 1833, des troubles surgissent encore et quelques individus acclament la république. L'insurrection est une nouvelle fois contenue par des militaires sardes. Mais le dénouement de cette situation va dépendre de l'évolution que connaîtra la monarchie absolue piémontaise.

En fait, l'avènement du prince Florestan Ier, en 1841, apaise un bref moment les tensions. Il abolit « l'exclusive » – c'est-à-dire le monopole – sur les blés et farines, et allège les tarifs douaniers. Nonobstant, la crise s'aggrave. Le 5 novembre 1842, une délégation mentonnaise se présente au palais, mais ses revendications sont rejetées. Dès lors, le processus révolutionnaire se met une nouvelle fois en marche.

LA RÉVOLUTION MENTONNAISE : 1848-1860

L'équilibre européen établi au lendemain de 1815, fondé sur des régimes absolutistes, voit évoluer ses principes, dans la région, au cours de l'année 1847. En octobre, le roi Charles-Albert de Piémont-Sardaigne met fin au gouvernement autoritaire et promulgue le Statut fondamental. Dans la ville de Menton, les premiers troubles éclatent le 4 novembre 1847. Deux jours plus tard, les consuls et quelques personnalités réclament des réformes constitutionnelles identiques à celles dont jouit le royaume de Sardaigne, ainsi qu'une diminution des taxes qui frappent le commerce. Le 16 novembre, Florestan Ier accorde cette réduction, mais refuse de nouvelles institutions. Le 25 novembre, un détachement des troupes sardes stationnées à Monaco occupe Menton. De surcroît, le prince relève de ses fonctions le négociant mentonnais Charles Trenca, commandant de ses carabiniers et contrôleur général des Finances. Il offre ainsi un chef à l'insurrection.

Dessin d'Augero réalisé lors des troubles « pré-révolutionnaires » survenus à Menton au cours du dernier trimestre 1847. Menton, musée de Préhistoire régionale.

Le mouvement révolutionnaire mentonnais relève de deux types de causes : certaines sont locales, internes à la principauté ; d'autres découlent du protectorat sarde et de la situation internationale. Parmi les premières, il faut souligner l'absence d'assemblée représentative élue qui aurait pu faire le lien entre le souverain et ses administrés. L'organisation sociale ressemble à celle d'un

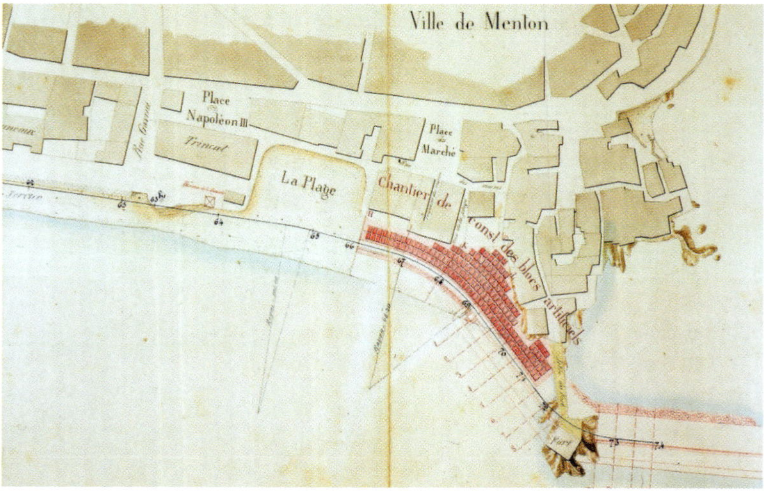

Maupassant à Menton

LORSQU'EN octobre 1881 Maupassant se rend chez Juliette Adam, à Golfe-Juan, il est fasciné par la Provence et par ce qui s'appelle déjà « la Côte d'Azur ». Il fait un séjour à Menton auprès de sa mère, du 7 au 14 mai 1882. MENTON le séduit. Après avoir visité les ruines du vieux château et le cimetière, d'où l'on découvre l'un des plus beaux panoramas du monde, il écrit : « De ce cimetière, la vue s'étend à gauche jusqu'à la pointe où Bordighera allonge dans la mer ses maisons blanches ; à droite jusqu'au cap Martin qui trempe dans l'eau ses flancs feuillus. »

fief du Moyen Âge : au sommet, le prince ; puis quelques fonctionnaires ; enfin l'ensemble de la population, dominée par de grandes familles, véritables clans aux intérêts opposés. Le système économique mis en place par Honoré V ne laisse aucune liberté ; il aggrave même les effets d'une crise locale, doublée d'une crise européenne à partir de 1846. Parmi les causes extérieures : l'ingérence de l'État protecteur dans les affaires de la principauté. Le traité de 1817 définissant les modalités du protectorat reconnaissait aux Monégasques une totale égalité des droits avec les sujets de Piémont-Sardaigne. Un réseau d'étroites relations s'étant alors créé, le royaume avait donc tout intérêt à voir éclater la principauté.

Charles Trenca est un grand propriétaire foncier et le premier négociant en huile et en agrumes, outre ses charges officielles auprès du prince. Après sa disgrâce, il réunit des notables mentonnais et organise la révolution. La passivité calculée du général Gonnet, qui entre dans Menton avec un bataillon le 4 janvier 1848, renforce sa détermination. Le 2 mars est créée une commission provisoire de gouvernement. Le 21 mars, elle proclame la déchéance des Grimaldi et l'érection de Menton et de Roquebrune en « villes libres placées sous la protection de la Sardaigne ». Le 24 avril, 70 députés sont élus, qui forment le Grand Conseil des villes libres. Le gouvernement est aussitôt présidé par Charles Trenca, et la municipalité place à sa tête un neveu de celui-ci, Auguste Massa.

En juin 1848, le gouvernement des villes libres procède à un plébiscite en faveur de l'annexion au royaume sarde. Mais, le 18 septembre, peu de temps après la défaite du roi Charles-Albert face aux armées autrichiennes à Custozza, le gouvernement de Turin temporise. Il décrète que Menton et Roquebrune seront administrés selon les lois en vigueur dans le royaume, dans l'attente de mesures définitives. L'impasse dure dix ans. Seule l'évolution du contexte international peut permettre d'en sortir. Napoléon III est désigné comme arbitre, mais il agit selon ses propres intérêts. En 1860, les deux communes participent au plébiscite organisé en vue du rattachement du comté de Nice à l'Empire. Menton vote son annexion : sur 1 120 inscrits, on compte 853 voix favorables, contre 54 avis négatifs et 2 nuls. L'accord passé entre Napoléon III et Charles III (successeur de Florestan Ier en 1856) est conclu par le traité de Paris du 2 février 1861. Menton devient définitivement français.

Page précédente : *Plan de l'enrochement du port de Menton (1862).* Menton, Archives municipales.

• • • Menton, de 1861 à 1945

Le rattachement de Menton à la France coïncide avec l'essor du tourisme et le lancement de grands travaux d'urbanisme. La conséquence des orientations nouvelles est l'abandon progressif de l'agrumiculture, de l'oléiculture et du commerce.

LE GRAND TOURISME : 1861-1914

Le développement d'une politique touristique rend nécessaire la réalisation d'infrastructures adaptées. La construction du port de pêche et de commerce débute en 1857 ; il est amélioré en 1869 et achevé neuf ans plus tard. En 1869, la Compagnie de chemins de fer PLM (Paris-Lyon-Méditerranée) lance les travaux afin d'assurer une liaison entre Monaco, Menton et Vintimille, le réseau s'arrêtant auparavant à Nice. Le Second Empire prend l'initiative du chantier de la corniche du bord de mer, terminée en 1881, tandis que la moyenne corniche est réalisée entre 1900 et 1930.

À partir de 1872, Menton s'agrandit. Des artères sont percées : l'avenue de la Gare (1878) ; la promenade du Soleil (1863-1878) ; le boulevard de Garavan, surnommé « le Rêve babylonien » (1882-1887). Menton accueille alors des visiteurs illustres, telles l'impératrice Eugénie et la reine Victoria.

Arrivée d'un train à Menton, au début du XXe s.

Phare de Menton, construit à la fin du XIXe s. Menton, musée de Préhistoire régionale.

Monument à la reine Victoria, square Victoria.

Les principaux architectes de Menton

CERUTTI-MAORI Henri • Menton, 1899 – 1972.
Fils du peintre Guillaume Cerutti-Maori, il est grand prix de Rome (1922). On lui doit quelques bâtiments dans l'Indochine des années 1930. Il est nommé architecte en chef pour l'Afrique-Occidentale française (1950).
À Menton, auteur de plusieurs bâtiments de style Art déco dont :
• ITINÉRAIRE 3 : **immeuble**, 26, place des Victoires → p. 77 ; ***Casa Isabella***, 14, avenue Édouard-VII → p. 79.
• ITINÉRAIRE 4 : **immeuble**, 19, rue Partouneaux → p. 98 ; **cinéma *Éden*** (1927), 11, rue de la République → p. 100 ; **immeuble**, 13, rue Guyau → p. 107 ; **villa *Val Rahmeh*** (1926) et **villa *Flora***, avenue Saint-Jacques ; **immeubles *Sorellina*** et ***Turrel*** (rue Guyau).

GARNIER Charles • Paris, 1825 – Paris, 1898.
Architecte de la Ville de Paris, son œuvre est représentative de l'éclectisme qui dominait sous le règne de Napoléon III. Il signe de nombreux édifices prestigieux, tels l'Opéra de Paris (1862-1875) et le théâtre de Monte-Carlo (1878).
Il est également l'auteur de deux villas à Bordighera (sur la Riviera italienne), dont l'une à son usage. À Menton, on lui attribue les plans de trois édifices :
• ITINÉRAIRE 2 : **villa Foucher de Careïl** (1892-1895), 81, boulevard de Garavan → photo p. 39 ; **villa *Maria Serena*** (v. 1886), 21, promenade Reine-Astrid → p. 62 ; **villa *Le Paradou*** (1878, remplacée par l'actuelle résidence *Les Gardénias*), 75, boulevard de Garavan → p. 67.

GLENA Abel • Menton, 1865 – 1932.
Collaborateur de l'architecte Scipion Jeansoulin (1844-1895), Abel Glena lui succède et devient l'un des architectes mentonnais les plus féconds de la Belle Époque. À partir des années 1910, il a Alfred Marsang comme collaborateur. L'œuvre de Glena épouse les fluctuations stylistiques de son temps, qui mêlent l'éclectisme de Garnier – c'est-à-dire le style Napoléon III –, l'italianisme si fréquent à Menton et l'Art nouveau qui se répand à la croisée des deux siècles.
À Menton, Glena a signé plusieurs édifices dont :
• ITINÉRAIRE 2 : **fondation Alphand-Bariquand** (1905), 41, boulevard de Garavan → p. 68.
• ITINÉRAIRE 3 : ***Riviera Palace*** (1898, surélevé par Marsang en 1910), 28, avenue Riviera → p. 78 ; **immeuble *Little Palace***, 3, avenue Thiers → p. 79, **immeuble *Flower Palace***, 5, avenue Thiers → p. 79 ; **villa Cochrane** (1918-1920), 10, avenue Cochrane → p. 80.
• ITINÉRAIRE 4 : **maison Glena** (1902), 2, rue Guyau → p. 108 ; **presbytère** (v. 1900, attribué à Glena), 22, rue Saint-Michel → p. 110 ; **lotissement du quartier des Carmes** (1904-1920, actuel quartier du musée de Préhistoire régionale).
• ITINÉRAIRE 5 : **oratoires du chemin du Rosaire** (1932), colline de l'Annonciade → p. 117 ; **villa *Mers et Monts*** (1905), route de Gorbio ; **sanatorium** (1903), route D 223 à partir de la route de Gorbio.

GRAY Eileen • Comté de Wexford (Irlande), 1878 – Paris, 1976. • → **p. 137.**

JAUFFRET Sylvain • Lauris, 1846 – Nice, 1925.
Architecte de la Ville de Menton, de 1876 à 1891, il est notamment l'auteur de :
• ITINÉRAIRE 1 : **chapelle de l'Immaculée-Conception** (1890, restauration après le tremblement de terre de 1887), place de la Conception → p. 54.
• ITINÉRAIRE 2 : **percement du boulevard de Garavan** (1882-1887) → p. 64.
• ITINÉRAIRE 4 : **hôtel des postes** (1885-1886, actuelle Caisse d'épargne), 21, rue Partouneaux → p. 97 ; ***Grand Hôtel d'Orient*** (1884, façade originelle), 1, rue de la République → p. 98.

LE CORBUSIER • La Chaux-de-Fonds (Suisse), 1887 – Roquebrune-Cap-Martin, 1965. • → **p. 139.**

LIVIERI René • Nice, 1908 – 1995.
Formé à l'école des arts décoratifs de Nice, René Livieri, dont le vocabulaire élargi épouse les problématiques d'un demi-siècle d'histoire architecturale, débute sa longue carrière dès les années 1930. On lui doit, entre autres, un certain nombre d'édifices à Nice. À Menton, Livieri est l'architecte de :
• ITINÉRAIRE 4 : **résidence *Paris Palace*** (1962), promenade du Soleil et 4, avenue Félix-Faure → p. 114.

MARSANG Alfred • Menton, 1878 – Denain, 1924.
Collaborateur d'Abel Glena, il est l'un des principaux architectes du Menton de la Belle Époque. Après la Première Guerre mondiale, il se fixe dans le Nord et contribue à la reconstruction. Parmi les édifices de Menton dont il est l'auteur, on peut citer :
• ITINÉRAIRE 3 : ***Riviera Palace*** (construit par Glena, 1898 ; exhaussé par Marsang, 1910), 28, avenue Riviera → p. 78 ; **villa *Renée*** (1918), 13, rue Morgan → p. 80 ; **hôtel *Astoria*** (1912-1914), 2, avenue Édouard-VII → p. 90 ; **maison Widmer** (1913), 19, avenue Carnot → p. 90.
• ITINÉRAIRE 4 : **hôtel *Leubner*** (1909, actuelle résidence *Majestic*), 1, rue Partouneaux → p. 96.

RANDON Philippe • Nice, 1833 – 1911.
Architecte dont le nom reste essentiellement associé à la ville de Nice, où il est l'auteur du musée des Beaux-Arts et du temple du parc Chambrun. Une place de Nice porte aujourd'hui son nom. À Menton, on lui doit :
• ITINÉRAIRE 4 : **aménagement de la place Ardoïno** (1861) → p. 101.

REY Adrien • Menton, 1865 – Nice, 1959.
Architecte du département des Alpes-Maritimes (1912) et architecte en chef du gouvernement pour les Alpes-Maritimes (1925). On lui doit un grand nombre d'édifices, dont la chambre de commerce de Nice (1924). À Menton, Rey a signé plusieurs bâtiments, comme le collège de

jeunes filles (1934), 6, rue Saint-Charles, démoli à la fin du XXe s., ainsi que :

• ITINÉRAIRE 2 : ***Garavan Palace*** (1912), 7, avenue Blasco-Ibáñez → p. 71.

• ITINÉRAIRE 3 : **villa *France***, 19, place des Victoires → p. 77.

• ITINÉRAIRE 4 : **maison Burkard** (1896), 38, rue Partouneaux → p. 97 ; **musée de Préhistoire régionale** (1907-1909), 46, rue Lorédan-Larchey → p. 106 ; **magasin *Les Dames de France*** (1920, actuelles *Nouvelles Galeries*), 27, rue de la République → p. 108 ; **halles municipales** (1898), quai de Monléon → p. 110.

RIVES Gustave • 1858 – 1926.
Architecte en chef des Palais nationaux, Rives est l'auteur de nombreux immeubles (Meudon, Neuilly-sur-Seine...) et d'établissements tels que l'ancien casino du Havre. Il collabore à la construction du Grand Palais et du musée Grévin, à Paris. À Menton, Rives a signé :

• ITINÉRAIRE 3 : **hôtel *Alexandra*** (1884, chantier supervisé par Tersling), 10, rue Paul-Morillot → p. 83 ; **kiosque à musique** (1884-1885, jardins Biovès ; démoli en 1932).

SABATIER Victor • Agen, 1825 – Nice, 1891.
Élève de Viollet-le-Duc, Sabatier devient, en 1854, inspecteur et premier dessinateur de Lefuel, lequel dirige les travaux d'agrandissement du Louvre. Sabatier est nommé en 1861 architecte diocésain de Nice, auquel s'ajoute celui de Fréjus en 1884.
À Menton, il est l'auteur de :

• ITINÉRAIRE 1 : **hôpital Saint-Julien** (1860-1862), avenue Laurenti → p. 48.

• ITINÉRAIRE 4 : **Cercle des étrangers** (1861, devenu hôtel de ville en 1902), place Ardoïno → p. 101.

SEASSAL Roger • Nice, 1885 – Paris, 1967.
Premier grand prix de Rome en 1913, Seassal est nommé architecte des Bâtiments civils et des Palais nationaux. Membre de l'Académie des beaux-arts en 1960, il est l'auteur de nombreux édifices, tels le monument aux morts de Nice, le *Palm Beach* de Cannes, le casino de Deauville, la faculté des sciences de Jussieu, à Paris, le monument Napoléon d'Ajaccio. Nice a honoré l'architecte en donnant son nom à l'une des places de la ville.
À Menton, Seassal a signé :

• ITINÉRAIRE 4 : **casino municipal** (1934), 2, avenue Félix-Faure → p. 114.

TERSLING Hans Georg
• Karlebo, Danemark, 1857 – Menton, 1920.
Architecte diplômé de l'École royale des beaux-arts de Copenhague, Tersling est l'auteur d'une trentaine d'édifices (hôtels, villas...) construits sur la Côte d'Azur, tels l'*Hôtel du Cap* à Roquebrune-Cap-Martin, le *Château de l'Ermitage* à Cap-d'Ail, la rotonde de Beaulieu. L'œuvre de Tersling témoigne d'une remarquable maîtrise du vocabulaire architectural de la Belle Époque dont il est l'un des plus illustres représentants. À Menton, on lui doit, entre autres :

• ITINÉRAIRE 3 : **église du Sacré-Cœur** (1913, achevée dans les années 1920 par Félix Vérola), 15, avenue Édouard-VII → p. 79 ; **hôtel *Impérial*** (1913), 9, avenue de la Madone → p. 81 ; **la Maison russe** (1882, actuelle clinique Saint-Georges), 18, rue Paul-Morillot ; **église orthodoxe russe** (1892, réalisée par Tersling d'après les plans de Térémine), 14, rue Paul-Morillot → p. 83 ; **hôtel *Alexandra*** (1884, réalisé par Tersling d'après les plans de Gustave Rives), 10, rue Paul-Morillot → p. 83 ; **palais Célestin Viale** (1906), 21, avenue Carnot → p. 90 ; **villa *Carla*** (v. 1898), angle avenue Carnot et rue Albini → p. 91.

• ITINÉRAIRE 4 : **casino *Kursaal*** (1909, actuel palais de l'Europe), 8, avenue Boyer → p. 94 ; **villa *Les Citronniers*** (remodelée par Tersling en 1895), 5, avenue Pasteur → p. 95.

TOURNAIRE Albert • Nice, 1862 – Paris, 1958.
Grand prix de Rome en 1888, se rend à Delphes (Grèce) en 1894 et participe aux fouilles archéologiques du sanctuaire d'Apollon. Il est l'auteur d'un grand nombre d'édifices tels que la villa *Arnaga* d'Edmond Rostand (1903), à Cambo-les-Bains, l'hôpital Pasteur à Nice (1937), l'Institut médico-légal de Paris et l'aile du quai des Orfèvres du Palais de justice de Paris (1911-1914). À Menton, il est l'auteur de :

• ITINÉRAIRE 3 : ***Winter Palace*** (1907), 20, avenue Riviera → p. 78.

TOURNON Paul • Marseille, 1881 – Paris, 1964.
Gendre du physicien Édouard Branly, Tournon devient architecte diplômé en 1912 ; il crée son agence à Paris deux ans plus tard. Ce « moderniste sage » a signé un grand nombre d'édifices, tels que l'église du Saint-Esprit à Paris (1928), l'église du Sacré-Cœur à Casablanca (1930-1940), la résidence universitaire Pierre-de-Coubertin, à Paris (1930). À Menton, on lui doit :

• ITINÉRAIRE 3 : **monument aux morts** (1928, sculpteur : Antoine Sartorio), place des Victoires → p. 77.

VÉROLA Félix • Coaraze (Nice), XIXe – XXe s.
Diplômé de l'école des arts décoratifs, Vérola installe son agence à Menton (4, rue de la Marne), où il signe quelques édifices, tels que :

• ITINÉRAIRE 2 : **villa *Hoche*** (boulevard de Garavan) ; **villa *Le Logis bleu*** (1930), 1, avenue Aristide-Briand.

• ITINÉRAIRE 3 : **hôtel *Lutétia*** (1914), chemin du Lutétia → p. 78 ; **église du Sacré-Cœur** (1913, Tersling ; achevée dans les années 1920 par Vérola), 15, avenue Édouard-VII → p. 79 ; **Grand Palais** (1905), 7, avenue Édouard-VII → p. 90.

Le Riviera Palace, construit en 1898 d'après les plans d'Abel Glena et surélevé en 1910 par Alfred Marsang.

Afin d'agrémenter la ville, Émile Biovès, au cours de sa mandature (1896-1905), entreprend la couverture du Careï et crée des jardins sur l'espace ainsi récupéré. En 1898, l'architecte Adrien Rey dessine les plans du marché couvert ; de 1907 à 1909, il bâtit l'édifice qui abrite aujourd'hui le musée de Préhistoire régionale. Au cours de cette année 1909 est inauguré le casino *Kursaal*, dû à Hans Georg Tersling.

C'est un Britannique, le docteur Henry Bennet, qui propulse Menton au rang de station climatique. Une trentaine d'hôtels – financés par des capitaux allemands, anglais, suisses et autrichiens – offrent 1 500 chambres. Puis apparaissent les grands hôtels de luxe : le *Riviera Palace*, construit par Abel Glena et Alfred Marsang (1898-1910) ; le *Winter Palace*, dû à Albert Tournaire (1907), avec ses célèbres pyramides d'écailles vernissées ; le monumental hôtel *Leubner*, de Marsang (1909) ; l'hôtel *Impérial*, par Tersling (1913)...

En 1913, Menton est riche de 62 établissements hôteliers, qui proposent quelque 4 500 chambres. Pour les touristes britanniques, allemands, austro-hongrois et russes, la saison débute en octobre et s'achève vers la mi-mai. À leur intention, le comité des fêtes organise bals et feux d'artifice, ainsi que les célèbres *corsi* carnavalesques et les batailles de fleurs. Tout au long de leur séjour se succèdent les tournois de tennis et de golf, les courses automobiles et les régates dans la baie de Menton, qui conserve encore le souvenir du *Lysistrata* et du *Namouna*, les deux yachts du milliardaire américain James Gordon Bennett, propriétaire du *New York Herald Tribune*.

Portrait du docteur Henry Bennet.

« Le prestige des illustres endroits... »

« CE DÉCOR du haut Menton, ces clochers, ces églises, ces vieilles maisons ont pour nos yeux et nos cœurs le prestige des plus illustres endroits de la terre. »

PAUL VALÉRY

Ancien marché de la place aux Herbes.

Le casino Kursaal, *l'année de son inauguration (1909). Il est bâti d'après les plans de l'architecte danois Hans Georg Tersling, à qui l'on doit plusieurs édifices luxueux à Menton.*

LA PREMIÈRE GUERRE MONDIALE

Le 1er août 1914, le maire de Menton reçoit un ordre de mobilisation. Le lendemain, vers 18 heures, l'administration municipale, totalement désorganisée face à un semblable événement, enregistre les premiers départs de conscrits. Les communications sont interrompues entre la France et l'Italie. La crainte des Mentonnais a tout d'abord pour objet la position italienne. La ville, qui ne se trouve pas sur le front des opérations, transforme rapidement ses bâtiments et certains hôtels en hôpitaux militaires et en maisons de convalescence pour les blessés.

L'état d'esprit de la population se dégrade. Les prix des denrées et services ne cessent d'augmenter, le ravitaillement est rendu difficile et les finances communales sont en péril. S'ouvre alors une ère nouvelle…, celle des restrictions et du marché noir, qui dureront tout le temps du conflit. Le 5 février 1917, des carnets pour l'obtention du sucre sont distribués. Le 9 février, la municipalité démissionne car elle ne peut plus faire face à ses obligations. À partir de juillet 1918, le ravitaillement fait toujours défaut, mais la présence des troupes américaines rassure. Le *Riviera Palace*, le *Winter Palace*, *Les Îles Britanniques* et le *Beau Rivage* se proposent pour accueillir les soldats d'outre-Atlantique. Le 11 novembre 1918, l'annonce de l'armistice provoque une immense manifestation de joie. Dès le mois de décembre, chacun songe à la reprise des affaires, qui se fera attendre encore deux années.

Affiche du 15e corps des armées italiennes.

L'ENTRE-DEUX-GUERRES

Après la Première Guerre mondiale, la croissance démographique se ralentit. En 1921, la population sédentaire compte 18 645 habitants ; elle ne s'élèvera qu'à 21 703 en 1936. Menton attire toujours des résidents, mais la puissante colonie britannique réduit les autres nationalités à un rôle de minorités, voire d'intruses. Les Anglais ne viennent plus pour se soigner, mais pour jouir d'une existence agréable dans un cadre ensoleillé. Les saisons se suivent et se ressemblent dans l'insouciance de la paix retrouvée, jusqu'à la crise de 1930.

De 1929 à 1935, le nombre d'hivernants diminue fâcheusement, passant de 32 486 à 14 488. En 1936, les quinze jours de congés payés annuels accordés aux travailleurs sont utilisés pour un séjour sur la Côte d'Azur, mais malgré la succession de deux saisons, celle d'hiver et celle d'été, le tourisme mentonnais est confronté à de sérieux embarras. Durant l'hiver 1937-1938, cinq hôtels ferment leurs portes. À cette crise s'ajoutent des problèmes sociaux aigus. Des conflits naissent à la faveur d'événements nationaux et internationaux, mais également locaux. En 1932, une coalition de gauche prend la direction de la municipalité et installe à sa tête un médecin radical-socialiste, le docteur Adrien Camaret. L'année suivante, la construction du nouveau casino provoque la scission des Mentonnais en deux blocs irrémédiablement opposés. Mais à partir de 1938, la population pressent l'inévitable drame avec la menace d'une guerre contre l'Italie. Manifestations et heurts ne cessent entre partisans et adversaires du fascisme. On craint le pire. Dès septembre 1939 est élaboré un plan d'évacuation du Bassin mentonnais.

LA SECONDE GUERRE MONDIALE ET L'ANNEXION À L'ITALIE : 1940-1943

En raison de la situation sensible pour Menton, qui compte un grand nombre d'habitants risquant de refluer sur la « position de résistance », le haut commandement exige l'évacuation de la ville.

Le 3 juin 1940, dans la soirée, l'ordre est exécuté. La population est alors répartie entre Antibes-Juan-les-Pins et Cannes. Le 7 juin, un nouvel ordre réclame la poursuite de l'exode vers les Pyrénées-Orientales ; lorsque surviendront les tragiques inondations de la Têt en octobre 1940, les Mentonnais seront de nouveau obligés de trouver un ultime refuge, dans le département du Var.

Le 11 juin 1940, l'Italie déclare la guerre à la France déjà vaincue. Le 24 juin, malgré la remarquable résistance de l'armée des Alpes, l'armistice livre Menton à l'occupation italienne qui, très vite, se transforme en une véritable annexion.

L'organisation administrative, judiciaire et militaire de la ville est réglée par un décret du Duce en date du 30 juillet 1940. Le rôle clé du dispositif mis en place est dévolu au commissaire civil, qui se substitue au préfet

La ligne de démarcation au poste de passage du pont de l'Union.

vis-à-vis de l'administration communale, ce qui n'empêche pas un petit noyau de résistants d'assurer la liaison clandestine et administrative de Menton avec la zone occupée.

La population ressent de plus en plus la volonté d'une italianisation forcée de la part des troupes occupantes. Au début de 1943, les grands hôtels situés sur les collines abritent le siège de la 4e armée italienne, avec le général Vercellone et son état-major. Cependant, en juillet, l'Italie s'effondre. Le retour de Menton au sein de la communauté française intervient le 8 septembre 1943 ; une nouvelle occupation débute… allemande cette fois.

DE L'OCCUPATION ALLEMANDE À LA LIBÉRATION : 1943-1945

La ville est administrée par une délégation spéciale, présidée par un préfet honoraire, mais elle est de fait contrôlée par les Allemands, qui occupent aussi toute la zone sud du pays. Pourtant, dès la fin de l'année 1942, les forces alliées ont débarqué en Afrique du

Les bombardements de juin 1944 à l'entrée du cap Martin (le fort du cap).

Nord, préludant à la reconquête du territoire, qui débute avec la libération de la Corse à la fin 1943. En février-mars 1944, la Feldkommandantur fait évacuer le bord de mer afin d'avoir une totale liberté d'action. Il est désormais interdit de vivre dans la ville à moins d'en justifier l'impérieuse nécessité.

Le 6 juin 1944, les Alliés sont en Normandie. Le 15 août, ils débarquent à Dramont (Var) et libèrent la Provence. Le 25 août, Menton est coupé du monde extérieur. Du 2 au 3 septembre, les canons de la marine alliée bombardent le mont Agel, point culminant du bassin versant monégasque, où se sont retranchées des arrière-gardes. Le 6 septembre, les Allemands quittent Menton ; le lendemain, le fort du mont Agel est enlevé par les troupes françaises.

Le 8 septembre, les parachutistes canadiens et américains entrent dans Menton. La ville est libérée. Mais la haute vallée de la Roya et le massif de l'Authion, face à la frontière italienne et au col de Tende, sont toujours aux mains des Allemands, qui remettent en état les fortifications et poursuivent les bombardements. Le 4 octobre 1944, la population civile encore présente est évacuée. Devant la menace permanente des Allemands, la région est déclarée « zone réservée ». Il est impossible d'y pénétrer ou d'en sortir sans un laissez-passer. Le 8 février 1945, les quelque 1 000 personnes qui n'avaient pas souhaité quitter Menton sont à leur tour évacuées. Le 1er mars est créé le commandement du front des Alpes, avec à sa tête le général Doyen. À son arrivée dans les Alpes-Maritimes, la 1re DFL (Division française libre), « noyau dur » des Forces françaises libres,

Les nouveaux aménagements de la baie orientale (1960-1964).

Le nouveau port de Menton à Garavan, aménagé en 1967.

est renforcée. Le 10 avril, elle passe à l'attaque; deux jours après, l'Authion est enlevé au prix de nombreux morts. Il faut attendre le 18 juin 1945 pour que la région Sospel-Roya soit enfin libérée.

• • • La reconquête et le temps présent

Une fois la région reconquise, seuls 13 864 Mentonnais reviennent d'un long exil, pour retrouver une ville qui a souffert sous les bombes : 75 % des immeubles sont endommagés; 10 % d'entre eux sont détruits. Le 11 novembre 1948, Menton est cité à l'ordre du Corps d'armée et reçoit la croix de guerre avec étoile de vermeil. Mais la ville ne retrouvera son aspect d'avant-guerre qu'au cours des années 1960. Profitant de l'essor

économique et de l'accroissement de sa population consécutif à la décolonisation, les trois municipalités successives conduiront une politique de grands travaux d'aménagement et de modernisation de la station climatique.

LES GRANDS TRAVAUX

Partiellement détruite en 1944 par les armées allemandes en déroute, la jetée portuaire est restaurée entre 1957 et 1960, élargie puis dotée de l'équipement nécessaire aux plaisanciers. Entre 1960 et 1964, une contre-jetée et des épis d'amarrage complètent le port, qui sera encore rénové de 1992 à 1995. De 1965 à 1973, l'aménagement de la baie orientale est réalisé, et le complexe du port privé de Garavan est inauguré en 1967. Nouvelle voie littorale, promenade piétonnière, plages, stade, centre commercial et établissements résidentiels et commerciaux voient le jour. La double artère qui part de la frontière pour rejoindre le quai Bonaparte et le tunnel du vieux Menton est achevée en 1973. Dans les vallées, est entreprise la couverture des torrents, qui permet d'ouvrir des voies de circulation. Une gare routière est alors bâtie, ainsi qu'un groupe scolaire et divers équipements sportifs. Un nouveau quartier voit le jour, Saint-Roman, qui se développe encore à l'aube du XXIe s.

Au cours des années 1980, en face du marché couvert, les travaux de transformation de la baie ouest sont lancés. Un endiguement permet de mettre le Bastion en valeur. Un jardin suspendu sur le rivage, un parking sous terre et de surface, un équipement sportif complètent l'ensemble. Au cours de la décennie suivante, on entreprend la construction d'une station d'épuration souterraine, qui manquait cruellement. Toujours dans cette baie, surgissent de grands édifices résidentiels qui modifient la physionomie du front de mer. Le centre-ville n'est pas oublié. Deux collèges sont inaugurés : Guillaume-Vento, en 1993 ; André-Maurois, en 2003. Une place est aménagée, qui offre au vieux musée mu-

Le collège Guillaume-Vento, dessiné par les architectes niçois Danielle Dogliani, Pierre Baptiste et Pierre Bernasconi. Il a été inauguré en 1993.

Le jardin du Campanin, créé en 1998.

Villa Foucher de Careïl construite boulevard de Garavan en 1892-1895. Les plans de cet édifice sont attribués à l'architecte Charles Garnier.

nicipal une remarquable perspective. Enfin, à partir de 1974, la rue Saint-Michel devient une artère piétonnière jusqu'à la place du Cap, rendue à la population en 1987, qui voit son débouché oriental orné du jardin du Campanin en 1998.

LE TOURISME TOUJOURS...

Conséquence de la guerre, 18 hôtels cessent leur activité entre 1946 et 1948. Malgré la reprise économique des années 1960, la situation de l'hôtellerie ne s'améliore guère. En 1969, 9 hôtels ferment leurs portes. Aussi les hôteliers sont-ils obligés de trouver des solutions innovantes pour rentabiliser leurs investissements. Deux formes d'aménagement sont associées : un immeuble de rapport et un hôtel moderne. Mais, à la fin du XXe s., on assiste toujours à la cessation d'activité de certains établissements.

En réalité, la vie de la station climatique a bien changé. Un nouveau type d'accueil tend à se développer, avec les maisons de vacances ou de retraite. À chaque saison correspond une clientèle spécifique, plus jeune et plus cosmopolite l'été, d'une génération plus aisée l'hiver. Bien que les saisons intermédiaires soient des périodes parfois délicates pour l'économie touristique, malgré le rajeunissement de l'image de Menton, la vieille « perle de la France » si chère au géographe Élisée Reclus a su tout à la fois conserver son prestige et se métamorphoser.

Témoignage bien vivant des grandes heures de la Côte d'Azur, par ses musées, son patrimoine architectural ancien, la luxuriance de ses villas et de ses palaces de la Belle Époque, ses jardins d'exception, Menton est un écrin qui renferme sept siècles d'histoire, sans qu'y soit jamais occultée celle du temps présent.

le Guide
de Menton

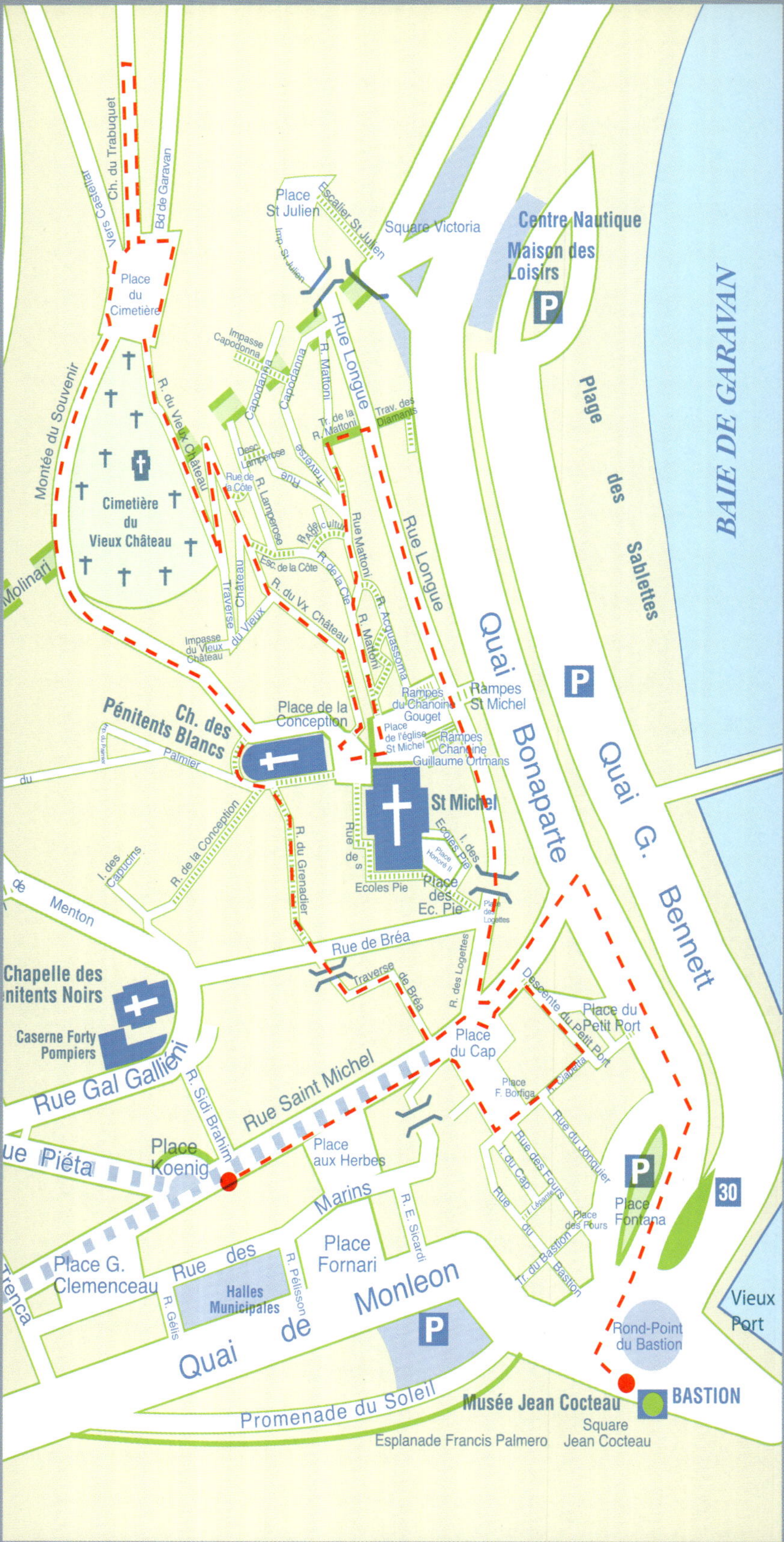

Vers Castellar
Ch. du Trabuquet
Bd de Garavan
Place du Cimetière
Place St Julien
Escalier St Julien
Imp. St Julien
Square Victoria
Centre Nautique
Maison des Loisirs
P
BAIE DE GARAVAN
Plage des Sablettes
Impasse Capodanna
Capodanna
R. Mattoni
Rue Longue
Tr. de la R. Mattoni
Trav. des Diamants
Montée du Souvenir
Cimetière du Vieux Château
R. du Vieux Château
Desc. Lamperose
Rue de la Côte
R. Lamperose
Traverse
Esc. de la Côte
R. de la Côte
Rue Mattoni
Molinari
Traverse du Vieux Château
Impasse du Vieux Château
R. du Vx Château
Quai Bonaparte
Quai G. Bennett
Rampes du Chanoine Gouget
Rampes St Michel
Place de la Conception
Ch. des Pénitents Blancs
Palmier
du
Place de l'église St Michel
Rampes Chanoine Guillaume Ortmans
St Michel
R. du Grenadier
Rue des Ecoles Pie
Ecoles Pie
Place Honoré II
Place des Ec. Pie
Place des Logettes
R. de la Conception
I. des Capucins
de Menton
Rue de Bréa
Traverse de Bréa
R. des Logettes
Descente du Petit Port
Place du Petit Port
Chapelle des Pénitents Noirs
Caserne Forty Pompiers
Place du Cap
Rue Gal Gallieni
R. Sidi Brahim
Rue Saint Michel
Place F. Borfiga
R. Ciapetta
Rue du Jonquier
Place Koenig
Place aux Herbes
ue Piéta
Rue des Fours
I. du Cap
Rue du Bastion
Place Fontana
30
Marins
R. E. Sicardi
Place Fornari
Place des Fours
Tr. du Bastion
Place G. Clemenceau
Rue des
R. Pélisson
Halles Municipales
R. Gélis
Trenca
Quai de Monleon
Vieux Port
Rond-Point du Bastion
Musée Jean Cocteau
BASTION
Square Jean Cocteau
Promenade du Soleil
Esplanade Francis Palmero

Le centre historique

Du Vieux-Port à l'hôtel Adhémar de Lantagnac

Formant un véritable labyrinthe, les rues et ruelles qui dévalent les pentes du vieux Menton depuis le cimetière du Vieux-Château rejoignent la mer dans le quartier du Vieux-Port. Toutes portent des noms évocateurs : Aquassoma, Capodanna, Lampedusa, Mattoni, noms de pirates et… peut-être de légendes.

1

2

3

4

1. La rue Longue.
2. Vue générale de la vieille ville.
3. Le parvis Saint-Michel, un soir de festival.
4. Le Vieux-Port.

Le Vieux-Port

Quais Napoléon-III, Impératrice-Eugénie, Gordon-Bennett

Capitainerie : quai Napoléon-III
Téléphone : 04 93 35 80 56

JUSQU'AU MILIEU du XIXe s., il n'existait à Menton aucun ouvrage pour accueillir les bateaux, hormis un mouillage de fortune au Portigliolo, petit port dévolu aux embarcations des patrons pêcheurs, et à la Grava (la « grève »), une plage destinée à l'amarrage des bâtiments de commerce.

LE CHANTIER de construction du port de commerce et de pêche commence en 1869 et ne s'achève qu'en 1878, tout au moins en ce qui concerne la grande digue de protection. Les travaux de la jetée, du quai et de l'endiguement – compris entre l'ancienne place de halage, la Grava et le Bastion – ne se terminent qu'en 1883. Le mur d'abri et celui de la contre-jetée sont bâtis en 1886.

APRÈS LA DESTRUCTION partielle du Bastion, de la grande digue et du quai lors de la Seconde Guerre mondiale, le port est restauré entre 1956 et 1958. Le quai est élargi et prend le nom de l'empereur Napoléon III. À partir de 1959 et jusqu'en 1965, une contre-jetée et un quai dédié à l'impératrice Eugénie viennent fermer le havre de Menton. L'aménagement du port est complété par une suite de nouvelles voûtes qui abritent bars et restaurants. Un quai est enfin agencé ; son nom honore la mémoire de Gordon Bennett (1841-1918). Il dirigea durant quarante ans, depuis sa villa de Beaulieu ou à bord de

3

1-2. Vieux-Port.
3. Quai Bonaparte.
4. Jardin du Campanin.

1

2

4

ses yachts amarrés dans la baie, une véritable institution de la presse : le *New York Herald Tribune*.

EN 1970, le centre nautique et la Maison des loisirs sont créés dans le prolongement de la promenade de la mer. Des œuvres d'art agrémentent ce site : une sculpture en cuivre martelé de Volti, *Saint Michel de la mer* (quai Impératrice-Eugénie) ; un panneau de céramique d'Henri Plisson, *La Mer* (façade de la Maison des loisirs) ; un bas-relief de Joseph Gazan, *Saint Michel, défenseur de Menton* (escalier des Sablettes).

LE VIEUX-PORT, désormais affecté à la seule navigation de plaisance, accueille près de 1 300 embarcations. Rénové à partir de 1992, il est doté d'une nouvelle capitainerie, édifiée en 1995.

À l'extrémité du quai Gordon-Bennett, l'escalier des Sablettes nous conduit sur le quai de Monléon, face au jardin du Campanin.

Jardin du Campanin

À la jonction des quais de Monléon et Bonaparte

À LA FIN DU XIXe S., le Petit-Port a laissé place à ce qui était appelé autrefois « le Jardinet », où s'élevait un édicule à décor de faïence dû à l'architecte mentonnais Adrien Rey [→ p. 30]. Remplacé dans les années 1960 par une station-service, le Jardinet, qui retrouve une nouvelle vie en 1998, se nomme désormais « le jardin du Campanin » (« campanile »).

SA CONCEPTION est confiée au paysagiste Olivier Chardin qui prend le parti de créer sur un petit espace une atmosphère évocatrice de la Provence, de l'Italie et de l'Andalousie. À l'ombre d'un pin parasol, adossés au mur d'une maison, des bancs inspirés de ceux du jardin de *Fontana Rosa* [→ p. 69] encadrent une gloriette. Les colonnades de la tonnelle, sur laquelle s'étire une glycine, représentent le classicisme. Les céramiques rendent hommage à l'écrivain Blasco Ibáñez. Clin d'œil à la Provence, la jarre introduit ici un élément familier et, bien mieux que ne le ferait un peintre coloriste, une grande variété de plantes décline la plus subtile gamme des bleus : plumbagos, sauges, agapanthes, asters, lavandes... L'olivier révèle toute sa valeur emblématique et confère son unité à cette composition complexe constituée d'un cuvier italien posé sur une calade (sol de galets juxtaposés) délimitée par des céramiques bleues et entourée de jolies colonnades antiques. Enfin, la présence de palmiers et de plantes tropicales (jacarandas, daturas, pittosporums, cycas...) rend compte des introductions multiples faites surtout depuis le XIXe s.

Nous sortons du jardin du Campanin, et nous empruntons, à gauche, le quai Bonaparte.

Quai Bonaparte

EN 1796, le général Bonaparte souhaite qu'on entreprenne le contournement de la vieille ville afin de rendre plus aisée la circulation. Le quai, réalisé de 1806 à 1811, est plaqué aux maisons-tours qui, jusqu'alors, avaient leurs soubassements dans l'eau. En 1902, le quai Bonaparte, parallèle à l'actuel quai Gordon-Bennett, est élargi par l'adjonction d'une série de voûtes à l'aplomb de la vieille ville. Les travaux sont achevés en 1903. Quelque

1

1. Place Honoré-II.
2. Place des Logettes.
3. Rue des Logettes.
4. Rue Longue.

2

3

4

temps plus tard, un trottoir est aménagé et orné d'un alignement de platanes et palmiers.

Nous poursuivons notre itinéraire sur le quai Bonaparte en direction de la rue Saint-Michel, puis nous empruntons, à droite, la rue des Logettes.

Place des Logettes

CETTE PETITE PLACE, à la jonction du quai Bonaparte et de la rue des Logettes (ancienne voie romaine), tire son nom de sa situation en belvédère au-dessus de la place du Port. Ornée d'une pergola et d'un décor de céramique qui rappelle l'histoire mentonnaise, la place s'étend de la porte Saint-Antoine jusqu'à la place du Cap, où a été réinstallée une fontaine datant du XVIIIe s.

LORS DE L'EXTENSION de la ville, le fort Saint-Antoine, n'ayant plus d'utilité, a été arasé, mais son infrastructure demeure sous la place actuelle.

Depuis la place des Logettes, nous nous dirigeons vers la rue des Écoles-Pies, puis nous gravissons ses quelques marches pour rejoindre la place Honoré-II.

De la place Honoré-II à la porte Saint-Antoine

INAUGURÉE en 1975, la place Honoré-II porte le nom du prince de Monaco (1597-1662) auquel on doit l'édification de la basilique Saint-Michel, du Bastion, des couvents des Capucins et de la Madone, ainsi que le percement de la rue Neuve. Pour la célébration du tricentenaire de la consécration de Saint-Michel (1975), plusieurs maisons ont été démolies afin de dégager ses fondations, faites sur les fortifications du Moyen Âge. En effet, l'ancienne redoute Saint-Jean a servi d'infrastructure à la basilique.

LE LONG de la rue des Écoles-Pies se dressent les murs de ce fortin – on aperçoit toujours une bouche à feu – qui protégeait l'une des portes de la ville jusqu'à la hauteur de l'ancien chemin de ronde.

LA VILLE MÉDIÉVALE était ceinte de remparts percés de huit portes, dont trois subsistent aujourd'hui. La porte Saint-Antoine, accès principal de la ville, du côté ouest, présente encore une antique échoppe. En ces lieux s'élevait une chapelle dédiée à saint Antoine, transformée en habitation en 1793.

Nous laissons pour l'instant la basilique Saint-Michel et passons la porte Saint-Antoine pour emprunter la rue Longue, nommée successivement *carriera Subtranea*, *carriera Recta*, rue Grimaldi, puis rue de la République.

Rue Longue

SITUÉE parallèlement au quai Bonaparte, la rue Longue est l'artère principale de la vieille ville. Entre la porte Saint-Julien, à l'est, et la porte Saint-Antoine, au sud-ouest, elle suit le tracé de la voie romaine Julia Augusta. Le long de celle-ci s'élevait, jusqu'au début du XVIe s., le rempart qui protégeait la ville du côté mer et prenait fondation sur les rochers du rivage ; il a disparu en raison des endiguements successifs. À partir du XVIe s., la ville se développe et des maisons sont construites sur ce rempart, comme en témoignent quelques linteaux sculptés aux n°s 4 (1513), 45 (1533),

1

2

3

1. Les Rampes.
2-4. Hôtel Pretti de Saint-Ambroise : vestibule, décor plafonnant de l'escalier, décor du vestibule.

4

56 (1534) et 129 (1543). De ravissantes portes aux jambages en pierre de taille rythment cette artère étroite et obscure : n°s 5, 22 *bis*, 23, 27, 30, 33.

LA FAÇADE MARITIME présente de nos jours un étagement allant jusqu'à neuf niveaux, par ajout d'étages inférieurs et supérieurs (quatre niveaux, depuis la rue Longue jusqu'au quai Bonaparte).

Après avoir parcouru environ le tiers de la rue Longue, nous atteignons ce qui est communément nommé « les Rampes ».

Les Rampes

Les Rampes ont été construites au cours de deux périodes. En 1753, Honoré III, en accord avec la commune, fait raser un pâté de maisons près de Saint-Michel, pour pouvoir construire un escalier qui permette de rejoindre la rue Longue depuis la basilique située en surplomb. Les travaux sont confiés à l'architecte niçois Michel Castellinard. Les Rampes, inaugurées en 1757 lors de la visite du prince, sont alors constituées de deux volées : les rampes du Chanoine-Ortmans et du Chanoine-Gouget. Ces deux noms évoquent des prêtres de la paroisse : Guillaume Ortmans (1865-1950) est le fondateur du patronage Saint-Louis-de Gonzague (1898), qui donna naissance, deux ans plus tard, à l'Association de la garde de Menton ; Charles Gouget (1893-1966) dotera celle-ci d'une fanfare, en 1925.

EN 2000, après un effondrement de la voûte supportant les escaliers, l'ancien collecteur des eaux pluviales aménagé lors du premier chantier a été retrouvé. Dans les années 1940-1941, les Rampes sont prolongées de la rue Longue au quai Bonaparte par les Italiens, qui avaient annexé Menton ; les quelques bâtiments qui se trouvaient à cet endroit avaient été bombardés. D'une certaine manière, les autorités occupantes ont achevé avec ce nouvel escalier (la rampe Saint-Michel) la perspective commencée deux siècles auparavant, mais ce prolongement ne possède qu'une seule volée de marches. Les Rampes nous font bénéficier, depuis la rue Longue, d'une vue remarquable sur la mer, la frontière et les montagnes de Bordighera.

Face à la rampe Saint-Michel se dresse l'hôtel Pretti de Saint-Ambroise.

Hôtel Pretti de Saint-Ambroise

45, rue Longue

EN 1533, la famille Pretti fait construire l'un des plus beaux édifices présents dans cette rue. En 1705, Antoine Ier Grimaldi anoblit Alexandre Pretti et lui accorde le fief de Saint-Ambroise (dans l'actuel quartier Carnolès). La masse imposante de cette demeure patricienne est assez caractéristique de l'architecture baroque de type génois, en cours à Menton au XVIIe s. La façade principale s'élève sur trois niveaux, qui comprennent un rez-de-chaussée rehaussé d'un *mezzanino*, un premier étage noble et un deuxième étage en attique. Sur cette façade, on peut lire une inscription gravée, extraite du Magnificat : *MISERICORDIA EIUS A PROGENIE IN PROGENIES TIMENTIBUS EUM*, suivie de la mention : *ANNO DOMINI MDCIL*. Dans le vestibule se

1. Vue aérienne de la rue Longue.
2. Vieille ville (partie supérieure).
3. Rue Longue (partie supérieure).
4. Ancien palais princier.

trouvait une lance turque rapportée de la bataille de Lépante par Barthélemy Pretti. À ce combat livré aux Turcs par don Juan d'Autriche participèrent deux galères des Grimaldi, chacune sous la direction d'un Mentonnais : *La Patrona*, commandée par Lorenzo Rossi, portait l'insigne ; *La Capitana*, commandée par Giacomo Laurenti, portait le fanal.
À LA SUITE du tremblement de terre de 1887, un décor « à la pompéienne » se substitue à l'ornementation baroque de l'hôtel. De fines guirlandes de verdure encadrent des tableaux à décor de lions (rappelant les armes de la famille) et de masques. Des rinceaux de feuillage et une frise de grecques soulignent la partie basse lambrissée.

De la rue Longue à la traverse des Diamants

EN POURSUIVANT notre chemin dans la partie supérieure de la rue Longue, nous découvrons, au n° 61, une maison reliée par un pont à celle qui lui fait face : il s'agit de l'unique témoignage de l'élégant style XVIIIe présent dans cette artère. Le rang social de la famille qui la fit bâtir est attesté par l'ampleur du vestibule, où l'on pouvait mettre à l'abri deux chaises à porteurs. Au-dessus des portes, les lignes courbes de la voûte et les cartouches rappellent le style rocaille.
UN PEU PLUS LOIN, dans la rue Longue, nous voyons sur notre droite la traverse des Diamants.

Traverse des Diamants

115, rue Longue

CE PETIT PASSAGE voûté permettait d'accéder directement à la mer, au pied du rocher de la vieille ville ; se trouvait là un débarcadère destiné aux princes, afin qu'ils rejoignent sans détour leur palais. Selon une légende, les dames de la suite princière égaraient souvent leurs bijoux dans cette traverse obscure et les Mentonnais, à la recherche des pierres précieuses, accouraient après chacun de leur passage. Plus vraisemblable est ce fait qu'on rapporte : la nuit venue, le scintillement des reflets de la lune sur la mer ressemblait à des éclats de diamants.

À quelques pas de la traverse se dresse, à droite, la façade de l'ancien palais des princes de Monaco.

Ancien palais princier

123, rue Longue

L'ANCIENNE MAISON seigneuriale bâtie au XVe s. pour Jean Ier Grimaldi dans la rue Longue est totalement transformée, deux siècles après, par Honoré II. Ce palais, dont la surface est augmentée par l'achat de deux maisons qui le jouxtaient, est achevé en 1650. Le prince y fait alors apposer une plaque commémorative, sur laquelle on peut lire : « Honoré II, pour remplacer l'antique citadelle détruite par l'ouvrage des guerres [...], agrandit et embellit cette maison réservée auparavant à l'usage d'un particulier, maintenant à celui des princes. »
AU XVIIIe S., la résidence, délaissée au profit du palais Carnolès, accueille les services du gouverneur de Menton.
Sous la Révolution, elle est tout d'abord réaménagée pour abriter la mairie, puis vendue comme bien national. L'édifice a la particularité d'avoir l'étage noble au troisième niveau. Le décor de la façade d'origine et l'aménagement intérieur ont disparu.

1

2

4

1. Quartier Saint-Julien.
2. Porte Saint-Julien.
3. L'ancien hôpital.
4. Rue Mattoni.

À proximité de l'ancien palais princier, nous remarquons, au n° 129, la maison Gaspard de Bottini (XVIe s.), qui présente un beau linteau de pierre en façade. Celui qui orne la maison Clavesana (XVIe s.), au n° 131, est en schiste rouge. Face à cette dernière, au n° 76, s'élevait, avant le rattachement de Menton à la France en 1861, le premier temple de l'Église réformée, dont les offices furent célébrés pendant quelques années dans une pièce du rez-de-chaussée.
Arrivés à l'extrémité de la rue Longue, nous atteignons le quartier Saint-Julien.

Quartier Saint-Julien

SITUÉ AU-DELÀ de la porte orientale de la ville, ce quartier placé sous le vocable de saint Julien possédait un oratoire qui a disparu aujourd'hui. Sur une façade de la place, on remarque une fresque peinte au XIXe s., qui représente Julien éduquant les petits enfants.
LA PORTE SAINT-JULIEN, anciennement nommée *Porta Julia,* fermait la ville. Par un édit du 18 janvier 1687, on y percevait les droits sur les marchandises en provenance du comté de Vintimille. Cette porte étant alors barrée par une chaîne, la taxe d'importation prit le nom de « droit de chaîne » (*caena*).
SURPLOMBANT la place Saint-Julien, un vaste bâtiment arcadé à la florentine a accueilli jusqu'en 1981 l'hôpital Saint-Julien, actuellement en restructuration. Cet établissement a été construit sur les plans de Victor Sabatier [→ p. 31], élève de Viollet-le-Duc, nommé architecte des Alpes-Maritimes en 1860. Il est situé sur une propriété d'Henriette de Monléon – veuve du baron Honoré Ardoïno – qui la céda à la Ville en 1861.

3

Avant de revenir sur nos pas, nous pouvons apercevoir, à droite, entre les maisons, une partie de l'ancien rempart médiéval. Nous redescendons la rue Longue et empruntons à droite la rue Mattoni.

De la rue Mattoni à l'arc d'Antoine

AVANT LA CONSTRUCTION des Rampes, au milieu du XVIIIe s., la rue Mattoni permettait d'accéder directement à la basilique Saint-Michel depuis le palais princier. Son nom serait dû à son pavage en briques pleines (*mattoni*, en italien). Cette artère où se trouvait, sous l'Ancien Régime, la maison commune (l'équivalent de l'hôtel de ville) fut nommée « rue des Patriotes » entre 1793 et 1801. Dans la rue Mattoni débouchent la traverse et la rue Capodanna ; dans son prolongement, on trouve les rues Lampedose (ou Lampedusa) et Aquassoma. Ces noms ont fait naître une légende qui rapporte que Menton fut fondé par des pirates venant de Lampedusa (petite île, entre Malte et la Tunisie) : ils se seraient établis sur la colline rocheuse de Menton et y auraient bâti une ville à leur convenance, tenant du labyrinthe. De là, ils pouvaient faire s'égarer facilement les assaillants qui réussissaient à franchir l'enceinte. Ces pirates auraient donné aux trois premières rues construites les noms des

1

2

3

1. Intersection des rues Mattoni et de la Côte.
2. Arc d'Antoine.
3. Arc d'Antoine (aquarelle de Rino Golinelli).

leurs : Capodanna, Mattoni, Aquassoma. Au-delà de la légende, il est certain que cette urbanisation en chicanes et en ruelles tortueuses a dû faciliter la défense des Mentonnais contre leurs agresseurs, pirates ou barbaresques.
CAPODANNA est en fait une altération de *Capuana* : la *carriera Capuana* est la rue haute, par opposition à la *carriera Subtranea*, la rue inférieure (rue Longue). Le nom de la place des Fours, près de cette artère, nous rappelle que se trouvaient ici les fours banaux de la commune.
CES FOURS ont été indirectement l'une des causes de la révolution mentonnaise de 1848. En effet, le prince possédait en propre les moulins et les fours. Lorsque les Mentonnais voulaient moudre leurs grains ou presser leurs olives, le prince mettait ses moulins à leur disposition en échange d'une redevance en nature, c'est-à-dire un impôt. Quand ils souhaitaient cuire leur pain, ils étaient obligés de le faire dans les fours princiers ; à cette opération correspondait une redevance en argent. Pour les habitants, fours et moulins entraînaient des taxes jugées à la longue abusives.
Quelques traces visibles sur les façades témoignent de l'un des rares incendies qu'ait connus la ville, la propagation des flammes ayant été favorisée par l'abondante réserve de bois.
DANS LA DESCENTE Capodanna, qui surplombe la place des Fours, nous pouvons voir des corbeaux, pierres qui servaient à poser des claies destinées au séchage des fruits et légumes (raisin, jujubes...) ainsi que des filets de pêche dans la partie basse de la ville. Nous pouvons aussi noter l'épaisseur des murs des maisons et leurs clés de bois dans la muraille.

LA RUE AQUASSOMA est une ruelle en partie voûtée, qui prend son nom d'un abreuvoir où l'on menait les bêtes ; l'expression *aiga-sauma* est constituée de deux mots : *aiga* (eau) et *sauma* (ânesse). C'est dans ce quartier que Jacques Doillon a tourné *Un sac de billes*, film adapté du célèbre roman de Joseph Joffo.

En remontant la rue Mattoni, nous nous dirigeons vers le parvis de Saint-Michel.

Arc d'Antoine et parvis de la basilique Saint-Michel

SUR LE PARVIS de la basilique, nous nous trouvons dans le décor d'un véritable théâtre en plein air qui met en situation la façade de la basilique et celles de la chapelle de l'Immaculée-Conception (dite des Pénitents blancs), de l'ancien collège, de l'ancien hôpital et de l'arc d'Antoine. Le parvis, rythmé par les verticales des clochers de l'Immaculée-Conception et de Saint-Michel, et par son campanile, s'ouvre par des rampes divergentes qui descendent vers la mer. Ce que nous pouvons considérer aujourd'hui comme une œuvre harmonieuse, synthèse de la scène urbaine et du paysage naturel, a nécessité, depuis la pose de la première pierre de Saint-Michel en 1619, jusqu'à l'achèvement de sa façade orientale en 1819, deux siècles de travaux.
EN 1701, Antoine Ier fait transformer l'arc de soutien de la rue Mattoni (qui consolidait la verticalité des maisons) en arc de triomphe pour commémorer le début de son règne. En 1757, Honoré III fait orner le parvis de la basilique d'une calade de galets blancs et noirs. Celle-ci associe les losanges des armes princières et le *H* arrondi, initiale du souverain.

Le festival de musique

André Böröcz, journaliste à la radio hongroise, est envoyé en mission à Paris, en 1946. En août 1949, au cours d'un séjour sur la Côte d'Azur, il découvre Menton, gravit le double escalier monumental de la vieille ville, se promène sur le parvis de Saint-Michel. Posé sur une fenêtre, un poste diffuse une partita pour violon de Jean-Sébastien Bach : c'est la révélation.

PARVIS DE LA BASILIQUE SAINT-MICHEL

Festival annuel, au mois d'août (en nocturne)

RENSEIGNEMENTS : **palais de l'Europe**
8, avenue Boyer – 06500 Menton
Téléphone : 04 92 41 76 95
Télécopie : 04 92 41 76 96
Courriel : ot-pro@villedementon.com

LA RENCONTRE entre la mer, le ciel, le parvis et la musique donne à Böröcz l'idée folle de fonder un festival ! Quatre ans plus tard, le 5 août 1950, le quatuor Végh inaugure une série prestigieuse de près de six cents concerts.

DURANT CINQUANTE ANS, jusqu'à sa mort, André Böröcz (1920-1998) fut l'infatigable et génial directeur musical du festival, aidé les premières années par son ami et compatriote Thomas Eördös. Personnalité attachante, il déborde d'idées, pétille d'intelligence et d'humour ; il sait mettre à l'aise, encourager et séduire les musiciens qu'il invite à Menton.

LE PARVIS est comme un balcon donnant sur la mer, enchâssé entre la basilique, une piazzetta en encorbellement dominée par la souriante chapelle des Pénitents blancs et les façades de la vieille ville entre lesquelles s'enfoncent les ruelles. Dans ce décor féerique à l'acoustique naturelle, les plus grands interprètes ont été chaleureusement accueillis.

ONT ÉTÉ PRÉSENTS des compositeurs reconnus tels que Benjamin Britten ou Francis Poulenc... Parmi les pianistes, qui furent les plus nombreux à honorer de leur présence le festival : Marguerite Long, Arthur Rubinstein, Emil Guilels, Samson François, Sviatoslav Richter, Georges Cziffra, Alfred Brendel, Maria João Pires, Martha Argerich... pour ne nommer que quelques figures mythiques.

COMMENT ne pas citer des violonistes tels que Jacques Thibaud, Isaac Stern, Yehudi Menuhin, Arthur Grumiaux, Igor et David Oistrakh..., des altistes à l'instar de Yuri Bashmet et de Gérard Caussé..., des violoncellistes aux noms prestigieux comme Pierre Fournier, Mstislav Rostropovitch, Paul Tortelier, Janos Starker, Yo-Yo Ma... ?

PRÉSENTES ENCORE, les flûtes de Jean-Pierre Rampal et de James Galway, la trompette de Maurice André, la harpe de Lily Laskine, les guitares d'Ida Presti et Alexandre Lagoya. Comment oublier les voix sublimes de Christa Ludwig, Elisabeth Schwarzkopf, Dietrich Fischer-Dieskau, Galina Vichnevskaïa, Ruggero Raimondi, Barbara Hendricks... ?

IL NE FAUDRAIT PAS omettre la musique de jazz, Dizzy Gillespie, Ray Charles, Keith Jarrett... ni celle des grandes traditions avec Ravi Shankar, Mikis Theodorakis, Paco de Lucía...

LES ENSEMBLES VOCAUX, les ensembles baroques et, surtout, les formations de musique de chambre ont été l'âme de ce festival... Tous les plus grands sont venus pour des instants d'éternité, pour des rencontres de rêve nées de l'imagination amoureuse d'André Böröcz : Karl Münchinger et Sviatoslav Richter, Wilhelm Kempff et l'Amadeus Quartett, les quatuors Végh, Bartók...

BERNARD GAVOTY exprimait en quelques mots l'atmosphère du festival : « L'étroit parvis de l'église Saint-Michel, haut lieu suspendu entre le ciel et la terre. »

Basilique Saint-Michel

Une première église placée sous le vocable de saint Michel, particulièrement vénéré dans le diocèse de Vintimille dont elle dépendait, est citée dans un acte de 1302, mais aucun texte ne précise le lieu où elle fut édifiée.

Ouverte tous les jours, sauf samedi matin et dimanche après-midi

- *Du 16 décembre au 30 octobre : de 10 h à 12 h et de 15 h à 17 h*
- *Du 1er novembre au 15 décembre : de 15 h à 17 h*

Cette première église était aussi un lieu de proclamation d'actes politiques et un lieu de sépulture pour les seigneurs et pour les Mentonnais.

Une deuxième église a été construite, au XVe s., pour accueillir une population plus nombreuse. Un dessin du XVIIe s. nous la montre bâtie sur la pointe de l'éperon rocheux, orientée est-ouest. Le modeste édifice de trois ou quatre travées en voûtes d'arêtes était surmonté d'un clocher au niveau du chœur.

Au début du XVIIe s., le prince Honoré II « réveille » la bourgade médiévale ; il la transforme par de grands travaux d'urbanisme. Elle est dotée d'un fortin sur la mer, les remparts sont percés pour créer de nouvelles rues.

Le souverain décide également de faire élever une belle et grande église en lieu et place de celle qui avait été bâtie au XVe s. Il pose la première pierre le 27 mai 1619.

La direction des travaux est confiée à Laurent Lavagna, *capo maestro della fabrica*, venu de Gênes. Les difficultés financières et techniques se révèlent assez nombreuses, aussi le chantier ne débute-t-il qu'au mois de mai 1639.

En 1653, l'église est ouverte au culte, mais il faut attendre le 8 mai 1675 pour que Mgr Maur Promontorio, évêque de Vintimille, la consacre en présence du prince Louis Ier. Elle n'est pas pour autant achevée, notamment en ce qui concerne les chapelles latérales. Quant à la façade, elle restera provisoire jusqu'au début du XIXe s. Le clocher, dénommé « la tour de l'Horloge », jugé trop petit, est complété en 1701 par un campanile de 53 mètres de haut.

1

4

2

L'intérieur

En pénétrant dans la basilique, nous sommes saisis par l'atmosphère émanant du lieu. Le baroque se prive résolument des grandes baies vitrées, leur préférant les petites lucarnes percées à la naissance de la voûte. La lumière apparaît ainsi un peu irréelle, forçant le visiteur à lever les yeux vers Dieu.

LA NEF. – Saint-Michel est construit selon un plan basilical en croix latine, sans déambulatoire ni transept saillant. La vaste nef de quatre travées, doublée de collatéraux percés de chapelles latérales, est prolongée par un chœur plus étroit dont l'entrée est marquée par un arc triomphal. Les supports de la nef centrale sont d'épaisses colonnes toscanes, leurs chapiteaux recevant les retombées des grandes arcades. La voûte de cette nef est en berceau plein cintre sans doubleau. La voûte primitive, en maçonnerie, a été remplacée après le tremblement de terre de 1887 par une voûte sur voliges beaucoup plus légère. Les lunettes de pénétration sont occupées par de simples baies aux vitres teintées et dépolies. Le décor plafonnant (fin XIXe s.) est dû à Guillaume Cerutti-Maori [→ p. 78]. Des tentures en damas de Gênes couleur amarante, offertes par le prince Honoré III lors de son mariage avec Marie-Catherine de Brignole-Sale en 1757, ornent la basilique à certaines

En 1819, grâce à une donation, la façade définitive est enfin mise en place, mettant un terme à deux siècles de travaux. En 1999, la Congrégation pour le culte divin et la discipline des sacrements confère à l'église Saint-Michel le titre et la dignité de basilique mineure. Un an plus tard, a lieu la proclamation solennelle en présence du prince héréditaire de Monaco, de l'archevêque de Monaco, des évêques de Nice et de Vintimille, assistés de nombreux membres du clergé.

AU COURS de la seconde moitié du XVIIe s., tous les chantiers ouverts dans le comté de Nice et dans la principauté se réfèrent au baroque italien. Menton, partie intégrante de la principauté, échappe aux influences piémontaises et adhère sans réserve au baroque génois, qui se caractérise par la permanence du style maniériste. L'Annunziata de Gênes va servir de modèle à Saint-Michel.

3

5

6

7

1. La nef.
2. La chaire.
3. Ange en bois doré, XVIIe s.
4. Le décor peint de la voûte : saint Michel.
5. Le buffet d'orgues.
6. Détail du retable d'Antoine Manchello.
7. Détail de la voûte.

périodes, accentuant le caractère baroque de l'édifice.

LE CHŒUR. – Clairement séparé du reste de l'édifice par l'arc triomphal, le chœur profond est monumentalisé par les ors et les faux marbres des pilastres. Son dallage de carreaux blancs et noirs est typique du classicisme. Le maître-autel du XVIIe s., en marqueterie de marbres polychromes, est composé, selon la tradition italienne, de tablettes curvilignes faisant converger les regards vers le tabernacle, point central de l'autel. Allégé de fines colonnettes, il est surmonté d'une surprenante statue de saint Michel du XIXe s. à l'allure théâtrale qu'encadre une parure d'autel; les chandeliers et les anges en bois doré datent du XVIIe s. Une couronne de bois doré surmonte l'ensemble. Elle supporte un lourd baldaquin de damas de Gênes amarante à galon doré.

LE RETABLE D'ANTOINE MANCHELLO. – Au-dessus des stalles, du côté épître (à droite de l'autel), ce retable signé du peintre monégasque Manchello est daté du 1er août 1565. Dans la partie centrale, saint Michel est entouré par saint Jean Baptiste (à gauche) et par saint Pierre (à droite), revêtu des insignes de la papauté; la tête ceinte d'une tiare, les épaules enveloppées d'une riche chape, il tient à la main les clés qui ouvrent les portes du ciel. Les personnages se détachent sur une vallée verdoyante où des angelots brandissent les instruments de la Passion. Dans la prédelle, partie inférieure du retable, est représentée la Cène. Dans la partie supérieure, la Vierge des douleurs porte son fils descendu de la Croix. Cette représentation, entourée par l'ange et la Vierge de l'Annonciation, est surmontée du buste de Dieu le Père. Face au retable de Manchello se trouvent une grande toile représentant Notre-Dame des Neiges, invoquée en temps de peste, ainsi que le diptyque de l'Annonciation.

LE BUFFET D'ORGUES. – Pièce maîtresse du chœur, le buffet d'orgues (XVIIe s.) placé dans la tribune, contre le chevet, attire le regard dès que l'on pénètre dans l'église. Conçu comme une façade, il est doté de belles colonnes en bois peint et doré qui soutiennent un entablement et un fronton brisé.

Ces orgues de facteur inconnu, comprenant 17 jeux, ont été classées monument historique en 1970.

LES CHAPELLES sont pour la plupart des chapelles funéraires de grandes familles mentonnaises.

1

1. Chapelle de l'Immaculée-Conception.
2. Détail du fronton.
3. L'autel.
4. Façade (dessin de G. Sadlier).

2

3

En sortant de la basilique Saint-Michel, nous remarquons, en face, une maison qui a abrité jusqu'en 1861 l'hôpital de la ville. Nous gravissons les marches jusqu'à la place de la Conception où se dresse, à gauche, l'ancien collège, devenu établissement scolaire, puis nous arrivons à la chapelle de l'Immaculée-Conception.

Chapelle de l'Immaculée-Conception

DITE AUSSI ***des Pénitents blancs***

Place de la Conception

Ouverte exceptionnellement
Renseignements à la basilique Saint-Michel

LA CONFRÉRIE des Disciplinants (ou des Pénitents blancs) apparaît à Menton en 1485 ; elle regroupait les gens de la terre : propriétaires et ouvriers agricoles qui, lors des grandes processions, devenaient anonymes devant Dieu, sous la bure du pénitent. Le rôle social des pénitents est important, aussi bien dans l'assistance des malades que dans celle des nécessiteux.
À L'ORIGINE, leur oratoire était situé dans l'actuelle rue du Vieux-Château. Au XVIIe s., ils l'abandonnent pour venir s'installer dans cette chapelle, près de la basilique Saint-Michel.

4

LA CHAPELLE a été édifiée entre 1680 et 1687, dans le quartier du Capitole, sur des terrains situés hors les murs de la cité médiévale, offerts par Louis Ier et la famille de Monléon. Témoin de l'extension de la ville vers l'ouest, elle est ouverte au culte en 1687. Jusqu'à la Révolution, elle sera le siège de la confrérie des Pénitents blancs. Fermée au culte en 1793, elle est transformée en club patriotique, puis en hôpital.
RENDUE à ses desservants traditionnels en 1808, elle est restaurée une première fois, de 1814 à 1818, mais sa voûte est détruite par le tremblement de terre de 1887. Trois ans plus tard, la voûte est relevée et décorée à la fresque par deux artistes de la région : Patrizio Rogolini et Guillaume Cerutti-Maori [→ p. 78], sur des plans dressés par l'architecte Sylvain Jauffret [→ p. 30].
LA CHAPELLE échappe aux lois sur les congrégations et la séparation des Églises et de l'État ; elle est de nouveau menacée lors des bombardements de 1944-1945. Classée monument historique en 1947, elle est entièrement rénovée et transformée en 1987.
CETTE CHAPELLE à nef unique est un très bel exemple de l'art de la Contre-Réforme. Les sculptures monumentales des divers saints vénérés par la confrérie scandent la nef et le sanctuaire. On peut remarquer les belles tentures en damas de Gênes cramoisi qui habillent tous les murs de la chapelle. Un chemin de croix du XVIIIe s. et des miroirs réflecteurs de lumière ponctuent ces tentures.

Depuis le parvis de la chapelle, nous empruntons les marches qui conduisent à la rue du Vieux-Château. Mais avant que nous les montions, notre regard se porte sur un pan de muraille long de 40 mètres et épais de plus de 2 mètres, avec plusieurs mâchicoulis. Des travaux récents ont permis d'établir que cette muraille continuait au-delà de la place, semblant englober sous sa protection la basilique Saint-Michel.

1

2

1-2-3. Rue du Vieux-Château.

4. Rue du Vieux-Château (dessin de F. Octobon).

3

Rue du Vieux-Château

LE NOM de la rue rappelle l'ouvrage fortifié qui couronnait la ville médiévale et était destiné à la protéger contre les envahisseurs génois, les barbaresques et autres pirates. Elle permet d'imaginer ce que pouvait être Menton à cette époque. De petites maisons basses, à un étage, s'échelonnent le long de ruelles étroites et sinueuses.

4

ARRÊTONS-NOUS devant la maison du Pénitent, au n° 4. Bâtie au XVIe s., elle a une demie-voûte brisée de brique et des petites fenêtres au linteau en bois dont la menuiserie est encore à petits châssis. Au Moyen Âge, les maisons sont toutes bâties selon le même type. Les matériaux employés pour les murs sont des pierres provenant de l'épierrage des champs, des galets et des réemplois de terrailles (tuiles, briques et vaisselle usagée) ; l'ensemble, lié par un mortier de chaux non étanche, permet au bâtiment de « respirer » et de lutter contre l'humidité ambiante. Les murs sont très épais, pouvant atteindre plus de 1 mètre, et posés directement sur le rocher, sans fondation ; non crépis, ils laissent apparaître les matériaux de construction.

TOUTES CES MAISONS ont subi nombre de transformations au cours des siècles, ce qui explique leur état actuel : fenêtres agrandies, voûtes brisées, surélévations... Des clés de soutien – certaines de bois, la plupart de fer – ont été posées après les tremblements de terre qui ont affecté la région. Les ouvertures sont extrêmement réduites, afin d'assurer une bonne protection contre le froid en hiver et la chaleur en été, mais surtout afin de ne pas affaiblir le bâti. La couverture des toits est faite en tuiles canal. Les maisons imbriquées les unes dans les autres forment ici une véritable ville de défense.

NOUS REMARQUONS la demeure au n° 14, avec sa porte en ogive du XVe s. et son unique étage. Elle est un bon exemple de ce que pouvaient être ces maisons médiévales, qu'on ne surélevait qu'au moment du mariage de l'héritier, habitude prise par un souci constant de la défense de la cité. On préférait exhausser plutôt que bâtir, car il ne fallait pas agrandir démesurément l'enceinte au risque de ne pas pouvoir contraindre les assaillants. Les escaliers sont dallés de schiste. Il ne faut pas, ici, chercher du marbre de l'époque : il est trop loin, trop cher et très difficilement transportable

AU n° 32, un arc de soutien relie une maison-tour au bâti qui lui fait face, afin de solidariser l'ensemble. Cet arc est un des plus beaux de la partie médiévale. Face à la maison-tour, une plaque signale la demeure natale du père Albini. Une fois passé la porte d'enceinte, nous voyons deux placettes qui n'existaient pas au Moyen Âge. Avec la diffusion des théories hygiénistes à la fin du XIXe s., qui incitent à assainir les vieux centres urbains, les bâtiments menaçant ruine sont démolis. Ces placettes permettent

1. Cimetière du Vieux-Château.
2-3. Monuments funéraires dans le cimetière du Vieux-Château.

1

2

Le père Albini

FILS D'UN CULTIVATEUR, Charles Dominique Albini est né à Menton le 26 novembre 1790. Entré au grand séminaire de Nice en 1809, il est ordonné prêtre cinq ans plus tard. Il regagne sa ville natale et se met au service du curé Trenca, qui a la charge de la paroisse Saint-Michel – celle-ci s'étend jusqu'à Castellar, Gorbio, Sainte-Agnès et Saint-Roman. Le prince de Monaco, souhaitant créer un hôpital, fait venir des religieuses hospitalières, qui s'installent à Carnolès en 1820 dans l'ancien couvent des Récollets de la Madone. L'hôpital est ouvert en 1821.
LE PÈRE ALBINI est chargé d'assurer l'aumônerie du couvent. En 1823, il est nommé professeur au grand séminaire de Nice ; il devient religieux oblat l'année suivante et se consacre alors à une vie de missions. Il s'installe en Corse, où il meurt en 1839. En 1968, le pape Paul VI le déclare « vénérable ».

d'aérer et d'ensoleiller un ensemble de bâtis de grande densité. Les travaux se conjuguent alors avec l'adduction d'eau potable distribuée grâce à des fontaines réparties dans la ville. Près de la fontaine datée de 1885, se trouve la rue de la Côte, à l'extrémité de laquelle on bénéficie d'un beau panorama sur les collines de Menton.

En amorçant la descente, nous pouvons remarquer un affleurement de grès qui atteste la construction des maisons directement sur le rocher. Puis nous remontons la rue du Vieux-Château afin de nous rendre aux cimetières.

Cimetières du Vieux-Château et du Trabuquet

Place du Cimetière ; chemin du Trabuquet

Ouverts tous les jours, de 8 h à 20 h

À L'ÉPOQUE MÉDIÉVALE, la forteresse de Menton se dressait sur l'emplacement du cimetière actuel, dit du Vieux-Château, à environ 78 mètres d'altitude. Construite vers 1249, la forteresse appartenait aux Vento, alliés des comtes de Provence. À l'époque de la Révolution, elle devient bien national et est acquise par la Ville, pour être transformée en cimetière. Les travaux d'aménagement débutent alors par la destruction des vieilles murailles qui tombaient en ruine. La paix revenue, les travaux reprennent dès 1814 et se poursuivent jusqu'en 1875.

Cimetière du Vieux-Château

LA NÉCROPOLE, dont la superficie atteint plus de 5 000 mètres carrés, comprend quelque 1 300 concessions funéraires.
LES SÉPULTURES de la colonie étrangère avoisinent celles des familles les plus réputées du pays : Partouneaux, Massa, Biovès, Fontana, Adhémar de Lantagnac, Rostagni, Laurenti, Monléon... Non loin de la tombe du prince Troubetskoï, adossée à la chapelle russe (bâtie en 1886 en mémoire de Mme de Tagliakoff), on remarque celle de Stein von Kamienski, lieutenant général prussien décédé en 1894. D'autres noms connus passent sous nos yeux : l'historien anglais John Richard Green ; l'historien allemand Alfred Woltmann ; l'inventeur du rugby William Webb Ellis ; le botaniste anglais John Moggridge ; les architectes Abel Glena, Alfred Marsang et Hans Georg Tersling...

3

1

2

1. Cimetière du Trabuquet.
2. Rue Bréa : maison Monléon.
3. Rue Bréa : maison Faraldo.

3

Quand Flaubert visitait le cimetière de Menton

LE SÉJOUR de Gustave Flaubert à Menton date de 1845. L'écrivain revenait d'un voyage à Gênes, où il avait admiré *La Tentation de saint Antoine* du peintre Breughel, qui deviendra un thème obsessionnel dans son œuvre. UN ROMANTISME pathétique habite le jeune Flaubert ; la visite du cimetière de Menton nous vaut une tirade shakespearienne et une description macabre dans le goût des « Jeunes-France » des années 1830-1840 : « Cimetière – Figure pâle du fossoyeur, homme maigre sous son bonnet de laine grise. Quel admirable cimetière, en vue de cette mer éternellement jeune ! Pas une croix, pas un tombeau ! L'herbe est haute et verte ; à peine s'il y a ces ondulations légères qui font ressembler les champs des morts à des champs de blés fauchés. »

Cimetière du Trabuquet

Après le rattachement à la France, en 1861, Menton devient rapidement une station climatique qui accueille pendant l'hiver les familles en villégiature. La ville est réputée pour son climat considéré comme bienfaisant contre la tuberculose. Par chemin de fer arrivent des malades qui espèrent une guérison, mais décèdent à Menton. Le cimetière du Vieux-Château commence à être trop étroit. En 1880, il est décidé d'aménager une nouvelle nécropole sur la colline du Trabuquet.
PARMI LES NOMBREUSES sépultures, on peut voir notamment : celle du dessinateur anglais Aubrey Beardsley, qui s'éteignit à Menton en 1898 ; la tombe de l'écrivain Stanislas André Steeman, auteur de romans policiers tel *L'assassin habite au 21*, celle du grand cinéaste René Clément.

Depuis la place du cimetière du Vieux-Château, nous pouvons admirer la baie de Garavan, de la vieille ville jusqu'à Bordighera. Nous redescendons à présent vers le centre de Menton en empruntant la montée du Souvenir ; cette charmante rue, ancien chemin muletier de Castellar, nous permet d'avoir un joli point de vue sur la baie occidentale, jusqu'au cap Martin. Arrivés en bas, nous contournons la chapelle de l'Immaculée-Conception afin de rejoindre la rue Bréa par la rue du Grenadier.

Rue Bréa

EN 1615, le prince Honoré II fit percer une nouvelle voie afin de donner accès au couvent des Capucins. Celui-ci fut transformé, après le départ des religieux en 1793, successivement en mairie, en école et en caserne de pompiers, avant de devenir un immeuble de rapport.
LA RUE NEUVE d'Honoré II changea de nom dans la seconde moitié du XIXe s. et devint rue Bréa.
AU n° 1, une plaque apposée sur la maison de la famille de Monléon signale le passage du pape Pie VII à Menton, en 1814. En face, au n° 2, une autre rappelle la mémoire du général Jean-Baptiste Bréa, né à Menton en 1790, assassiné à Paris en juin 1848, lors des journées révolutionnaires. Au n° 3, une troisième évoque le passage du général Bonaparte en 1796, alors qu'il partait pour la campagne d'Italie [→ p. 24].

1. Place du Cap en 1900.
2. Quartier de la Ciapetta.
3. Place aux Herbes.

À l'extrémité de la rue Bréa, du côté de la mer, nous empruntons la rue des Logettes, que nous descendons afin de gagner la place du Cap.

Quartier de la place du Cap

DÈS LA FIN DU XVe S., passé la porte Saint-Antoine, commence l'urbanisation du cap Saint-Sébastien. Aux magasins bâtis au XVIe s. pour les marchands, les négociants, les artisans et les pêcheurs, qui servaient à la gabelle du sel destiné au Piémont, viennent ensuite s'ajouter des maisons d'habitation. Ce faubourg, fréquemment appelé « bourgade des Pêcheurs », se développe alors autour de l'ancienne chapelle Saint-Sébastien, dédiée à l'un des saints invoqués contre la peste.
EN 1622, Honoré II confie la chapelle à la confrérie des Pénitents noirs, qui a vu le jour en 1604 et dont le prince est le premier prieur. Elle restera le siège de la confrérie jusqu'en 1793 [→ p. 109], puis l'édifice est vendu comme bien national. Son nouveau propriétaire élève une maison à son emplacement, et dispose la Vierge de Miséricorde dans une niche sur la façade.

De la place du Cap, nous nous dirigeons vers la place François-Borfiga (félibre mentonnais, 1877-1957) qui la jouxte, afin de pénétrer dans le quartier de la Ciapetta.

Quartier de la Ciapetta

L'ARTÈRE qui permet de relier le Vieux-Port à la promenade du Soleil est percée vers 1890. De ce fait, le quartier de la Ciapetta s'éloigne du rivage, et l'ancien rocher (la *ciapetta*) sur lequel est bâtie la vieille ville disparaît sous un terre-plein qui devient la place Fontana.
AU DÉBUT DU XXe S., la circulation est de plus en plus dense dans la rue Saint-Michel ; le remblaiement du quartier de la Ciapetta permet alors le raccordement du Vieux-Port à la route nationale 7.
La nouvelle voie prend le nom de quai de Monléon ; elle prolonge vers l'ouest le quai Bonaparte. En ce début du XXe s., le quartier de la Ciapetta vit ses derniers jours les pieds dans l'eau. Entrepreneurs et négociants de la ferme du sel ou marins au cabotage, qui animaient les lieux, vont bientôt disparaître.
DANS CE QUARTIER populaire de la ville, nous pouvons remarquer des ruelles bordées de modestes maisons, celles des pêcheurs et des marins.

Nous revenons sur la place du Cap et empruntons, à gauche, la rue Saint-Michel.

Rue Saint-Michel

CETTE ARTÈRE, qui suit le tracé de la voie romaine Julia Augusta, a été jusqu'au XIXe s. l'unique voie menant en Italie.
À la fin du XIXe s., la municipalité décide l'alignement de cette rue. Un corps de bâtiment est adjoint à l'hôtel Adhémar de Lantagnac et à la maison Ardoïno. Des commerces viennent s'installer dans ce quartier qui devient le centre actif de la ville. Au mois de juin, la procession de la Fête-Dieu empruntait son parcours ; communiantes et communiants, conduits par les sœurs de Saint-Thomas, tentaient de se frayer un passage parmi les étalages à l'ombre des bâches au drapé baroque.

1

2

Hôtel Adhémar de Lantagnac.
1. Façade.
2. Détail d'un trumeau.
3. Un des salons.

À PARTIR DE 1974, sur l'initiative de la jeune chambre économique, la rue est transformée en zone piétonnière. À la fin du XXe s., cette artère est totalement rénovée et dallée.

Hôtel Adhémar de Lantagnac

SERVICE DU PATRIMOINE

24, rue Saint-Michel

Salle d'exposition, boutique et accueil

Ouvert du mardi au samedi, de 10 h à 12 h 30 et de 13 h 30 à 18 h

Téléphone : 04 92 10 97 10
Télécopie : 04 93 28 46 85

AU XIXe s., la famille Adhémar de Lantagnac, dont trois de ses membres ont assumé la tâche de gouverneur de Menton, entre en possession d'un hôtel particulier construit au siècle précédent, auquel elle donne son nom.

L'ORIGINALITÉ architecturale de cette demeure réside dans sa conception : un plan quadrilatère à quatre façades – sur rues, sur cour et sur jardin.

Le portail à carrosses ouvrant sur la rue Saint-Michel a été englobé dans le bâti d'une boutique. L'aile située entre la place aux Herbes et la cour à carrosses a pu être adjointe ultérieurement pour abriter les services du gouverneur. La façade sur ladite cour est très sobre, seul ressort le portail (muré actuellement) permettant d'accéder au grand escalier ; il a conservé son architecture classique : double pilastre plat à faible décrochement supportant un tympan cintré et surbaissé au-dessus d'une forte corniche moulurée.

La présence de nombreux commerces ne permet plus une bonne lecture de la façade.

AU REZ-DE-CHAUSSÉE et au rez-de-jardin, se succèdent les pièces de réception, la salle à manger et le salon d'apparat ; de part et d'autre de l'entrée (arrière), un escalier conduit aux chambres et aux dépendances. Une ferronnerie Louis XVI accompagne cette montée. Les pièces de ces deux niveaux sont ornementées de peintures à trumeau placées au-dessus des portes, des cheminées et des glaces ; elles ont reçu un encadrement, sculpté de motifs ciselés pour la plupart d'entre elles. Des glaces à encadrement de même style, des consoles dorées, des cheminées de marbre complètent le décor.

3

CET AMÉNAGEMENT présente des styles divers : style rocaille Louis XV à motifs d'arabesques et de feuillage, pour les trumeaux et les glaces ; style Louis XVI, plus dépouillé, pour d'autres peintures ; un troisième genre, celui des peintures « à fresque », dans une chambre d'époque Directoire.

L'ENSEMBLE du décor est assez semblable à celui que l'on peut voir dans les hôtels aixois ou les châteaux de Provence de la même époque. La qualité des peintures, la finesse du ciselé des encadrements des trumeaux et des glaces laissent supposer un artiste habile en cet art décoratif très spécifique de la Provence.

La Colle
Les Colombières
Domaine des Colombières
Garavan
Bd de Garavan
Route de Super Garavan
Super Garavan
Chemin Bella Vista
Tunnel
ITALIE
Pont St Louis
Esp. Jojo Arnaldi
St Ludovic
Esp. Schuman
Voie Romaine
Prom. Reine Astrid
Av. A. Briand
Av. Porte de France
Square Lesseps
Ch. du Perroquet
Ch. St Laurent
GARE
Chemin Fleuri
R. Webb Ellis
R. F. Bac
Route des colombières
Sentier Puraina
Av. Blasco Ibanez
Parc du Pian
STADE LUCIEN RHEIN
Av. St Jacques
Ch. St Jacques
Sentier Villa Noël
St Jacques
Ste Anne
St Julien
Av. Laurenti
Porte de France
Promenade de la Mer
Sentier des Oliviers
Cimetière du Trabuquet
Ch. du Trabuquet
Ch. de la Colle Supérieure
Ch. de la Colle Inférieure
Route de Castellar
Bd du Fossan
Corniche des Ciappes
Ch. des Ciappes
Castellar
Sentier du Plateau St Michel
Tunnel Pascal Molinari
Promenade du Val de Menton
Montée du Souvenir
Rue Longue
Quai Bonaparte
Quai Gordon Bennett
Rue Bréa
Rue St Michel
Rue Guyau
R. Loredan-Larchey
Rue St Michel
Marché
Quai de Monléon
Esplanade Francis Palmero
Square du Souvenir Français
Quai Napoléon III
Vieux Port
Jetée Imp. Eugénie
Baie de Garavan
STADE RONDELLI
Square Baden Baden
Port de Garavan

« Le Rêve babylonien »

Des Rochers rouges à la vieille ville

1

2

Des grottes des Rochers rouges au sommet de la vieille ville, nous voyageons à travers le temps, qui nous conduit vertigineusement de quelque 25 000 ans avant notre ère jusqu'à la Belle Époque... En effectuant cet itinéraire, où l'automobile est de rigueur, nous avons le sentiment que le temps se condense et qu'en l'espace d'une avenue, d'une promenade, d'un boulevard se déroule toute l'aventure humaine.

3

1. L'Homme de Menton.
2. Villa Maria Serena.
3. Fondation Alphand-Bariquand.
4. Les Rochers rouges.

Les Rochers rouges et les grottes de Grimaldi

Grimaldi (Italie), à 350 mètres de la frontière franco-italienne

MUSEO DEI BALZI ROSSI
MUSÉE DES ROCHERS ROUGES

Ouvert tous les jours, sauf le lundi, de 8 h 30 à 19 h 30

Téléphone : 00 39 0 184 381 13

LES GROTTES DE GRIMALDI (ou des Rochers rouges, ou encore dei Balzi Rossi) sont situées en bord de mer, entre Menton et Vintimille. Cet ensemble est constitué des grottes du Prince (en l'honneur du prince Albert Ier de Monaco), des Enfants, du comte Costantini (fondateur de l'Institut italien de paléontologie), du Cavillon, de Florestan (prince Florestan Ier) et de la Barma Grande (« grande grotte »). À celles-ci s'ajoutent trois autres sites mineurs : les abris Lorenzi et Mochi, et le rocher de la Tour. LE MUSÉE, dont les bâtiments actuels ont été construits en 1994, a été créé en 1898 par Sir Thomas Hanbury [→ p. 127] afin d'y conserver et exposer le résultat des fouilles archéologiques du site. Dès 1872, les grottes firent l'objet d'une exploration scientifique par Émile Rivière ; elles sont à juste titre considérées comme un des gisements préhistoriques les plus riches au monde. La sépulture triple de la Barma Grande, fort impressionnante, comprend les ossements de deux adolescents et d'un adulte de grande taille appartenant au type Cro-Magnon, la forme plus ancienne d'*Homo sapiens*, arrivé en Europe aux alentours de – 37 000 avant notre ère. Quant aux vénus – statuettes en pierre de femmes enceintes – trouvées dans la Barma Grande, elles témoignent déjà de la vive sensibilité de nos ancêtres du Gravettien (– 27 000 / – 19 000). Un escalier et une passerelle qui traverse la voie de chemin de fer nous conduisent aux autres grottes, où l'on peut admirer notamment un cheval gravé à environ 4 mètres de hauteur (paroi orientale de la grotte du Cavillon). Un petit bâtiment, le Museo Vecchio, complète la visite. EN QUITTANT ces lieux, on peut à loisir se promener au bord de la mer, d'où l'on découvre un superbe point de vue sur la baie de Garavan et la plage des Œufs, en contrebas de la grotte du Prince.

4

1

2

3

1-2-3. Villa Maria Serena.

Nous reprenons la route en direction de Menton, pour découvrir, près du poste-frontière, en territoire français, la villa *Maria Serena*.

Villa *Maria Serena*

21, promenade Reine-Astrid

Visites guidées, tous les mardis à 10 h, organisées par le Service du patrimoine (renseignements : 04 92 10 97 10)

ÉRIGÉE dans un parc de 1 hectare, avec les Rochers rouges et la baie de Garavan comme écrin, la villa *Maria Serena* a été bâtie en 1886 sur des plans attribués à Charles Garnier, pour le comte Louis Foucher de Careïl. Son style quelque peu ostentatoire n'est pas sans évoquer celui de la propre villa de l'architecte de l'Opéra de Paris, à Bordighera.
L'ÉDIFICE, où l'on remarque une alternance des volumes, des pleins et des vides, possède des loggias et des terrasses. La villa *Maria Serena* a toutefois subi des dommages provoqués par les bombardements de la Seconde Guerre mondiale ; c'est ainsi que son belvédère a été partiellement amputé du quatrième niveau.
EN 1922, la propriété est acquise par un banquier britannique, Henry Konig, qui la lègue à la Ville en 1947. Depuis, elle sert de cadre aux réceptions d'hôtes illustres tels qu'Élisabeth de Bavière, le président René Coty..., ainsi qu'à de hautes personnalités des arts et des lettres.

Le jardin de *Maria Serena*

LE JARDIN, qu'il serait plus pertinent de nommer « palmeraie », est un hymne à la verticalité ébouriffée. Dès que nous franchissons l'entrée, notre regard est sollicité par des formes longilignes qui paraissent s'articuler entre elles, car les deux plans sont ici séparés par un talus très pentu.
LE PLAN INFÉRIEUR est occupé par un ensemble de palmiers où l'on reconnaît *Caryota urens, Phoenix canariensis, Washingtonia, Chamaerops humilis*, auxquels se mêlent de superbes cycas. Le plan supérieur, coiffé d'un alignement de cyprès, a l'apparence d'une sombre muraille végétale. Dans un éventail de feuilles semblables aux plumes d'un grand oiseau vert, la puissante gerbe de *Strelitzia augusta* assure une continuité entre les deux plans.
Le niveau supérieur occupe une sorte de promontoire au-dessus de la route et de la rivière Saint-Louis. Le parti pris pour son aménagement a consisté à découper l'espace en de nombreux petits jardins, de forme plutôt arrondie, ce qui permet de densifier l'ensemble des cheminements et de multiplier les courbes, en accentuant ainsi l'impression d'un vagabondage en sous-bois. Le nombre et la dimension des arécacées, le jaillissement des stipes, mais aussi l'absence de fleurs suggèrent l'image d'une oasis. L'un des éléments du jardin fragmenté, de forme ovale, n'est pas sans rappeler, avec ses grands palmiers périphériques droits comme des colonnades et son bouquet central de petits palmiers (*Phoenix roebelinii*), un temple à cella à demi ruiné. Plus loin, un lourd rideau de *Strelitzia reginae*, de yuccas et de cycas ferme l'horizon vers le sud. Au bord du ravin du torrent Saint-Louis a été conservé un pan de mur avec son volet bleu. Tout laisse croire – surtout avec les jarres posées au pied de la ruine – que le lieu va s'animer et que la fenêtre s'ouvrira bientôt.
LE BASSIN, avec sa fontaine au dragon, apporte un peu de fraîcheur dans cet

1

2

3

4

1. Fontaine Hanbury.
2-3-4-5. Le Clos du Peyronnet.

environnement minéral. Au milieu des liliacées, le dragonnier (*Dracaena draco*) – tel un être fabuleux, entre pieuvre géante et harpie diabolique – lève ses multiples bras aux terminaisons chevelues alors que son stipe ventru et balafré saigne en laissant exsuder d'épaisses gouttes d'un suc vermeil.

En sortant de la villa *Maria Serena*, nous nous dirigeons vers la fontaine Hanbury, édifiée en 1897 à l'intersection de la promenade Reine-Astrid et de l'avenue Aristide-Briand, que nous empruntons jusqu'au passage à niveau.

Le Clos du Peyronnet

Avenue Aristide-Briand

Propriété privée

LA VILLA aux couleurs passées, noyée dans la végétation, se singularise par une longue galerie à colonnade dont la moitié est colonisée par une magnifique glycine très ancienne.

5

AU DÉBUT DU XXe S., Humphrey Waterfield, architecte paysagiste anglais autodidacte, dessine le jardin qui s'étend sur quelque 6 000 mètres carrés.

IL IMAGINE un « escalier d'eau », c'est-à-dire une succession de bassins aux dimensions identiques, dénivelés les uns par rapport aux autres et séparés par les restanques (terrasses). Plus bas, il fait creuser deux pièces d'eau beaucoup plus grandes, rectangulaires et pareillement dénivelées. Entre les deux ensembles de bassins, il aménage une tonnelle posée sur des piliers de pierre servant à la fois de passage et de lieu de repos. Du haut de la propriété, le regard « rebondit » sur chaque miroir d'eau qu'il entr'aperçoit, plutôt qu'il ne les voit, pour se perdre à travers une étroite fenêtre végétale dans l'immensité bleue de la Méditerranée.

AFIN DE BÉNÉFICIER d'un autre regard sur ce jeu de miroirs, Waterfield n'hésite pas à élargir considérablement l'escalier de pierre qui escalade les deux dernières restanques. Cette flaque de lumière sur l'espace minéralisé ocre accentue plus fortement encore l'illusion de naturel de ces biefs successifs enveloppés d'une couronne herbeuse épaisse et sensuelle. L'association du jeu d'eau et du grand escalier est une référence implicite aux aménagements classiques des parcs des grands châteaux. Chez les Waterfield, l'escalier de prestige était un lieu où l'on pouvait se retrouver et se rassembler.

LE CLOS DU PEYRONNET est maintenant la propriété de William Waterfield, neveu de Humphrey. Son objectif ? Sauvegarder le jardin en respectant l'aménagement conçu par son oncle. Néanmoins, il lui apporte sa propre touche, car le lexicologue s'est fait jardinier. De ses voyages en Afrique du Sud, il revient avec une passion : les bulbes. Sa collection compte actuellement plus de 300 taxons.

AUJOURD'HUI, *Le Clos du Peyronnet* est un lieu merveilleux où l'ordre n'exclut pas la fantaisie. Saturé de parfums, de chants d'oiseaux et de sensualité, il oscille entre luxuriance folle et austérité savamment calculée.

1

1. Frontière franco-italienne (vers 1950).
2. Pont Saint-Louis.

2

Depuis l'avenue Aristide-Briand, nous nous dirigeons vers le poste-frontière du pont Saint-Louis.

À la frontière

Esplanade Jojo-Arnaldi

APRÈS AVOIR dépassé les bâtiments des douanes françaises, construits dans les années 1950 – et fixés à jamais, grâce à Gérard Oury (*Le Corniaud*, 1964), dans l'iconographie cinématographique –, on parvient à un site chargé d'histoire : un viaduc monumental enjambe la faille qui forme une frontière naturelle avec l'Italie. La vision des bâtiments « mussoliniens » des douanes italiennes, juchés à flanc de coteau sur de massifs contreforts en pierre de taille, est surprenante. En contrebas, les jardins maraîchers soigneusement entretenus apportent une note familiale à l'ensemble, avec le linge qui sèche sur les étendoirs.

À L'ENTRÉE du pont, une plaque honore la mémoire d'un résistant mort à dix-huit ans, Jojo Arnaldi, dont le nom a été donné à l'esplanade du poste-frontière. Cet endroit enchanteur a été le théâtre d'événements dramatiques, que vient nous rappeler la présence d'un fort au pont Saint-Louis.

EN 1973, est ouverte une seconde voie, qui permet de se rendre au poste-frontière Saint-Ludovic, aperçu en contrebas, esplanade Robert-Schuman.

Nous empruntons, à droite de l'esplanade Jojo-Arnaldi, le boulevard de Garavan.

Le nom de Garavan a donné lieu à nombre de controverses. Pour certains, il serait issu de l'italien *garar in vano* (« rivaliser en vain ») ; pour d'autres, le nom viendrait de l'expression *garer du vent*, une interprétation qui paraît toutefois fantaisiste. Enfin, a été proposé le celte *kaër a van* (« le village des rochers »), qui semblerait indiquer l'habitat préhistorique tout proche.

LE BOULEVARD de Garavan, qui s'étire sur 3 kilomètres environ, est bordé de caroubiers et de poivriers. Il nous conduit de la frontière à la vieille ville. Son percement, réalisé entre 1882 et 1887, est dû à l'architecte Sylvain Jauffret [→ p. 30]. Ce boulevard est également connu sous l'expression « Rêve babylonien », par allusion aux jardins mythiques de Babylone.

Menton, « ma ville est un jardin »

VERS LE MILIEU DU XIXe S., Menton est encore un gros bourg où, exception faite de la vieille ville et du bord de mer, les espaces non construits occupent de vastes superficies. Sur les anciennes cartes postales on distingue de grandes plages marquées par le moutonnement des frondaisons des arbres du grand verger local. Sur les restanques qui sculptent les pentes, le vert pâle des oliviers contraste avec le vert cru des citronniers qui constituaient alors une grande richesse pour le pays.

EN DEHORS de ces plantations, une riche végétation méditerranéenne parfumée, faite d'essences au feuillage persistant, occupe les zones non cultivées. On reconnaît très vite l'association de myrtes (*Myrtus communis*), pistachiers-lentisques (*Pistacia lentiscus*) avec leur gomme à odeur forte, oléastres (*Olea europaea*, var. *sylvestris*) et caroubiers (*Ceratonia siliqua*) aux longues gousses aplaties remplies d'une pulpe sucrée dans laquelle sont noyées

Garavan
ou « le Rêve babylonien »

1

les graines de poids constant qui auraient servi d'unité de mesure (le carat). À ce groupement de plantes il faut ajouter le ciste cotonneux (*Cistus albidus*), le romarin (*Rosmarinus officinale)* et un genévrier aux feuilles piquantes : le cade, ou oxycèdre (*Juniperus oxycedrus*).

SUR LES ROCHERS et dans les lieux les plus chauds, se trouve *Opuntia ficus indica*, plante originaire d'Amérique introduite en Espagne puis en Afrique du Nord, qui aurait été rapportée de Tunisie sur le littoral méditerranéen français, par les troupes de Charles Quint, où elle s'est naturalisée. Sur tous les talus, sur le bord des chemins, les restanques et les versants rocailleux et ensoleillés, le vent caresse les gerbes d'or du genêt à balai (*Genista scoparia*) et joue avec les houppes bleues du *Trachelium caeruleum*. Le figuier de Barbarie, avec ses raquettes charnues entourées de fruits comestibles aux couleurs changeantes, voisine avec le figuier commun (*Ficus carica*), aux feuilles très singulières et aux petits fruits assez savoureux.

DANS LES VALLONS et le long de leur ligne de fond (le talweg), la canne de Provence (*Arundo donax*) forme de larges peuplements, jouant le rôle d'écrin à quelques rares lauriers-roses (*Nerium oleander*) ; dans les zones les plus humides, parfois à l'ombre, l'acanthe (*Acanthus mollis*) aux feuilles longuement pétiolées et aux limbes dentés jette en juillet et août, avant de disparaître, ses hampes garnies de fleurs blanches.

DE LOIN EN LOIN, parfois groupés en bosquets, voici les pins pignons ou pins parasols (*Pinus pinea*) à l'écorce crevassée brun-rouge, les pins d'Alep (*Pinus halepensis*), d'une hauteur de 15 à 20 mètres, au tronc gris argenté, et quelques rares chênes verts, les yeuses (*Quercus ilex*). Voici le charme-houblon

1-2. La flore du boulevard de Garavan.

2

(*Ostrya carpinifolia*) aux longs chatons mâles et aux inflorescences femelles en forme de serpentins, et le cerisier sauvage qui fait la joie des oiseaux. Autour des maisons, les arbres fruitiers – orangers, citronniers, amandiers, cerisiers, figuiers – voisinent avec les plantes ornementales : le cyprès d'Italie (*Cupressus sempervirens*) au port étalé ou dressé, d'une longévité exceptionnelle dépassant trois siècles ; l'arbre de Judée (*Cercis siliquastrum*) introduit en Europe au temps des croisades ; le mimosa (*Acacia dealbata*), plante rapportée d'Australie à La Malmaison par le navigateur et botaniste Nicolas Baudin, vers 1804, mais introduite dans le Midi au début du Second Empire.

1

2

3

4

L'OUVERTURE de larges avenues bordées de platanes accompagne l'urbanisation des vallées. Éloigné des maisons, sur ces pentes livrées régulièrement aux flammes, l'arbre à perruque (*Cotinus coggygria*) recolonise le milieu après l'incendie et prend en automne la couleur du feu.

Menton, « le désir des tropiques »

VERS LA FIN DU XIXe S., le paysage de la Côte d'Azur a subi un profond remaniement. Sans doute l'expansion coloniale a-t-elle conduit les sociétés européennes à retrouver un petit territoire qui puisse rappeler ces vastes espaces tropicaux où vivent les plantes les plus merveilleuses et les fleurs les plus parfumées. Pas étonnant que d'aucuns veuillent réinventer les tropiques, mais des tropiques contrôlés, bien policés et aseptisés.

ABRITÉ DES VENTS du nord par la retombée du Massif alpin, que souligne une corniche qui se colore d'ocre au soleil couchant, Menton connaît des hivers doux et subit de courts épisodes de gel, rarement dommageables à la végétation. L'été est très chaud, voire suffocant, et l'humidité atmosphérique est toujours forte. Les pluies, selon les années, sont très irrégulières et tombent en grosses averses accompagnées parfois de violents orages. Cette ambiance climatique de chaleur et de moiteur confère à Menton comme au liséré littoral – appelé Côte d'Azur en France et Riviera en Italie – une atmosphère propice aux acclimatations végétales. C'est là, entre Bordighera et Beaulieu-sur-Mer, que les aristocrates bâtissent à grands frais leurs paradis, n'hésitant pas à y introduire les arbres les plus rares, les plantes les plus précieuses. Parcs et jardins commencent alors à se multiplier. Plantes ornementales aux fleurs et aux feuilles extraordinaires, espèces fruitières aux fruits de formes et de couleurs étranges, essences au port singulier effacent peu à peu le paysage ancien. Dans le cortège des nouveaux venus, le palmier est certainement la plante qui possède la plus grande charge d'exotisme, la flore française ne disposant à cette époque que d'un seul représentant des arécacées : *Chamaerops humilis*.

LES ÉVÉNEMENTS vont se précipiter et l'arrivée, en 1869, du chemin de fer à Menton accentue ce mouvement.

5

6

Chaque villa devient une île semée de fleurs et plantée d'arbres aux feuilles, aux fleurs et aux fruits surprenants. Une symphonie de couleurs submerge le boulevard de Garavan. Les villas si somptueuses sont rapidement noyées sous un déferlement de végétaux, tous plus rares et plus beaux les uns que les autres.

La naissance d'un paysage

De propriété à propriété, on fait des échanges. Un chassé-croisé de plantes bouleverse progressivement l'image de Menton. Un paysage nouveau est en train de naître. Le faux-poivrier (*Schinus molle*) est largement mis à contribution, mais le palmier des Canaries (*Phoenix canariensis*) – introduit à Nice par le vicomte Vigier en 1864 – et le dattier sont les plus sollicités. D'autres essences – *Ficus elastica, Casuarina equisetifolia, Jacaranda, Eucalyptus sp., Albizzia julibrissin* (l'arbre à soie), etc. – sont judicieusement dispersées le long des rues ou des avenues et viennent orner et ombrager les parcs. Insensiblement, Menton « ville-jardin » adopte un profil tropical.

DEPUIS SA CRÉATION, le boulevard de Garavan n'a cessé d'attirer les grands de ce monde dans un cadre réellement paradisiaque aux hivers si doux. De belles villas, au style éclectique et aux noms évocateurs de destinations lointaines, ornent les deux rives de cette bucolique corniche : *La Vista* (où séjourna le duc d'Aumale), *Ispahan*, *Bella Vista* (résidence du duc de Sutherland), *Himalaya* (propriété de la famille américaine Caroll of Carolton), *Le Paradou* (domaine de la famille britannique Kennedy, puis de la famille Bariquand),

7

8

La Favorite et combien d'autres encore, qui se nichent ici, au cœur d'une végétation luxuriante.

La flore du boulevard de Garavan.
1. Palmiers.
2. Nénuphars.
3. Cycas.
4. Dombeya.
5. Passiflore.
6. Succulente.

7. Villa Foucher de Careil.
8. Villa La Favorite.

1

3

4

1. Fondation Alphand-Bariquand.
2-3. Le Clos du Roman gris.
4. Parc du Pian.

Fondation Alphand-Bariquand

41, boulevard de Garavan

DANS UNE PROPRIÉTÉ qui s'étend sur 7 hectares, Marie-Jeanne Alphand, fille de Jean-Charles Alphand, ingénieur des Travaux publics, responsable des parcs de la Ville de Paris, fait construire un hôpital destiné aux enfants malades. Le 8 avril 1905, elle pose la première pierre de l'édifice, dont les plans sont conçus par l'architecte Abel Glena [→ p. 30].
LE BÂTIMENT, long de 45 mètres, présente une arcade florentine, avec des galeries ornées de motifs floraux et géométriques par Guillaume Cerutti-Maori [→ p. 78].
L'hôpital se dresse sur une plate-forme naturelle d'où l'on découvre montagnes et mer, dans un superbe paysage. Marie-Jeanne Alphand, décédée en 1927, avait été mariée à l'industriel Émile Bariquand.

Domaine *Le Clos du Roman gris*

41, boulevard de Garavan

LE CLOS DU ROMAN GRIS, situé dans le domaine Alphand-Bariquand, est bâti dans les années 1890 pour Lord Mountbatten, père du dernier vice-roi des Indes. L'acquéreur « officiel » de ce domaine de 24 000 mètres carrés, entretenu par vingt jardiniers, est John Edward Power Wallis, conseiller privé de la Couronne et ancien gouverneur de Madras (Inde).
LORD MOUNTBATTEN reçoit au *Clos du Roman gris* la reine Victoria. Autre invitée de marque, Agatha Christie, qui séjourne dans la maison occupée actuellement par les gardiens, en bordure du boulevard de Garavan, face au parc du Pian. Elle y écrit un roman policier qui s'inspire directement d'un crime commis dans le quartier.

2

Parc du Pian

Boulevard de Garavan, avenues Blasco-Ibáñez et Saint-Jacques

DOMINANT la baie de Garavan, le parc du Pian est une belle oliveraie de quelque 3 hectares, qui compte plus de 600 arbres, certains plusieurs fois centenaires.
SITE CLASSÉ depuis 1960, cette ancienne propriété de la famille Faraldo, acquise par la municipalité, a été aménagée en parc public. Merveilleux lieu de détente, il sert aussi de cadre aux fêtes conviviales et aux manifestations nocturnes d'été.
PENDANT des siècles, l'olivier a été un élément économique majeur pour tout le Bassin méditerranéen, particulièrement pour Menton ; utilisé dans l'alimentation, (huile d'olive), il sert aussi à fabriquer des onguents, à préparer des décoctions (avec les feuilles)... et son bois est un excellent matériau pour l'éclairage et le chauffage. Arbre mythique, l'olivier est un symbole d'abondance, de gloire, de sagesse et de paix. Considéré comme immortel, il est depuis toujours lié à la vie du peuple méditerranéen.

Depuis le boulevard de Garavan, nous empruntons, à gauche, l'avenue Blasco-Ibáñez pour nous rendre au domaine de *Fontana Rosa*.

Fontana Rosa

le jardin des Romanciers

Né à Valencia, en 1867, le romancier espagnol Vicente Blasco Ibáñez est séduit par Menton. En 1921, il décide de s'installer dans le quartier de Garavan. Sept ans plus tard, le célèbre auteur de *La Barraca* s'éteint dans cette ville aimée.

Avenue Blasco-Ibáñez

Visites guidées, le vendredi à 10 h, organisées par le Service du patrimoine (renseignements : 04 92 10 97 10)

LE LOURD PORTAIL du domaine de *Fontana Rosa* est surmonté d'un fronton mouluré sur lequel se détachent les portraits en céramique de Balzac et de Dickens entourant celui de Miguel de Cervantès. Il est barré d'un long bandeau reposant sur six écussons de fruits et de roses. Derrière ce portail se cache l'un des jardins les plus originaux de Menton, peut-être aussi l'un des plus rares : *el jardin de los Novelistas*, le jardin des Romanciers. Il est la création étrange et délirante d'un personnage extravagant.

LORSQUE Blasco Ibáñez acquiert cette propriété, elle se compose de bâtiments relativement imposants (deux villas et plusieurs pavillons). Elle possède un puits, deux fontaines, deux parcelles consacrées à l'agriculture et à l'arboriculture (oliviers et citronniers), et, sans doute, quelques petits carrés que l'ancien occupant des lieux a probablement utilisé pour y installer son potager et cultiver quelques plantes ornementales.

BLASCO IBÁÑEZ réaménage cet ensemble, qui doit à la fois répondre à ses besoins et illustrer ses tendances et ses passions. La partie haute, où sont situés les vergers, n'est pas modifiée. La partie basse, architecturée, est divisée en deux par des constructions : le garage, la maison du gardien, un aquarium posé sur des chapiteaux ioniques.

La rotonde de Cervantès

EN FRANCHISSANT l'espace dévolu au jardin, par un escalier prestigieux conduisant à un bassin rectangulaire, on accède tout d'abord à la rotonde de Cervantès. En arrière du bassin, un bas-relief blanc de 1 mètre de haut représente des enfants nus jouant dans la nature : d'un côté, un cortège de musiciens, avec flûtes, tambourins,

cors et cymbales, parmi des oliviers et des roseaux ; de l'autre, sous un pommier, une farandole d'enfants qui tiennent des guirlandes de grappes de raisin.

AU-DESSUS, a été aménagée la rotonde proprement dite. Il s'agit d'un portique semi-circulaire à double colonnade, dont l'entablement est orné de fruits et de roses; des bancs ont été placés ici, décorés de carreaux de céramique illustrant les aventures de Don Quichotte. Ce portique était, à l'origine, entouré d'un écran de cyprès; il est aujourd'hui incomplet.

BLASCO IBÁÑEZ avait disposé dans tout le jardin des stèles qui supportaient les bustes en bronze – œuvres du sculpteur Léopold Bernstamm – des géants de la littérature universelle : Charles Dickens,

Gustave Flaubert, Victor Hugo, Fedor Dostoïevski, Alexandre Pouchkine, Honoré de Balzac, Émile Zola et, naturellement, Cervantès.

La bibliothèque et la salle de cinéma

DANS LA PARTIE orientale du jardin, on distingue encore très nettement la symétrie de la composition, une sorte d'agora où l'on se promène, où le visiteur peut s'asseoir pour prolonger la discussion. Tous les bancs, de style valencien, font face à la partie habitée, au parc et à la montagne. Un grand bassin octogonal orné de céramiques bleues et blanches, de style andalou, devait être chapeauté par un dôme « liquide » lorsque étaient mis en marche les jets d'eau distribués autour de ce bassin. Entre ce dernier et le banc, une grande allée, dans l'alignement de la bibliothèque, était entourée de six colonnes doriques, aujourd'hui couchées. De part et d'autre de ce promenoir sont installés deux bancs semi-circulaires. Tous sont ornementés de divers motifs de céramique, tels que légumes, fruits, fleurs et couples de danseurs.

EN FACE DE L'AGORA, au bas du parc aménagé sur le versant, une longue pergola-tunnel (l'allée de Bacchus) supportée par des colonnes quadrangulaires, toutes reliées entre elles par des bancs au décor de céramique, sert de limite à la partie habitée ; elle permet de passer de la villa et de la salle de cinéma à l'aquarium et d'établir ainsi un circuit comprenant des rampes et des escaliers le long desquels ont été posées des jardinières recouvertes de céramiques valenciennes. Un belvédère est construit au-dessus de la salle de cinéma – une partie de l'œuvre de Blasco Ibáñez ayant été acquise par des firmes américaines de production, l'écrivain désirait pouvoir projeter les films tirés de ses romans (*Les Quatre Cavaliers de l'Apocalypse*, *Arènes sanglantes*, *Mare nostrum*...).

L'ENSEMBLE est complété par une bibliothèque-bureau de 40 000 volumes, où Blasco Ibáñez se réfugiait pour écrire et exalter son inspiration. Classée monument historique en 1990, *Fontana Rosa* est en cours de réhabilitation.

Le Garavan Palace.

Face au domaine de *Fontana Rosa*, on peut voir le *Garavan Palace*, grand vaisseau blanc, témoin de la Belle Époque, dont le clocheton se dresse face à la mer. Cet ancien hôtel a été édifié par Adrien Rey [→ p. 30].

Nous passons à présent sous le pont du chemin de fer ; à gauche, s'élevait la villa du philosophe Alfred Fouillée. Celui-ci, son épouse – auteur du *Tour de France par deux enfants*, sous le pseudonyme de G. Bruno – et son fils, le jeune philosophe Marie-Jean Guyau, vécurent ici leurs dernières années.

La rue Webb-Ellis (inventeur du rugby, mort et inhumé à Menton en 1872), nous conduit vers la gare de Garavan, bâtie en 1882 pour accueillir la reine Victoria. Après la gare, nous gagnons, vers l'est, l'avenue Katherine-Mansfield. À droite, chemin Fleuri, un mémorial nous rappelle que cette femme de lettres a vécu dans le quartier de Garavan.

Depuis l'avenue Katherine-Mansfield, nous nous dirigeons vers l'avenue Porte-de-France et le port de Garavan.

1

2

1. *Portrait de Katherine Mansfield.*
2. *Le jardin d'*Isola Bella.
3. *La villa* Isola Bella *dessinée par Katherine Mansfield.*

Katherine Mansfield

NÉE À WELLINGTON (Nouvelle-Zélande) en 1888, décédée à Fontainebleau en 1923, Katherine Mansfield a vécu à Menton de janvier 1920 à avril 1921 (elle séjourna à *L'Hermitage*, puis dans les villas *Flora* et *Isola Bella*). Ses lettres témoignent de son émerveillement de se trouver à Menton, où elle se soigne contre la tuberculose.

ISOLA BELLA, qu'elle loue au mois de septembre 1920, lui inspire une description emplie de bonheur. Ici, semble se réaliser le rêve paradisiaque, le rêve de l'île heureuse, exotique, ensoleillée.

« MA PETITE MAISON jaune clair, avec le mimosa qui pousse devant et qui est d'un jaune tout juste un peu plus soutenu, le jardin plein de plantes, la terrasse aux piliers ocre, qui s'effritent et que recouvrent des feuillages, retraite des lézards, tout cela fait partie d'un tableau ou d'une histoire.

« JE VEUX DIRE qu'ils ne sont pas éloignés de votre idéal, de votre rêve. La maison a sa façade vers la mer, mais vers la droite il y a une vieille ville avec son petit port, un quai minuscule planté de poivriers et de platanes. Cette vieille ville, bâtie tout contre le coteau, muraille solide, dirait-on, de formes et de couleurs, est la plus jolie chose que j'aie jamais vue. Chaque fois que je vais en voiture de ce côté, j'y découvre un changement. »

3

La baie et le port de Garavan.

Baie de Garavan

L'AMÉNAGEMENT de la baie de Garavan, ceinturée par le quai Bonaparte, l'avenue Porte-de-France et la promenade Reine-Astrid, est entrepris à partir de 1965. La Ville obtient alors une concession d'endigage de 18 553 mètres carrés située à hauteur de l'ancien épi Saint-Jacques. DE 1965 À 1971, les Sablettes et les autres plages de la baie orientale sont aménagées sur 30 000 mètres carrés. Ainsi disparaissent les rochers de la vieille ville, chers aux cœurs de tous les Mentonnais : Rocca Longa, Patata et Païus, plongeoirs naturels qui ont fait le bonheur des adolescents jusque dans les années 1970. Disparaissent également les « pointus », bateaux multicolores de pêcheurs qui étaient amarrés sur la plage... mais aussi le souvenir piquant et tachant du varech, des oursins et du goudron qui maculait les galets de la baie. Quant aux filets de pêche, étendus le long des parapets du quai Laurenti, les fibres synthétiques les ont fait remiser au fond des entrepôts du Vieux-Port, entre le quai Napoléon-III et la jetée Impératrice-Eugénie.

Port de Garavan

LE SUCCÈS de la navigation de plaisance et le développement du yachting sur la Côte d'Azur ont eu pour conséquence de rendre insuffisant le nombre pourtant non négligeable de ports publics. Le coût des travaux de construction ne pouvant être supporté ni par la Ville ni par l'État, on fit appel à l'initiative privée. EN 1966 est créé le deuxième port de Menton. Sa longueur totale – y compris l'avant-port – est de 750 mètres, avec une largeur moyenne de quelque 200 mètres. Sa capacité d'accueil est de 800 bateaux en secteur privé et 200 en secteur public, de différents tonnages et de longueurs variant de 8 à 40 mètres. Les travaux de construction ont duré quatorze mois. L'inauguration, le 21 juillet 1967, a fait l'objet d'une fête populaire inoubliable. LE PORT DE GARAVAN est en évolution constante pour faire face à la demande d'une clientèle internationale.

Nous nous dirigeons vers la vieille ville et nous gravissons l'avenue Saint-Jacques qui fait face au stade Rondelli. Le petit édifice qui donne son nom à cette artère a été bâti en 1688 ; de style baroque, aux teintes chaudes, il a été classé monument historique en 1948. C'était à l'origine un oratoire de voyageurs ; il devint la chapelle funéraire de la famille Bertrand, puis des Pretti de Sainte-Marie. Aujourd'hui désacralisé, il accueille des expositions temporaires.
Contigu à la chapelle Saint-Jacques, à laquelle il offre un saisissant contrepoint, se trouve l'immeuble *Garavan Beach*, séduisant exemple de l'architecture riante des « sixties ». Construit en 1963 par l'architecte monégasque Raymond Mare, il fait un clin d'œil très pertinent au langage baroque, avec le motif de feston en volutes contrariées qui sculpte verticalement les façades, offrant un écho au fronton-campanile de la chapelle. La composition présente une large corbeille centrale en arc de cercle épaulée de deux sections obliques rectilignes ; le dessin dynamique des garde-corps confère à l'ensemble une indéniable impression de légèreté.

Jardin botanique exotique Val Rahmeh

En 1922, sir Percy Radcliffe, général de l'armée britannique, époux de Rahmeh Theodore Swinburn, est au soir d'une carrière tout au service de l'Empire. En séjour à Menton, il découvre cette magnifique propriété qui deviendra le jardin botanique Val Rahmeh.

Avenue Saint-Jacques

Téléphone : 04 93 35 86 72

Ouvert tous les jours sauf mardi

• Du 1er novembre au 30 avril : de 10 h à 12 h et de 14 h à 17 h
• Du 1er mai au 31 octobre : de 10 h à 12 h et de 15 h à 18 h

Percy Radcliffe décide de s'installer sous ce ciel lumineux, dans cet amphithéâtre naturel où fleurissent déjà de luxueuses résidences et d'orgueilleux palaces, dans ce cadre où poussent les plantes les plus rares. Amoureux des jardins, il est assez probable qu'il ait lui-même introduit les premières plantes exotiques de Val Rahmeh et conçu la belle allée plantée de *Phoenix canariensis* qui conduit à la villa, réaménagée dans les années 1920 par Henri Cerutti-Maori [→ p. 30]. Au cours de la décennie suivante, une aile supplémentaire est ajoutée au sud-ouest, en harmonie avec les bâtiments existants. De style néoprovençal, cette demeure aux nombreuses terrasses couvertes abrite les services locaux du Muséum d'histoire naturelle de Paris, un laboratoire et deux salles d'expositions temporaires. LA DERNIÈRE propriétaire, une riche Anglaise capricieuse et excentrique aimant les fleurs jusqu'à la passion, accentuera l'aimable confusion du jardin en occupant tous les espaces encore libres. May Campbell fera de son domaine un lieu magique plein d'odeurs et de couleurs.

Du jardin d'agrément au jardin botanique

ÉTOURDIE par la volupté des fragrances et la magnificence des réceptions, May Campbell ne peut ou ne veut pas voir les signes qui annoncent l'écroulement de son univers. En 1966, il faut vendre. Le ministère de l'Éducation nationale se porte acquéreur et la propriété est affectée au Muséum national d'histoire naturelle, qui la transforme en jardin botanique exotique ouvert au public dès l'année suivante.

LE ROUGE ÉBLOUISSANT de l'hibiscus, l'orange lumineux de *Streptosolen*, le bleu profond de la sauge mexicaine captent un instant le regard avant que la diversité des formes n'entraîne de nouvelles émotions.

LE JARDIN BOTANIQUE remplit trois fonctions essentielles. La fonction pédagogique se traduit par l'accueil des écoliers, des collégiens et des lycéens de Menton, par l'organisation de stages pour les élèves des écoles spécialisées ou pour les étudiants des universités. La fonction muséologique est présente dans les salles du rez-de-chaussée de la villa. La troisième fonction du jardin est la conservation, avec *Sophora toromiro*, l'emblématique plante endémique de l'île de Pâques, aujourd'hui disparue et sauvée de l'extinction par l'équipe de Thor Heyerdahl qui préleva, en 1956, quelques gousses sur un petit arbuste dans le cratère du volcan Rano Kao. Les graines rapportées à Göteborg (Suède) ont miraculeusement germé et les plants ont fructifié. Les toromiros du jardin sont les descendants par bouturage de ces « miraculés ».

D'UNE SUPERFICIE de 1 hectare, le jardin Val Rahmeh juxtapose une suite de petits territoires de diverses affinités biogéographiques. On dénombre près de 1 500 taxons cohabitant dans ce domaine, dont l'aménagement comme le choix de ses composants répondent d'abord à des critères esthétiques. Comme tous les jardins, Val Rahmeh a cherché l'excellence dans quelques collections. Les fruitiers tropicaux et subtropicaux, les arécacées et les solanacées constituent la force et la fierté de ce domaine.

1

2

1. Vue de Garavan.
2. Vue de la vieille ville.

De Garavan à la vieille ville

AU CŒUR du jardin Val Rahmeh, nous gravissons, à droite, les marches du chemin Saint-Jacques, pour rejoindre le boulevard de Garavan en direction de la vieille ville et du belvédère. Le souvenir de quelques écrivains est encore bien présent dans l'atmosphère de ce quartier bucolique : Louis-Ferdinand Céline, Lesley Blanch, auteur des *Sabres du Paradis* et épouse de Romain Gary... et combien d'autres ! Parmi tous ces familiers des lieux, certains nous offrent à voir la beauté saisissante qui unit Garavan à la vieille ville et au-delà. Octave Mirbeau écrit : « C'est le vieux Menton avec ses escalades rapides de maisons tassées l'une sur l'autre, étrange et vivant grouillement de taches claires et de taches d'ombre, d'angles de soleil et de clochers bleus qui se découpent sur le fond de velours opalin des montagnes. Au-delà de la vieille ville, séparé d'elle par une large nappe d'eau brillante, le cap Martin s'avance, fendant la mer de sa masse sombre qui s'amincit comme l'étrave d'un gigantesque navire. Puis la Tête de Chien, accroupie dans le ciel, pareille à un formidable sphinx. »

Vers Gorbio
Val de Gorbio
Les Castagnins
Vers Ste Agnès
Route du Val de Castagnins
Av. de Prades
Av. des Acacias
Vallée du Borrigo
N.D. de Fatima
Carrefour Saissi Henry
Torrent de Gorbio
Route de Gorbio
Rue Peglion
R. Peglion
Corniche des Serres de la Madone
Allée des Arbousiers
Corniche des Serres de la Madone
Sentier du Vallon
Chemin de Ste Agnès
Av. Guillaume 1er de Provence
Parc Gorre
Av. Cernuschi
Cours René Coty
Av. des Alliés
Rue des Sœurs Munet
Av. Riviera
La Madone
Allée du 8 Mai 1945
A. des Hespérides
R. Vallière
Impasse de la Maison Russe
Route C. des Serres de la Madone
Ch. du Pigautier
Tr. de la Vierge
Rue des Sœurs Munet
GARE
Av. de la Gare
Av. Mal Juin
Chemin du Pigautier
Av. Cochrane
Rue Albert 1er
R. Massena
R. V. Hugo
Av. Thiers
Eglise Russe
Rue Paul Morillot
Av. Fiorette
Chap. de la Madone
Parc de la Madone
R. P. Morillot
Synagogue St Christophe
Av. des Bruyères
Sacré Cœur
Rue Morgan
Cours du Centenaire
Av. Edouard VII
C. Georges V
Av. de Verdun
Jardins Biovès
PTT
St John
Aristide Briand
Jean Monnet
Pont de Union
Av. du Gal de Gaulle
Av. de la Madone
Av. du Pigautier
R. Frères Picco
R. Am. Courbet
Rue H. Bennet
Square Elisabeth
Promenade du Soleil
Av. Carnot
R. Albert
Baie du Soleil
Vers Monaco et Nice
Mer Méditerranée

À l'ouest de Menton

De la place des Victoires à la villa Carla

Menton est rattaché à la France en 1861. Un des premiers soucis du Second Empire est de désenclaver la région par la création d'un important réseau routier et ferroviaire. En 1869, le chemin de fer arrive à Menton ; il va contribuer au bouleversement de la petite cité, qui part à la conquête de l'Ouest et devient une station climatique réputée.

1. Fronton de l'hôtel Alexandra.
2. Riviera Palace.
3-4. Place des Victoires et monument aux morts.
5. Pilastre anthropomorphe de la tour Saint-Ambroise.
6. Église orthodoxe russe.

Place des Victoires

LA PLACE des Victoires est sans doute l'un des lieux les plus suggestifs de la cité. Une impression de sérénité se dégage de cet harmonieux espace elliptique. Dressé au centre, le monument aux morts, inauguré en 1928, est dû à l'architecte Paul Tournon [→ p. 31] et au sculpteur Antoine Sartorio (1885-1988) à qui l'on doit, entre autres, le bas-relief du palais de justice de Menton et la façade du palais de la Méditerranée à Nice. Autour de la place, nous pouvons remarquer deux beaux immeubles Art déco à l'élégante modénature.

• AU N° 19, la villa *France*, édifiée par Adrien Rey [→ p. 30], présente un portail cintré, surmonté d'un oculus encadré d'un gracieux motif de colombes. Les deux bow-windows qui articulent la courbe sont couronnés de frontons en arc de cercle d'inspiration italienne.

• AU N° 26, la façade dessinée par Henri Ceruti-Maori [→ p. 30] prend une forme concave. L'attique percé de trois doubles-fenêtres cintrées apparaît comme un hommage à l'architecture florentine. D'élégants fers forgés ornent les balcons et un bas-relief couronne la façade.

1

2

3

4

1-2. Riviera Palace.
3. Winter Palace.
4. Résidence Lutétia.

À l'arrière-plan de la place des Victoires, on aperçoit deux masses de rose et de blanc qui se détachent des collines : le *Riviera Palace* et le *Winter Palace*.

Riviera Palace

28, avenue Riviera

L'ANCIEN hôtel *Riviera* a été construit par l'architecte Abel Glena [→ p. 30] en 1898. Les trois étages d'origine ont été surélevés de deux autres par son collaborateur Alfred Marsang [→ p. 30] en 1910.
CE VASTE BÂTIMENT de 250 chambres offrait à sa clientèle un théâtre et un jardin ombragé de tonnelles de rosiers. La façade, où se mêlent éclectisme et Art nouveau – comme dans de nombreux édifices mentonnais –, est ornée d'une frise de Guillaume Cerutti-Maori, ponctuée de céramiques turquoise de la manufacture Saïssi. La frise évoque les principaux pays (États-Unis, France, Grande-Bretagne…) dont l'hôtel s'honorait de recevoir la clientèle.
À L'INTÉRIEUR, le faste de la Belle Époque s'exalte à nouveau : hall d'entrée, grand salon, salon de musique, remarquable escalier de marbre, avec les décors peints par Cerutti-Maori, glaces, verrières et vitraux. À l'instar des somptueux hôtels de Menton, le *Riviera* a été reconverti en appartements privés en 1958.

Winter Palace

20, avenue Riviera

RICHE de 220 chambres, le *Winter Palace* a été édifié par Albert Tournaire [→ p. 31] en 1907. Au-dessus des terrasses, ses deux clochetons à tuiles vernissées jaunes se profilent sur le ciel et les montagnes en arrière-plan. La qualité de l'édifice a motivé l'inscription de sa façade et de ses toitures au titre des monuments historiques en 1975. À l'intérieur, quelques éléments d'époque – le hall notamment – ont été préservés, mais le décor a été en grande partie modifié. Comme le proche *Riviera Palace*, le *Winter* a été réaménagé en appartements.

Guillaume Cerutti-Maori

Menton, 1866-1955

PEINTRE RÉPUTÉ pour ses fresques ornementales, Guillaume Cerutti-Maori, père de l'architecte Henri Cerutti-Maori, a décoré – outre le *Riviera Palace* – de nombreux édifices mentonnais : la voûte de Saint-Michel [→ p. 52] et celle des Pénitents blancs [→ p. 54] ; les galeries de la fondation Alphand-Bariquand [→ p. 68] ; une maison bâtie par l'architecte Viale [→ p. 80] ; sa propre demeure [→ p. 105] ; une façade à l'angle des rues Ardoïno et Partouneaux [→ p. 96] ; la maison d'Abel Glena [→ p. 108].

Résidence *Lutétia*

Chemin du Lutétia

NON LOIN du *Riviera* et du *Winter*, l'architecte Félix Vérola [→ p. 31] édifie, en 1914, l'hôtel *Lutétia* pour un groupe financier allemand. Mis sous séquestre durant la Première Guerre mondiale, il est vendu et transformé en appartements. Il n'a jamais rempli sa fonction hôtelière.

1

2

3

1. Casa Isabella : *détail de ferronnerie.*
2-3. Casa Isabella.

En opposition à ces grands vaisseaux de l'industrie hôtelière, fiers de s'exposer à tous, *Château Marly* est une grande villa du début du XIXe s. qui se niche dans le vert profond des cyprès et les gris des eucalyptus – en ses murs, la famille de Partouneaux a accueilli l'impératrice douairière de Russie en 1857.
EN DESSOUS, rue des Sœurs-Munet, on remarque la villa *La Vierge*, construite à la fin du XIXe s. Elle abrite la communauté des sœurs missionnaires fondée par Alice Munet, ce qui explique la présence, dans le jardin, d'une réplique de la grotte de Lourdes, dominée par un imposant araucaria.
En quittant la place des Victoires et en descendant l'avenue Édouard-VII, nous entrons dans le quartier de La Condamine, dit aussi « de l'Entente cordiale », urbanisé à partir des années 1900. À cette époque, les vergers laissent place aux courts de tennis (1901) et à l'église du Sacré-Cœur (15, avenue Édouard-VII) construite par l'architecte danois Hans Georg Tersling [→ p. 31] en 1913. La Grande Guerre interrompt les travaux, qui seront repris dans les années 1920 par Félix Vérola [→ p. 31].

Casa Isabella

14, avenue Édouard-VII

LA *CASA ISABELLA*, dessinée par Henri Cerutti-Maori [→ p. 30], perpétue l'esprit du classicisme français. L'élévation de la façade, assez solennelle, est encadrée de deux travées à pilastres surmontées d'un fronton triangulaire brisé. Entre les fenêtres de l'attique, habillées en plein cintre, la nouvelle tendance ornementale a réduit les fresques (tant à l'honneur au cours des décennies précédentes) à l'état de tympans peints couleur bleu ciel.

LA CORNICHE affirme son autorité par la présence de deux frontons saillants. La comparaison avec le bâtiment contigu est significative : à l'ornementation toute classique de Cerutti-Maori, il oppose la panoplie complète du style Art déco, qui triomphe au lendemain de la Première Guerre.

Nous poursuivons notre chemin dans l'avenue Édouard-VII et nous tournons à droite, dans l'avenue Thiers, où nous remarquons deux beaux immeubles, le *Little Palace* (n° 3) et le *Flower Palace* (n° 5), œuvres d'Abel Glena [→ p. 30]. Ils témoignent de la même inspiration que la *Casa Isabella* d'Henri Cerutti-Maori. Frontons, moulurations et fers forgés néo-Louis XVI arborent flambeaux et carquois entrecroisés – un motif de fonte industrielle très présent sur le territoire mentonnais.
Nous reprenons l'avenue Édouard-VII, puis nous tournons à droite, cours du Centenaire, percé en 1960. Son nom honore le rattachement de Menton à la France par le traité de Paris du 2 février 1861. Avant de poursuivre dans le cours du Centenaire, nous empruntons la première voie à gauche, la rue Henry-Bennet.

Rue Henry-Bennet

CETTE RUE porte le nom du médecin anglais Bennet (1816-1891), à qui l'on doit d'avoir favorisé la promotion de Menton au rang de station climatique de première importance – dans la rue de la République, un monument est dédié à sa mémoire [→ p. 97].
CETTE PETITE artère, qui aboutit à la mer, possède une belle unité stylistique. Le côté impair présente une succession

1

2

1. Rue Henry-Bennet.
2. Collège Guillaume-Vento.

de charmantes maisons de ville à deux ou trois étages bâties au cours du premier tiers du XXe s. Toutes différentes, elles offrent un savoureux échantillonnage de styles déployés à cette époque.

• AU N° 19, immeuble *Les Fruits d'or*, d'Henri Cerutti-Maori : une rigoureuse façade des années 1930, dont l'austérité ne tolère, au-dessus de la porte, qu'un petit panneau peint figurant des grappes de citrons.

• AU N° 15, la façade attire le regard par sa couleur ocre. Ce savoureux petit immeuble, élevé sur trois niveaux, a été construit par l'architecte Viale. Son style est empreint de l'esthétique Art nouveau. Un décor d'agrumes, œuvre du fresquiste Guillaume Cerutti-Maori, orne le débord de la toiture.

• AU N° 13, le bâtiment, dont la façade est à dominante jaune, est d'une facture nettement plus sévère que le précédent, malgré son bow-window central. Seule fantaisie, les cabochons de céramique turquoise qui ponctuent la façade, où alternent cercles et pointes de diamants.

• AU N° 11, l'édifice, par contraste, fait montre ici d'un traitement plus souple, déroulant l'inflexion du bow-window. La rhétorique architecturale est un joli compromis entre l'Art nouveau de la Belle Époque et l'Art déco de l'entre-deux-guerres. Quant aux ferronneries industrielles des balcons, elles sont résolument de style 1925.

Nous reprenons maintenant le cours du Centenaire. Les façades affichent ici, en pleine ville, la modernité architecturale des quarante dernières années du XXe s. Le collège Guillaume-Vento (n° 400) en est un excellent témoignage. Il porte le nom d'un noble génois, premier seigneur de Menton en 1262. L'établissement a été construit en 1993 d'après les plans des architectes niçois Danielle Dogliani, Pierre Baptiste et Pierre Bernasconi. Son dessin, d'un modernisme qui ne renie pas un certain classicisme, est emblématique du style des années 1990, avec son arche monumentale qui marque l'entrée.

Nous traversons la rue Morgan, où nous apercevons la villa *Renée* (n° 13), maison familiale de l'architecte Marsang [→ p. 30], caractéristique des constructions mentonnaises des années 1880-1914 avec les frises en sgraffite (décor en camaïeu résultant du grattage d'un enduit clair sur fond de stuc sombre) et la tourelle-belvédère. Après la rue Morgan, nous découvrons, à gauche, l'ancien théâtre de verdure, puis nous atteignons l'avenue Cochrane. En tournant à gauche, nous nous rendons au conservatoire.

Villa Cochrane

DITE AUSSI ***villa* La Victoire**

CONSERVATOIRE DE MUSIQUE, DE DANSE ET D'ART DRAMATIQUE

10, avenue Cochrane

Téléphone : 04 93 35 82 95

QUELQUE PEU cachée par les orangers et les oliviers de l'ancien théâtre de verdure, la villa Cochrane a été affectée, depuis 1950, au conservatoire municipal. Cette belle demeure, édifiée entre 1918 et 1920 par Abel Glena [→ p. 30] pour de riches Anglais, lord et lady Percy Cochrane, est une fantaisie aimable librement inspirée du répertoire italianisant. Colonnettes, moulurations et arcades y abondent. Une loggia à arcades abrite l'escalier d'accès à l'entrée latérale.

L'ENSEMBLE n'est pas dépourvu de grâce, avec son imposante corniche en doucine et ses beaux balcons dont les ferronneries à volutes sont encore imprégnées du style

1

2

4

3. Villa Fred-Anny.
4. Chapelle Saint-Christophe.
5. Résidence Impérial.

1-2. Villa Cochrane.

5

Art nouveau déjà en déclin à cette époque. Ce conservatoire accueille aujourd'hui 450 élèves dans plusieurs disciplines : musique, chorégraphie et art dramatique.

Après le rond-point Georges-Pompidou et l'avenue Cernuschi, nous voyons, sur notre gauche, le square de Sotchi, inauguré en 1973 ; son nom évoque le jumelage de Menton avec la grande station balnéaire de Russie, au bord de la mer Noire. Le « monument » placé ici n'est autre qu'une stalactite vieille de sept millions d'années, extraite du tunnel de la Giraude lors des travaux destinés à la construction de l'autoroute.

Nous traversons un lotissement, *Le Clos des Lucioles*, et gagnons l'avenue du Pigautier. À l'angle, nous remarquons la villa *Fred-Anny* (n° 5), à beau décor de sgraffite. Un peu plus bas, à l'angle de l'avenue de la Madone, nous voyons la chapelle Saint-Christophe, construite en 1874 dans la propriété de Gaspard Médecin, alors maire de Menton. De style néogothique, cet édifice privé fut mis à la disposition du curé de l'église du Sacré-Cœur (avenue Édouard-VII) en 1955. Les pèlerinages qui s'y déroulaient à l'intention des automobilistes et des voyageurs étaient de véritables fêtes populaires, aujourd'hui tombées dans l'oubli. Cette chapelle est actuellement un lieu pour des expositions temporaires.

En empruntant, à droite, l'avenue de la Madone, nous nous approchons d'un portail monumental qui ferme le parc de l'hôtel *Impérial*.

Résidence *Impérial*

9, avenue de la Madone

SUR CETTE PLAINE littorale qui s'étire entre la mer et la colline de la Madone, Pierre Alberti, comte de La Brigue, était propriétaire, à l'est du palais Carnolès, d'un immense domaine juxtaposant des parcelles, les unes boisées, les autres à usage agricole. Ces carrés de bigaradiers, de citronniers, d'oliviers et de vignes constituaient un délicat patchwork qui s'animait au moment de la récolte. C'est sur ce domaine, vendu au début du XXe s., que sera construit l'*Impérial*, destiné au célèbre hôtelier Joseph Aletti, et que sera aménagé son parc. Le style de la façade est simple, avec un souci de retour aux sources locales qui semble marquer la fin de la Belle Époque.

INAUGURÉ en décembre 1913, l'*Impérial* est le dernier des grands établissements dus à l'architecte Tersling [→ p. 31]. C'est aussi l'un des derniers à clore la grande tradition de ces somptueux palaces qui, de l'*Alexandra* (1884) – dont le chantier fut supervisé par le même Tersling, alors au début de sa carrière –, au *Riviera* (1898) et au *Winter* (1907), attiraient la *gentry* cosmopolite dans l'élégance et le luxe d'un décor faisant écho à ceux de la clientèle. Mais les lumières de l'*Impérial* s'éteindront après une seule année d'activité.

3

1. *Parc de la résidence* Impérial.
2. *Hôtel* L'Aiglon.
3. *Chapelle de la Madone.*

La Première Guerre mondiale marque la fin des villégiatures de familles aisées. Les palaces comme les villas se vident brusquement ; Menton devient un vaste hôpital où affluent les blessés. Réquisitionné en février 1915, l'*Impérial* devient – avec l'aide financière de deux Anglais résidant habituellement à Menton, Percy Cochrane et Stanley Randall – l'hôpital auxiliaire n° 222, dit aussi « de l'Entente cordiale ». En 1947-1948, l'*Impérial* est transformé en appartements par les soins de l'architecte niçois Milon de Peillon.

Le parc de l'*Impérial*

L'environnement végétal inhabituel du parc de l'hôtel répond aux choix de Tersling, désireux d'effacer l'impression de monotonie née de la présence d'une grande façade nue. Un rideau végétal s'impose, constitué de palmiers (*Phoenix canariensis, Washingtonia robusta, Butio capitata, Chamaerops humilis*), d'araucarias et de pins parasols – aujourd'hui hauts d'une trentaine de mètres –, de *Ficus elastica*, d'eucalyptus, ces derniers paraissant peu en harmonie dans cet ensemble qui joue parfaitement son rôle en créant un bel effet de perspective. Depuis la somptueuse grille qui clôture le domaine, le regard glisse sur la pelouse tachée de quelques plages de couleur et piquetée d'agrumes et de cycas, butte contre la riche palmeraie d'où jaillissent les silhouettes élégantes des pins parasols et des araucarias, et rencontre en arrière-plan la partie haute de l'hôtel, qui apparaît comme un immense château bâti au milieu d'un vaste ensemble boisé. L'illusion est totale. Le parc de l'hôtel *Impérial*, d'une superficie de 1 hectare, est un merveilleux jardin qui témoigne du savoir-faire de son concepteur et conserve l'image et l'atmosphère de ces grands palaces qui appartiennent au paysage et à l'histoire de Menton.

Jouxtant le parc de l'*Impérial*, l'hôtel *L'Aiglon* (7, avenue de la Madone), bâti en 1885 par Tersling, est caractéristique du style de la fin du siècle. Son architecture et son décor quelque peu prolixe font penser aux pavillons construits en Europe centrale. *L'Aiglon* est surélevé en 1951.

Après avoir dépassé *L'Aiglon*, nous longeons le parc de la Madone. À son extrémité, nous quittons l'avenue de la Madone pour remonter, à droite, la rue Paul-Morillot.

Chapelle de la Madone

2, rue Paul-Morillot

Ce sanctuaire, aujourd'hui désaffecté, est dédié à la Vierge. Construit aux XIe et XIIe s., au bas des pentes gréseuses de la colline des Serres-de-la-Madone, il longe l'antique Via Julia Augusta.

En 1482, Lambert Grimaldi autorise la création d'un couvent de frères mineurs attenant à la chapelle. Au XVIe s., celle-ci devient un lieu de pèlerinage réputé où les fidèles se rassemblent autour de Fra Schiavone, son prieur, qui mourra de la peste en 1529. La tradition locale rapporte que, la nuit venue, le sentier qui reliait le couvent à la tour Saint-Ambroise, où résidait Fra Schiavone, se transformait en un long ruban de lumière et que s'y produisaient de nombreux miracles. À sa mort, la chapelle tombe dans l'oubli. Elle est reconstruite en 1550 par les soins du tuteur du jeune prince Honoré Ier, Étienne Grimaldi – son monogramme figure avec les armes des Grimaldi sur l'un des chapiteaux de la chapelle [→ p. 17].

1

2

4

1. Autel de la chapelle de la Madone.
2. Résidence Alexandra.
3. Tour Saint-Ambroise.
4. Église orthodoxe russe.

EN 1640, la chapelle et le jardin sont donnés par le prince Honoré II aux pères réformés de l'ordre de Saint-François. Ils y demeurent jusqu'à la Révolution. Rouverte au début du XIXe s., elle reçoit les religieuses de l'ordre de Saint-Thomas-de-Villeneuve, appelées par le prince Honoré V pour prendre en charge l'hôtel-Dieu et l'école de filles. Après le rattachement de Menton à la France, Charles III vend les bâtiments à un particulier (1862), qui les transforme en villa. Un siècle plus tard, le détenteur des biens est exproprié par le département des Alpes-Maritimes et le site est transformé en parc. Les bâtiments sont rasés en 1967; la chapelle est sauvegardée *in extremis*.

Tour Saint-Ambroise

Entrée par les jardins du palais Carnolès

ÉDIFIÉE à l'origine sur un puits, la tour Saint-Ambroise est un petit monument de plan hexagonal à trois niveaux, couvert d'un dôme de tuiles vernissées en écailles de poisson. Sa partie supérieure a été modifiée au XVIIIe s. LES DEUX premiers niveaux sont d'un dessin relativement simple. En revanche, le troisième est scandé par des pilastres anthropomorphes (atlantes et cariatides à figurations de grotesques) et des baies en plein cintre. La tour Saint-Ambroise, seul monument de style maniériste qui subsiste à Menton, a été inscrite sur l'Inventaire supplémentaire des monuments historiques en 1961.

Résidence *Alexandra*

10, rue Paul-Morillot

L'ANCIEN HÔTEL *Alexandra* est élevé en 1884 sur les dessins d'un architecte parisien, Gustave Rives [→ p. 31]. Le jeune Hans Georg Tersling [→ p. 31] veille à l'exécution des travaux. C'est le début de sa carrière mentonnaise, à une époque où naissent les premiers palaces de la ville; l'*Alexandra* en est un bon exemple. L'ORIGINALITÉ de l'édifice réside en deux imposantes tourelles, chacune surmontée d'un bulbe couvert d'ardoise, lui-même sommé d'un belvédère à clocheton. Ces couronnements ont été supprimés lors de la réfection de la toiture, au début des années 1980, ce qui a ôté sa légèreté à la façade. L'hôtel est agrandi en 1925. Une façade ouest néo-Renaissance est ajoutée. À L'ORIGINE, le parc possédait des courts de tennis et un terrain de cricket, ainsi qu'un kiosque à musique, aménagements aujourd'hui disparus. L'hôtel *Alexandra* a été transformé en résidence.

Église orthodoxe russe Notre-Dame-Joie-des-Affligés-et-Saint-Nicolas-le-Thaumaturge

14, rue Paul-Morillot

Visites guidées, le quatrième samedi du mois à 14h30 (sauf période estivale), organisées par le Service du patrimoine (renseignements : 04 92 10 97 10)

À LA FIN DU XIXe S., une importante colonie russe fréquente la Côte d'Azur. La grande-duchesse Anastasia, tante de Nicolas II, fonde l'Association Sainte-Anastasie afin de permettre à de jeunes tuberculeux de son pays de séjourner à Menton. Un établissement hospitalier voit le jour en 1882; son église est érigée dix ans plus tard. La maison de convalescence, transférée dans la vallée de Gorbio en 1908, est toujours en activité.

3

1. Église orthodoxe russe : l'iconostase.
2. Jardin de La Palmosa.
3. Chapelle Saint-Ambroise.

LES PLANS DE L'ÉGLISE sont donnés par l'architecte russe Térémine et exécutés par Tersling [→ p. 31], le plus élégant et le plus grand architecte mentonnais. Dédiée à Notre-Dame Joie des affligés et à saint Nicolas le Thaumaturge, elle est consacrée le 26 novembre 1892.

TRÈS ENDOMMAGÉE lors des combats de 1940 et par les pillages de la guerre, elle est restaurée en 1958 et entièrement rénovée en 1992-1993. Cette église, qui reprend le schéma centré des édifices orthodoxes – ainsi que la forme traditionnelle de flamme des bulbes –, ne présente pas un pur style russe, mais un mélange des styles occidental et byzantin.

L'INTÉRIEUR a conservé sa décoration, dont l'iconostase, cloison de marbre ornée d'icônes qui sépare de la nef le sanctuaire, où est encore célébré le culte orthodoxe russe. La juridiction de l'Église orthodoxe étant différente de celle de l'Église catholique, les Russes peuvent choisir leur rattachement hiérarchique. L'église Notre-Dame-Joie-des-Affligés-et-Saint-Nicolas-le-Thaumaturge dépend de l'archevêque de Genève mais est rattachée au patriarcat de New York, qui représente l'Église russe en exil.

Square Armand-Fernandez

DIT AUSSI ***jardin de* La Palmosa**

20, rue Paul-Morillot

À PROXIMITÉ de l'église orthodoxe a été dessiné, en 1995, un jardin situé sur l'emplacement d'une ancienne villa, *La Palmosa*. Cet espace boisé est dédié à Armand Fernandez (1903-1964), un maître de l'art floral et un pépiniériste distingué dont le nom est intimement lié aux célèbres batailles de fleurs du pays mentonnais des années 1950.

LES CONCEPTEURS ont imaginé un parc arboré, recouvert d'une pelouse et traversé par un large sentier revêtu d'un asphalte lisse pour assurer le confort des promeneurs. Orientés nord-sud, dix palmiers (*Phoenix canariensis*) constituent un élément de structuration du jardin. Filaos, cyprès, ifs, araucarias, *Cedrus atlantica*, pittosporums et quelques touffes de bambous sont placés sur le pourtour, mais ils ne donnent jamais une impression d'enfermement. On remarquera le magnifique cocotier du Chili (*Jubaea spectabilis*) au port trapu et au stipe lisse, dressé telle une colonne, un superbe *Acacia malanoxylon* et deux oliviers centenaires décharnés comme des mains de patriarche. L'aire de jeux conçue pour les enfants est ombragée par la frondaison épaisse d'une très belle rosacée (*Cotoneaster pannosa*) originaire de Chine.

LA PELOUSE piquetée de *Chamaerops humilis* est ouverte aux promeneurs, pour lesquels des bancs ont été fixés le long du chemin. Ce square se distingue par l'absence de fleurissement, hormis une haie de lauriers rouges en bordure de l'hôpital et un buisson aux fleurs blanches à l'entrée. La façade de verre de l'établissement hospitalier, construit en 1979, se fond dans la végétation ambiante, reflétant le port altier de *Washingtonia robusta*.

Nous revenons sur nos pas, rue Paul-Morillot, et nous tournons à droite afin de descendre l'avenue Florette. Nous regagnons l'avenue de la Madone. Une petite chapelle funéraire appartenant aux Pretti-Galeani de Saint-Ambroise rappelle aux promeneurs le souvenir de l'une des plus importantes familles de Menton.

Palais Carnolès Musée des Beaux-Arts

Antoine Ier Grimadi décide de faire bâtir une résidence d'été dans l'esprit du Grand Trianon de Versailles (1687). Une tradition rapporte que les plans de la villégiature du prince de Monaco auraient été réalisés par l'architecte Robert de Cotte, associé à Jacques Gabriel.

3, avenue de la Madone

Ouvert tous les jours
sauf mardi et fêtes légales
de 10 h à 12 h et de 14 h à 18 h

Téléphone : 04 93 35 49 71

Courriel : musees@villedementon.com
Site internet :
www.villedementon.com/fr/musee.htm

1

1. Palais Carnolès.
2. Dessin en élévation de la façade du palais avant modification.

On est en tout cas certain que Jacques Gabriel a conçu des plans pour le palais Carnolès et que l'architecte monégasque Antoine Latour a été chargé de les adapter.
En 1725, il dresse un plan d'ensemble, puis prend en charge la construction de la résidence et de ses dépendances. Outre les bâtiments, le domaine comprend un jardin potager, un jardin ornemental, dit « fleuriste » et un grand jardin-parc avec bassins et jeux d'eau. En 1731, la mort d'Antoine Ier marque le début d'une longue série de malheurs qui entraîne progressivement le domaine vers une inéluctable dégradation que la plantation de mûriers – en vue de promouvoir la sériciculture – ne fera que retarder sans pouvoir l'enrayer.

2

Guerre de Succession d'Autriche, Révolution française, révolution mentonnaise, confiscation des biens des Grimaldi par la ville libre de Menton puis leur restitution, vente en 1863 du domaine de Carnolès par le prince Charles III à Jean-Baptiste Gellot, transformation du palais en casino puis en villa meublée pour têtes couronnées… sont autant d'avatars qui finiront par dénaturer la propriété, mais le palais sortira sans trop de dommages de cette longue crise.

En 1896, le domaine est acheté par Edward Phels Allis, zoologiste américain spécialiste des poissons, qui confie à l'architecte Tersling [→ p. 31] les travaux de remodelage de la propriété.

Du côté jardin, la façade est profondément modifiée par la suppression du grand escalier extérieur à double révolution ainsi que par la construction de deux ailes latérales conférant à l'édifice une facture néoclassique linéaire et imposante. Les deux niveaux du bâtiment n'étant plus reliés par un escalier, Tersling choisit d'en créer un à l'intérieur. Ainsi, sur la façade ouest, viennent s'ajouter deux petits retours comprenant un escalier d'honneur, éclairé par une verrière, donnant accès aux salons de l'étage noble, et deux escaliers desservant les pièces sous combles. Ces adjonctions se traduisent, sur la façade, par des éléments concaves percés de niches surmontées d'oculus de facture très élégante. La belle ferronnerie du garde-corps de l'escalier et la galerie ornée de marbres polychromes révèlent l'époque à laquelle elles ont été réalisées.

En 1947, Edward Phels Allis meurt. En 1961, l'industriel belge Philippart, dernier propriétaire, est exproprié afin de créer un parc public. Huit ans plus tard, le palais et le jardin sont inscrits sur l'Inventaire des monuments historiques. Le palais est alors affecté au musée des Beaux-Arts, qui est inauguré en 1977.

1

2

1. Décor du grand salon du palais Carnolès.
2. Louis Bréa, Vierge à l'Enfant.

Les collections

Une partie des collections provient du fonds de l'ancien musée de la rue Lorédan-Larchey, qui abrite aujourd'hui le musée de Préhistoire régionale [→ p. 106]. Constitué à partir de la fin du XIXe s., ce fonds a été considérablement enrichi par le legs, en 1959, de Charles Wakefield Mori, amateur de la peinture du XIXe s. et créateur du musée national de Monaco, dont il était le conservateur. Achats, donations et legs viennent enrichir les collections du musée, en particulier la belle donation d'un orientaliste, le général roumain Georges Bagulesco, riche d'importantes estampes japonaises. Enfin, les Biennales d'art contemporain de Menton viennent alimenter le fonds du musée en œuvres du XXe s. – tous les premiers prix de cette manifestation sont achetés par l'État et déposés au palais Carnolès.

Les collections, exposées sur deux niveaux, offrent un beau panorama de la peinture du XIIIe au XXe s.

• Au premier étage, sont accrochées les œuvres des primitifs français, italiens, espagnols et flamands, telle une Vierge à l'Enfant toscane (XIIIe s.). Les écoles européennes du XVe au XIXe s. sont également bien représentées. Des XVe et XVIe s., on remarque

une Présentation de la Vierge au Temple rhénane (XVe s.), une Vierge (fin XVe s.) attribuée à l'école de Léonard de Vinci, la Vierge à l'Enfant (début XVIe) de Bernardino Luini, l'un des artisans de la Renaissance lombarde. À ces noms, il faut ajouter ceux de Louis Bréa, peintre niçois actif de 1473 à 1523, du Maître de San Lorenzo (XVIe s.) et de Bronzino, grande figure du second maniérisme florentin (XVIe s.).

POUR LE XVIIe s., on s'attachera tout particulièrement à des œuvres telles que *L'Embarquement* de Jan Baptist

1

Weenix, *Portrait d'un seigneur italien* par Ferdinand Voet, sans oublier Philippe de Champaigne avec l'admirable *Saint Benoît recevant Maur et Placide*.

LE XVIIIe S. figure ici en bonne place, avec la belle toile de François Guillaume Ménageot, *Les Adieux de Polyxène à Hécube*, et *Le Sacrifice d'Iphigénie* dû au talent du peintre anglais Benjamin West. Le XIXe est également mis en valeur avec *L'Approche de l'orage* de John Constable, son compatriote, qui aura une influence marquante sur le jeune Delacroix.

TOUJOURS au premier étage, une salle est consacrée aux modernes, parmi lesquels on remarque : Charles Camoin, qui exposa avec les fauves de 1905 ; Suzanne Valadon, qui posa pour Renoir et Toulouse-Lautrec avant de devenir l'un des peintres importants de sa génération ; Moïse Kisling, artiste de l'école de Paris ; le grand coloriste Othon Friesz.

• AU REZ-DE-CHAUSSÉE, sont présentés les joyaux de la collection Wakefield Mori (notamment Suzanne Valadon, Vlaminck, Utrillo, Dufy, Braque et Picabia), accompagnés d'acquisitions (Gleizes, Piaubert...) et de nombreux dépôts de l'État (Sutherland, Poliakoff, Saura...).

À CES TABLEAUX, il faut ajouter du mobilier, des tapisseries, des dessins, estampes et affiches, ainsi que des œuvres statuaires installées tant à l'intérieur du palais Carnolès (Carpeaux, Dubois...) que dans son parc (Bernstamm, Janniot, Sigaldi...).

OUTRE LA PRÉSENTATION permanente des collections, le musée des Beaux-Arts de Menton organise au cours de l'année plusieurs expositions temporaires (au rez-de-chaussée du palais) qui s'attachent le plus souvent à faire connaître les œuvres d'artistes contemporains.

2

1. La collection d'agrumes du parc de Carnolès présente 137 variétés différentes.
2. Jardin de sculptures du parc de Carnolès.

Le parc de Carnolès

LE PARC DE CARNOLÈS, qui s'étend sur 1 hectare, est orné de sculptures. La large allée qui le traverse nous permet d'accéder à l'entrée du musée. Elle est bordée de grands palmiers (*Phoenix canariensis*, *Chamaerops humilis*) et de cycas. Le musée des Beaux-Arts est niché dans un écrin de verdure. Parmi les vieux et beaux arbres, on peut voir un magnifique pin parasol dont le tronc mesure près de 2 mètres de diamètre, un chêne vert à l'immense frondaison, deux podocarpus et un *Washingtonia filifera* de 20 mètres de haut.

ENTRE l'allée et les courts de tennis qui bordent le parc, a été installée une belle collection d'agrumes constituée de 137 variétés, dont : l'oranger commun (*Citrus sinensis*), le bigaradier (*Citrus aurantium*), le citronnier (*Citrus limon*) et quelques raretés comme le bigaradier *bizzaria* et le cédratier Rhobs et Arsa.

EN 1999, le Conservatoire français des collections spécialisées a distingué la collection de *Citrus*. En 2005, le parc obtient le label « Jardin remarquable ».

1. Hôtel Prince de Galles.
2. Résidence Le Florentina.
3. Promenade du Soleil.

1

2

3

Avant de sortir du parc, nous pouvons admirer, du côté mer, l'hôtel *Prince de Galles* (4, avenue du Général-de-Gaulle et 69, promenade du Soleil), l'un des plus anciens établissements de tourisme de Menton. Il a été édifié sous le Second Empire, sur l'emplacement de l'ancienne caserne des carabiniers.

Nous quittons le parc de Carnolès et gagnons le bord de mer par une artère située en prolongement de la rue Paul-Morillot : la rue Panaït-Istrati, dont le nom conserve le souvenir de l'écrivain roumain (1884-1935). Istrati a résidé à Menton, à l'hôtel *Les Sapins* (chemin de la Maison-Russe), à partir de 1926. Une de ses œuvres, intitulée *Codine* (1926), a été adaptée au cinéma en 1962 par Henri Colpi et a obtenu le grand prix du scénario à Cannes l'année suivante.

Résidence *Le Florentina*

Angle rue Panaït-Istrati et promenade du Soleil

LE FLORENTINA est un exemple réussi parmi les barres d'habitation qui s'ouvrent au rivage. L'immeuble a été construit en 1966, au plus fort de la vogue balnéaire, par l'architecte Yves-André Parquet. MALGRÉ sa taille imposante, c'est une impression de légèreté qui prime. La très sensible inflexion de la façade suffirait à elle seule à briser la sensation de masse ; s'ajoute à cela une série de subtils détails. Le plan frontal est gommé par un travail systématique de biseautage : ainsi la base maçonnée des allèges des balcons est inclinée vers l'extérieur, par opposition aux lisses métalliques des garde-corps qui se replient vers l'intérieur, donnant le sentiment de lutter contre les vents marins, en évacuant ainsi l'idée de pesanteur.

« DES BOSQUETS d'orangers, de citronniers parfument l'atmosphère ; des villas élégantes, des châteaux à colonnades et à terrasses se montrent au milieu de la verdure et des fleurs ; de profondes vallées aux versants ombragés d'oliviers prolongent au loin dans le cœur des montagnes et se ramifient en gorges rocailleuses ; des villages, semblables à des forteresses, couronnent les cimes abruptes qui se dressent autour du cirque verdoyant. »

ÉLISÉE RECLUS.

Nous longeons la promenade du Soleil et nous nous reposons un instant sous la pagode du square qui évoque le séjour à Menton du géographe Élisée Reclus, dans les années 1860, créateur malgré lui du premier « slogan » de la ville : « Menton, perle de la France ». Avant de regagner le centre-ville, à l'angle de la promenade du Soleil et de l'avenue Carnot, nous remarquons la résidence *Admiral Plaza*.

Résidence *Admiral Plaza*

2, avenue Carnot et promenade du Soleil

DANS LA VAGUE de constructions de la fin du XXe s., l'*Admiral Plaza* occupe, avec deux autres immeubles de l'avenue Félix-Faure (le *Victoria Palace* et le *Victoria*

1. Résidence Admiral Plaza.
2. Hôtel de Londres.

1

2

3. Résidence Gloria Maris.
4. La sirène de Gloria Maris.

3

Beach, édifiés à la même époque), une place prépondérante sur le front de mer. Plus homogène que le *Victoria Palace*, l'*Admiral Plaza* s'inscrit dans le courant historiciste qui a marqué les années 1990, après la remise en cause de l'esthétique moderne. Bâti en 1996 par les architectes Robert Milon de Peillon et Dan Costa-Foru, il représente, par ses choix et ses proportions, un effort honorable pour s'inscrire dans la tradition mentonnaise éclectique de la Belle Époque, revisitant d'une certaine manière l'héritage d'architectes comme Adrien Rey, à qui l'on doit le marché couvert du quai de Monléon et le musée de la rue Lorédan-Larchey.

AU REZ-DE-CHAUSSÉE, un porche monumental d'inspiration romaine est flanqué de doubles colonnes ; il ouvre sur un passage reliant l'avenue Carnot à la promenade du Soleil. Cet ensemble immobilier a été bâti sur l'emplacement de plusieurs villas, dont *La Perle blanche* de Cléo de Mérode, égérie du Second Empire.

Hôtel de Londres

15, avenue Carnot

LORS DE SES SÉJOURS à Menton, en 1873 et 1874, Robert Louis Stevenson, auteur de *Docteur Jekyll et Mister Hyde* et de *L'Île au trésor,* a résidé à l'*Hôtel de Londres*. Cet établissement dont la façade est d'une grande sobriété s'élève sur quatre niveaux ; il fut partiellement détruit lors du tremblement de terre du 23 février 1887. Venu à Menton dès 1863, Stevenson y revient au cours de la décennie suivante : « Curieuse ironie du sort qui veut que les endroits où l'on nous envoie soient souvent d'une singulière beauté. On couve le paysage d'un regard aussi avide de ses beautés… qu'un homme qui recouvre la pleine jouissance d'un domaine dont on l'avait jusque-là injustement floué […]. Ce n'est qu'une fois installé dans le coin qu'il s'est choisi, que le convalescent commence à mesurer le changement qui l'affecte. À ses pieds et sous ses yeux, les oliveraies et la mer indigo. Et l'éternelle magnificence du profil des Alpes nues, derrière Menton, que rien ne peut altérer. »

Résidence *Gloria Maris*

16, avenue Carnot

Dressé entre la promenade du Soleil et l'avenue Carnot, l'édifice est d'un style caractéristique des années 1950. Comme son nom l'indique, il exalte, dans ces années de l'après-guerre, les vertus balnéaires à travers le triomphe du « plan courant », dont il est un bon archétype. Du côté mer, à chaque heureux propriétaire est dévolue une portion de façade, parfaitement encadrée, conférant à l'ensemble une allure de motel. Du côté avenue Carnot, une double entrée qui encadre un imposant relief en céramique verte de Vallauris, figurant une sirène, dessert les deux ailes du bâtiment. Les sobres portes rehaussées d'un filet de laiton sont agrémentées d'originales poignées en forme de dauphin. La qualité de la céramique de G. Vidal-Maurion, la stylistique typographique affirmée de GLORIA MARIS et la forte symétrie de l'ensemble concourent à l'efficacité de cet hommage rendu aux éléments marins.

4

1

1. Maison Widmer.
2. Le portail du palais Célestin-Viale.

3

3. Palais Célestin-Viale.
4. Hôtel Astoria.

4

Le long de l'avenue Carnot, on peut encore remarquer nombre d'édifices intéressants. La maison Widmer, due à Alfred Marsang [→ p. 30], date de 1913 (19, avenue Carnot) ; son propriétaire, d'origine suisse, Joseph Arthemi Widmer, est le fondateur du *Riviera Palace*. En traversant la rue Henry-Bennet, nous passons devant le palais Célestin-Viale

2

(21, avenue Carnot), construit en 1906 par Tersling [→ p. 31] pour une famille de banquiers. Ces deux immeubles, avec leur décor à bossage en pierre de taille, sont une adaptation locale de l'architecture haussmannienne. Jouxtant le palais Viale, se dresse le Grand Palais (7, avenue Édouard-VII), dû à Félix Vérola [→ p. 31] et construit en 1905 ; il s'inspire des deux immeubles précédents et participe à l'harmonie qui émane de l'architecture de ce quartier.

À L'ANGLE des avenues Édouard-VII et Carnot s'élève l'hôtel *Astoria*, construit en 1912 par Marsang. Cet important édifice de style parisien nous présente les ultimes choix décoratifs de la Belle Époque. Dans cet hôtel, réaménagé en résidence, a séjourné en février 1960 l'écrivain Vladimir Nabokov, auteur de *Lolita* (1955) et de *La Transparence des choses* (1972).

Square des États-Unis

23, avenue Carnot

Jardin ouvert au public, de 9 h à 18 h

UNE RÉHABILITATION d'une certaine ampleur, qui portait sur un ensemble immobilier constitué de deux longues barres d'immeubles de direction nord-sud, fermé au nord, mais ouvert au sud, a contraint les promoteurs et les pouvoirs publics à restructurer complètement le modeste jardin situé dans ce puits de lumière.

COMPTE TENU de la situation de la zone à aménager, la création d'un véritable jardin composé de plantes ligneuses, d'herbacées et de végétaux susceptibles d'intervenir dans d'harmonieuses compositions florales était une véritable gageure.

LIEU DE PASSAGE, de promenade, de repos ou de méditation, le jardin devait être conçu en évitant d'en faire un simple espace vert coupé par une rue traversière.

LE PARTI CHOISI a consisté à créer une grande couronne végétale discontinue de largeur irrégulière avec, en son centre, deux noyaux végétalisés de dimensions inégales, séparés l'un de l'autre par un jardin d'eau dans lequel se déverse une cascade.

LES ALLÉES piétonnières permettent au promeneur, comme au simple passant, d'être au plus près des végétaux, tout en mettant en communication les avenues Édouard-VII et Carnot. Le cheminement intérieur, en forme de 8, enjambe un bassin par une longue et large passerelle, que couvrent en partie les branches d'un néflier du Japon et d'une érythrine, et à

1

1. Chevet de l'église anglicane Saint-John.
2. Vitrail de l'église anglicane Saint-John.
3. Square des États-Unis.
3. Villa Carla.

3

4

l'extrémité de laquelle on aperçoit la fontaine à la Naïade située sur la place voisine.

PARMI les grands sujets, apparaissent d'abord (côté sud) les trois ficus (*Ficus elastica*) géants sauvegardés de l'ancien jardin. Puis se déploie un cortège de palmiers : de vénérables dattiers des Canaries (*Phoenix canariensis*) bien distribués dans l'espace, deux splendides bouquets de *Chamoerops humilis*, un élégant *Caryota urens* et la cohorte de *Phoenix roebelenii*. Plus loin, la frêle silhouette de l'*Araucaria cunninghamii* fait ressortir la rondeur de la frondaison du *Phytolacca dioica*. Du côté nord, un *Grevillea robusta* bénéficie du soleil de l'après-midi. En revanche, au coin sud-ouest, dans l'angle de l'hôtel *Astoria*, la zone d'ombre est occupée par la trilogie des bambous, fougères arborescentes et araliacées, qui habillent une ruine romantique. Enfin, les taches de couleur des rosiers, daturas, acanthes, tradescantias, hortensias, strelitzias occupent surtout le côté ouest. L'aspect didactique n'est pas négligé : le nom de la plante et l'empreinte de sa fleur sont gravés dans le béton du sentier.

Église anglicane Saint-John

31, avenue Carnot

L'ÉGLISE, placée sous le vocable de saint Jean l'Évangéliste, a été construite en 1867 sur l'initiative du pasteur William Barber, originaire de Leicester, en poste à Menton de 1864 à 1878.

Édifiée dans un style néogothique, elle est l'un des rares bâtiments religieux ornés de vitraux que l'on puisse trouver dans la ville. Ce charmant lieu de culte, où la reine Victoria vint se recueillir lors de son séjour à Menton en 1882, atteste la ferveur religieuse de la communauté britannique, très importante à la Belle Époque.

L'ÉDIFICE possède les caractéristiques des églises de la campagne anglaise du XIXe s. L'intérieur du bâtiment, avec sa voûte à charpente apparente, illustre bien les propos de Nikolaus Pevsner, lorsqu'il évoque une « coque de navire renversée » (*Histoire de l'architecture européenne*). Les murs de l'abside sont décorés de marbres et de mosaïques italiens dans le style préraphaélite ; les étoiles d'or sur un fond bleu dessinent les cieux sur la voûte. Tout autour de l'église, le jardin d'agrumes a été conservé.

2

Villa *Carla*

DITE AUSSI ***villa Albini***

Angle avenue Carnot et rue Albini

FACE à l'église Saint-John se dresse la façade très ouvragée de la villa *Carla*, prénom de la fille du notaire Paul Albini, alors premier adjoint du maire Émile Biovès. Construite vers 1898 d'après les plans de Hans Georg Tersling [→ p. 31], elle se remarque par son pittoresque décor de céramique turquoise et jaune citron de la manufacture mentonnaise Saïssi.

Av. de Prades
Le Borrigo
Av. des Acacias
VERS A8 Sauf Bus et P.L.
Tardieu
Route de Sospel
Val Careï
Sentier des Moulins
Sentier Saint Jeanne d'A
Sentier des Acacias
Monastère de l'Annonciade
Chemin du Rosaire
Allée Maréchal de Lattre de Tassigny
Chemin des Moulins de la Ville
Route de l'Annonciade
Ch. de la Croix
Vallée du Careï
Sentier Pépin
Borrigo
N.D. de Fatima
Sentier du Funiculaire
Promenade du Val de Careï
Chemin
Impasse des Sources
Route des Vignasses
VERS A8
Av. de Sospel
Sentier des Caguendries
Mont Gros
Av. Riviera
Rosaire
Prom. M. Leclerc de Hauteclocque
Rue Pietra Scritta
R. Harpignies
Les Ciappes
Route du Mont Gros
Corniche des Ciappes
Chemin du Lutetia
Allées des Eucalyptus
Route de Castellar
GARE ROUTIÈRE
Marché du Careï
R. Col. Hébert
Square Namur
Plateau St Michel
Corniche des Ciappes
Ch. des Ciappes
Tr. du Paropent
Route de Castellar
Av. de la Gare
All. de Namur
A. des Acacias
Rue des Terres Chaudes
Escaliers des Rigaudis
Sentier du Plateau St Michel
Ch. du Collège
Bd du Fossan
R. Massena
R. V. Hugo
Av. Thiers
Av. Boyer
Allée du Louvre
Rue du Louvre
Rue Henri Greville
Av. de Verdun
Jardins Biovès
C. Georges V
Imp. Botta
PTT
Rue Partouneaux
Rue Urbana
Rue Prato
Rue Ardoino
Rue Isola
Ch. du Trabuquet
Rue H. Bennet
Av. Edouard VII
St John
Allée Louis Moreno
Rue de la République
Rue St Charles
R. Loredan Larchey
Rue Magenta
Rue Guyau
Tr. du Palmier
Promenade du Val de Menton
Montée du Souvenir
St Julien
Av. Lau
Tunnel Pascal Molinari
Porte de
Promenade
Carnot
R. Albini
Av. Felix Faure
Place St Roch
Rue Longue
Rue Brea
Montée du Souvenir
Quai Bonaparte
Quai Gordon Bennett
Jetée Imp. Eugénie
du Soleil
Prom. du Soleil
oleil
Rue St Michel
Marché
Quai de Monléon
Esplanade Francis Palmero
Vieux Port
Square du Souvenir Français
Quai Napoléon III

Le centre-ville

Des jardins Biovès au casino municipal

Dès le début du XIXe s., l'urbanisation s'étend sur la plaine littorale. L'économie de la cité, qui s'organisait autour de l'agriculture et du négoce, se transforme pour faire place au « grand tourisme », ce dont témoigne cet itinéraire, notamment avec ses résidences et ses casinos.

1. Musée de Préhistoire régionale : la section des Arts et Traditions populaires.
2. Clocher de la chapelle des Pénitents noirs.
3. Le Bastion, où se trouve le musée Jean-Cocteau.
4. L'une des statues placées sous les arcades du musée de Préhistoire régionale.

Les jardins Biovès

Avenues Boyer, de Verdun et Félix-Faure

EN 1899, Émile Biovès, maire de la ville, entreprend la couverture sur voûtes du torrent du Careï, dans la partie située entre le pont de la rue Partouneaux et le pont suspendu de l'avenue Félix-Faure. On y aménage des jardins d'agrément ouverts sur la mer, destinés à embellir la station climatique. Ces jardins Biovès, qui attirent les hivernants, participent à la scénographie urbaine et mettent en valeur le nouveau casino *Kursaal* (1909).

EN FÉVRIER 1929, un hôtelier organise une exposition de fleurs et agrumes dans les jardins du *Riviera Palace*. L'année suivante, le Carnaval des fruits d'or a lieu rue de la République. En 1934, les organisateurs qualifient la manifestation de « Fête du citron ». Deux ans plus tard, l'exposition orne les jardins Biovès et ne les quittera plus. En 1954, sont créés les défilés de chars ornés d'agrumes. Chaque année, 120 tonnes d'agrumes sont utilisées pour la joie des quelque 400 000 visiteurs présents au cours des deux semaines que dure la période carnavalesque. En 2011, Menton orchestre sa 78e édition !

1

2

3

1. Vue des jardins Biovès avec, à droite, la façade du palais de l'Europe.
2-3. Les jardins Biovès lors de la Fête du citron.

HORMIS la période de ces festivités qui enfièvrent le quartier, les jardins Biovès sont un agréable lieu de promenade, orné de bigaradiers et de palmiers, de cycas et de yuccas, agrémenté de fontaines et de statues. En descendant vers la mer, nous remarquons : le *Monument à la mémoire d'Émile Biovès* (1925), haut-relief taillé dans le grès dû à Edmond Guillaume ; *La Déesse aux fruits d'or* (1958), vénus en pierre de La Turbie allongée sur la pelouse, sculptée par Volti ; le *Monument du rattachement de Menton à la France* (1896), de Denys Puech, où l'on voit Marianne accueillant Menton sous les traits d'une jeune fille. Dans le second jardin : *Stèle commémorative d'Albert Ier de Belgique* au centre d'une petite pièce d'eau ; *Les Fauconniers* (1903), deux bronzes du sculpteur russe Eugène Lanceray.

Dans l'avenue Boyer – sur l'emplacement de l'ancienne rive gauche du Careï –, qui longe les jardins Biovès, s'élevaient des villas (*La Celle*, *Raydor*…), ainsi que la pension *Mimosa*. Mais l'aspect de cette avenue champêtre a bien changé. Les villas et la pension ont fait place à des immeubles imposants bâtis entre 1920 et 1980, tels que le *Palais Ausonia* ou l'hôtel *Chambord*. Toutefois, subsiste encore de la Belle Époque, dressé au milieu de l'avenue, le casino *Kursaal*, aujourd'hui palais de l'Europe.

Palais de l'Europe

ANCIEN ***casino* Kursaal**

8, avenue Boyer

LE *KURSAAL* a été construit en 1909 sur les plans de Tersling [→ p. 31], qui, exceptionnellement, a signé et daté le bâtiment sur un pilier de la façade. « L'architecte y a mêlé une décoration néoclassique à un parti plus éclectique, inspiré des grandes halles d'exposition des années 1850-1880. L'intérieur, outre des salles bien proportionnées et éclairées, contient un ravissant théâtre de style classique conçu aussi par Tersling » (M. Steve).

OUVERT sur les jardins Biovès, le *Kursaal* est le quatrième casino à avoir été érigé dans la ville, après le palais Carnolès, l'actuel hôtel de ville (à l'origine Cercle des étrangers) et le casino Villarey, édifices maintenant tous transformés ou fermés. Lieu de prestige et de distraction, le *Kursaal* a reçu les musiciens et les troupes d'opéra, les corps de ballet et les compagnies théâtrales les plus réputés. Acquis par la Ville à la fin des années 1950, puis réaménagé, il est devenu, à partir de 1961, le palais de l'Europe. Il abrite l'office du tourisme, la bibliothèque municipale, le théâtre Francis-Palmero, une galerie et des salles de congrès.

BIBLIOTHÈQUE MUNICIPALE

8, avenue Boyer

Téléphone : 04 92 41 76 60

Ouverte tous les jours (sauf dimanche, lundi et fêtes légales)
• Mardi, jeudi, vendredi, de 13 h 45 à 17 h 30 • Mercredi, de 9 h 30 à 12 h et de 14 h à 18 h • Samedi, de 9 h 30 à 12 h et de 14 h à 17 h

LA BIBLIOTHÈQUE est fondée en 1898 par l'écrivain Lorédan Larchey, conservateur de la bibliothèque de l'Arsenal à Paris, en retraite à Menton. Tout d'abord logée dans une salle du musée municipal, elle est transférée au rez-de-chaussée du palais de l'Europe en 1964.

Le palais de l'Europe.

1

2

3

1. Façade actuelle.
2. La salle à l'italienne telle qu'elle se présentait à l'époque de l'inauguration.
3. Le Kursaal, achevé en 1909, futur palais de l'Europe.

CONSTITUÉ d'environ 65 000 ouvrages, parmi lesquels figurent quelques éditions rares, le fonds de la bibliothèque s'est enrichi au cours du temps, grâce à diverses acquisitions et donations. On peut y voir de belles éditions en latin, en italien et en français, des XVIe, XVIIe et XVIIIe s., notamment le *Dictionarium* (1598) d'Ambroise Calepin, l'édition de 1668 du théâtre de Corneille et plusieurs éditions de l'*Histoire naturelle* du comte de Buffon : celle de 1752 (32 vol.), *Histoire naturelle des oiseaux* (1770, 18 vol.) et *Histoire naturelle des minéraux* (1783, 9 vol.). On y relève également l'édition de 1777 de l'*Encyclopédie* de Diderot et d'Alembert (33 vol. + planches) et de belles collections d'œuvres complètes, telles celles de Bossuet (1821, 21 vol.) et de Rousseau (1819, 22 vol.). LA BIBLIOTHÈQUE possède en outre un exemplaire de la célèbre *Description de l'Égypte*, recueil des observations et des recherches qui ont été faites pendant l'expédition de l'armée française, publié sous les ordres de Napoléon Ier et daté de 1809. Cet exemplaire fut offert par le roi Louis XVIII, le 1er septembre 1824, au général Louis de Partouneaux, qui en fit don à la Ville de Menton.

THÉÂTRE FRANCIS-PALMERO

8, avenue Boyer

Téléphone : 04 92 41 76 50

Au sein du palais de l'Europe, le théâtre Francis-Palmero reçoit le public dans une salle à l'italienne, due à Tersling. Celle-ci, entièrement restaurée, a de nouveau été inaugurée en 1971. Le théâtre, qui fait partie de la vie mentonnaise, accueille, d'octobre à mai, des spectacles qui se veulent le plus variés possible.

OFFICE DU TOURISME

8, avenue Boyer

Téléphone : 04 92 41 76 76

Télécopie : 04 92 41 76 78
Courriel : tourisme@menton.fr
Site internet : www.villedementon.com

Ouvert du lundi au samedi, de 8 h 30 à 12 h 30 et de 14 h à 18 h, le dimanche, de 9 h à 12 h 30

LE PALAIS de l'Europe abrite l'office du tourisme, l'un des lieux essentiels pour l'activité touristique et culturelle de la ville.

En quittant le palais de l'Europe, on remarque, à gauche, jouxtant celui-ci, la villa *Les Citronniers*, bâtiment remodelé en 1895 par l'architecte Hans Georg Tersling, qui en fit sa demeure. La façade principale, avenue Pasteur, est ornée de deux énormes cariatides qui soutiennent un balcon avec cabochons de faïence de la manufacture Saïssi.

Francis Palmero

FRANCIS PALMERO (1917-1985) est l'une des hautes figures de Menton. Maire (1954-1977), conseiller général (1958-1973), député des Alpes-Maritimes (1958-1968), sénateur de 1971 à son décès, il a transformé Menton par une politique de grands travaux. Par ailleurs, il s'est intéressé à la défense du chemin de fer de Provence et au développement du complexe de Valbonne-Sophia-Antipolis.

1. Louis de Partouneaux.
2. Résidence Majestic.
3. L'Orangeraie, *ancien* Grand Hôtel de Venise.
4. Hôtel des Ambassadeurs.

2

4

1

3

Nietzsche à Menton

FRIEDRICH NIETZSCHE (1844-1900), qui fit plusieurs séjours à Nice, a passé deux mois à Menton, en novembre et décembre 1888, où il a séjourné à l'*Hôtel des Étrangers*. Le Sud et les paysages méditerranéens, dont la découverte, selon le philosophe, le libère des pesanteurs germaniques, offrent à son regard la puissance fécondante et régénératrice de la lumière.

LES PAGES qu'il écrit sur Nice, Èze, Gênes, Menton rayonnent d'allégresse. Pour l'auteur du *Gai Savoir*, Menton est un espace de beauté, de calme, où le solitaire revendique son droit à l'isolement. « Le site est magnifique, j'ai découvert huit promenades. Que nul ne vienne m'y retrouver. J'ai besoin de cette tranquillité absolue. »

Rue Partouneaux

CETTE ARTÈRE porte le nom d'une vieille famille de Menton, les Partouneaux, qui a donné trois généraux à la France : Louis (1770-1835), Maurice (1799-1865), Paul (1871-1947).

• AU Nº 1, l'hôtel *Leubner*, aujourd'hui résidence *Majestic*, a été construit par Marsang [→ p. 30] en 1909. Élevé sur six niveaux – dont un rez-de-chaussée en pierre de taille de La Turbie – à gros bossage, l'édifice possède, aux deux premiers étages, une vaste terrasse bordée d'une balustrade à vases turquoise de Saïssi. Ce bâtiment emprunte le vocabulaire architectural haussmannien : nombreux décrochements, modénature imposante, cartouches et médaillons à enroulements de rubans et de guirlandes de fleurs...

• AU Nº 3, l'*Hôtel des Ambassadeurs*, bâti en 1863, est l'un des rares témoins de la grande hôtellerie naissante encore en fonction aujourd'hui.

• AU Nº 7 *bis*, nous remarquons l'hôtel *Grimaldi*, construit en 1961 par Cave de Beaulieu, dont la façade n'est pas dépourvue d'originalité. Ses balcons en épis, coiffés de pergolas à redan, jouent plaisamment des variations de lumière, surtout au soleil couchant. Des ébauches de fers forgés andalous alternant avec des allèges pleines trahissent néanmoins les limites d'un programme économique.

• ANCIENNE pension *Les Hespérides*. Dans ce quartier, avant le commissariat de police (nº 9), une impasse donnait accès à la pension *Les Hespérides*, qui a accueilli l'écrivain Vladimir Nabokov en 1937-1938. En face, à l'angle des rues Prato et Partouneaux, s'élevait l'ancien *Hôtel des Étrangers*, devenu *Queen's Hôtel*, où résida le philosophe allemand Friedrich Nietzsche en 1888.

• AU Nº 15 nous voyons, précédée d'un grand jardin d'agrumes et de plantes exotiques, la façade blanche de la maison de vacances *L'Orangeraie*, qui a succédé au *Grand Hôtel de Venise*. Son entrée imposante est surmontée d'une élégante marquise Belle Époque. Un groupe de lions évoquant ceux de San Marco, à Venise, couronnait la façade ; un seul subsiste aujourd'hui. En face, à l'angle des rues Partouneaux et Ardoïno, une très belle frise signée Guillaume Cerutti-Maori [→ p. 78] figure des enfants dans un

1. Angle des rues Ardoïno et Partouneaux.
2. Maison Burkard.
3. Caisse d'épargne.
4. Monument à la mémoire de Henry Bennet.

Vladimir Nabokov à la pension *Les Hespérides*

QUE MENTON ait été un des lieux privilégiés de l'histoire de la littérature, l'œuvre de Vladimir Nabokov l'atteste. C'est à Menton que Nabokov (1899-1977) a écrit en partie et achevé l'un des ouvrages les plus exceptionnels du XXe s., *Le Don*, dernier roman que ce polyglotte a écrit en russe, avant son départ pour les États-Unis.

SI LES SOUVENIRS niçois de l'auteur remontent à l'enfance, à l'hiver 1903, Menton et Moulinet seront les témoins d'une création littéraire qui pose les véritables problèmes de l'art. Il serait vain, en dehors de sa correspondance, d'essayer de trouver une image réaliste de Menton chez un écrivain dont le projet est de réinventer l'univers à la dimension de ses rêves et de ses fantasmes.

EN OCTOBRE 1937, les Nabokov quittent Cannes et s'installent à Menton, à la pension *Les Hespérides*. « Ils se baignaient, barbotaient et se rôtissaient sur la plage des Sablettes », précise Brian Boyd, biographe du romancier.

EN 1939, les Nabokov quittent la France exposée à l'invasion allemande. Ils embarquent à Saint-Nazaire pour l'Amérique où l'écrivain enseigne la littérature et publie *Lolita*. Revenu en Europe, il visitera la Côte d'Azur dans les années 1960, de l'Esterel à l'Italie. Èze et La Turbie susciteront son émerveillement. Installé en Suisse, à Montreux, il écrit *Feu pâle* (1962) et *Ada ou l'Ardeur* (1969).

décor champêtre rehaussé de clous de céramique bleue et de cabochons dorés à la feuille.

• AU N° 21, l'ancienne poste (actuelle Caisse d'épargne) a été construite par Sylvain Jauffret [→ p. 30] en 1885. Sur sa façade occidentale, un square ombragé par un énorme *Ficus elastica*, abrite le *Monument à la mémoire de Henry Bennet*.

• AU N° 38, la maison Burkard (1896), édifiée par Adrien Rey [→ p. 30], présente un beau décor de façade en sgraffite ocre et jaune. Cet édifice de forme triangulaire possède, dans son pignon le plus étroit, une suite de baies encadrées de colonnes.

Nous empruntons maintenant la rue de la République.

Monument à la mémoire de Henry Bennet

Face au n° 1, rue de la République

ADOSSÉ à l'ancien hôtel des postes, le *Monument à la mémoire de Henry Bennet* (1816-1891) a été réalisé par le sculpteur Fabbio Stecchi. Inauguré en 1884, il est dédié au médecin obstétricien de la reine Victoria. James Henry Bennet découvre Menton lors d'un séjour thérapeutique. Guéri de la tuberculose pulmonaire, il écrit, en 1861, *Mentone and the Riviera as a winter climate*. Grâce à cet ouvrage, Henry Bennet participe au « lancement » de la station de Menton.

Angle rue Partouneaux et square Henry-Bennet.

Immeuble Art déco

19, rue Partouneaux et rue de la République

FACE AU MONUMENT dédié à Henry Bennet, nous remarquons un ravissant petit immeuble à la façade très soignée, construit par l'architecte Henri Cerutti-Maori [→ p. 30]. Le décor en à-plat, très sage, jette les bases d'une variante Art déco, qui conjugue diverses influences mentonnaises et italiennes. Au premier étage, les balcons à balustres font encore écho à l'architecture classique ; au second, l'académisme des garde-corps en fonte à motifs « flambeaux et carquois », que l'on retrouve sur de nombreux édifices de l'époque, est tempéré par l'italianité des fenêtres en plein cintre. La corniche à métopes complète l'élégance de cette demeure.

Orient Palace

ANCIEN **Grand Hôtel d'Orient**

1, rue de la République

LORS DE SA CONSTRUCTION par Sylvain Jauffret [→ p. 30], en 1884, le *Grand Hôtel d'Orient* affiche un néoclassicisme de bon ton ; mais, vers 1920, afin de répondre à un désir d'exotisme et à l'enchantement des contrées lointaines, ses façades sont entièrement remodelées « à l'orientale » : fenêtres à la mauresque, décors de céramique, coupoles azurées, minarets miniatures, jardins « à l'égyptienne ».

LE JARDIN, qui met en valeur la façade, présente une remarquable collection de palmiers et de cycas, colorée de rosiers odorants.

L'architecture de quelques édifices publics et hôteliers témoigne de l'engouement orientaliste de la seconde moitié du XIXe s.

La peinture, l'opéra et le théâtre revisitent un Orient idéalisé, à l'instar de la flamboyante *Salomé* (1894) d'Oscar Wilde, illustrée par Aubrey Beardsley qui meurt et est inhumé à Menton en 1898, à l'âge de vingt-six ans. À l'évidence, l'Orient apparaît comme la grande affaire des Anglais, surtout sous le règne de la reine Victoria, impératrice des Indes, hôte elle-même de Menton. De leur côté, les Français consolident leurs positions politiques et économiques, en Afrique noire, au Maghreb et en Indochine. Cette situation favorise du même coup un tourisme de luxe, certes avide de « terres chaudes », mais qui recherche avant tout un exotisme assez confortable. Pour répondre à ce désir, des palaces sont construits sur toute la Côte d'Azur. Altiers, ils s'agrémentent de fioritures empruntées à l'architecture des pays convoités. À Menton s'élèvent, entre autres, le *Riviera Palace* (1898), le *Winter Palace* (1907) [→ p. 78], le *Grand Hôtel d'Orient* (1884, « orientalisé » vers 1920). Quant au casino municipal (1934) – « cadet » de la Mamounia de Marrakech, construite en 1923 par des architectes français –, il est un élégant compromis entre l'Art déco et le style mauresque. Dans les années 1920, Ferdinand Bac réalise le surprenant jardin des *Colombières* [→ p. 120] dans les restanques de Garavan où se distingue un mausolée rouge inspiré des marabouts arabes, destiné à lui servir de sépulture – où il ne repose d'ailleurs pas. Menton s'approprie aussi les architectures d'un Orient plus lointain. Celle de l'empire du Milieu, par exemple, incite Adrien Rey à décoller la toiture ajourée du marché couvert (1898) [→ p. 110], quai de Monléon.

LA SOIF D'UN EXOTISME policé accompagne les ressortissants européens dans leur quête d'une douceur hivernale qui leur soit salutaire, plus particulièrement les nantis de l'Empire britannique, tels ce James Matheson

Menton et les parfums de l'Orient

1. Façade de l'Orient Palace.
2. Succulente dans le parc de l'Orient Palace.

mort à Menton en 1878 – compagnon en fortune de William Jardine, et créateur, avec lui, du comptoir britannique de Hong Kong – ou Brian Houghton Hodgson, spécialiste du Tibet et du bouddhisme, qui baptisera *Himalaya* sa villa de Garavan, pour se souvenir de ses séjours à Darjeeling et Katmandou.

L'AMÉNAGEMENT de jardins luxuriants autour des villas cossues de Garavan fait appel à des essences lointaines. On rapporte des antipodes arbres et fleurs rares qui s'adaptent merveilleusement à l'ensoleillement mentonnais. Grâce à une poignée d'amateurs éclairés, anglais pour la plupart, à l'exemple de Humphrey Waterfield, « inventeur » en 1913 du *Clos du Peyronnet* [→ p. 63], où se côtoient cyprès du Cachemire, néfliers du Japon, manias du Siam et la glycine dragon noir de Chine. À l'ouest de la ville, sir Lawrence Johnston façonne, à partir de 1920, *Serre de la Madone* [→ p. 123], vaste propriété à la végétation « cosmopolite » du plus grand intérêt où l'Orient est bien représenté. Quant à lord Percy Radcliffe, ancien gouverneur de Malte, il offre à son épouse indienne, en 1922, un havre miraculeusement paradisiaque qu'il baptise *Val Rahmeh* [→ p. 74] en son honneur (*Rahmeh*, son prénom, signifie « chat » en hindi).

Un tiers des plantes du domaine de Val Rahmeh, aujourd'hui transformé en jardin botanique exotique, provient d'Orient et d'Extrême-Orient.

DEPUIS l'acclimatation de l'emblématique citronnier, le paysage mentonnais n'a cessé d'enrichir sa latinité de tropicales fragrances, un atout indéniable qui contribuera à attirer aussi d'intrépides voyageurs et de valeureux soldats à l'heure du repos.

PREMIÈRE FEMME occidentale à être entrée dans Lhassa (1924), la ville interdite du Tibet, Alexandra David-Néel honore Menton de sa présence dix ans après l'exploit qui fit sa gloire ! Le général Henry Frey finira ses jours à Menton – il s'était illustré au Tonkin, lors de la consolidation du pouvoir colonial, ainsi qu'à Pékin pendant la révolte des Boxers (1900).

POUR SA PART, l'ancien diplomate roumain Georges Bagulesco, qui fut en poste au Japon dans les années 1930, léguera à la Ville, en témoignage d'amitié, une belle collection d'estampes et de peintures maintenant présentée au palais Carnolès [→ p. 85].

1

1. *Cinéma Éden.*
2. *Temple écossais.*
3. *Casino Villarey.*

2

3

Temple écossais

SALLE DES CONFÉRENCES
SAINT-EXUPÉRY

8, rue de la République

AVANT la construction de ce temple, le culte était célébré par le pasteur James Ewing Somerville dans le hall de la villa *Les Grottes* (quai Laurenti, aujourd'hui avenue Porte-de-France), qui est devenue plus tard l'hôtel *L'Amirauté.*
L'ÉGLISE ÉCOSSAISE, construite entre 1889 et 1890, est ouverte au culte en janvier 1891 par le pasteur Somerville. Nommé à Menton en 1886, celui-ci reste chapelain de l'église jusqu'en 1920 ; il est remplacé par le révérend Arnott qui dirige la paroisse jusqu'en 1933. À la déclaration de guerre, l'église écossaise est fermée ; elle ne sera jamais rouverte au culte. En 1958, le conseil de l'Église d'Écosse, à Édimbourg, propriétaire de l'immeuble, le vend à la Ville de Menton.
L'ÉDIFICE, devenu salle polyvalente, garde de son ancienne fonction religieuse une ambiance de temple rural anglais. Une façade simple, surmontée d'une élégante flèche recouverte de cuivre, donne accès à un vestibule qui précède la nef. Nous pouvons remarquer la très belle et très imposante charpente.
AU COURS DE L'ANNÉE, conférences, pièces de théâtre, concerts et réunions viennent animer cet ancien lieu de culte.

Au n° 11 de la rue de la République, à l'angle de la rue Villarey, on remarque la façade Art déco moderniste du cinéma *Éden*, édifié en 1927 par Henri Cerutti-Maori [→ p. 30] : quasi aveugle, elle est percée de trois oculus, conformément à une tendance futuriste des années 1930. Cet édifice est aujourd'hui l'unique salle de cinéma de Menton.

Nous remontons quelques mètres la rue Villarey, où se dresse, face à nous, le *Grand Casino.*

Grand Casino

12, rue Villarey

DURANT LES ANNÉES de l'entre-deux-guerres, le *Grand Casino*, de l'architecte Hélain et du décorateur Novarro, était un des lieux de plaisir privilégiés de la cité mentonnaise. L'inauguration, en 1887, a donné lieu à une fête magnifique. « Le Casino Central, édifice de style mauresque renfermait cafés, restaurants, salons de lecture, salles de jeu, de concert et de spectacle. Construite, décorée et meublée en six mois, cette œuvre vapeur qui s'élevait au milieu de vastes jardins faisait honneur à son architecte et à son décorateur » (Stephen Liégeard).
La partie centrale du *Grand Casino* est flanquée de deux corps plus bas, de plan semi-cylindrique. L'ensemble, désaffecté, semble être en attente...

1. Place Ardoïno.
2. L'hôtel de ville dans les années 1950.
3. Monument à la mémoire de Louis Laurenti.

1

2

Nous revenons sur nos pas afin de nous rendre rue de la République. Une fois traversée la rue Saint-Charles, nous nous trouvons, à gauche, place Ardoïno.

3

Hôtel de ville

17, rue de la République

Téléphone : 04 92 10 50 00

Ouvert tous les jours (sauf samedi et dimanche), de 8 h 30 à 12 h 30 et de 13 h 30 à 17 h

Après le rattachement de Menton à la France (1861), la mairie emménage dans les anciens bâtiments du couvent des Capucins qui jouxtent la chapelle des Pénitents noirs (rue du Général-Gallieni). En 1882, elle s'installe dans un ancien hôtel de la place Nationale (actuelle place Georges-Clemenceau), où elle se trouve vite à l'étroit. En 1902, l'administration municipale s'établit dans les locaux actuels.

L'édifice a été construit en 1861 par Victor Sabatier [→ p. 31], pour le baron Honoré Ardoïno (1819-1874), botaniste et historien de Menton, afin d'abriter le Cercle des étrangers. À la fin du Second Empire, l'architecte Philippe Randon réalise, face au Cercle, une place et deux immeubles inspirés du style piémontais. En 1920 est élevé au centre de cette place le *Monument à la mémoire de Louis Laurenti* (maire de Menton, conseiller général), réalisé par le sculpteur Léopold Bernstamm. Après le décès du baron Ardoïno, le bâtiment abrite le théâtre des Folies-Bergère, puis il est cédé à la municipalité en 1898, qui le transforme en hôtel de ville.

En 1957, Jean Cocteau réalise le décor de la salle des mariages dans les locaux précédemment occupés par les services de la justice. La salle de théâtre Second Empire, devenue salle du conseil municipal, est ornée de tapisseries de Perrot (1961).

Salle des mariages

En 1957, l'écrivain, peintre et poète Jean Cocteau décore et aménage la salle des mariages de l'hôtel de ville de Menton; peu de temps après, il dirigera les travaux de réhabilitation d'un fortin du XVIIe s. (le Bastion), afin d'y installer un musée consacré aux diverses facettes de son œuvre.

Hôtel de ville

17, rue de la République

Téléphone : 04 92 10 50 29

Ouvert tous les jours (sauf samedi, dimanche et fêtes légales), de 9 h à 12 h et de 14 h à 17 h

Visites guidées organisées par le Service du patrimoine (renseignements : 04 92 10 97 10)

EN 1955, Jean Cocteau (1889-1963) avait déjà réalisé le décor de la chapelle Saint-Pierre, à Villefranche-sur-Mer; en 1959, il effectuera celui de la chapelle Saint-Blaise-des-Simples, à Milly-la-Forêt. Ces années 1950 représentent pour Cocteau une période faste dans son œuvre de fresquiste. AVEC LA SALLE DES MARIAGES, Cocteau offre à la Ville une œuvre éblouissante.

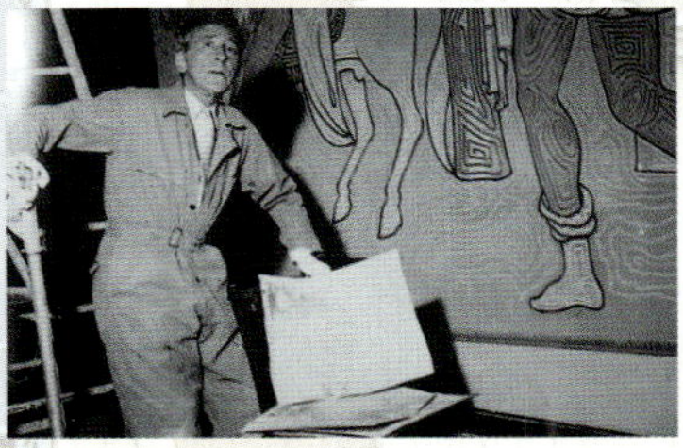

2

3

Lorsque l'on y pénètre, on remarque au plafond une fresque sur le thème de Pégase, le cheval ailé de la mythologie, né du sang de Méduse et dompté par Bellérophon. Selon la légende, d'un coup de sabot sur un rocher de l'Hélicon, Pégase fit jaillir la source Hippocrène où se réunissaient les Muses et dont on buvait l'eau pour connaître l'inspiration poétique.

SUR LE MUR de gauche, la fresque représente une noce barbare, dans un village ; sur celui de droite figurent Orphée et Eurydice (thème présent également dans l'œuvre cinématographique de Cocteau), ainsi que des centaures. Enfin, sur le mur du fond, les mariés sont représentés par une jeune fille coiffée d'une capeline et un garçon portant un bonnet de pêcheur caractéristique de la Méditerranée.

UNE SALLE DES MARIAGES devant comporter une allégorie de la République, Cocteau fit graver sur des miroirs se faisant face deux Marianne, dont le reflet se multiplie à l'infini.

Cocteau parle de la salle des mariages

« Je me dictai ou cru me dicter des thèmes et m'acharnai à organiser une fois encore, les mystérieuses noces du conscient et de l'inconscient de la beauté reproduite, figurative et de la beauté produite, abstraite ; l'une mise en branle par l'art grec, reproduisant les formes de la nature, l'autre par l'art nègre, produisant des tatouages et des déformations physiques aptes à contrarier les formes naturelles jusqu'à leur substituer un monde imaginaire où l'homme commande. [...]

« UNE SALLE DES MARIAGES doit présenter quelques fastes, c'est ainsi que travaillant parois et plafond, je n'ai jamais oublié qu'ils dussent avoir un cadre assez théâtral fait de velours et d'or ; mais tout en n'oubliant pas le style officiel des moquettes rouges et des plantes vertes, je le transporte un peu plus haut, un peu plus loin. Rien ne porte au songe le cortège qui pénètre dans une mairie, rien ne lui offre la chance des candélabres, de l'encens et des orgues. Je me suis donc attaché faute de mieux, à lui suggérer quelques pompes : un chemin de peau de panthère, des torchères rappelant des figuiers de barbarie et des aloès qui hérissent nos jardins de trophées sauvages. L'or à la feuille, les fauteuils et les chaises espagnoles, les miroirs gravés, les jardinières de bambou et les traditionnelles plantes vertes du vestibule, voilà l'ensemble qui m'aide à rendre moins sévère la rigueur du code Napoléon. »

1. Façade de l'hôtel de ville.
2. Jean Cocteau à l'œuvre.
3-4. Détails des fresques de la salle des mariages. © Adagp, Paris 2006.

4

1. Temple protestant.

2. Collège André-Maurois.

Nous sortons de l'hôtel de ville et nous nous retrouvons place Ardoïno. Près de là, au 19, rue de la République, se dresse le temple protestant, bâti sur un terrain acheté au baron Bati de Partouneaux en 1867. L'édifice religieux est inauguré dès l'année suivante. Les deux architectes Bourrit et Simmler travaillent ici avec l'entreprise de construction d'Honoré Laurenti – les Laurenti appartiennent à une famille mentonnaise protestante.
Le temple présente un dessin et un aménagement respectueux des règles de l'Église réformée : aucune décoration, ni œuvre peinte ni statue, une simple croix accueillant les fidèles.

Nous empruntons, le long du temple, la rue de la Marne, puis nous tournons à gauche, dans la rue Magenta.

Collège André-Maurois

4, rue Magenta

S'IL REPREND les couleurs traditionnelles de l'architecture de l'hôtel de ville, juste en contrebas, le collège André-Maurois rompt résolument avec toute tentation de pastiche architectural. Construit en 2000, cet établissement, qui accueille environ 400 élèves, s'inscrit dans la lignée moderniste héritée du Bauhaus.
L'ÉDIFICE tire son expressivité d'un triple jeu de contrastes entre formes, matériaux et couleurs. Il oppose volumes pleins et parties ajourées, pans de béton et résille d'acier, ocres rouge et blanc-gris.
LES ARCHITECTES (Causse, Rigault et Benaïm) ont imaginé un effet d'encastrement géant de portiques irréguliers rouge et blanc sur une structure en coursives d'acier et de verre. Ils jouent habilement de la dissymétrie, conférant à chaque angle de vue une importance spécifique.
LA FAÇADE SUD, rue Magenta, met en évidence l'entrée du collège sous une triple arche blanche en saillie qui sert également de brise-soleil dans sa partie supérieure. L'arche est épaulée par deux monolithes rouges découpés de bandeaux tantôt verticaux, tantôt horizontaux. L'important perron rattrape le dénivelé du terrain – nous pouvons remarquer le clin d'œil au bâtiment préexistant, dont on a récupéré le portail en fer forgé peint en bleu. Le soin apporté à la réalisation des détails, notamment ceux des ouvrages métalliques, le raffinement des couleurs et la prise en compte évidente des données géoclimatiques confèrent à cet ensemble une fort belle tenue architecturale.

Après nous être rendus rue Magenta, pour voir l'entrée principale du collège, nous la poursuivons jusqu'à la place Lorédan-Larchey.

Place Lorédan-Larchey

DITE AUSSI ***place du Musée***

AUTRE LIEU de modernité, la place Lorédan-Larchey, réalisée en 1994 par l'architecte parisien Jean-Paul Viguier, résulte d'un pari audacieux. Sous un espace en dénivelé, autrefois encombré par les automobiles, il s'agissait de créer un parking souterrain et d'aménager en surface un espace piétonnier.
NOUS SOMMES LÀ en présence d'une conception tout en finesse, qui respecte avec une modestie méritoire le cadre architectural d'alentour. Le projet repose sur l'harmonie de l'alliance entre l'eau, la pierre et la végétation. Au milieu d'une double allée de ficus ombragée de tonnelles d'acier et de verre court une longue cascade en paliers. L'eau, à partir

1

1. Place Lorédan-Larchey.
2-3. Frises peintes en sgraffite.
4. Maison Cerutti-Maori.

2

3

d'une fontaine sommitale, s'écoule sous des claies de carrare blanc, à l'exemple de l'aménagement réalisé par Buren place du Palais-Royal, à Paris. Les effluves capiteux des jasmins enroulés aux mâts lumineux des tonnelles, mêlés au murmure de l'eau souterraine, font de ce lieu une étape agréable à la fin des torrides après-midi d'été.

LA PLACE LORÉDAN-LARCHEY et les rues environnantes offrent de beaux exemples de frises et de décors peints des XIXe et XXe s. Nous pouvons voir aussi la maison familiale de Guillaume Cerutti-Maori [→ p. 78]. L'immeuble, de 1909, présente des frises peintes sous l'avant-toit. L'entrée, au 20, rue de la Marne, s'ouvre sur une cage d'escalier décorée à fresque. L'une des façades borde le square Ernest-Lessieux à côté du musée de Préhistoire régionale – le buste du peintre et aquarelliste Ernest Louis Lessieux (1848-1925), réalisé par le sculpteur Léopold Bernstamm, a été inauguré en 1926, dans ce même square.

Le décor peint

LE PAYS MENTONNAIS présente plus de 250 frises peintes en décor de façade. Réalisées pour la plupart entre 1860 et 1930, elles sont de style néoclassique, Belle Époque, éclectique ou, pour les récentes, d'inspiration Art déco. Cet art est maîtrisé alors par les ouvriers piémontais. À Menton, c'est l'entreprise de Guillaume Cerutti-Maori [→ p. 78] qui détient le marché du décor peint.

LA TECHNIQUE du sgraffite (de l'italien *sgraffito*) permet d'obtenir un décor en camaïeu par grattage d'un enduit clair sur fond de stuc sombre. Présente en Italie depuis la Renaissance, cette technique sera peu à peu abandonnée, parce que trop coûteuse, au profit de la fresque peinte sur enduit frais et, surtout, du *fresco secco* (sur enduit sec) et de la détrempe (pigments délayés à l'eau et fixés au moyen de colle organique ou de gomme végétale).

4

Musée de Préhistoire régionale

Le musée de Préhistoire régionale permet au public de suivre les grandes étapes de l'aventure humaine, à travers celle de ces divers groupes de chasseurs et d'agriculteurs qui, des Alpes maritimes à la Ligurie, ont campé sur le bord du littoral, entre mer et montagnes, depuis leur arrivée il y a un million d'années.

Rue Lorédan-Larchey

Téléphone : 04 93 35 84 64
Télécopie : 04 92 10 05 40

Ouvert tous les jours, sauf mardi, de 10 h à 12 h et de 14 h à 18 h

ÉDIFIÉ sur la place Lorédan-Larchey, que bordent deux rangées de maisons datant de la Belle Époque, le musée de Préhistoire régionale propose un beau répertoire architectural : une loggia à cinq arcades ornées de statues figurant les quatre saisons, trois fenêtres à l'étage surmontées de frontons triangulaires, aux proportions palladiennes, une respectable frise d'attique sous la corniche à métopes... Ce monument a été bâti entre 1907 et 1909 par Adrien Rey.

Les collections

STANISLAS BONFILS (1823-1909), réputé pour ses fouilles archéologiques dans les grottes de Grimaldi [→ p. 61] au cours de la seconde moitié du XIXe s., fut nommé en 1878 conservateur du premier musée de Menton – celui-ci était alors installé dans l'ancien hôtel de ville de la place Georges-Clemenceau. Vers 1890, Bonfils initia à l'archéologie le jeune François Octobon (1881-1969), lequel effectua à son tour de nombreuses recherches en diverses régions. Octobon, qui légua plusieurs de ses collections à sa cité natale, sera à l'initiative d'autres donations et legs privés.

LE BÂTIMENT de la rue Lorédan-Larchey abrita dès 1909 l'ensemble des collections municipales d'art et d'archéologie. En 1977, elles furent partagées entre le musée des Beaux-Arts, installé dans le palais Carnolès [→ p. 85], et l'édifice de la rue Lorédan-Larchey, affecté au futur musée de Préhistoire régionale – ainsi qu'à la section Arts et Traditions populaires – qui sera inauguré en 1988, après les travaux d'aménagement nécessaires.

LA PRÉSENTATION des collections, réparties entre plusieurs salles, a été conçue par Henry de Lumley, qui dirige l'étude de la grotte du Vallonnet, à Roquebrune-Cap-Martin. Quoique propriété de l'État, les nombreuses pièces issues de ces fouilles (outils de pierre, ossements d'animaux...) ont été déposées au musée de Menton. Toutes les autres collections sont propriété de la Ville.

• PALÉOLITHIQUE INFÉRIEUR
Grotte du Lazaret (150 000 ans), à Nice : outils (notamment de superbes bifaces), quelques ossements d'animaux tels que des éléments crâniens de cerfs et de bouquetins, gibier habituel d'*Homo erectus* du Lazaret.
• PALÉOLITHIQUE MOYEN ET SUPÉRIEUR
Grottes de Grimaldi : quelques outils de l'homme de Neandertal (v. 50 000 ans), riche collection de l'époque de l'homme de Cro-Magnon (35 000 à 12 000 ans), outils en silex et en os, objets d'art mobilier, éléments de parure, ossements humains et animaux.
• MÉSOLITHIQUE
Abri Martin (10 000 ans), à Gréolières : outils caractéristiques des derniers peuples chasseurs, éléments de parure, ossements animaux.
• NÉOLITHIQUE
Grotte de Beaulieu-sur-Mer. Grotte des Perles (7 000 à 4 000 ans), à Vence : céramiques, outils, parures et ossements humains. Vestiges provenant d'autres sites.
• ÂGE DU BRONZE (4 000 à 2 800 ans)
Grotte des Poteries, à Vence : nombreuses céramiques. Aven Cresp, à Caussols : un rasoir et une pendeloque de ceinture en bronze.
• ÂGE DU FER
Camp du Castellas (2 500 ans), à Escragnolles : céramiques et une perle d'ambre.
• ANTIQUITÉ ROMAINE
Beaulieu-sur-Mer. Vintimille. Grotte Bianchi, à La Colle-sur-Loup. Mont Bastide, à Èze. Nombreuses céramiques (200-500 apr. J.-C.).
• ÉPOQUE MÉROVINGIENNE
Sépulture d'Ilonse (600 apr. J.-C.) : objets de parures et ossements d'une jeune femme.

OUTRE LA RICHESSE de son fonds archéologique et la qualité didactique de la présentation des sites préhistoriques majeurs de la Côte d'Azur, le musée de Préhistoire régionale possède des objets d'arts et traditions populaires ayant trait à la vie mentonnaise des siècles passés (meubles, objets domestiques, costumes...), ainsi qu'une section consacrée aux sciences de la nature (géologie, minéralogie, paléontologie, entomologie, ornithologie...).

1

2

1. Immeuble 13, rue Guyau.
2. *Villa* Les Mouettes.

En sortant du musée, nous empruntons la rue Lorédan-Larchey. Au n° 15, nous remarquons une maison construite en 1910 par Abel Glena [→ p. 30]. Les frises en sgraffite de l'avant-toit, les façades et la toiture sont inscrites sur l'Inventaire supplémentaire des monuments historiques. En face, au n° 20, nous pouvons admirer la villa *La Source*, construite en 1920 par le même architecte. **Nous tournons** dans la première voie à gauche, la rue Magenta. À l'extrémité de celle-ci nous trouvons la rue Guyau.

Rue Guyau

DANS CETTE RUE, dont le nom évoque le philosophe Marie-Jean Guyau (1854-1888), on peut remarquer quelques édifices particulièrement intéressants.
• AU N° 13, un petit immeuble des années 1920, dû à Henri Cerutti-Maori [→ p. 30], semble figé dans son état originel, nous projetant dans un passé nostalgique. Le crépi ocre jaune d'époque rehausse une modénature soignée de style italianisant. Encadrée de deux avant-corps en bow-window très « bourgeois », la façade dénote une influence Art déco dans les fenêtres en plein cintre et la loggia tripartite à doubles colonnettes de l'attique. Ce nouveau style gomme l'ornementation chargée de la Belle Époque, dont les seuls résidus ici sont les écoinçons des bow-windows et l'entablement des ouvertures cintrées en partie supérieure (une curieuse dichotomie avec le premier étage tout en balustres).
• AU N° 8 *bis*, la villa *Les Mouettes* étage sa construction le long de l'escalier Léopold-Bernstamm. Une frise sous l'avant-toit rappelle le nom de la demeure : elle figure un vol de mouettes au-dessus de la végétation. Les façades et les frises

1

1. Villa Les Mouettes.
2-3. Maison Glena.
4. Nouvelles Galeries.

2

3

4

ont été classées monuments historiques. C'est dans cette villa que le sculpteur Léopold Bernstamm (1859-1939) a résidé, des années de la Grande Guerre jusqu'à sa mort. Artiste réputé, Léopold Bernstamm a vu défiler dans son atelier parisien, pendant trente ans, les élites intellectuelles et les célébrités de l'Europe entière, dont il fut aussi l'invité. Dans le vaste atelier qu'il avait fait aménager dans la villa *Les Mouettes*, il a poursuivi son œuvre – près de là, place Ardoïno, on peut voir le *Monument à la mémoire de Louis Laurenti.* Ami du romancier Vicente Blasco Ibáñez, il réalisa pour *Fontana Rosa* [→ p. 69] un grand nombre de bustes destinés à orner son jardin.

• AU N° 2 (angle de la rue du Général-Gallieni), la maison Glena, résidence du célèbre architecte mentonnais [→ p. 30], qui date de 1902 (Glena avait installé son agence au n° 4), est à remarquer pour son décor peint sous les toits, dû à Guillaume Cerutti-Maori [→ p. 78] : des enfants y symbolisent les beaux-arts ; la frise est illuminée par des cabochons à la feuille d'or. La façade, entièrement en pierre de taille (ce qui est peu fréquent à Menton), est animée de bossages et d'éléments de décors néoclassiques plaqués autour des baies. Un portail en ferronnerie Art déco donne accès à une cage d'escalier ornée d'une frise en rinceaux. Les portes palières de style Art nouveau témoignent d'un certain luxe.

• FACE À la maison Glena, au 27, rue de la République, se trouve un ancien grand magasin, *Les Dames de France* (aujourd'hui *Nouvelles Galeries*), œuvre tardive d'Adrien Rey [→ p. 30]. Au début des années 1920, l'auteur du marché municipal s'essaie à un autre programme fonctionnaliste, mais plus de vingt ans ont passé… Spécialiste de l'architecture

Marie-Jean Guyau

ON PEUT considérer que Menton, où Marie-Jean Guyau (1854-1888) a longuement séjourné, fut le révélateur d'une philosophie baignée de lumière, d'espérance. De la petite villa située à Garavan, récemment détruite, Marie-Jean Guyau découvre chaque jour « la mer toujours recommencée », mais encore la mer ludique et ses joutes allègres, la mer sereine et qui rassérène, l'élan de la nature et de la vie, la joie claire de la lumière et de la chaleur nourricière.

VERS D'UN PHILOSOPHE (1881), poèmes composés à Nice, à Menton, ou en Italie, témoigne de l'évolution intellectuelle de Guyau, de sa prise de conscience : « Je n'ai plus cette ardeur, cette foi qui soulève. Je suis las », écrit-il au cours d'une période d'un pessimisme douloureux.

LA MÉDITERRANÉE, rédigée au pont Saint-Louis à Menton, est l'un des derniers recueils de ce poète philosophe de vingt-quatre ans, qui a découvert toute l'énergie des mondes et se donne pour vocation de célébrer l'ordre et la dynamique de l'univers.

La rencontre de Marie-Jean Guyau et de Menton a été en quelque sorte décisive. Menton et son climat ensoleillé ne sont pas étrangers à l'épanouissement d'une philosophie tonique de l'existence chez ce tuberculeux qui meurt à trente-quatre ans, en 1888, alors que Nietzsche écrivait son *Zarathoustra*.

1

2

1. Vue des Nouvelles Galeries.
2. Frise à l'angle des rues Général-Gallieni et Pieta.
3-4. Chapelle des Pénitents noirs.

3

éclectique, qui maniait habilement les formules des Beaux-Arts, Rey est tout à coup confronté à une nouvelle modernité, prônant la rigueur et la ligne droite. Il se sort de cette situation en dressant une manière de façade rideau, rythmée par de larges verrières, et en résolvant l'écueil du traitement d'angle grâce à l'emploi du pan coupé à 45°. Il couronne toutefois cet édifice rationaliste par un hommage au grand style de la corniche à métopes et de la balustrade.

En face des *Nouvelles Galeries*, le square Henry-Longfellow rappelle que le poète américain (1807-1882) a séjourné dans la ville; il est orné du buste de l'écrivain. À l'arrière du square, une façade offre un décor peint Belle Époque à guirlandes de fleurs sur un étonnant fond turquoise.

Nous remontons à présent la rue du Général-Gallieni pour nous diriger vers la chapelle des Pénitents noirs.

4

Chapelle des Pénitents noirs

DITE AUSSI

de la Miséricorde

9, rue du Général-Gallieni

Ouverte lors des messes

Du lundi au samedi, de 17 h à 18 h 30, le dimanche, de 9 h à 10 h

EN 1615, le prince Honoré II et le père Laurent de Brindes, général des Capucins de la province de Gênes, posent la première pierre du couvent mentonnais confié à cet ordre.
En 1617, Nicolas Spinola, évêque de Vintimille, consacre la chapelle. L'année suivante, Honoré II fait percer la rue Neuve (actuelle rue Bréa), pour faciliter l'accès au couvent. Les capucins desservent cet établissement jusqu'en 1793. Fermé par la Convention, il abrite la mairie de Menton de 1861 à 1881; puis il est transformé en caserne et la chapelle est utilisée comme magasin de sel. En 1808, cette dernière est confiée à la confrérie des Pénitents noirs (installée auparavant dans le quartier de la place du Cap [→ p. 58]), qui entreprend de nombreuses transformations. La façade, autrefois simple muraille, est totalement remaniée en 1875; la statue de la Vierge de Miséricorde offerte par la princesse Caroline est placée dans la niche centrale. Le clocher est construit en 1875. De 1875 à 1877, l'intérieur de la chapelle est modifié par l'adjonction de deux nefs latérales.
PIÈCE remarquable du mobilier, le maître-autel (XVIIe s.) est d'inspiration italienne; sa face antérieure est en marqueterie de buis, citronnier, palissandre, acajou et noyer. En 1987, il a été classé monument historique. Les orgues de 1894, placées dans un buffet du début du XIXe s., ont été classées en 1982 et restaurées en 1993.

De la rue Sidi-Brahim au quai de Monléon

DEPUIS la rue du Général-Gallieni, nous nous rendons rue Sidi-Brahim, dont le nom évoque les combats de 1845 menés en Algérie par les chasseurs alpins face aux cavaliers de l'émir Abd el-Kader.
À L'EXTRÉMITÉ de cette artère, nous arrivons rue Saint-Michel. Au n° 22, la

1

1. *Maison Ardoïno.*
2. *Fronton de l'ancienne mairie.*
3. *Place Fornari.*
4. *Cabochon de céramique sur l'une des façades des halles municipales.*
5. *Halles municipales.*

2

3

maison Ardoïno abrite aujourd'hui le presbytère de la basilique Saint-Michel. L'édifice de style néo-Renaissance, à grandes baies cintrées ornementées de vitraux, a été construit vers 1900, sans doute d'après les plans d'Abel Glena. La frise (angelots et guirlandes) qui couronne la demeure est traitée en sgraffite.
À CÔTÉ du presbytère se trouve la place du Général-Kœnig (1898-1970), qui honore l'un des grands combattants de la Seconde Guerre mondiale, nommé commandant des Forces françaises de l'intérieur en 1944. Dans le jardin a été érigé le *Monument de la Résistance* dû au sculpteur Morlaix (1956).
NOUS ARRIVONS à présent place Georges-Clemenceau (ancienne place Nationale), où s'élève, au centre d'une fontaine, une colonne à fût cannelé qui supporte un buste de Marianne. Sur le pourtour de la place, nous voyons l'hôtel Trenca de Monléon, affecté à la mairie en 1882. Depuis la place du Général-Kœnig, nous nous dirigeons vers les halles.

5

Halles municipales

DITES AUSSI ***Marché couvert***

Accès par les rues des Marins, Gélis, Pélisson et le quai de Monléon

Ouvertes tous les matins, de 7 h à 14 h

4

CE LIEU DE VIE et d'échanges est le rendez-vous privilégié des habitants de la ville. La construction des halles a été décidée à la fin du XIXe s. En effet, au mois d'avril 1897, le conseil municipal accorde à cinq Mentonnais le droit de bâtir et d'exploiter un marché couvert. Les concessionnaires font appel à Adrien Rey [→ p. 30], qui achève les travaux en septembre 1898. L'architecte donne à ce bâtiment éminemment utilitaire une apparence agréable, tout en évitant de le rendre disparate par rapport au quartier. Une de ses particularités est la marquise établie sur toutes les façades et formant porche abrité pour les entrées. L'aspect est égayé par une grande diversité de couleurs des matériaux : moellons du soubassement, enduits, briques variées, céramiques de la manufacture Saïssi…, ainsi que par les motifs ajustés aux portes et au campanile.
LA PLACE AUX HERBES, où se tenait l'ancien marché aux fruits et légumes, nous permet, à l'ombre des platanes, de nous rafraîchir près de la fontaine ornée d'une statue de Mentonnaise due à Marcel Bouraine.

Nous traversons la place Fornari et nous poursuivons le quai de Monléon pour aller au Bastion, sur le Vieux-Port, qui abrite aujourd'hui le musée Jean-Cocteau.

Musée Jean-Cocteau

Le Bastion, qui sert de cadre au musée dédié à l'œuvre de Jean Cocteau, est un édifice militaire dont la construction, prévue en 1619 par Honoré II pour protéger Menton, fut achevée en 1636. À cette époque, les Espagnols exerçaient un protectorat sur la principauté de Monaco.

Le Bastion

Quai Napoléon-III

Téléphone : 04 93 57 72 30

Ouvert tous les jours (sauf mardi et fêtes légales), de 10 h à 12 h et de 14 h à 18 h

1

1. Jean Cocteau, Innamorati. *© Adagp, Paris 2006.*
2. Vue du Bastion.

LE FORTIN, en avancée dans la mer entre les deux golfes, était relié à la plage par une passerelle. On accédait à son premier étage par un escalier de bois. La salle des gardes, à ce même étage, a perdu son aspect militaire, comme le rez-de-chaussée, autrefois magasin à munitions.
DU XVIIe s. subsistent la cuisine avec son four et la voûte en brique de la grande salle. Les échauguettes, qui flanquent le bâtiment aux quatre angles, ont été refaites (1960-1965).
JEAN COCTEAU (1889-1963), qui en 1957 décora la salle des mariages, avait exprimé le désir de créer dans le Bastion un musée destiné à recevoir ses œuvres. Il a présidé lui-même aux restaurations de l'édifice. Il a dessiné les mosaïques du sol, celle de la salamandre au rez-de-chaussée,

2

et celles des embrasures des fenêtres au premier étage. Il a conçu les vitrines en fer forgé pour abriter ses céramiques zoomorphes. Mais il n'a pas pu voir l'achèvement de son œuvre, le musée ayant été inauguré en 1967, quatre ans après sa mort.

Le musée expose un grand nombre d'œuvres et de documents : outre les céramiques, on peut y voir rassemblés des dessins, des tableaux, des séries de pastels (*Innamorati*, *Les Animaux fantastiques*), deux tapisseries (*Judith et Holopherne* et les *Visages*), des photographies, des manuscrits...

Cet ensemble permet d'apprécier Jean Cocteau, l'écrivain, l'homme de théâtre, le poète, le cinéaste, le décorateur, le peintre, celui qui semblait chercher en tout à illustrer son propre aphorisme : « Comprenne qui pourra : je suis un mensonge qui dit toujours la vérité. »

Jean Cocteau, portrait au crayon et pastel.

En 2005, la ville a reçu une extraordinaire donation de la part de l'homme d'affaires américain Severin Wunderman. Passionné par la créativité multiforme de Cocteau, il a acquis quelque 1 800 œuvres originales qui constitueront la part la plus importante d'un nouveau musée Jean-Cocteau, situé en face du marché couvert et en bordure de cette Méditerranée chère au poète ; sa construction, confiée à Rudy Ricciotti, devrait s'achever à l'automne 2011.

Résidence du Midi.

Depuis quarante ans, les municipalités qui se sont succédé ont conduit les travaux nécessaires à la réalisation d'un terre-plein en avancée sur la mer, que prolonge le quai Napoléon-III. Cela a pu permettre le contournement du quartier du Marché et divers aménagements : parkings, jardin, jeu de boules... Sous cet espace gagné sur la mer, une station d'épuration des eaux a été mise en place. L'esplanade Francis-Palmero a été agencée en reprenant les thèmes du décor du marché et agrémenté d'une fontaine où sont utilisés les motifs de masques en céramique qui ornent les halles.

Nous quittons l'esplanade et allons maintenant emprunter la promenade du Soleil en direction du casino.

Résidence du Midi

1652, promenade du Soleil

Cette résidence (ancien *Hôtel du Midi*) présente, face à la mer, une volumétrie intéressante. Originellement, elle devait ressembler à une traditionnelle demeure mentonnaise, mais elle a été parée, dans les années 1920, de la panoplie du plus pur style Art déco. Un examen attentif révèle en effet, sous cet habillage, une structure génoise récurrente. Son charme indéniable tient à la rencontre heureuse entre un archétype historique de villa et une décoration « à la mode » qui lui sied à merveille.

L'élévation méridionale est constituée de deux avant-corps saillants réunis au rez-de-chaussée par une loggia à cinq arcades, encadrant un corps central en retrait. C'est l'imposante corniche en visière qui confère une grâce martiale à la résidence. Colorée de tonalités de glace vanille-fraise-cassis, elle nous apparaît délicieuse avec ses six grandes poteries

1

2

3

4

1. Hôtel Vendôme.
2. Hôtel Royal Westminster.
3. Hôtel Balmoral.
4. Résidence Victoria Palace.

de Vallauris qui ponctuent le balcon de la loggia. La cannelure, caractéristique de la décoration des années 1920, est ici l'élément fédérateur : elle donne une dynamique verticale aux angles des avant-corps, sculpte les fûts des colonnes de la loggia et dessine les frises qui soulignent la corniche. Les fers forgés à corbeilles de fruits sont bien sûr typiques du style Art déco épanoui. Nous pouvons aussi remarquer les petits chapiteaux carrés à motifs géométriques et l'entrée latérale, avec son joli porche.

ENTRETENUE avec goût, cette maison originale résume tout le calme et la douceur que l'on attend de Menton. Immobilisée entre l'actualité éphémère et l'immuable tradition, elle est un lieu d'harmonie face auquel on se plaît à rêver.

Tout le long de la promenade du Soleil, les premiers grands hôtels de tourisme sont édifiés en bord de mer, dès la fin du Second Empire : le *Royal Westminster*, le *Vendôme*, le *Balmoral* – tous trois encore résidences hôtelières – et le *Régina*, transformé en appartements. En façade sur la mer, le *Royal Westminster* présente quelques jolis palmiers, un beau spécimen d'*Oreopanax nymphaeifollium*, ainsi qu'un ensemble harmonieux de yuccas, de cycas et d'euphorbes géantes.

Résidences *Victoria Palace* et *Victoria Beach*

1500, promenade du Soleil

LE GOÛT DU « rétro », symptomatique d'une autocommisération passéiste qui, à maintes reprises, a servi d'argument à de célèbres propositions architecturales du dernier quart du XXe s., s'est pleinement épanoui à Menton à l'aube de notre siècle. Des résidences comme *Victoria Palace* et *Victoria Beach* en sont de bons exemples. Plusieurs programmes importants fidèles à cette tendance ont vu le jour au cours de ces années. Celui-ci est l'un des plus marquants, tant par sa superficie que par la complexité de son traitement. Il a modifié à lui seul la physionomie de cette portion du front de mer et de la place Saint-Roch attenante.

L'EXUBÉRANTE décoration imaginée en 1996 pour ces deux résidences accumule tous les poncifs de la « méditerranéenneté historique ». Les balustres soutiennent des colonnes qui encadrent des fers forgés parfois dissimulés sous des pleins cintres… C'est dire toute la prouesse dont a su faire preuve l'imagination du concepteur. Le programme se décline en plusieurs coloris de volets pour satisfaire au goût chromatique de la clientèle : vert pour l'Italie, bleu pour la France, blanc dans le meilleur des cas ! Objet de polémiques, cet ensemble qui oscille entre le *cosy* et le *kitsch* a maintenant sa place dans le panorama de l'agglomération mentonnaise.

Nous quittons la promenade du Soleil, pour prendre, à droite, la rue Adhémar-de-Lantagnac, qui nous conduit place Saint-Roch.

Fontaine de la place Saint-Roch

LA RUE Adhémar-de-Lantagnac sépare le *Victoria Palace* du *Victoria Beach*, à l'endroit où a été préservé un superbe *Ficus macrofila*. Elle donne accès à la place Saint-Roch. Ici, c'est toujours la référence à l'antique qui prime, avec la fontaine conçue par le sculpteur Sacha Sosno en 1996. Elle est représentative

1

2

1. Résidence Paris Palace.
2. Le casino municipal peu de temps après sa construction en 1934.

de la démarche de cet artiste niçois, de réputation internationale, très présent dans sa ville natale. Sa problématique illustre toujours le contraste entre forme brute et art policé, faisant émerger des silhouettes antiques de blocs colossaux. Dans le cas présent, la masse de carrare blanc posée sur un socle gris est éclatée en quatre blocs regardant chacun les voies formant le carrefour. Un nu masculin couronné fait face à la mer, du côté de la rue Adhémar-de-Lantagnac ; un nu féminin se drape de dos face à la section occidentale de l'avenue Félix-Faure ; un deuxième torse masculin apparaît dans l'axe de la rue Partouneaux ; face à la vieille ville, sur le tronçon oriental de l'avenue, se dresse une colonne. L'eau qui glisse, caressant les statues, est recueillie dans un vaste bassin. En opposition à l'alibi folklorique des réalisations attenantes, la démarche archéologique se double ici d'une interrogation sur l'essence de la modernité.

Nous regagnons la promenade du Soleil pour aller en direction du casino.

Résidence *Paris Palace*

1360, promenade du Soleil

LA RÉSIDENCE, érigée en 1962, est l'un des premiers jalons posés sur le rivage par la systématisation des « barres » de la modernité triomphante. Hommage de René Livieri, excellent architecte niçois, à un glorieux aîné, Roger Seassal, auteur du casino voisin, l'immeuble occupe une position privilégiée sur la promenade du Soleil. Sa masse imposante est parfaitement maîtrisée par un art impeccable du dessin. Le bâtiment, rigoureusement symétrique, offre l'intérêt notable d'être soigné sur toutes ses façades.

CONSTITUÉ d'un parallélépipède percé en son milieu d'une arche traversante, il est flanqué de quatre tourelles d'angle sur cinq niveaux. L'élévation du côté de l'avenue Félix-Faure est plus sobre que l'opulente façade du front de mer. Les vitrages des cages d'escalier y introduisent deux césures verticales. La façade sur la mer, elle, utilise le principe du balcon filant, modulé par un décroché en cascade qui permet d'en varier la largeur – le jeu d'ombres ménagé amorce les rotondes d'extrémité.

L'ARCHITECTE, déjà en activité dans les années 1930, avait su durant sa longue carrière se constituer un vocabulaire formel étendu, qu'il utilise ici avec une grande maîtrise. Les tourelles d'angle relèvent encore des stylèmes de l'entre-deux-guerres, mais, présentement, René Livieri leur donne une valeur d'actualité. Elles sont soutenues par des consoles en doucine dont il s'est fait la spécialité, tout comme pour les fers forgés modernes, hérités du grand style français.

LA SOBRE efficacité de cet ensemble désormais historique contraste avec la surenchère *kitsch* de son voisinage postérieur.

Casino municipal

2, avenue Félix-Faure

C'EST À L'OUEST du *Paris Palace*, face à l'esplanade des jardins Biovès, toujours en front de mer, qu'a été bâti en 1934 le casino conçu par Roger Seassal [→ p. 31], spécialiste du genre – il était déjà l'auteur du *Palm Beach* de Cannes et du Sporting Club d'été de Monte-Carlo. Le casino figure parmi les quelques rares bâtiments à avoir échappé à l'iconoclastie de la modernité – récemment restauré, il n'a pas subi de modifications structurelles

1. Casino municipal.
2. Détail de la façade du casino municipal.

1

fondamentales. Son architecte érudit, membre de l'Institut, a opté pour une stylistique conforme aux goûts de la clientèle de la Côte d'Azur orientale : un modernisme sage, rehaussé d'Art déco exotique. L'édifice surprend par sa conception résolument dichotomique, comme si Roger Seassal avait souhaité imbriquer entre eux deux corps de bâtiment différents possédant chacun sa logique et son langage propre.
AU NORD, face aux jardins, on trouve l'entrée principale du casino qui, avec la savoureuse dentelle de son fronton, pourrait sembler l'émanation d'une certaine tendance « rétro » actuelle.
DU CÔTÉ SUD, face à la mer, la partie qui donnait autrefois de plain-pied sur la plage comporte une pergola en arcades terminée en partie ouest par une rotonde desservie par un double escalier, autrefois kiosque à musique. L'aménagement de la voie de circulation automobile entre la pergola et la plage a privé l'ensemble de son identité balnéaire, lui ôtant du même coup une grande partie de son sens. La pergola a toutefois gardé intacte sa référence au baroque mexicain qui, à première vue, semble avoir inspiré ce complexe si hétéroclite.
L'AILE OCCIDENTALE est peut-être la plus réussie. Ce qui fut un cinéma à toit ouvrant – spécificité de l'architecture méditerranéenne de l'époque – a été dévolu au casino, aujourd'hui exploité par le groupe Barrière. Le quadrilatère du cinéma, grâce à un habillage virtuose, devient un écrin précieux. Les façades nord et sud sont en effet allégées par leurs inflexions convexes, entaillées par trois niches concaves monumentales. Là aussi, les réminiscences baroques fédèrent cet ensemble savamment *kitsch*. Mais la corniche d'inspiration Louis XV est pourtant bien méditerranéenne, avec ses enroulements de vagues, rappelant un motif grec. Les impressionnants pots à feu sont, quant à eux, une réinterprétation d'un des stylèmes archétypes du baroque triomphant. Ce motif est d'ailleurs repris sur les frontons chapeautant les niches. Si la verticalité monumentale est soulignée par la juxtaposition des niches et des oculus placés au-dessus – aveugles eux aussi –, elle est contredite par un parement uniforme de damier en losanges. Cet habillage très élégant préfigure étonnamment une tendance décorative des années 1950 ; pourtant, c'est bien le style mauresque que salue ici cet architecte archéologue. Nous pouvons admirer la prouesse de Seassal, qui a su réintroduire dans l'architecture du XXe s. les problématiques initialement exportées par les navigateurs génois quelque quatre siècles auparavant et réinvesties ici par le biais d'une mythologie exotique tout droit issue du cinéma hollywoodien. Cet enchevêtrement subtilement architecturé paraît aujourd'hui riche de sens et mérite l'hommage qui lui est rendu au détour d'une aussi belle restauration.

2

Mer Méditerranée
Baie du Soleil
Baie de Garavan
Port de Garavan
Vieux Port
ITALIE
Tunnel
Garavan
Les Colombières
Le Baousset
La Colle
Vallée du Fossan
Les Ciappes
Vallée du Careï
Monastère de l'Annonciade
Vallée du Borrigo
N.D. de Fatima
Les Castagnins
Val de Gorbio
Vers Gorbio
La Madone
Parc Gorre
Plateau St Michel
GARE
GARE ROUTIÈRE
Sacré Cœur
Synagogue St Christophe
Eglise Russe
St John
St Julien
Ste Anne
St Jacques
Ste Jeanne d'Arc
Vers Monaco et Nice
Vers Ste Agnès
VERS A8 Sauf Bus et P.L.
VERS A8
Vers Monti et Sospel
Vers Castellar
Vers CASTELLAR
A8 Esterel - Côte d'Azur
Promenade du Soleil
Av. Porte de France
Av. A. Briand
Route de Gorbio
Route de Sospel
Corniche André Tardieu
Route des Cabrolles
Route de Castellar

Les collines du pays mentonnais

De l'Annonciade à Serre de la Madone

La cité mentonnaise est entourée d'un amphithéâtre de collines et de montagnes qui l'enserrent et la protègent des vents. Ainsi s'explique le microclimat dont bénéficie Menton. Cet itinéraire, au-dessus du golfe de la Paix, peut être envisagé par des randonneurs. Toutefois, les visiteurs pressés pourront découvrir aisément paysages et points de vue en utilisant leur véhicule.

1. Céramique de Serre de la Madone.
2. Chemin du Rosaire.
3. Fontaine de Serre de la Madone.
4. Monastère de l'Annonciade.
5. Les Colombières : *le jardin clos.*

Colline de l'Annonciade

Ce haut lieu mentonnais est accessible en automobile par la route de l'Annonciade, qui prend naissance au n° 99 de la route de Sospel, dans la vallée du Careï. Les amateurs de randonnée pédestre peuvent emprunter le chemin du Rosaire.

Chemin du Rosaire

FACE À LA GARE routière, au-dessus du marché du Careï, nous laissons la route de Sospel et nous nous engageons sur le chemin du Rosaire, bordé d'agaves, de pins et d'aloès. Ce sentier en pas d'âne longe l'arrière des palaces et nous mène au monastère de l'Annonciade.

AU XVIIe s., Isabelle Grimaldi, sœur du prince Louis Ier de Monaco, de retour de Terre sainte où elle a contracté la lèpre, invoque Notre-Dame. Elle obtient une guérison miraculeuse. En remerciement, elle fait édifier, sur le chemin de la chapelle de Puypin, 15 oratoires consacrés aux mystères de la Vierge. Après la Première Guerre, les oratoires tombent en ruine. En 1930, une souscription publique est ouverte pour les reconstruire. Le chantier est confié à l'architecte Abel Glena, qui conçoit des petites chapelles en cul-de-four couronnées de tuiles canal. Un décor à la fresque d'inspiration Art nouveau, rehaussé de cabochons dorés – œuvre de Guillaume Cerutti-Maori [→ p. 78] –, orne l'intérieur de l'abside.

LE CHEMIN du Rosaire est inauguré en 1932. En 1931, devant le mauvais état des fresques, on place devant celles-ci un nouveau décor, exécuté sur panneaux amovibles.

1

2

3

1. Monastère de l'Annonciade (dessin, milieu du XIXe s.). 2. Monastère de l'Annonciade. 3. Intérieur de la chapelle.

Monastère de l'Annonciade

Ouvert tous les jours, de 9 h à 17 h

À LA FIN du XIe s., la petite cité fortifiée de *Podium Pini* (ou Puypin) s'élève au sommet de la colline qui sépare les vallées du Careï et du Borrigo. À partir de 1316, Puypin fait place à une nouvelle ville, installée depuis quelque temps déjà sur une autre colline proche du rivage de la Méditerranée : Menton. Au milieu du XIVe s., rien ne subsiste de cet antique Puypin, si ce n'est une humble chapelle dédiée à Notre-Dame de l'Annonciade, invoquée par les marins et les personnes en danger – nous ne connaissons pas précisément la date de sa construction. À partir du XIVe s., la petite chapelle est citée dans les différents textes parvenus jusqu'à nous. Édifice à nef unique, à voûte en berceau et à chevet plat, cette chapelle est agrandie au XVIIe s. On y adjoint des bâtiments conventuels pour y accueillir la congrégation de Puypin, fondée en 1694 par des prêtres de la région mentonnaise. Venant couronner le sommet de l'oppidum, ces bâtiments, qui forment une masse imposante visible de la mer, servent de point de repère aux navigateurs. Tout au long des siècles, ces derniers ont déposé dans l'église des ex-voto, qui témoignent de la piété populaire. En 1641, le prince Honoré II de Monaco, soutenu par ses sujets mentonnais, chasse l'occupant espagnol de ses États. Un de ses lieutenants, Jean Jérôme de Monléon, offre en remerciement à Notre-Dame de l'Annonciade un très bel ex-voto en bois doré. L'ensemble de ces œuvres pieuses a été déposé dans une salle afin que visiteurs et pèlerins puissent les admirer.

DEVENUES biens nationaux, la chapelle et ses dépendances sont acquises en 1808 par Jérôme de Monléon. En 1866, son fils Charles Gratien abrite à l'Annonciade des pères capucins chassés de Gênes par le gouvernement italien. En 1893, ils sont remplacés par des capucins de la province de Lyon ; ces derniers y restent jusqu'en 1999.

EN 2000, des annonciades, religieuses de l'ordre de la Vierge, se substituent aux capucins. Depuis, elles accueillent les Mentonnais et les fidèles de la région lors des fêtes mariales, le 25 mars et le 8 septembre. Berceau de Menton et véritable colline inspirée, l'Annonciade demeure un havre de recueillement et de paix. Ici, les vergers et les pâturages ont tendance à faire place à une végétation subtropicale, le vignoble demeurant le seul souvenir des temps ancestraux.

En redescendant du monastère par la corniche André-Tardieu, en direction du nord, nous nous arrêtons un instant devant la villa *La Tête du Commandant*, résidence d'André Tardieu.

Villa *La Tête du Commandant*

1072, corniche André-Tardieu

ANDRÉ TARDIEU, personnage politique éminent de la IIIe République (onze fois ministre, trois fois président du Conseil), abandonne la vie politique et s'installe à l'*Hôtel de l'Annonciade*, situé près du monastère. En 1935, l'écrivain André Maurois lui rend visite : « Je le trouve goguenard, cynique, gentil. Il nous emmène voir l'emplacement d'une maison qu'il fait construire plus haut, sur un pic ; devant nous, un vallon, les caps, la mer. » Mais Tardieu ne connaîtra le bonheur

1

2

1-2. Villa La Tête du Commandant.

3

3. La Citronneraie.

de sa villa que quelques années ; en 1939, il est frappé par la maladie, qui le rend invalide, et il meurt en 1945. Tardieu est inhumé dans le petit cimetière de Monti, où un monument funéraire à sa mémoire a été inauguré en 1957. Homme politique brillant, surnommé « le Mirobolant », il est « agile et solide, atténuant la rigueur de la méthode par la hardiesse conciliante des suggestions ». Raymond Poincaré disait de lui : « M. Tardieu a hautement mérité d'être classé parmi les plus grands chefs. Il a l'esprit aussi lucide et aussi ordonné que la volonté prompte et soutenue. » Dans sa résidence, il travaille dans une immense bibliothèque qui lui sert de bureau et où il rédige ses ouvrages sur l'avenir politique de la France, notamment *La Révolution à refaire*, publiée en 1936-1937.

LA VILLA *La Tête du Commandant* a été réalisée par Pierre Patout au cours des années 1930. L'architecte, qui laisse ici une large place aux arts décoratifs, est encore influencé par son propre travail d'aménagement de trois transatlantiques (*Le Normandie*, *L'Atlantique* et *L'Île-de-France*). Il conçoit cette grande villa toute blanche avec des coursives héritées des bastingages, qui lui donnent des allures de paquebot.

Arrivés au n° 69 de la corniche André-Tardieu, nous découvrons un domaine accroché aux flancs de la colline, le mas *Flofaro*, plus souvent appelé *La Citronneraie*.

La Citronneraie
Mas Flofaro
CITRONNERAIE FRANÇOIS MAZET

69, corniche André-Tardieu

Visite toute l'année, sur rendez-vous

Visites guidées organisées par le Service du patrimoine (renseignements : 04 92 10 97 10)

FACE AU SOLEIL levant, avec en toile de fond un décor de montagne, *La Citronneraie* est en quelque sorte le dernier des grands vergers d'agrumes de Menton ou le premier qui annonce le renouveau de la culture du citron.

ACQUISE EN 1950 par son propriétaire actuel, *La Citronneraie* compte trois ans plus tard – outre les 200 oliviers déjà présents – une cinquantaine d'agrumes, tous regroupés autour d'une maison de caractère construite en 1820. La résidence principale – restaurée et aménagée – et ses trois dépendances s'étendent de nos jours sur quelque 1 000 mètres carrés, sans que soient altérés le charme et la magie du lieu. De 1957 à 1965, les achats de parcelles se succèdent ; le domaine atteint une superficie de 4,5 hectares. En raison d'une pluviométrie irrégulière sous le climat méditerranéen, préjudiciable au développement des fruits, il est urgent de réhabiliter les systèmes de récupération et de stockage de l'eau : celle qui est issue des ruissellements du haut du versant est canalisée par le chemin muletier qui ceinture et longe la partie supérieure de la propriété. Dès 1957, sont entreprises les premières plantations de citronniers de la variété dite « Menton », la seule exploitée ici, réputée pour être la plus gustative de toutes. À ce jour, le domaine est riche

2

1

1. Les Colombières.
2. Les Colombières (dessin de Ferdinand Bac).

de 450 citronniers, pour une production d'environ 150 à 200 kilogrammes de fruits par arbre selon les années. Toutes les récoltes issues du mas *Flofaro* sont destinées à un marché où l'on retrouve les plus grands noms de la gastronomie française. Outre les citronniers, on trouve aussi des mandariniers, des cédratiers de Corse, des clémentiniers, des pomelos, des bigaradiers et des kumquats.

TOUTEFOIS, l'arboriculture fruitière n'est pas seule à trouver place dans ce vaste domaine. De nombreuses plantes tropicales et subtropicales font du mas *Flofaro* un jardin d'agrément où les fleurs délicates voisinent avec des arbres géants (camphriers, eucalyptus, palmiers), et où les essences de contrées plus froides (érables, cèdres, ginkgos...) ajoutent un charme supplémentaire. Jasmins et rosiers mêlent leur parfum, tandis que vignes (cépages noah et chasselas) et passiflores courent sur les pergolas et les clôtures. Quant à la terrasse de la maison, elle est ombragée par une belle glycine centenaire (*Wisteria sinensis*).

Collines de Garavan

Arrivés au terme de notre parcours sur la colline de l'Annonciade, nous nous rendons aux confins de la commune, en direction de l'Italie. Afin de partir à la découverte des collines de Garavan, nous conseillons aux visiteurs d'emprunter leur véhicule.

NOUS DESCENDONS la vallée du Careï en direction du bord de mer, puis nous empruntons la promenade du Soleil et la promenade Porte-de-France qui, toutes deux, longent la baie de Menton. Nous gagnons ensuite le pont Saint-Louis.

AVANT d'arriver aux anciens bâtiments des douanes, nous trouvons, à gauche le boulevard de Garavan. À la hauteur du n° 67, nous prenons la route des Colombières, afin de nous rendre à l'étonnante propriété réalisée par Ferdinand Bac.

Les Colombières

312, route de Super-Garavan

Visites guidées, du 1er juillet au 10 août, organisées par le Service du patrimoine (renseignements : 04 92 10 97 10)

Dessinateur, illustrateur et caricaturiste de talent, écrivain et romancier habitué des salons parisiens, Sigismond Ferdinand Bach (1859-1952), plus connu sous le pseudonyme de « Ferdinand Bac », est une personnalité phare de la Belle Époque. Témoin de son temps, mettant sa plume et son trait au service de la presse, Bac est l'auteur de sulfureuses chroniques mondaines. Familier de l'ex-impératrice Eugénie, reçu à la table des puissants de ce monde, il est également un bâtisseur qui s'applique à donner forme et âme à la matière. Homme de savoir, Bac ne se satisfait pas de simples spéculations intellectuelles. Il se veut homme d'action et devient architecte, décorateur, concepteur de jardins.

À LA DEMANDE des Ladan-Bockairy, une famille proche de Ferdinand Bac, celui-ci a pour mission d'aménager un espace d'une superficie de 11 hectares sur les hauteurs de Garavan. Il se consacre à ce projet de 1920 à 1928 et réalise une œuvre déconcertante que l'on pourrait qualifier de délirante. Pourtant, la singularité de cet ensemble, malgré son aspect totalement atypique, en fait une création dont la qualité tant esthétique que symbolique se révèle exceptionnelle.

1

2

1. Entrée du domaine des Colombières.
2. Les Colombières : *la rotonde de l'Obélisque.*

3. Les Colombières : *le jardin d'Homère (aquarelle de G. Sadlier).*

3

Sans vouloir décrypter la totalité de ce message, qui nous parvient inscrit dans la pierre et dans le végétal, il nous paraît fondamental de donner quelques clés pour comprendre la démarche de ce créateur qui a eu l'élégance de nous fournir un guide publié en 1925 sous le titre *Les Colombières : ses jardins et ses décors*.

CONÇUES comme une entité indissociable, *Les Colombières* se composent d'une villa et d'un parc. Les végétaux et la quinzaine de fabriques (petits édifices pittoresques) qui ponctuent la promenade du parc doivent, dans l'esprit de Bac, s'interpénétrer. Le vivant doit acquérir une beauté sculpturale et la matière être animée d'un souffle vital. Bac s'attache à abolir toute séparation entre le jardin et la résidence, entre le minéral et le végétal. Dans l'espoir d'escamoter les murs et de fortifier l'illusion du rêve, il a recours à la fresque et à la céramique. « Tromper ses sens, tromper ses yeux », tel est le mot d'ordre, car Bac déteste les murs nus que les Anciens prenaient pour des prisons. Tromper certes, mais pour mieux faire vivre l'illusion.

LES COLOMBIÈRES, moderne Villa Adriana – que l'empereur Hadrien se fit bâtir à Tivoli –, sont l'hommage fervent rendu à la Méditerranée par une personnalité jouissant d'une culture raffinée. C'est une grand-messe païenne, un feu d'artifice éblouissant, un temple où l'homme doit pouvoir communier avec son passé et se remémorer les lieux sacrés qu'il a jadis fréquentés.

SON OBJECTIF étant clairement affiché, Bac souhaite inscrire son projet dans le paysage en traitant l'environnement, qui ne peut être que méditerranéen, et en installant en quelques points privilégiés des éléments qui soient autant de signes manifestes pour évoquer cette divinité qu'est la Méditerranée.

POUR LA VILLA, Bac réutilise quelques murs de la modeste maison de l'ancien propriétaire du lieu, le philosophe Alfred Fouillée, et il s'emploie à bâtir un petit palais aux façades d'ocre rouge, avec un atrium et son bassin, qui ouvre sur le jardin d'Homère. Pour orner les murs de l'atrium et ceux de plusieurs pièces de la demeure, Bac peint lui-même quelques fresques.

POUR L'ENVIRONNEMENT, le parti repose sur la juxtaposition de jardins jalonnés de statues et de fabriques, d'une colonnade, d'un pont, de bassins et de fontaines..., chacun de ces jardins étant consacré à un thème particulier, à un personnage mythologique ou à un objet à forte charge symbolique : la fontaine des Colombes, le *Faune dansant*, le jardin du Trompe-l'œil, l'*Enfant au papillon*, la fontaine de Nausicaa, l'*Esclave au collier*, le bassin espagnol, le mausolée de style byzantin, la rotonde de l'Obélisque avec son miroir d'eau sur la margelle duquel un vers de Lucrèce vient nous rappeler que « les choses que l'on croit mortes à jamais, renaissent »... Une partie seulement du domaine est aménagée ; quant au dernier jardin, dédié à Orphée, il n'est plus que « cette trinité immense, du ciel, de la mer et des arbres ».

LE PARC des *Colombières* est aussi une mise en scène grandiose de la nature. Ce n'est pas le moindre des paradoxes que ce domaine singulier soit aussi le seul lieu d'exception à Menton à avoir proscrit le matériel végétal exotique. Ici les plantes introduites (oliviers, cyprès, caroubiers) sont de véritables « barbares » et, à ce titre, exclues du paradis classique. Pour d'autres motifs, notamment esthétiques, les fleurs sont

1. Les Colombières : le mausolée (dessin de Ferdinand Bac).

2

3

2-3. L'Esquinade.

des espèces sauvages : « Madame, méfiez-vous de cette mégalomanie florale », murmure Ferdinand Bac à sa belle visiteuse. Il accepte toutefois la présence du laurier-rose et des rosiers blancs, et s'attendrit curieusement sur la délicieuse capucine, cette charmante immigrée venue des Amériques.

Nous poursuivons la route de Super-Garavan en direction de *L'Esquinade*. Sur les contreforts des Préalpes appelés « le Pas de la Mort », les sentiers de la contrebande des années 1950 conduisent – mais pas toujours à bon port ! – les marcheurs infatigables jusqu'au quartier de Super-Garavan. Pour desservir les collines agricoles en cours de mutation, la Ville décide de réaliser, de 1953 à 1965, un nouvel axe routier : la route de Super-Garavan, véritable balcon sur la Riviera. Entre 1965 et 1970, sont aménagés les routes du Baousset, de La Colle-Supérieure et le sentier de La Colle-Inférieure. Sur les hauteurs des collines de Garavan, une troisième voie de circulation, l'autoroute, règle, pour un temps, le problème de la circulation dans les rues de Menton : au cours de ces années 1965-1970, le flot journalier d'automobiles était de 9 000 à 10 000 véhicules environ.

L'Esquinade

2629, route de Super-Garavan

Visites guidées organisées par le Service du patrimoine (renseignements : 04 92 10 97 10)

LE JARDIN de *L'Esquinade* est l'archétype même du jardin de collectionneur. Son aventure commence en 1968, lors de l'ouverture du grand chantier autoroutier et des travaux de génie civil qui l'accompagnent : réalisation des viaducs, percement des tunnels et creusement d'une large tranchée dans la masse rocheuse. Pour permettre aux camions d'accéder à ce chantier, on transforme un sentier en route de Super-Garavan, qui devient une voie de pénétration pour ceux qui sont à la recherche de terrains à bâtir.

EN 1972, Édouard et Simone Mazzola, anciens propriétaires d'une jardinerie, décident de se fixer sur la terre qui les a vus naître et de vivre comme l'esquinade – crabe ou araignée de mer –, parmi les rochers et les végétaux. Ils acquièrent un vallon d'environ 1 hectare, au-delà du grand viaduc qui enjambe la vallée. Mais il leur faut d'abord combler ce vallon, puis créer leur jardin en aménageant de larges bandes de terre séparées les unes des autres par de puissantes restanques (petits murets de pierre sèche) et étagées sur un dénivelé de 50 mètres. Au terme de 5 000 rotations de camions de 10 mètres cubes – mais *L'Esquinade*, dont le nom évoque le verbe *s'échiner*, stimule les titans plutôt qu'elle ne les rebute –, la plate-forme est prête. La villa est bâtie en 1976 et l'aménagement des surfaces cultivables s'achève en 1990.

CES TERRASSES, de forme légèrement arquée, à l'abri des vents, bien exposées au sud-sud-ouest, enregistrent en hiver des températures inférieures de 2 à 3 °C par rapport à celles du littoral. À Menton, *L'Esquinade* peut ainsi être vue comme un centre expérimental pour l'acclimatation des plantes. Son alimentation en eau est assurée par une source qui couvre les besoins du jardin tout au long de l'année.

JARDIN de collection, *L'Esquinade* est un lieu remarquable par l'ensemble végétal

2

3

1

1. Une allée fleurie à L'Esquinade.
2. Vue depuis Super-Garavan.
3. Vallée de Gorbio.

que l'on y trouve et par son paysage, d'une rare beauté. D'ici, la vue n'est que couleurs, du rouge des toits de la vieille ville au bleu infini de la mer. Dans la partie haute du jardin sont regroupées 160 espèces ou sous-espèces d'agrumes, notamment de nombreuses variétés de citronniers, dont celle dite « de Menton ». Puis vient le cortège des arécacées, avec 130 espèces ou sous-espèces de palmiers, qui expriment dans la rudesse et l'étrangeté de leur stipe et le délire joyeux ou inquiétant des feuilles toute la richesse et l'extravagance de la biodiversité. Enfin, dans la partie inférieure, la plus chaude, sont réunis les fruitiers et les plantes à épice. De riches collections d'hibiscus, de mimosas et de brugmansias, et de nombreuses espèces ornementales subtropicales font de ce jardin d'altitude l'antichambre du paradis.

GRÂCE à leur talent, Édouard et Simone Mazzola ont su renouveler l'œuvre de création des grands aristocrates du XIXe s., tout en conservant cette générosité et cette modestie qui font le charme de leur accueil. Leur préoccupation essentielle est la recherche de plantes d'exception qu'ils traquent partout, particulièrement lors de leurs voyages aux Caraïbes. Après trente années d'efforts continus, un grand jardin est né.

Nous quittons *L'Esquinade* et reprenons la route de Super-Garavan en direction de l'ouest. Arrivés au terme de cette route, nous empruntons celle du Baousset pour rejoindre la route de Castellar, que nous descendons jusqu'au centre de Menton. De là, nous regagnons le bord de mer et nous nous dirigeons vers Roquebrune. À l'extrémité de cette commune, nous tournons à droite, pour gagner la vallée de Gorbio.

Vallée de Gorbio

Entre Roquebrune-Cap-Martin, à l'ouest, et la vallée du Borrigo, à l'est, la vallée de Gorbio est enserrée par un cordon montagneux qui la préserve des froids alpins. Son territoire est constitué de collines boisées et de massifs rocheux, dont les cimes de Gorbio (929 mètres) et des Cabanelles (1 084 mètres) – le village de Gorbio [→ p. 133] se trouve à l'extrémité de la vallée.

À 2 KILOMÈTRES du bord de mer, au n° 74, route de Gorbio, sur le versant d'une véritable crête de montagne, nous découvrons l'un des plus remarquables jardins de Menton, classé monument historique, et aujourd'hui propriété du Conservatoire du littoral.

Serre de la Madone

74, route de Gorbio

Téléphone : 04 93 57 73 90
Télécopie : 04 93 28 55 42
Courriel : visites@serredelamadone.com
Site internet : www.serredelamadone.com

Ouverte tous les jours (sauf lundi)
• Avril à octobre, de 10 h à 18 h
• Novembre à mars, de 10 h à 17 h
À 15 h, visites commentées (histoire du jardin et de son architecture, découverte des plantes acclimatées)

NÉ À PARIS, en 1871, de parents fortunés originaires des États-Unis, Lawrence Johnston est un citoyen britannique. Il cherche à établir sa demeure et à créer un jardin où il pourrait installer les plantes les plus rares qu'il rapporterait du bout du monde. Johnston, qui a toujours prêté attention à la nature et plus spécialement

1-2. Serre de la Madone.

1

2

3. Portrait du major Lawrence Johnston.
4. Décor de céramique à Serre de la Madone.

à la culture des plantes, découvre la riche flore de l'Afrique du Sud au cours de la révolte des Boers, à laquelle il participe en tant que marin de Sa Majesté britannique. En 1907, sa mère lui achète la propriété de Hidcote, dans les Costwolds, où il réalise en l'espace de dix ans un nouveau modèle de jardin. Après la Première Guerre mondiale, il reprend ses voyages de prospection botanique, mais se rend vite compte des limites que peut avoir l'introduction des plantes des « pays chauds ». Il se met donc en quête d'une terre d'accueil possédant un climat plus clément que celui de l'Angleterre. Il choisit un site proche des palaces où sa mère descend chaque hiver et s'installe à Menton en 1924.

LE DOMAINE qu'il acquiert mesure à peu près 6 hectares; il est cultivé dans sa partie basse, alors que la partie haute est boisée. Une petite ferme de style mentonnais sépare la zone agricole et l'espace forestier. Johnston garde cet aménagement initial, conserve les oliviers, les figuiers, les pêchers et la vigne, mais il ajoute des tonnelles et fait construire des escaliers pour ouvrir des perspectives et multiplier les passages entre les deux parties de la propriété.

Il réalise ou modernise douze citernes, soit une réserve de quelque 1 000 mètres cubes d'eau, et consolide les restanques. Il se plaît aussi à animer l'ensemble par des statues représentant des personnages de l'Antiquité ou des animaux fabuleux.

3

4

Les trésors de *Serre de la Madone*

UNE ROUTE bordée de cyprès donne accès à la propriété. Au milieu des fougères, elle grimpe à flanc de coteau, puis elle tourne brusquement et s'élargit en une sorte de place en demi-lune au fond de laquelle sont dressés deux gros piliers servant de portail, d'un modèle similaire à ceux de Val Rahmeh [→ p. 74]. Le long de cette rampe d'accès, on découvre de superbes essences, qui font l'originalité et la qualité de ce beau jardin : le chêne tropical de l'Himalaya, dont la feuille n'a rien d'une feuille de chêne; les deux immenses pins des bouddhistes (*Podocarpus*), aux fines feuilles en faucille et à l'ombre épaisse; les deux palmiers jupons (*Washingtonia filifera*), dont l'un est encore paré de sa longue jupe protectrice; le grand *Magnolia delavayi* du Yunnan; l'exceptionnelle agavacée *Nolina* du Mexique, ou pied d'éléphant, qui serait tricentenaire.

QUANT À LA SERRE, qui devait à l'origine être chauffée, elle n'est plus aujourd'hui, malgré sa verrière, qu'un grand abri de jardin qui sert de refuge à quelques plantes fragiles.

RESTAURÉE en 1990, elle a le mérite d'être une sorte de hall d'où l'on découvre le

1

2

3

1-2-3-4. Serre de la Madone.

4

vaste berceau du grand jardin central avec, en premier plan, le bassin, qui a retrouvé sa fonction, et son double alignement de jardinières. En arrière, un autre plus petit, avec une statue en son centre, prolonge le miroir d'eau ; la perspective se ferme sur un rideau végétal qu'entourent deux socles sur lesquels sont posés des angelots assis. Depuis ce bassin, la structure du jardin apparaît avec une grande clarté. Sur la partie haute, entre les troncs rouges des beaux pins parasols, court le grand escalier qui franchit les différents gradins pour conduire à l'élégante villa. L'ANCIENNE ferme, qui a été réaménagée, conserve tout son charme, les agrandissements n'ayant pas bouleversé sa belle harmonie. Au-delà de la maison, cyprès, pins et autres arbres indigènes ferment la perspective.
En contrebas du bassin, sur un espace particulièrement large, Lawrence Johnston a installé l'une de ces unités paysagères qu'il a multipliées dans son domaine. Dans un jardin à la française centré sur un bassin circulaire au bord duquel sont couchés des angelots, quatre pelouses d'angle entourées de buis sont plantées de quatre platanes d'allure provençale. La différenciation de cet espace par rapport à l'ensemble est si évidente qu'elle nous apparaît comme un véritable mode d'emploi. Car ce jardin se présente comme une juxtaposition de tableaux cloisonnés, comme l'était déjà celui de Hidcote. Ainsi découvre-t-on successivement : deux grandes aires de protéacées, qui s'offrent comme un hommage au concepteur et un rappel de ses voyages en Afrique du Sud ; le belvédère circulaire et son toit de glycine ; la cour du Mandarinier et sa calade ; le Jardin « espagnol » avec son bassin aux nénuphars et ses bancs recouverts de carreaux de céramique à l'abri d'un appentis prenant appui sur la maison ; l'allée d'Auguste avec ses alignements d'oliviers ; l'immense tonnelle, d'une centaine de mètres, posée sur des piliers de pierre et tous les parterres qui sont autant de faire-valoir pour une essence tropicale particulièrement intéressante, l'arbousier des Canaries, à l'écorce lisse couleur chocolat qui se détache en lambeaux ; l'arbre de feu (*Brachychiton acerifolium*) et la cohorte flamboyante de tous les arbres rapportés d'Asie ou bien d'Afrique dont certains, à l'instar des mahonias, se sont naturalisés ici. En 1937, Johnston quitte Menton. Il n'y revient qu'en 1949, mais les premiers symptômes de la maladie marquent déjà gravement l'homme.
Il meurt à Menton en 1958. Neuf ans plus tard, la propriété est rachetée par Berings, puis elle passera aux mains d'une société monégasque en 1986.
Mal entretenu, plus ou moins laissé à l'abandon, le beau jardin ne sera bientôt plus qu'une grande friche et le domaine bâti une merveilleuse ruine.
EN 1990, le domaine est classé monument historique, ce qui le protège de l'appétit des promoteurs mais ne ralentit pas sa dégradation. En 1999, il est racheté par le Conservatoire du littoral. Depuis lors, un gigantesque travail de réhabilitation est en cours.

1902
Lavage Interdit

Aux alentours de Menton

Nous partons à la découverte des alentours de Menton et des villages juchés sur les collines. D'est en ouest, notre itinéraire nous mène des jardins botaniques Hanbury (La Mortola, Italie) jusqu'au village de Castellar, sur la colline Saint-Sébastien. Nous nous dirigeons ensuite dans la vallée du Careï, pour nous rendre à Castillon et à Monti. À l'extrémité de la vallée du Borrigo, se trouve le village médiéval de Sainte-Agnès. Enfin, pour clore notre périple dans ce qui se révèle être un véritable écrin pour le pays mentonnais, nous rejoignons, tout à l'ouest, Gorbio et Roquebrune-Cap-Martin.

Page précédente : Roquebrune-Village.
1. Gorbio : église Saint-Lazare.
2. Castellar : église Saint-Pierre.
3. Jardins botaniques Hanbury.
4. Roquebrune-Cap-Martin : église Sainte-Marguerite.

Jardins botaniques Hanbury

Giardini botanica Hanbury

Corso Montecarlo, 43 - La Mortola
18039 Ventimiglia (Italie)

Téléphone : (39) 0184 22 95 07
Télécopie : (39) 0184 22 92 20
Site internet :
www.parks.it/giardini.botanici.hanbury

Fermés de novembre à mars
Ouverts tous les jours, sauf mercredi (visite de 2 à 3 h) :
- du dernier dimanche de mars au 14 juin, de 10 h à 17 h (fermeture à 18 h)
- du 15 juin au dernier dimanche de septembre, de 9 h à 18 h (fermeture à 19 h)
- du dernier dimanche de septembre au 31 octobre, de 10 h à 18 h (fermeture à 19 h)

NÉ À LONDRES en 1832, Thomas Hanbury est âgé de trente-quatre ans lorsqu'il décide, en 1866, de revenir en Europe après ses multiples périples. Il s'installe durant l'hiver dans un grand palace mentonnais. Au cours d'une excursion en Italie, il découvre le promontoire de La Mortola, dont il apprécie immédiatement la beauté. Il perçoit également les potentialités du site. Hanbury achète en mai 1867, à Ambrosine Grandis, au lieu-dit Punta della Croce, un immense domaine de 18 hectares. Au centre, se dresse le vieux *palazzo* Orengo d'une riche famille de Vintimille qui possédait la propriété depuis le XVIIe s. Sur ce domaine planté d'oliviers, d'agrumes et de vignes, Thomas Hanbury décide de créer une œuvre colossale, l'un des plus beaux et

1-2-3. Jardins botaniques Hanbury.

des plus importants jardins botaniques au monde; la moitié des terres y est réservée à l'acclimatation de plantes exotiques originaires de différents pays, et l'autre, à la végétation méditerranéenne. Son frère Daniel, botaniste et pharmacien, participe au projet et lui apporte une caution scientifique.

LES TRAVAUX de transformation du domaine s'étendent sur six années, menés conjointement aux opérations de plantation. Daniel Hanbury, disparu en 1875, avait noué d'étroites relations avec les établissements horticoles de la région et les jardins botaniques les plus réputés, comme celui de Montpellier. Le projet peut donc se poursuivre grâce à des botanistes italiens, français, mais surtout allemands (Cronemeyer, Kurt Dinter et Alwin Berger), qui prêtent leur concours. L'intervention de Ludwig Winter est déterminante pour le dessin du jardin et l'introduction de plantes exotiques, notamment des palmiers. Le jardin de collectionneur devient peu à peu un jardin botanique. En 1883 paraît la première édition de l'*Index Seminum*, riche de 559 références. Six ans plus tard, l'inventaire recense 3 500 taxons.

DÈS LORS, avec sa graineterie, son herbier, sa bibliothèque et sa photothèque, La Mortola est au cœur d'un vaste réseau mondial d'informations et acquiert un statut de centre de recherches de niveau international où se donne rendez-vous le gotha de la systématique végétale.

APRÈS LA MORT de Thomas Hanbury, en 1907, sa femme, Katherine Aldam Pease – aidée d'Alwin Berger – poursuit son œuvre, relayée après la guerre par lady Dorothy, l'épouse de leur fils Cecil, qui va jouer un rôle essentiel dans le remodelage du domaine. Sensibilisée aux idées modernes, avertie des tendances de l'horticulture anglaise, elle offre au jardin une nouvelle respiration: des plages de couleur sont créées grâce à l'introduction de plantes ornementales, des perspectives sont redessinées et le paysage s'ouvre sur la mer. Mais après la dernière guerre, le bilan se révèle terrible. Lady Dorothy, sans moyen et sans appui, se dépense en vain. Malade, puis paralysée, elle s'enferme dans la solitude de « la petite villa ».

ACHETÉS par l'État italien en 1960, les jardins botaniques sont gérés à partir de 1987 par l'université de Gênes. Celle-ci organise les replantations ainsi que le recensement botanique et restaure les bâtiments. Le domaine Hanbury retrouve une partie de sa splendeur. Une superficie de 9 hectares est aménagée, qui reçoit quelque 7 000 espèces végétales d'une valeur patrimoniale inestimable.

DANS LES JARDINS Hanbury les plantes sont réparties dans différents secteurs et ordonnées par thèmes et collections. On peut les admirer selon deux itinéraires.

Itinéraire de descente

1. Aire Nirvana : bassin orné de rocailles et de plantes aquatiques. • 2. Aire des Quatre-Saisons (nom du petit temple) : collection d'agaves. • 3. Collection d'aloès. • 4. Pergola; collection de *Bignoniaceae* : *Pandorea*, *Jacaranda*, *Pyrostegia*, etc. • 5. Collection de succulentes (plantes qui possèdent des organes charnus gorgés d'eau) : *Euphorbiaceae*, *Cactaceae* et *Aloaceae*. • 6. Collection de cyclamens. • 7. Fontaine du Dragon (sculpture en bronze provenant de Kyoto) ornée de papyrus. • 8. Jardin des Parfums, créé par

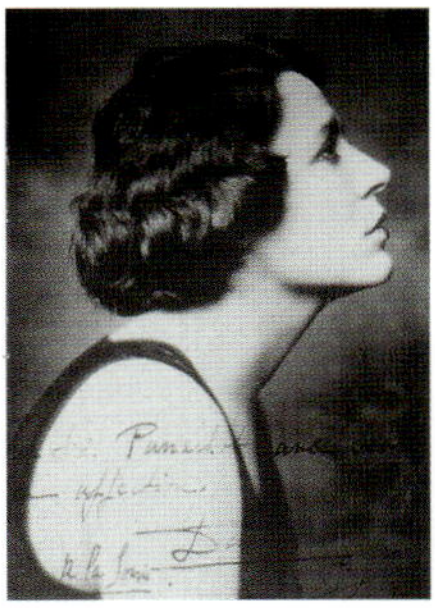

1

2

3

4

1. Eileen Gray.
2-3-4. Villa Tempe a Pailla.

Dorothy Hanbury en 1928 : collections de plantes aromatiques (*Heliotropium*, *Cymbopogon*, *Pelargonium*, *Jasminum*, *Rosmarinus*, *Calycanthus*, *Citrus*...). • 9. Mausolée mauresque où ont été déposées les cendres de Thomas Hanbury et de son épouse. • 10. Verger exotique : *Acca*, *Corinocarpus*, *Diospyros*, *Persea*... • 11. Allée des Oliviers.

Itinéraire de montée

1. Pinède, avec un grand *Pinus halepensis*. • 2. Puits vénitien, avec un *Olmediella betschleriana*. • 3. Pergolas; collections de passiflores, glycines et *Thunbergia*. • 4. Collection de *Brugmansia*. • 5. Forêt australienne : eucalyptus, callistèmes, *Melaleuca*, *Brachychiton*... • 6. Allée des cycas. • 7. Palmeraie : *Trachycarpus*, *Brahea*, *Chamaerops*, *Phoenix*...

Castellar

POUR SE RENDRE à Castellar, à partir de l'hôtel de ville de Menton, nous prenons, en direction de l'est, la départementale RD 24, dite « route de Castellar », voie étroite qui surplombe la vallée du Fossan. Après avoir passé le quartier Maglioc, la route s'élève sur la colline des Ciappes. Au n° 187, nous découvrons la villa d'Eileen Gray, avec sa façade Art déco.

Villa *Tempe a Pailla*

187, route de Castellar

La propriété ne se visite pas

DE 1926 À 1927, la designer irlandaise Eileen Gray (1878-1976) fait édifier sa villa *E 1027* [→ p. 136] à Roquebrune-Cap-Martin. En 1932, sur un bassin en bordure de la route serpentant de Menton à Castellar, elle décide de construire une seconde maison sur la Côte d'Azur, où elle met de nouveau à profit ses talents d'architecte. Elle donne à cette demeure le nom de *Tempe a Pailla*, formé à partir d'un dicton mentonnais : « Le temps et la paille permettent aux nèfles de mûrir. » Le vieil adage s'applique à merveille à cet édifice dont la qualité architecturale n'est reconnue que depuis peu.

DU SOLEIL, Eileen Gray en aura dans sa nouvelle villa, et elle saura l'utiliser magistralement. Accrochée à la colline sur un soubassement de pierre sèche, avec ses volets bleus d'allure presque grecque, *Tempe a Pailla* nous apparaît comme une véritable maison de poupée. Les recettes géniales que l'architecte a expérimentées à Roquebrune-Cap-Martin y sont réemployées, mais avec beaucoup plus de simplicité et d'ingéniosité. Seule la façade orientale est visible depuis la route de Castellar.

À L'INSTAR de la villa *E 1027*, *Tempe a Pailla* évoque la proue d'un bateau. La façade donnant sur la route reprend en le simplifiant un dispositif inauguré à Cap-Martin – des volets bleus, à claire-voie, dont les lamelles orientables coulissent devant une fenêtre en bandeau –, à cette différence qu'ici tout est résolument modeste : pas de véranda précédant un grand séjour, mais une petite terrasse au sud, orientation qu'elle réserve parcimonieusement au séjour et au solarium. Les chambres sont situées au levant, la cuisine au nord. À l'ouest, seuls quelques hublots percent la façade sur le chemin de servitude. Pour sa demeure (inscrite sur l'Inventaire des monuments historiques en 1990), Eileen Gray conçoit également un mobilier approprié. Dans les années 1950, le peintre Graham Sutherland

1

1. Castellar.
2. Castellar : le palais Lascaris.
3. Castellar : église Saint-Pierre.

2

3

rachète la propriété. Il construit sa *Villa Blanche*, à l'arrière du domaine, sur cette exposition plein sud qu'Eileen Gray avait écartée.

Village de Castellar

Altitude : 375 mètres • 850 habitants
À 7 kilomètres de Menton

KATHERINE MANSFIELD, évoquant le village de Castellar, écrit : « Je pourrais vivre ici pendant des années et des années, je veux dire loin de ce qu'on appelle "le monde". » Pour y parvenir, elle devait emprunter des « routes [qui] tournent et tournent en montant. On dirait qu'on remonte aussi le cours des siècles ».
AVANT l'implantation du village actuel, au XVe s., l'ancien Castellar, bâti deux siècles auparavant, se dressait à environ 870 mètres d'altitude. Les ruines imposantes qui subsistent sont celles d'une enceinte polygonale fortifiée avec courtines, percée de meurtrières et flanquée de tours.
EN 1435, LES SEIGNEURS de Lascaris-Vintimille, possesseurs du fief, demandent aux habitants de construire, 500 mètres en contrebas, une *villanova* fortifiée par une enceinte. Quelques bâtiments existent encore de l'époque de la fondation de Castellar « le Neuf », mais le bourg va rapidement s'étendre vers le bas, comme en témoigne une maison dont la façade (rue de la République) porte l'inscription : S.G. 1570. Quant aux fortifications, elles seront rasées en 1751 par les troupes françaises et espagnoles, hormis la porte nord et trois tours.
CASTELLAR est un petit bourg aux voies étroites ponctuées de passages voûtés. Situé sur la colline Saint-Sébastien, on y bénéficie d'une vue remarquable sur la baie de Garavan.

• Palais Lascaris
58, rue de la République
CONSTRUIT au XVIIe s., l'ancien palais des Lascaris-Vintimille (inscrit sur l'Inventaire des monuments historiques en 1997) est en cours de restauration. Il a malheureusement été scindé en deux parties lors du percement de la rue de la République. À l'intérieur, on remarque des décors de stuc et des fresques associant les motifs habituels du baroque niçois de la fin du XVIIe s. La tour-porche, couverte d'un dôme à lanternon, abrite une collection d'uniformes, de décorations et de divers documents rassemblés dans un petit musée militaire.

• Église Saint-Pierre
Place du Maréchal-Foch
LORS de la fondation du village, au XVe s., est édifiée l'église paroissiale. Agrandie au siècle suivant, elle est partiellement rebâtie à partir du XVIIIe s., notamment pour la réorienter nord-sud. Endommagée lors du tremblement de terre de 1887, qui détruisit aussi la chapelle extérieure Saint-Jean-Baptiste – lieu de sépulture des Lascaris –, l'église est restaurée.
SA FAÇADE est d'ordonnance classique. Son clocher quadrangulaire est exhaussé d'un clocheton à bulbe. À l'intérieur, sur l'autel de la Vierge, la statue en stuc polychrome est entourée de quinze tableaux figurant les mystères du Rosaire (milieu du XIXe s.).

• Chapelle des Pénitents noirs
5, rue du Général-Sarrail
DITE AUSSI chapelle Notre-Dame-de-la-Miséricorde, l'édifice possède un clocheton baroque (XVIIIe s.) surmonté d'un petit dôme.

• Chapelle des Pénitents blancs
53, rue du Général-Sarrail
DITE AUSSI chapelle du Saint-Esprit, ce petit édifice à nef unique a été construit

1

2

3

1. Castellar : chapelle Saint-Sébastien.
2. Castellar : chapelle Saint-Bernard.
3. Castillon : le clocher.

au XVIIe s. Il renferme une belle collection d'objets de la confrérie, tels que lanternes et bannières de procession. Cette chapelle se trouve aujourd'hui enchâssée dans des maisons d'habitation.

• Chapelle Saint-Sébastien

Dans le cimetière

ÉDIFICE roman (XIIIe s.) inscrit sur l'Inventaire des monuments historiques, Saint-Sébastien a été église paroissiale avant le déplacement de Castellar au XVe s. La chapelle présente une abside en cul-de-four, un portail en arc brisé et un clocher-mur à deux baies. Restaurée en 1999, elle a perdu son rôle cultuel.

• Chapelle Saint-Antoine

Place Saint-Antoine (proche du parking)

CETTE petite chapelle rurale est précédée d'un porche ouvert. Peirineta Raibaudo, accusée de sorcellerie, fut étranglée puis brûlée ici, le 16 novembre 1623.

• Chapelle Saint-Roch

Route des Granges-Saint-Paul

L'ÉDIFICE à porche ouvert, comme le sont toutes les chapelles de pèlerinage, recevait le 16 août les confréries de pénitents.

• Chapelle Saint-Bernard

Chemin Saint-Bernard

POUR ACCÉDER à Saint-Bernard – l'une des trois chapelles éloignées du bourg –, il nous faut compter une bonne heure de marche à pied. Édifiée au XVIe s., sur la colline dont le nom honore la mémoire de Bernard de Clairvaux, elle est la seule à présenter un bon état de conservation.

• Abri de Pendimoun

Chemin Saint-Bernard

HABITÉ il y a 8 000 ans, ce site, considéré comme le gisement le plus riche de France pour la période du néolithique final, fait l'objet de fouilles attentives depuis le milieu du XXe s.

Castillon

Altitude : 535 mètres • 290 habitants
À 2 kilomètres au nord-est de Menton

DE CASTELLAR, à la sortie de la route des Condamines, nous empruntons, à droite, la route départementale 2566, afin de nous rendre à Castillon.

RECONSTRUIT au début des années 1950, le bourg actuel constitue une jolie réussite architecturale. C'est là un exemple rare d'intégration à son site, œuvre d'un seul concepteur, l'architecte niçois Richard Laugier, qui construira un peu plus tard le palais des expositions de Nice. Ce qui frappe dès l'abord, c'est la grande unité de la conception. Dans ce projet, Laugier opte pour une mise en œuvre traditionnelle, en ayant recours à la pierre de taille calcaire du pays pour toutes les parties apparentes. La même logique préside au choix des toitures, dans le respect de la tradition.

DE L'ÉGLISE, située en contrebas, la rue principale serpente entre les maisons basses jusqu'à un édifice à plusieurs étages qui domine l'ensemble. L'église est l'un des points forts du programme architectural. Richard Laugier témoigne ici d'une réelle maîtrise à combiner avec habileté les éléments du répertoire historique. Sa chapelle pourrait être assimilée à un édifice roman authentique, mais mâtiné de baroque.

LA FAÇADE en « chapeau de gendarme », avec son oculus en croix grecque, est délicieusement méridionale. Elle offre l'originalité d'intégrer, au-dessus d'une porte monumentale, un très imposant linteau en pierre verte qui provient de la vallée de la Roya. Le gracieux clocher d'inspiration baroque est aussi « habillé à l'ancienne » avec son parement de tuiles vernissées.

1. Castillon : le village reconstruit après le tremblement de terre.
2. Monti : chapelle Saint-Roman.
3. Sainte-Agnès : église Notre-Dame-des-Neiges.

LE BOURG actuel succède, en fait, à deux autres édifications. Attesté dès le XIIe s., le village, situé à l'origine au sommet du col de Castillon, fut en partie dévasté par le tremblement de terre de 1887 ; il ne reste que quelques vestiges de l'habitat et du château féodal, encore visibles à l'ouest du village actuel. Reconstruit à la fin du XIXe s., Castillon est de nouveau détruit lors des bombardements de 1944.
LE VISITEUR curieux pourra entreprendre une excursion jusqu'au col de Castillon pour admirer le panorama et découvrir le fort de la ligne Maginot et la ruine de la façade de l'église Saint-Michel, ultime vestige du village avant sa réédification au lendemain de 1887.

Monti

Altitude : 130 mètres
Hameau de la commune de Menton

DE CASTILLON, nous reprenons la route départementale en direction de Menton. Avant de pénétrer dans l'agglomération, nous traversons le verdoyant hameau de Monti.
LA CHAPELLE Saint-Roman, bâtie en pierres apparentes, est située à la limite de trois communes (Castellar, Menton et Sainte-Agnès), en bordure du torrent du Careï. Autrefois dépendante de Monti, cette jolie chapelle rurale est aujourd'hui incluse dans un nouveau quartier de Menton, auquel elle a donné son nom.
LONGÉE par le sentier muletier Menton-Sospel, la chapelle servait de cadre, au mois d'août, aux festins campagnards de la Saint-Roman. En 1840, Honoré V décide la construction, à Monti, d'un nouveau sanctuaire dédié à son saint patron. De style troubadour, alors en vogue à l'époque, l'église Saint-Honoré comprend un vaisseau central flanqué de deux collatéraux terminés par deux charmants petits autels. Le clocher élève avec fierté sa flèche de pierre vers les cieux. Grâce à la volonté d'irréductibles Mentonnais, cette église est de nouveau ouverte au public.

Sainte-Agnès

Altitude : 700 mètres • 1 100 habitants
À 10 kilomètres au nord de Menton

ON ACCÈDE à Sainte-Agnès par le val des Castagnins et le col de Garde (route départementale 22). En descendant de Monti, nous pouvons aussi emprunter la route des Cabrolles, à hauteur de l'échangeur de l'autoroute. Cette voie bucolique permet d'éviter la traversée de la ville et, de surcroît, offre de beaux points de vue tant sur Menton que sur Cap-Martin.
APRÈS le hameau des Cabrolles – sur le territoire de Sainte-Agnès –, nous passons à proximité de la petite chapelle rurale Saint-Pascal-Baylon, placée sous le vocable d'un franciscain espagnol de la seconde moitié du XVIe s. Construite en 1846, elle subsiste encore bien qu'elle ait été amputée de son parvis au moment des travaux de l'autoroute.
PLUS LOIN, au hameau des Castagnins, qui dépend aussi de Sainte-Agnès, un sentier nous mène à la chapelle Sainte-Lucie. Dissimulé parmi les oliviers, cet édifice de style Renaissance a conservé, grâce à sa lumineuse façade et à son petit porche, le charme des chapelles rurales. Chaque année, le 13 décembre, jour de la fête patronale, les habitants du hameau y font célébrer la messe et organisent un plantureux festin de *barbajuan* (beignets de courge rouge).

1-2-3. Gorbio.

1

2

3

De la route des Cabrolles, nous rejoignons la route départementale 22, en passant près de la mairie annexe du bourg, et nous montons jusqu'à Sainte-Agnès, le village littoral le plus haut d'Europe. À l'entrée se trouve la chapelle médiévale Saint-Sébastien, récemment restaurée et décorée par Floch et Poulain.
Dès le XIIIe s., il est fait mention du village de Sainte-Agnès. Un habitat fortifié se dressait à quelque 200 mètres à l'est du bourg actuel. Les ruines du château, visibles sur un rocher à pic, à 754 mètres d'altitude, évoquent la légende d'un cruel pirate, Haroun, qui aurait été séduit par la beauté d'une jeune chrétienne nommée Agnès et se serait converti à la religion de celle-ci.
Au XVe s., le bourg occupe le site actuel. Avec ses hameaux des Cabrolles et des Castagnins, Sainte-Agnès est caractéristique des villages alpestres, aux passages voûtés et aux rues à degrés, étroites et sinueuses.
L'église paroissiale Notre-Dame-des-Neiges, au centre du village, a été érigée en 1575. Sa façade principale, percée d'un oculus, présente un fronton triangulaire (XVIIIe s.). L'intérieur, élevé sur un plan à nef unique, est orné d'un tabernacle du XVIIe s. et de tableaux de même époque.
En face de l'église se dresse la chapelle de Pénitents blancs (XVIIe s.), aujourd'hui désaffectée et transformée en musée des Traditions populaires ; elle accueille aussi des expositions temporaires.
L'oratoire Sainte-Agnès, édifié en 1954, rappelle l'ancienne chapelle, détruite en 1931.
Sous le rocher de Sainte-Agnès a été construit, entre 1931 et 1934, l'un des quatorze forts de la ligne Maginot des Alpes. Lors de la Seconde Guerre, ce fort a contribué à la défense de Menton.
Du Righi, proche du fort, nous avons un remarquable panorama sur Menton, les vallées, la mer, la Riviera italienne et le cap Martin.
Du monument aux morts, nous pouvons admirer les à-pics grandioses des montagnes environnantes.

Gorbio

Altitude : 360 mètres • 1 200 habitants
À 7 kilomètres au nord-ouest de Menton

On accède à Gorbio en empruntant la route départementale 23. Mais en descendant de Sainte-Agnès (RD 22) nous pouvons aussi, à l'embranchement, prendre à droite la route de la Maura (RD 223) afin de rejoindre la RD 23. Ce dernier itinéraire permet de découvrir l'ancien sanatorium de Gorbio, construit par Abel Glena de 1898 à 1901.
La structure de cet établissement hospitalier conjugue les canons architecturaux d'inspiration florentine et les nécessités imposées par l'héliothérapie. Ce bâtiment est toujours un centre de soins destiné à la rééducation pulmonaire et cardiothoracique.
Nous redescendons dans la vallée afin d'aller au village de Gorbio, fondé au XIe s. par les seigneurs de Lascaris-Vintimille, et dont le nom est mentionné en 1301. La partie la plus ancienne du château, situé au sommet du bourg, présente des structures du XIIe s. ; elle est composée d'une tour à fenêtres géminées (XIIIe s.) et d'un corps de bâtiment rectangulaire. Au cours du XVe s., la famille Lascaris fait agrandir la demeure en utilisant une partie du jardin médiéval – aujourd'hui propriété privée, le château ne se visite pas.

1

2

1. Gorbio : chapelle des Pénitents blancs.
2. Gorbio : chapelle Saint-Lazare.
3. Roquebrune-Cap-Martin.

3

Au XVIIIe s., un second château est édifié par les comtes de Malaussène (branche des Lascaris-Vintimille), lequel appartient encore aujourd'hui à cette famille originaire d'Aix-en-Provence. LE VILLAGE médiéval, qui s'est développé autour du château, était entouré d'une muraille dont ne subsiste qu'une porte d'entrée ogivale. Comme dans nombre de petits bourgs de la région, on y trouve un lacis de ruelles avec passages voûtés. Parmi les villages du pays mentonnais, Gorbio demeure sans doute l'un des plus authentiques. Sur la place réaménagée récemment, on remarque une fontaine offerte par Thomas Hanbury, ainsi qu'un orme gigantesque (environ 6 mètres de circonférence) planté en 1713.

• Église Saint-Barthélemy

Rue Garibaldi

MODESTE édifice au décor intérieur de style baroque, l'église paroissiale a été construite en 1683, mais sa façade n'a jamais été achevée. À l'intérieur s'élève une nef voûtée en berceau; dans le décor des chapelles latérales, on remarquera principalement *L'Adoration des bergers*, attribuée à Orazio Ferrari, peintre génois du XVIIe s. De la même époque, on peut voir des œuvres de peintres anonymes, comme le *Martyre de saint Sébastien*, traité en clair-obscur. La statuaire est ici présente avec un christ du XVIIe s. et deux bois polychromes du XVIIIe s. : la *Vierge de Gorbio* et la *Vierge à l'Enfant*. Quant au bénitier de marbre noir, il date sans doute du XVe s.

• Chapelle des Pénitents blancs

Rue Piazza-Nova

L'ÉDIFICE, bâti en 1445, se dresse face à l'église Saint-Barthélemy. La confrérie, aujourd'hui encore active, perpétue les traditions religieuses, notamment la Fête des limaces. Chaque année, en juin, le jeudi qui suit la Fête-Dieu, une procession parcourt la ville, qui est éclairée par des lampes à huile confectionnées avec des coquilles d'escargots.

• Chapelle Saint-Lazare

Chemin de Sainte-Agnès

LA DATE d'édification de Saint-Lazare est toujours très incertaine. Pour certains historiens, elle remonterait au XVIIe s., tandis que d'autres s'accordent pour lui attribuer une origine médiévale.

Roquebrune-Cap-Martin

Altitude : 300 mètres • 12 000 habitants
À l'ouest de Menton, par la RN 7

OFFICE DU TOURISME
218, avenue Aristide-Briand
06190 Roquebrune-Cap-Martin
Téléphone : 04 93 35 62 87
Télécopie : 04 93 28 57 00

ENTRE MENTON et Monaco, la ville de Roquebrune-Cap-Martin s'étend le long du littoral : à l'ouest, le quartier Saint-Roman, à la frontière monégasque; à l'est, le quartier Carnolès, qui se prolonge sur Menton. La ville s'étage des pentes du mont Agel (1 145 mètres) jusqu'à la mer : au nord, Roquebrune-Village et son château féodal (300 mètres); au sud, le quartier de Cabbé, le long de la baie. Sur ce territoire de quelque 933 hectares, l'architecture offre des contrastes inouïs : audaces fonctionnelles d'Eileen Gray et de Le Corbusier; villas aristocratiques de la Belle Époque; bâti médiéval heureusement conservé... Cependant, son histoire remonte bien en deçà, avec des vestiges romains et, plus encore, avec quelques sites préhistoriques, dont le plus connu est la grotte du Vallonnet.

1

2

1. Site romain de Lumone.
2. Ruines du monastère Saint-Martin.
3-4. Roquebrune : chapelle de la Pausa et ruelle avec passage voûté.

3

4

• Grotte du Vallonnet

Quartier du Vallonnet, lieu-dit Lascasa

LA GROTTE du Vallonnet – l'une des plus anciennes d'Europe (900 000 ans) – est un site essentiel pour la connaissance de la faune préhistorique de cette époque et l'industrie lithique qui lui est associée.

• Site romain de Lumone

Cap-Martin, lieu-dit Lumone

DE L'OCCUPATION romaine de ce site nous sont parvenus de beaux vestiges d'un mausolée du Ier s. av. J.-C., constitués de trois arcades et de voûtes portant des traces de fresques. Situé à un embranchement de la Via Julia Augusta et de la Via Aurelia (face à l'actuelle mairie), il était dressé à l'emplacement d'un relais de poste de l'Empire romain.

• Monastère Saint-Martin

Près du sémaphore de Cap-Martin

AU PIED du sémaphore de Cap-Martin, dans une propriété privée, se trouvent les ruines du monastère Saint-Martin (XIe s.), ancien prieuré des moines de Lérins.

Roquebrune

LE CHÂTEAU féodal a été construit à flanc de colline, vers 970, par Conrad Ier, comte de Vintimille. Très tôt enchâssé dans les habitations du village, ce fief entre en possession de Charles Grimaldi en 1355. Dès lors, durant cinq siècles, le destin de Roquebrune est intimement attaché à l'histoire politique de la principauté de Monaco : suzeraineté du duché de Savoie au XVe s.; protectorat espagnol au XVIe s.; protectorat français aux XVIIe et XVIIIe; annexion à la France (1793-1814), puis retour à la principauté. En 1848, Roquebrune – comme Menton – s'érige en « ville libre », puis est rattachée à la France par le traité de 1861.

• Château féodal

ÉRIGÉ VERS 970, le château a été plusieurs fois réaménagé, restauré et partiellement reconstruit, notamment aux XIIe, XVe et XVIe s., pour augmenter sa puissance militaire. Vendu comme bien national en 1808, il est encore rénové au cours du XIXe, puis acheté par William Ingram en 1911, qui en fait don à la Ville en 1921. Le château est classé monument historique en 1927.

L'ARCHITECURE de l'édifice témoigne de ses capacités de défense : les murailles ont une épaisseur de 2 à 4 mètres; le donjon quadrangulaire, dans lequel on pénètre par un pont de pierre, a une silhouette massive; enfin, on remarque le dispositif défensif traditionnel, avec chemin de ronde, échauguettes, mâchicoulis, meurtrières et archières. À l'intérieur du château subsistent encore plusieurs salles voûtées ainsi que les cuisines, qui ont été restituées.

ROQUEBRUNE-VILLAGE

JUSQU'AU XIVe s., la forteresse possédait six portes, par lesquelles on accédait au donjon et au village enclos dans une même enceinte. Ce dernier conserve encore de nos jours son aspect médiéval, avec ses montées à degrés, ses ruelles étroites et ses passages sous voûtes. À l'entrée du village, on voit un olivier millénaire, au tronc phénoménal, considéré comme l'un des plus vieux du monde.

• Église Sainte-Marguerite

AU XVIe s., l'ancienne chapelle médiévale Notre-Dame-de-l'Apié devient église paroissiale placée sous le patronage de sainte Marguerite. Elle est profondément remaniée en 1618, par Honoré II, puis une nouvelle fois restaurée et agrandie au XVIIIe s. À l'extérieur, elle présente une façade classique et le parvis (1776) est mosaïqué noir et blanc.

1. Cap-Martin : villa Torre-Clementina.
2. Cap-Martin : villa Cypris.
3. Cap-Martin : Hôtel du Cap.
4. Cap-Martin : villa Trianon.

1

2

3

4

À l'intérieur : voûtes peintes par Gastaldi (fin XIXe s.), deux tableaux de Marc-Antoine Otto et une copie du célèbre *Jugement dernier* de Michel-Ange.

• Chapelle de la Pausa

POUR AVOIR été préservés d'une épidémie de peste en 1467, les Roquebrunois ont fait édifier, peu de temps après, une chapelle. À l'intérieur, nous pouvons remarquer des fresques rénovées par Gastaldi à la fin du XIXe s. CHAQUE ANNÉE, le 5 août, a lieu, de l'église Sainte-Marguerite à la chapelle de la Pausa (« la Paix »), une procession où les habitants costumés donnent une représentation de la passion du Christ. Cette commémoration de l'achèvement miraculeux de l'épidémie attire encore aujourd'hui des milliers de touristes.

Cap-Martin

MAJESTUEUX promontoire rocheux qui s'avance au-dessus de la mer, le cap Martin est aussi un havre joliment verdoyant que l'aristocratie européenne découvre à la fin du XIXe s. S'y retrouvent la duchesse d'Aoste, la princesse Lætitia de Savoie, l'empereur François-Joseph et son épouse Élisabeth (Sissi), l'impératrice Eugénie, le roi Édouard VII d'Angleterre, suivis par les multiples personnalités du monde artistique et politique que compte le continent, comme Winston Churchill qui en fut « citoyen d'honneur ». À leur intention, des architectes tels que Hans Georg Tersling [→ p. 31], auteur du bel *Hôtel du Cap* (1892-1908), érigent à la Belle Époque de somptueuses villas, telles que *Torre-Clementina*, *Cypris*, *Zamir*, ou *Cyrnos*, résidence construite en 1892 pour l'impératrice Eugénie.

• Villa *Torre-Clementina*

Avenue Impératrice-Eugénie

ÉDIFIÉE par l'architecte Lucien Hesse peu après 1904, pour la romancière Maria Star (pseudonyme d'Ernesta Stern), cette demeure privée, avec ses jardins, est inscrite sur l'Inventaire des monuments historiques. Les décors intérieurs, d'esprit orientalisant, et l'aménagement du parc (jardins géométriques avec fontaines, pièces d'eau, sculptures et une dizaine de fabriques) sont l'œuvre de l'architecte paysagiste Raffaëlle Mainella.

• Villa *Cypris*

Avenue Douine

DESTINÉE à Mme Robert Douine, épouse du directeur des *Grands Magasins du Louvre*, à Paris, cette demeure privée, de style byzantin, a été construite à la même époque que la villa *Torre-Clementina*. Œuvre de l'architecte Édouard Arnaud, elle est elle aussi inscrite sur l'Inventaire des monuments historiques, ainsi que ses jardins (pièces d'eau, fabriques, colonnade couverte, pergola aux piliers de marbre et arcs de brique) dus à Raffaëlle Mainella.

• Villa *E 1027*

Promenade Le Corbusier

AUTRE monument historique, cette villa a été édifiée en 1926-1927 par la designer irlandaise Eileen Gray, avec l'architecte Jean Badovici, à l'intention de ce dernier [→ p. 137].

• Site corbuséen du cap Martin

Promenade Le Corbusier

ENSEMBLE classé monument historique, conçu par Le Corbusier, le site corbuséen est constitué de plusieurs édifices : la guinguette *L'Étoile de Mer* (1948-1949), la baraque-atelier de l'architecte (1952), le « Cabanon » (1952) et cinq « unités de camping » (1954-1957) [→ p. 138].

Le cap Martin et le modernisme architectural

Habitué aux villas Art nouveau de la Belle Époque, le cap Martin est devenu, paradoxalement, un des hauts lieux de l'architecture moderniste qui se développe dans l'entre-deux-guerres. Dépouillement, fonctionnalité, lignes géométriques et qualité plastique des matériaux utilisés, tels sont les mots d'ordre sur lesquels s'appuient deux grands créateurs : Le Corbusier et Eileen Gray.

Eileen Gray et la villa *E 1027*

Promenade Le Corbusier

Pour les visites, se renseigner à l'office du tourisme de Roquebrune-Cap-Martin
218, avenue Aristide-Briand
Téléphone : 04 93 35 62 87

APRÈS AVOIR réalisé la maquette de la villa, sa première œuvre en tant qu'architecte, Eileen Gray en dirige le chantier, qui débute en 1926. Si le rôle de cette dernière paraît aujourd'hui prépondérant dans la conception elle-même, cette demeure résulte néanmoins de la collaboration avec son ami Jean Badovici.

LE NOM DE LA VILLA fournit peut-être une clé : dans *E 1027*, il y a *E* pour *Eileen* puis, en suivant l'ordre de

Eileen Gray
Comté de Wexford (Irlande), 1878-Paris, 1976

APRÈS des études à Londres, Eileen Gray poursuit sa formation à Paris, où elle s'installe définitivement en 1907. En 1919, elle réalise son premier décor complet pour un appartement parisien. En 1922, elle ouvre la galerie Jean-Désert, où elle présente meubles, miroirs, lampes et tapis qu'elle conçoit. En 1924, elle est remarquée par l'architecte Walter Gropius, puis côtoie Le Corbusier et Mallet-Stevens au Salon d'automne. Après la fermeture de la galerie en 1930, riche de sa première expérience avec la villa *E 1027*, elle s'intéresse de plus en plus à l'architecture et à la conception de mobilier. L'élégance fonctionnelle qui caractérise son œuvre place Eileen Gray parmi les personnalités marquantes du modernisme. Redécouvert dans les années 1970, son immense talent sera couronné par une rétrospective au Victoria & Albert Museum de Londres en 1976 et une exposition au Museum of Modern Art de New York en 1980.

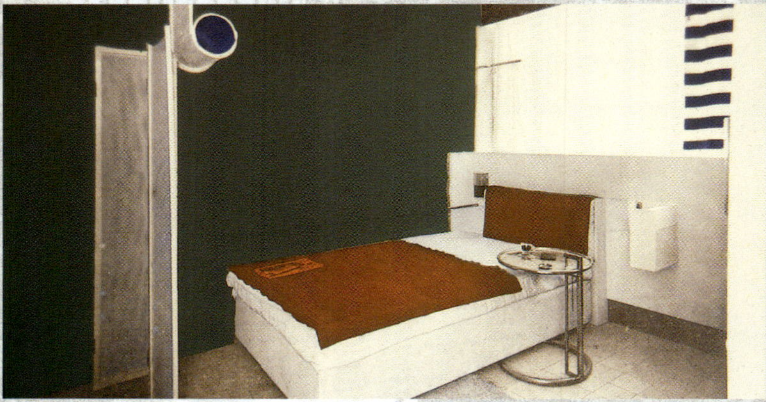

l'alphabet, *10* pour le *J* de *Jean*, *2* pour le *B* de *Badovici* et *7* pour le *G* de *Gray*.
LA MAISON s'élève à proximité de la mer, au centre d'un jardin en terrasses, avec une exposition nord-ouest-sud-est, qui favorise l'ensoleillement. La modernité est avant tout marquée, ici, par la présence de nouvelles techniques, le béton armé et l'ossature métallique. L'étage principal est un rez-de-chaussée surélevé, couvert d'une terrasse accessible à double épaisseur pour assurer l'isolation thermique, dont le plan libre, clos de quelques rares murs, s'entoure de terrasses d'agrément. Des fenêtres en longueur créées spécialement avec des persiennes et de grandes baies l'éclairent. La pièce de séjour donne sur la mer, sa façade n'est qu'une immense baie ouverte au soleil. Cet étage est porté par des pilotis qui définissent un vaste espace libre à l'étage de soubassement, adossé au sud-est à la forte pente de terrain. Mais l'attention portée par Eileen Gray au mobilier (celluloïd, câbles d'acier, aluminium...) et à l'aménagement intérieur en grande partie modulable, pour un confort strict, traduit aussi des préoccupations qui dépassent la simple observance des principes édictés par Le Corbusier.
Les pièces closes – salles de bains, cuisine, chambre principale en haut, chambres de domestiques et chambre d'amis en bas – ont des dispositions indépendantes et se superposent dans un bloc compact. Un escalier en vis les relie à la terrasse de couverture.
DÉPOURVUE de décor à l'origine, la maison fut ornée de huit peintures murales en 1938 par Le Corbusier lui-même au cours d'un séjour avec son épouse. Le mobilier a été dispersé dans les années 1990 – certaines pièces ont rejoint les collections du Centre Pompidou, à Paris.
PEU DE TEMPS après avoir édifié la villa *E 1027*, Eileen Gray construira en 1932 *Tempe a Pailla*, sur la route de Castellar [→ p. 129].

Le Corbusier et le site corbuséen

Promenade Le Corbusier

Pour les visites, se renseigner à l'office du tourisme de Roquebrune-Cap-Martin
218, avenue Aristide-Briand
Téléphone : 04 93 35 62 87

DEPUIS les années 1930, Le Corbusier fréquente la villa *E 1027* d'Eileen Gray et de Jean Badovici. Après la guerre, une brouille avec ses amis le conduit à rechercher un logement plus autonome, sur une parcelle voisine.
SUR UN TERRAIN pentu en bord de mer dominant la villa *E 1027*, se succèdent, d'est en ouest, la baraque-atelier de chantier, le « Cabanon », la guinguette *L'Étoile de Mer*, le bloc des « unités de camping ».
L'ÉLÉMENT majeur, le « Cabanon », jouxtant la guinguette et caché sous un caroubier, est aussi le moins visible. Sa construction associe le bois, ses dérivés (contreplaqué), ainsi que des matériaux industriels (plaques ondulées de fibrociment en couverture).
LES FAÇADES sont revêtues de dosses de pin imitant des rondins, mais le projet initial prévoyait un bardage d'aluminium qui aurait conféré une tout

2

1. Villa E 1027, d'Eileen Gray : la chambre à coucher.
2. La guinguette L'Étoile de Mer, jouxtant le « Cabanon » de Le Corbusier.

autre esthétique et aurait modifié le rapport au site. Une grande attention est portée aux détails.

LE VOLUME intérieur est divisé en un couloir d'accès et une pièce unique, soit un carré de 3,66 mètres de côté. Dans cet espace minimal mais très élaboré, conçu à partir du modèle théorique du plan libre, les fonctions de séjour, de toilette et de repos sont réparties autour d'un vide central réservé à la circulation. La vue exceptionnelle sur la mer, la maîtrise de la lumière, le mariage entre les couleurs vives du plafond et du sol et le ton chaud du bois des parois, l'animation apportée ponctuellement par le décor peint des volets repliables et du couloir, le caractère épuré mais fonctionnel du mobilier, tout concourt à l'agrément du séjour.

LES CINQ « unités de camping » sont regroupées dans un bloc allongé élevé sur pilotis ; toutes identiques, elles ne sont différenciées que par la couleur de leur porte. Prévu pour accueillir deux personnes, l'espace intérieur de chaque unité (8,27 mètres carrés) est divisé par une colonne sanitaire ; il est encore plus restreint que celui du Cabanon et son aménagement est sommaire.

APRÈS la mort de Le Corbusier, un ensemble sera bâti dans cette zone du cap Martin par l'équipe de l'architecte Candilis : *Le Parc Massolin.*

Le Corbusier

Charles-Édouard Jeanneret,
dit Le Corbusier
La Chaux-de-Fonds (Suisse), 1887-
Roquebrune-Cap-Martin, 1965

APRÈS des études de peinture et d'architecture, Le Corbusier s'installe à Paris en 1917. Très tôt, il prône une esthétique fonctionnelle et dépouillée, reposant sur des structures géométriques simples. Polémiste évident (revue *L'Esprit nouveau*, 1920-1925 ; *Vers une architecture*, 1923), il devient l'un des chefs de file de ce qu'il est convenu d'appeler « le style international ». En 1931, il réalise la villa *Savoye* (Poissy), où il tire parti de toutes les potentialités de l'angle droit, qui seront de nouveau exploitées dans les « unités d'habitation » de la Cité radieuse (Marseille, 1947). Toujours attaché à résoudre le dilemme entre architecture, urbanisme et habitat collectif, il a aussi été l'un des premiers à révéler les qualités esthétiques des matériaux industriels (par exemple, le béton brut de décoffrage), à se soucier de la rationalité des volumes et de l'interpénétration des espaces, à avoir recours à la standardisation d'éléments de construction... Dans les années 1950, l'auteur de la *Charte d'Athènes* (1942) et du *Modulor* (1950) nuancera le rigorisme présent jusque-là dans son œuvre au profit de lignes, de formes, de volumes assemblés en de véritables compositions plastiques (église Notre-Dame-du-Haut de Ronchamp, 1953).

Événements Manifestations

Expositions au musée des Beaux-Arts

● RENSEIGNEMENTS
Téléphone : 04 93 35 49 71

Expositions à la galerie d'Art contemporain du palais de l'Europe

● RENSEIGNEMENTS
Téléphone : 04 92 41 76 66

JUIN

Rendez-vous aux jardins et Mois des jardins

● RENSEIGNEMENTS
Téléphone : 04 92 10 33 66

JUILLET

Rencontres de danse contemporaine

● RENSEIGNEMENTS
Téléphone : 04 92 10 33 66

AOÛT

Festival de musique de chambre

● RENSEIGNEMENTS
Téléphone : 04 92 41 76 95

SEPTEMBRE

Journées méditerranéennes des jardins

● RENSEIGNEMENTS
Téléphone : 04 92 41 76 76

Journées du patrimoine

● RENSEIGNEMENTS
Téléphone : 04 92 10 33 66

OCTOBRE

Mois des colloques

Tous les samedis du mois d'octobre, conférences-débats autour de thèmes liés à l'actualité tels que : *Science et conscience*; *La Cité des hommes*; *Quelle philosophie pour notre temps?* *Rencontres sur les origines.*

● RENSEIGNEMENTS
Téléphone : 04 92 10 50 83

DÉCEMBRE

Noël à Menton

Marché de Noël. Chemin des Crèches. Animations.

● RENSEIGNEMENTS
Téléphone : 04 92 41 76 76

Adresses utiles

Palais de l'Europe
8, avenue Boyer – 06500 Menton

Bibliothèque municipale
Téléphone : 04 92 41 76 60
Télécopie : 04 92 41 76 69
Courriel : huguette.viale@ville-menton.fr

Office du tourisme
Téléphone : 04 92 41 76 76
Télécopie : 04 92 41 76 78
Courriel : tourisme@menton.fr

Festival de musique
Téléphone : 04 92 41 76 95
Télécopie : 04 92 41 76 96
Courriel : ot-pro@villedementon.com

Conservatoire de musique

10, avenue Cochrane – 06500 Menton
Téléphone : 04 93 35 82 95
Télécopie : 04 93 35 44 34

Hôtel Adhémar de Lantagnac

24, rue Saint-Michel – 06500 Menton
Téléphone : 04 92 10 97 10
Télécopie : 04 93 28 46 85

Hôtel de ville

17, rue de la République
BP 69 06502 Menton Cedex
Téléphone : 04 92 10 50 00

Palais Carnolès Musée des Beaux-Arts

3, avenue de la Madone – 06500 Menton
Téléphone : 04 93 35 49 71
Télécopie : 04 92 41 80 66
Courriel : musées@villedementon.com

Musée Jean-Cocteau

Quai Napoléon-III – 06500 Menton
Téléphone : 04 93 57 72 30

Musée de Préhistoire régionale

16, rue Lorédan-Larchey – 06500 Menton
Téléphone : 04 93 35 84 64
Télécopie : 04 92 10 05 40
Courriel : pierre-elie.moulle@ville-menton.fr

Service du patrimoine

5, rue Ciapetta – 06500 Menton
Téléphone : 04 92 10 33 66
Télécopie : 04 93 28 46 85
Courriel : josiane.tricotti@ville-menton.fr

Index des rues, des sites et des monuments

Cet index ne recense que les rues, les places, les sites et monuments directement liés à Menton et à ses environs. Lorsqu'un site fait l'objet d'une notice, son nom apparaît ici en gras, ainsi que les folios auxquels il renvoie. Quand un édifice fait l'objet d'un développement à l'intérieur d'un site, seul le folio est en gras.

CRÉDITS PHOTOGRAPHIQUES

VILLE DE MENTON : photos Thomas Bilanges, Paul Deverdun, Jacques Godard, Christian Goron, Jean-Jacques Laure, Élisabeth Rossolin, Pianetti, Josiane Tricotti.
SERVICE DU PATRIMOINE – MAIRIE DE MENTON.
SERVICE COMMUNICATION – MAIRIE DE MENTON.
SERVICE DES ESPACES VERTS – MAIRIE DE MENTON.
MUSÉE DES BEAUX-ARTS DE MENTON (PALAIS CARNOLÈS).
MUSÉE DE PRÉHISTOIRE RÉGIONALE.
ARCHIVES MUNICIPALES.
BIBLIOTHÈQUE MUNICIPALE.

ARCHIVES DU PALAIS DE MONACO.

CENTRE DES MONUMENTS NATIONAUX
Président : Isabelle Lemesle
Directeur général : Fabrice Benkimoun

ÉDITIONS DU PATRIMOINE
Directrice des éditions : Dominique Seridji
Responsable des éditions : Clair Morizet
Responsable adjointe : Karin Franques
Suivi de fabrication : Carine Merse

CONCEPTION GRAPHIQUE : Raymonde Branger
PHOTOGRAVURE : Payton, Bilbao, Espagne
IMPRESSION : Néo-Typo, Besançon, France
RÉIMPRESSION : Mame, Tours, France

Achevé d'imprimer en juin 2006
Dépôt légal : juin 2006
Réimpression : février 2011